BLAD...

"A hell-b... fo... h... l... of any novel and SF, set in a well-rea... nineteen-... as well as —ERIC ...

"Smart, ... fully real... and pace... ine finding herself via weapons of mass destruction, bionic strength, and the heartb... for ... h... ... *Seventeen* magazine mainlin... ..."
—JEFF LONG, *Ne...*

"A fun, fast-moving alt-history romp!"
—S. M. STIRLING,
author of *The Council of Shadows*

"G. T. Almasi's *Blades of Winter* is a smart, punchy deluge of radical thought packed into a febrific alternate-history thrill ride. Almasi is an author finding his stride, mind ablaze with kaleidoscopic insight, creativity, and action. And did I mention humor? Because there's a lot of that, too."
—JAMES WAUGH, senior story developer,
Blizzard Entertainment

"Almasi has created a vivid and entirely believable alternate history that is steeped in historical fact, future science, and international intrigue. *Blades of Winter* has all the action and excitement of today's hottest videogames and an absolutely unrelenting pace that will keep your heart pounding. The pages practically turn themselves."
—JAMES A. BROWN, lead level designer, Epic Games

"*Blades of Winter* starts with a freeze-frame bullet to the face and only takes off from there. Vicious action sequences and brilliant SF tech make for some of the best pacing I've consumed in a really long time."
—SAM STRACHMAN, writer, IP developer, Ubisoft

BLADES OF WINTER

A NOVEL OF THE SHADOWSTORM

G. T. ALMASI

BALLANTINE BOOKS • NEW YORK

Blades of Winter is a work of fiction. Names, places, and incidents either are products of the author's imagination or are used fictitiously.

A Del Rey Mass Market Original

Copyright © 2012 by G. T. Almasi

Excerpt from *Hammer of Angels* by G. T. Almasi copyright © 2012 by G. T. Almasi

All rights reserved.

Published in the United States by Del Rey, an imprint of the Random House Publishing Group, a division of Random House, Inc., New York.

DEL REY is a registered trademark and the Del Rey colophon is a trademark of Random House, Inc.

RANDOM HOUSE WORLDS and House colophon are trademarks of Random House, Inc.

This book contains an excerpt from the forthcoming book *Hammer of Angels* by G. T. Almasi. This excerpt has been set for this edition only and may not reflect the final content of the forthcoming edition.

ISBN 978-0-440-42354-6
eBook ISBN 978-0-345-52254-2

Printed in the United States of America.

www.delreybooks.com

9 8 7 6 5 4 3 2 1

To my family

BLADES OF WINTER

CHAPTER 1

Nothing pisses me off more than being shot at while I'm eating. It's the midday rush here in my new favorite restaurant, a cozy Hungarian joint on East 82nd Street. I'm jammed into a small table by the kitchen, with a Redskins cap pulled low over my face. The charming old dining room is packed, and the paneled walls echo the Eastern European barks of the broad, buxom waitresses as they dominate the good-humored customers. The food here is spectacular, but right now I'm kind of distracted by that bullet hurtling straight at my left eye.

Until this .22-caliber interruption, I was quietly noshing my yummy goulash. My unwitting target, an ugly little man named Hector, sits at his table across the room with some chick. It's not a very sexy mission. I'm just following this fucking jerk around. The brief said he was a former Russian Level, so I thought the job would be a lot more exciting than this. I did notice that he chews each bite of food exactly thirty-two times. *Whoop-dee-doo.*

At least it's a Level 12 Job Number. This'll be the highest-rated mission I've ever pulled, although it's not exactly mine. It was originally assigned to a coworker named Grey, but he called in sick this morning. The ExOps dispatcher is a total dingbat named Virgil, so it was a cinch to sucker—uh, I mean *persuade*—him to mix me up with my father and assign the mission to me. You'd think the fact that I'm a mid-five-foot, nineteen-year-old female Level 4 Interceptor named Alix would be a hint that I'm not a fortysomething Level 20 Liberator named Philip who's been dead for eight years. But who am I to correct a senator's son? If he's okay with putting me on a Job Number that's eight steps beyond my pay grade, I'm okay with it, too.

But back to that bullet flying my way. Five seconds ago, Hector stood up and put on his jacket to leave. Four seconds ago, I turned my head to look for my waitress. Three seconds ago, Hector's date plucked a small silver pistol out of her handbag. She's about my age and height but with dark hair and dark clothes, and she's suddenly wearing a pair of giant Jackie Onassis sunglasses. Two seconds ago, she pointed her puny gun at my face. One second ago, as this miniature Jackie-O chick pulled the trigger, I told my neuroinjector to get me ready to do some serious head stomping. As of this instant, I'm fully jacked on Madrenaline and time has slowed to a crawl.

The bullet has just emerged from Jackie-O's little fashion accessory, so I've got time to pull out my larger and much more impressive black pistol. It's a Lion Ballistics LB-505. I inherited this gun from my father, who spent a lot of time fiddling with the onboard artificial intelligence. After a particularly successful tinkering session he nicknamed her Li'l Bertha. I communicate with Li'l Bertha through the raised neural contact pad on her grip that snaps into a matching recess built into the palm of my left hand.

Like every pistol from Lion Ballistics, my LB-505 is built around the patented radar-assisted gyroscopic aiming system that made this company the Harley-Davidson of hard-core gun nuts everywhere. The AI transparently manages all the techno crap and feeds real-time target information to my Eyes-Up display.

One of the 505's coolest capabilities is that it can change caliber on the fly. This feature is called Multi Caliber, and it allows me to reduce my competitors to one or more meat piles, depending on what size bullets I select. As I take aim with my dad's gun, it scans Jackie-O to see if she's wearing any kind of armor and pops the ammunition selector into a corner of my field of vision:

Select Ammo Type:
  1. Standard
  2. Explosive
  3. Armor-Piercing
  4. Incendiary
  5. Pupu Platter

The scan of Jackie-O returns "null." There are so many goddamn people in here, the scanner can't isolate my target. Okay, fine. I tell Li'l Bertha to use .30-caliber Incendiaries. I've been taught that whether they're armored or not, nothing distracts the competition more than setting them on fire.

Jackie-O's bullet is halfway here. This isn't my first time being shot at, but it still makes my hands begin to tremble while my stomach knots up. My neuroinjector senses my anxiety and squirts a dose of Kalmers into my bloodstream. I change my mind about the ammo and decide to precede the Incendiary rounds with two .50-caliber Explosive slugs. I need to move this crowd out of the way so that the Incendiaries can work their subtle magic.

Christ, her bullet is so close that I can see its rotation! I've spent too much time putzing around with my gun. I hold my head still while my retinal cameras photograph this little chickie for posterity, then I dodge to the side. The bullet sizzles across the skin of my left cheekbone as I pump two Explosive shots into the ceiling above Jackie-O. This distracts her with falling debris and gets all the others to duck under their tables. Now she's totally exposed, so I mash down the trigger and unload my Incendiaries on her.

My flaming bullet fog hits her so hard that she doesn't even have a chance to be torn to bits. She simply goes up in a white cloud of smoke that fills the whole dining room. It's like the girl was never there. Her vanishing act (and perhaps all the noise, fumes, and fire) has scared the shit out of everybody, and they all start screaming their heads off. The smoke is so thick, I can't even see my table in front of me. I switch on my infrared vision just in time to spot Hector as he follows a group of terrified patrons out the front door. I charge after him and switch my infrared off as I storm into the bright sunshine outside.

As Hector escapes up the block, the street erupts in gunfire. *Damn it!* I was so smug about roasting Jackie-O with my full-auto bulletgasm that I've stumbled into her backup team.

A cloud of bullets and one rocket-propelled grenade streak toward me. I leap in the air as the grenade hits the sidewalk and detonates. The concussion kicks me up three stories. My cap flies off, and I crash through a window as the front of my ex-favorite New York eatery goes up in smoke. I hope their insurance covers them for an attack of the killer spies from Psychoville.

I land on all fours in a small bedroom. The floor dances under me while the maniacs outside pulverize the walls and windows and generally shoot the shit out of the apartment. The air is full of flying metal, wood splinters, and shards of glass. Plaster dust grinds in my teeth, and smoke burns my throat. I roll into the hall and then run up the fire stairs. As I burst onto the roof, the sound of a helicopter thuds through the air. This is a solo mission, so I know the air support isn't for me. I arm and drop my electromagnetic pulse grenade, then I jump through an open window across the back alley and land in a bathtub. The EMP grenade will roast the electronics of anything in its blast radius, so I take my Mods and Enhances offline while Li'l Bertha shuts down to protect herself.

A black, nasty-looking little chopper soars over the roof across the alley as I trigger my EMP. The electro-fried aircraft careens out of control and smacks into the building. The helicopter-shaped paperweight drops out of my sight, so I don't see the result, but I sure as hell hear and feel it. The explosions and squeals of terror are both particularly satisfying.

My hands start shaking again. The Kalmers have faded out of my bloodstream. Kalmers don't eliminate reactions to stress and fear; they simply suppress them. Once they wear off, you can be hit by what Med-Techs call emotional recoil. My mouth dries out, my lungs gulp for air, and my legs squeeze together to keep me from peeing my pants. I curl up into a ball and ride it out. After a few minutes I'm done crying and shaking. I lurch out of the tub, scram the apartment, and climb the stairs to the top of the building. My new knees let me rooftop jump all the way to 60th Street, where I slide down a fire escape and catch a taxi to Chelsea.

CORE (CATALOGUE OF RECORDS, ExOps)
PER-A59-001

Crystal City Gazette, July 8, 1972

Local Girl Dazzles at the Gymnastics National Championships

NEW YORK CITY—Crystal City's Alix Nico thrilled Madison Square Garden last night as she swept the all-around and the individual events in the 10–11-year-old division at this year's USAIGC Gymnastics National Championships. Her stunning performance was an emphatic finale to an extremely successful year for Nico, who set a USAIGC record for victories in a single season.

Nico is already considered a favorite to win gold at the Montreal Olympics. She is training at the Roosevelt Gymnastics Center in Washington, D.C., under the supervision of her coach Tasha Dovetsky.

CHAPTER 2

The cab takes me all the way down Broadway to 18th Street in Chelsea. I walk across Columbus Park and stop in front of a newsstand. My hands flip through a Spider-Man comic book while my eyes scan the street to see if I've been followed. Everyone seems normal; no lurky-jerkies. I cross the street against the signal and run through an alley, emerging on the other side of the block. Still nobody out of place, just people rushing hither and yon, doing their thing.

I take another taxi back uptown to Penn Station and catch a train to Washington, D.C. Then the nine-thirty VRE commuter train gets me to Crystal City, Virginia. The VRE stop is a twenty-minute walk from my house, but since my Mods enable me to run at over thirty miles per hour, I make it home in three minutes. It's already past ten o'clock when I leap up to the front porch roof, ease through the window into my bedroom, and try to sneak past my mom's room to the bathroom. She's got that mother hearing, though.

"Alixandra Janina Nico, is that you?" She walks into the hall as she ties on her robe. When she sees me, her voice shifts from pissed to scared and she gasps, "Oh, my God, what happened?" She looks at the left side of my face. I reach up and touch my cheek, which feels sort of crunchy. When I hold my hand away, I see that my fingertips have dried blood on them. You wouldn't think you could forget about a bullet wound to your head.

"Hmm," I mumble. "No wonder the people on the train were staring." I keep walking toward the bathroom. Nobody noticed me in Manhattan, of course. New Yorkers only turn their heads for free bagels or exploding dump trucks.

Mom follows me, her arms crossed over her chest. "Alix, please listen to me. I really am starting to think that ExOps is too dangerous for a girl your age." ExOps is short for Extreme Operations Division, where both Mom and I work in D.C. She's a senior personnel manager in the Admin Department, and I'm a Level 4 field agent trained and equipped as an Interceptor.

Extreme Operations is a non-public-facing U.S. intelligence agency that specializes in, well, extreme operations. Missions range from high-security black bag jobs to whacking well-protected people. When one of the aboveground U.S. agencies needs an especially nasty job done, it calls us.

I go to the bathroom sink and turn the water on. Mom stands behind me and watches me in the mirror. "I should have made you go to the Olympics when I had the chance."

Before I became a spy I was a sure thing to make the U.S. Olympic gymnastics team. ExOps is way more interesting though, plus I don't have to put up with all the bouncy little bitches who hated my guts because I kicked their star-spangled asses at every meet. I say, "Cleo, it's no big deal. It's just a scratch. I mean, gymnastics was dangerous, too." I grab the soap and hold my hands under the faucet. "Besides, Dad wasn't any older than me when he started doing fieldwork."

"He *was* much older, and this is different."

"No, it's not. I—"

She cuts me off. "It's different because he wasn't my nineteen-year-old daughter!"

"Cleo, it's only a scratch. I'm *fine*." Our reflections in the mirror show how much we look like each other. We're both on the petite side at five feet four inches, and we're both skinny with straight, dark red hair and fair skin. Our eyes are different. Hers are brown, whereas mine are blue-green, like my dad's were. When we're tense, our mouths both make the same tight little crescent-moon shape. People comment about our resemblance all the time. They say that if we didn't wear our hair differently, they'd have trouble telling us apart. That's fine with me. I think my mother is pretty. I just wish I was taller.

I wash my face, being careful to clean out the wound. After I dab myself dry with a towel, Mom gets a bandage out of the medicine cabinet and carefully tapes it on my cheek. She fusses around with it to make sure it sticks. After a minute I roll my eyes and mutter, "Cleo-o-o."

"For God's sake, Alix, don't you think I'll be a little concerned when you come home all bloody and cut up?"

Maybe she needs some affection. Work and school have been super busy lately, and I haven't been home very much. I put my arms around her and give her a big squoosh. "Oh, Mom, that's why I love you, because you're so concerned when I come home all bloody and cut up." She gives a start. That was over a dozen nice words in a row, all for her. I even called her "Mom" instead of using her first name. She's melting. I finish her off with "I'm starved. Can we make supper together?" What mother can resist cooking with her baby girl? I boil spaghetti while she whips up a butter and cheese sauce. Cleo tells me about her day while we eat. When we're done, she goes back to bed and I go downstairs to my workshop.

The shop occupies the entire basement. The cracked cement floor and fluorescent overhead lighting aren't exactly the height of fashion, but I'm more comfortable here than almost anywhere else. I've left it pretty much the same as when my dad had it. A heavy wooden workbench commands the front wall. Tall metal racks crammed full of gadgets, supplies, books, and other junk line the back wall. A row of combination-locked four-drawer filing cabinets full of confidential paperwork from Extreme Operations lurk under the stairs. The center of the room is inhabited by a faded green leather couch, a paint-stained coffee table, and two shop stools.

This dusty, musty wonderful space became mine after I graduated from Camp and moved back home. At first, I spent my time down here dismantling radios and putting them back together. Once ExOps assigned me my first real Job Numbers, I began to use the shop to maintain my Mods and Enhances.

I've received a bunch of mechanical modifications and biological enhancements. Mods are generally hardware, like my electrohydraulically accelerated joints or the nanoligaments that hold my limbs together while I leap tall buildings in a single bound. Enhances tend to be soft upgrades centered around my augmented nervous system. The heart of this system is called a neuroinjector, which manages the flow of drugs that help me react quickly and deal with stressful situations without losing my mind. My neuroinjector is a Nerve Jet, which is the best because the Med-Techs can program it to administer drugs to me when certain conditions are met whether I request it or not.

Some Enhances need to be refilled, but otherwise they're maintenance free. Mods, in contrast, need regular tinkering because they get so beaten up in the field. A few upgrades are hybrids of both Mods and Enhances, like the cameras they painted on my retinas. The cameras include solid state microhardware to transmit imagery, but with no moving parts they take care of themselves.

I rummage around on the workbench, looking for my testing console. Finally I find it hiding under a pile of gun magazines. I uncoil the console's sensor cable and plug it into the data socket on my hip. The console checks my fluids and looks for stress fractures in my modified joints. I run a special test to see if my internal wiring was damaged by the electromagnetic pulse I used on that helicopter.

Everything checks out fine, but I've felt some tightness

in my knees since that three-story jump I did earlier today. I unplug the console cable from my hip, pull off my jeans, and sit on one of the shop stools. My knees look perfectly normal if you only take a quick look. A closer inspection reveals that there isn't any skin there, only flesh-colored metal and plastic. My ankles and elbows are the same way, but since they don't hurt, I'll leave them alone.

I unscrew both kneecaps and use a flashlight to see inside. They look fine, so maybe they just need a lube job. I squirt some liquid graphite into both knees and use my fingers to rub it in. While I swing my legs back and forth to help spread the lubricant around, I imagine what Dr. Herodotus's reaction will be if I screwed up his shiny new knees. He's my primary Med-Tech, and he'll be ripped that I didn't break them in before I pulled a job. Well, that's too bad. If it weren't for people like me, he'd have nothing to do but install fake tits on porn stars and politicians' wives. I finish Midasizing my knees and leave them to soak for a few minutes.

Now for my best friend, Li'l Bertha. I take her apart, clean her out, and oil her up. While she's stripped, I take a good look at all her pieces. Sometimes Incendiary bullets ignite early, which can screw up her electrical components. I replace two switches that look questionable and pack in fresh ammunition until her ammo indicator reads "100%."

My dad thought his nickname for his pistol was a real hoot. Sometimes when he worked, he'd hum along to the radio and substitute "Li'l Bertha" for the normal lyrics. When he got killed, the brass at Extreme Operations assumed his gun had been destroyed or lost. I never told them I'd found it down here in the basement and kept it for myself.

I also found my dad's service record. He was one of the first Levels. None of our competitors had ever combined German Mods and Chinese Enhances in the same agent before. My father and the other original ExOps

Levels immediately became the baddest mofos in the Shadowstorm.

Dad's list of upgrades included:

Vision Mod 1: Distance.
Vision Mod 2: Infrared.
Vision Mod 3: Low-light.
Double adrenaline reserve.
Triple adrenaline reserve.
Legs: Reinforce joints and major tendons.
Arms: Reinforce joints and major tendons.
Polymetallic sheathing on long bones, rib cage, and skull.
WeaponSynch neural link to LB-505 (left hand).
Body-distributed audio recording suite.

His service record included a long list of repairs and adjustments made throughout his career. It was pretty crude compared with what I've got now. I got all my vision work done in one session, not three. He didn't even have Madrenaline, just a triple helping of the same old crap we've used for a million years. No wonder he drank so much.

While I wait for my knees to get nice and saturated, I grab a book from one of the metal shelves. I like to supplement my school's history classes with Dad's military history books. His collection covers a lot of historical periods, but most of them are about World War II. When I was barely ten, I already knew that the Germans had started the war in Europe by invading Poland in 1939. Within a year, the Fritzes had taken Western Europe. A year after that, they pulled off the biggest amphibious operation in history when they invaded Great Britain. The Brits fought like apes but the poor sods were cornered. The Luftwaffe bombed the crap out of them until the Wehrmacht had goose-stepped all the way across the British Isles.

The relationship between the United States and Germany stayed pretty tense until Hitler got iced by his own officers in 1942. His Nazi Party fell apart, and Germany returned to somewhat saner leadership. The war in Europe was over. This allowed America's armed forces to focus on the stupendously ambitious Japanese, who we crushed under a galactic quantity of explosive ordnance. The bombing campaigns were so devastating that some of the smaller contested islands simply vanished. While we occupied Japan, Germany and Russia carved up the Middle East and China's Chiang Kai-shek hacked up every Communist within two thousand miles of Beijing.

Next there was a little war in Korea. This ground on for two years before the U.S. dropped the world's first atom bomb on a Chinese army base in northern Korea. The end. The Korean War was where my father served as an army officer. After the war, he went into army intelligence, which led to his career as a covert agent at ExOps. There was plenty of work to do. The Chinese wanted Japan and Mongolia, the Germans wanted the Soviets' half of the Middle East, and the Russians just wanted everything.

After we gave Castro the boot and made Cuba a state, the U.S. wanted to be left alone to wallow in the American dream. But the dream kept getting messed up because we had to work so hard to stay touchy-feely with Greater Germany. President Nixon hated the Germans in general and their enslavement of Europe's Jews in particular. His attitude led us to the brink of war with Germany during the oil embargo. Bad times. I was only a kid when all that went down, but I still remember the air raid drills: all of us hiding under our desks like idiots.

I twist my kneecaps back on, pack up my tools, and put Li'l Bertha into my dad's gun safe. My father didn't always take his gun with him when he traveled; it depended on the Job Number. One day, eight years ago, he left for a job and never came back. When ExOps told us the Germans had executed him, I spent two terrible days and nights down here, shrieking and throwing stuff around. My mother tried to console me, but she was such a mess herself that she could barely get out of bed. The second night I dragged a chair over in front of the safe and climbed up to spin the dial. I'd swiped the combo by peeking while my father did it. I unlocked the door and found Li'l Bertha inside.

Of course I couldn't activate her since I didn't have my Mods yet, but she felt perfect in my hand, and after a few minutes I was doing a nice fast draw. I thought it was Dad's ghost teaching me. Sounds funny, I know, but c'mon, I was twelve. A few days later a very tall woman came to the house to clear out my dad's classified materials.

She also came for me.

CORE   HIS-MODS-018

Brief History of Mods and Enhances

In 1944, all of the four victors of World War II launched major initiatives to help them hold and consolidate their end-of-war positions. The Americans and Russians applied their industrial might to the production of vast navies and mechanized armies. The Germans and Chinese turned to their respective scientific communities to develop the soldier of the future.

These supersoldiers would require greatly expanded physical capabilities. To this end, scientists in Stuttgart implemented a range of mechanical modifications while researchers in Beijing experimented with a suite of chemical enhancements. Both programs eventually shifted their focus from mass-produced frontline troops to individually crafted superhuman spies.

These upgraded agents quickly came to rule the clandestine battlegrounds. It became clear that the Shadowstorm would not be won by fleets of ships and tanks but by the bionic and biotic agents from Germany and China, respectively. The question was which of the two superspy technologies would win out.

The answer arrived from an entirely unexpected source. Jakob Fredericks, a senior American intelligence officer at Extreme Operations Division, had his medical technicians install both chemical enhancements and mechanical modifications on several of his field agents. The results were stunning and heralded the world's first Levels. Within months, these dually enhanced and modified agents took command of the Shadowstorm.

Mods and Enhances have come a long way since those early days, of course. What was once a radical combination of two competing technologies is now practiced by all the major intelligence agencies. If the stealthy and sudden delivery of death and chaos can be considered a gift, the world has only to thank Jakob Fredericks.

CHAPTER 3

"Our Father who art in heaven, hallowed be caffeine." I swig my coffee and continue. "Now where the hell is my bus? Amen."

I'm down the street from my house, waiting for the number 23 bus. My sunglasses serve as a dam of hipness against my school uniform's ocean of dorkitude. My dark red hair, starched white shirt, and forest-green blazer conspire to transform me into a refugee from Christmas Freak Island. At least the pants are simple khakis.

ExOps agents who haven't finished college are required to pursue a bachelor's degree. A normal school would let us wear ripped jeans and Elvis Presley T-shirts, but we don't go to a normal school. We attend a special satellite of George Washington University called Saint Boniface Academy. It's basically a finishing school for government-spawned homicidal maniacs like me. The academy is modeled after private Catholic schools, hence my stupid outfit. The strict discipline and structure supposedly helps us become better agents, but after two years at St. Bony's I'm not sure it's the students who need discipline and structure.

To help me through my daily imprisonment, I begin every school day with a big travel mug of my mom's atomic-powered Cuban Blend. My father called it "Java Más Macho" and said it could put hair on a Dutchman's ass. This kind of language usually got a harrumph out of Mom while Dad would peek over his newspaper and wink at me.

I'm so tired this morning that I'd drink this coffee even if it put hair on *my* ass. My mind kept me awake all night, replaying yesterday's excitement in New York. The Med-Techs have named this type of insomnia Post-Stimulant Sleep Disorder. If you asked me, I'd just call it a freaking action hangover. Then this morning we had no hot water, so I haven't even had a shower. Blech.

A midsize black Cadillac glides up the street and stops across the road. The tinted driver-side window whirrs open to reveal my field partner, Patrick. ExOps teamed me with him after we graduated from Camp. We're the same age, and at five foot six he's taller than me by two inches. He's got light brown hair and a round face that always seems ready to break into a grin.

When we met back at Camp, he was in the middle of going through puberty. His voice broke during our first year, which led to some hilarious low- and high-pitched comm-training phrases like "TARget AcquIREd Alpha LEAder. Please adVISE." I teased him mercilessly about his squeaky voice, but he's so good-natured that he just laughed along with me. He's smart, he's funny, and his devotion to my every need plays out well in the sack. I couldn't have asked for a better partner.

Patrick leans out the window and calls, "Hello, little girl. Want some candy?"

I'm about to launch into my oversexed schoolgirl act when Raj leans forward from the backseat and growls at Patrick. "Knock it off, Solomon." Then to me: "Get in the car, Scarlet. The Front Desk wants to see you."

Raj and I just missed each other at spy school, which we called Camp A-Go-Go. He graduated the year before I started, but stories about me trickled up to him before I got out of Initial Training. Mom told me that some of the ExOps staffers started a pool, betting on how fast I'd get promoted, until their boss shut it down.

When Raj met me, I was the youngest agent ever to graduate into the field. The big guy had been ExOps' previous flavor of the month, and he didn't like being pushed aside by some pip-squeak fifteen-year-old no matter how famous her father had been. We were the big assholes on campus, and since we were both hopped-up, psychotically competitive youths with more pride than sense, that rivalry played itself out with elegance and grace.

Raj is six years older than me and carries 295 pounds on a six-foot-five frame. He tends to wear heavy motorcycle boots, black jeans, and big capelike duster overcoats. We're both seen as fast-track Levels, him because of his size and mission capabilities, me because of my speed and rapid progress through Camp A-Go-Go. Since Raj is a Vindicator, we don't compete for the exact same assignments, but competing for attention hasn't made us any friendlier.

I hop in the front passenger-side seat and say to Patrick, "Hi, Trick. How's tricks?"

"I've been busy, my dear," he answers as he drives the car away from the bus stop. "But not as busy as you've been."

The word "busy" has a few meanings in our business. What it means here is that he (and of course all of Extreme Operations) has figured out that Virgil's incompetence as a dispatcher allowed me to sneak onto a Job Number meant for a much higher Level. "Busy" also refers to the fact that I told my Med-Tech I had the proper clearance for my new Mods before that was, in fact, the case. Trick doesn't care so much about bureaucratic propriety, but he knows that the Front Desk really frowns on that kind of procedural chicanery.

Raj is bucking for another promotion, so he frowns on it, too. "Scarlet," he rumbles, "do you have any idea of the resources that have gone into your current system?" As a Level 8, Raj is my superior. He reminds me of this as often as possible. He insists on calling me by my ExOps field name, Scarlet. We field agents use each other's handles when we pull a mission, but it's more personable to use our regular names when we're just driving around. Raj isn't very personable. He's never even told any of us what his real name is. I tried convincing his former Camp classmates to tell me, but they all refused. Our boss knows, but by the time you're a Front Desk at Extreme Operations, you've learned how to keep a secret.

I pull the vanity mirror down so I can see Raj's big head and reply, "One million, six hundred sixty-nine thousand, eight hundred and fifty-two dollars." That kind of money used to produce a Level 10, but nowadays it's average for a Level 4 like me.

Raj does some calculating, then announces, "It's got to be more than that now."

We keep arguing while Patrick drives across the Williams Bridge into D.C. I keep it out of my voice, but I've started to regret my recent visit to Dr. Herodotus. I honestly thought the whole clearance thing was a load of bureautrash. While I pretend to listen to Raj, I mentally access my copy of the Administration Department's equipment manual. It lives in my head along with all the other files the Med-Techs stuffed in there when I had my Mods installed.

The virtual document appears in my Eyes-Up display and overlays my view of the physical world around me. I focus my gaze on the table of contents entry for maintenance, and the document scrolls to that chapter. Reading, reading . . . there's all kinds of stuff in here about how to maintain Extreme Operations property, including oneself. I run a search for the word "clearance" and get 179 matches from this chapter alone. Damn.

Raj finally finishes blathering: ". . . and now you've thrown off your Level Cycle and Development Schedule."

I turn around to look at Raj and say, "Look, Rah-Rah, I've already got one mother to deal with. Tell me something useful, like if I need to let anyone know that

I'll be out of school today." Raj glowers at me but doesn't answer. He hates it when I call him Rah-Rah.

Patrick answers my question. "We've already notified the head of your department, Alix."

I look over at Trick and inquire, "So what's happened to Miss Alixandra Nico that keeps her out of the academy today? Have I stopped to help a homeless band of gypsy children? Have I been abducted by aliens?" Normally, Trick would begin to trade progressively more ridiculous situations with me, but instead he laughs weakly and doesn't look at me.

This makes me uneasy. I grumpily cross my arms and turn my head to look out the window to hide my nervousness. I'm dying to talk to Trick over our implanted commmphones, but I'm worried that Raj will be able to tell and will insist on knowing what we're commming about. He's really observant, and little changes in our expressions can sometimes reveal that we're commming to each other.

Some people have trouble using a commmphone, but I picked it up easily. I got a head start from going to holiday dinners at my mom's parents' house. My grandparents expected everyone to carry on three conversations at once, so they would ask you a question even if you were already talking to someone else. The only time I experienced a similar cacophony was the day I went away to Camp with seventy-four other kids.

I decide to comm anyway. If I keep it short, hopefully Raj won't pick it up.

I comm to Trick, "What's going on?"

He comms back, "You're in the doghouse, Hot Stuff."

Now I don't care whether Raj hears us or not. I shriek, "Are you kidding? What for? I kicked ass!"

"I guess the Front Desk thinks you overstepped a bit," Patrick mumbles.

"How was I supposed to know it was such a crazy mission? It sounded like a basic Creep 'n' Peep."

Raj leans forward and shouts, "Scarlet, all Level 12 jobs are crazy!" He sits back and adds, "Dumbass."

I turn around in my seat and yell back, "Rah-Rah, the brief listed a single fucking objective: follow one goddamn guy. No big deal." Raj crosses his arms and glowers at me until I give up and face the front again.

Trick says, "We picked up a flurry of unusual comm calls after you got to the restaurant." He tells me the Info Department is still decrypting it all, but what's obvious is that the mission changed dramatically once I was in a static situation with Hector. The potential for sudden, unexpected shifts like this are why the job was Level 12 and not Level 4.

"By that time, it was too late to pull you out," Trick finishes. "But that kind of surveillance *is* what guys like Grey are for."

Grey is the Level 12 Infiltrator who was originally assigned to follow Hector. I happened to be in the Front Desk's office when Grey called in sick. When my boss asked me to make sure that Virgil, our notoriously slow dispatcher, set up a replacement right away, I ran downstairs to Virgil's desk, where I may or may not have ad-libbed that the Front Desk wanted the replacement to be me. Then I may have mistakenly given him my father's ID number instead of my own. But still, if he'd even bothered to check it . . .

I stare out the car window. Yesterday's mission seemed like a great idea until that Jackie-O chick took a shot at me. I decide not to tell Trick that I borrowed his precious Redskins cap and then lost it. I'm in enough trouble with my boss. I don't need static from my partner, too.

As we pull into the underground garage at Extreme Operations' headquarters, I grimly brace myself for a world-class chewing out.

A brief introduction to the Shadowstorm and Level Classes

The roots of today's hypertense political jungle were sown during World War II (1939–1944) as Germany, Russia, China, and the United States all found success on their respective battlegrounds. They also found myriad reasons to mistrust one another. The time and effort spent spying on their wartime foes was nearly matched by what they spent spying on their wartime friends. This mistrust turned to paranoia and the four megastates, now known as "The Four," launched what have become nearly constant intelligence operations against one another. Too often this cloak-and-dagger activity gets out of hand and the overworked embassies must put out yet another diplomatic fire.

Despite the underlying tension, a surface peace has been maintained. Rather than risk another all-out war, The Four have sought to resolve their conflicts in silent shadows with anonymous agents. Many of these spies endure a series of medical procedures to increase their speed, strength, endurance, and agility. Each series of modifications and enhancements brings the operative a new level of performance, hence the name for these agents: Levels.

The best-funded agencies train their Levels to be specialists, the most common of which include:

Infiltrator: Undercover specialist. Infiltrators receive highly covert long-term solo missions and receive Info support via commphone.

Protector: Security work and bodyguard. Protectors are well equipped, but their clearly visible optical equipment makes them suitable for noncovert work only.

Interceptor: Short and medium-length insertions, usually on foreign soil. An Interceptor typically works with an intelligence-enhanced partner known as an Information Operator.

Vindicator: Short-term insertions, heavy support, and leadership roles. Vindicators tend to receive noncovert missions and usually work as part of a team.

Malefactor: Long-range terminations and passive intel collection. To remain undetected until needed, these agents are sometimes injected with sleeper directives.

Liberator: Master of all specialties, extremely rare.

Most agencies prohibit nonenhanced field agents from engaging these terrifying marvels. It is no overstatement to say that because of their infiltration abilities, destructive potential, and mission dedication, Levels have become the most important field assets in the twentieth century's Shadowstorm.

CHAPTER 4

The Front Desk isn't a piece of furniture; it's a job title currently held by Cyrus El-Sarim. Cyrus runs the German Section, where I work. He's a sizable swarthy guy who looks like he could have started the Persian Empire. He was known as Sheik when he was an ExOps field agent back in the Stone Age.

Cyrus goes way back with my parents, so I've known him all my life. I can read his face and body language like a book. When he's happy, his mustache makes two hairy arches. When he's mad, his bushy eyebrows touch each other.

I get off the elevator. I can see all the way across the floor to his office. The eyebrows are grinding together like a pair of Latin dancers. The eyes shoot daggers at me as I walk across the bustling main office where telephones ring, secretaries scuttle, and dark suits huddle around stacks of paperwork. A few faces look up at me as I pass by. Levels are the rock stars here, so people notice when we're around—especially when the Front Desk is yelling at us before we've even made it into his office.

There's two ways I can deal with Cyrus right now. I can grovel and beg forgiveness, or I can act like a big shot. I dial up big shot, waltz into his office, and grace his guest chair with my ass. He continues to rage. It's impressive; he still hasn't paused for breath. He finishes his bluster about my reckless gunplay and launches a harangue about me losing Hector.

I examine my fingernails. I can't keep them nice doing

this kind of work. It's too bad. I'd have great-looking hands if my nails weren't so chipped.

Cyrus finally runs out of breath and plunks down in his chair. He groans. "I'll never hear the end of this. The damned job wasn't even in our section. We only picked it up because Hector is based in Germany's half of the Middle East." He winces and gingerly places his hand over his stomach. "Do you know how many Levels I have that give me the ulcers you do?"

I stop examining my nails and chirp, "Don't you want to see my new toys, Cyrus? Here, watch me pick up your desk."

He looks away and gives me the hand, like a cop stopping traffic. He gently rubs his midsection and mutters, "For Christ's sake, Alix. You've worked here for over four years. You know I can't have you accelerating your Development Schedule."

"Well, how about yesterday? I'd be a pile of paprikash right now if I hadn't gotten my new Mods."

Cyrus says, "Scarlet, your Development Schedule does more than extend your physical abilities. It also strengthens your emotional capacities." He's still rubbing his stomach. "I'm concerned about the effect this job may have had on you. You know, when I was your age—"

I cut him off. "You were blowing stuff up and killing people, just like me."

His hand comes off his stomach and slams the desk in front of him. "I was *not* pulling Level 12 missions by myself!" Cyrus stands up and paces around behind his desk. "I thought I was seeing things when I read your father's name on the mission summary yesterday. How the hell could you pull the sheet for that Job Number? You *knew* it was way too high for you."

"I knew I could do it, and Virgil didn't say anything—"

Now it's his turn to cut me off. "That's because Virgil is a well-connected moron! You haven't even done a solo 5 yet and you try to pull a solo 12—in the middle of Manhattan!" He's gotten loud again. "How much competition was in that restaurant besides Hector and the girl you terminated?"

Well, let's check the ol' memory cache and find out.

One of my Mods is a government-only device called Autonomous Single Day Memory Recall Loop, or Day Loop for short. It contains a digital record of everything I've seen and heard during the past twenty-four hours. Yesterday's lunch was only nineteen hours ago, so it's still in there. I center my Day Loop in my Eyes-Up display and rewind it to the event.

"Not sure," I say, "but I met her grieving friends outside."

Cyrus is not amused. He puts both hands on his desk and leans toward me to growl, "Exactly! You had no idea how much competition there was. What if the woman sitting behind you was working with the girl?"

"There was no woman behind me. It was two men in shirts and ties. One had a brown jacket."

While I continue to review my Day Loop, I completely miss what Cyrus is trying to tell me, that is, until he shouts, "Don't get smart with me, Alix! Not now. Your situational awareness was shallow at best. You had no backup. You could have wasted over thirty civilians with that goddamn barrage of yours. It risked everything we've put into you, and for all you know, it took out some of our own agents!" That had never occurred to me. A solo is a solo, I thought. Then again, it is ExOps.

"Was I alone?" I ask.

Cyrus leans back off his hands, stands up, and paces around some more. "Yes, but only because the Job Number was designed for an Infiltrator." Cyrus lectures me that following a Russian Level like Hector requires proper experience and training. Hector is retired, but he still has his Mods and Enhances.

The CIA wanted us to find out who he was visiting in New York. They think Hector is freelancing for someone, and if that someone is an American, he's probably up to no good.

Cyrus says, "We expected *something*, but that situation escalated much faster than we thought it would."

"Who was the chick with the big sunglasses?"

He looks out the window and answers, "Your picture of her told us she was a Protector, but we don't know who she was working for."

A Protector. Of course. Those weren't sunglasses; they were external optics.

Cyrus continues, "We've been trying to trace her origin since yesterday afternoon, but the Information Department hasn't found any connections to the Germans, the Russians, or the Chinese." Cyrus adds that it's odd that her employer would send a Level like her on that kind of job. Protectors usually work as high-visibility bodyguards, not undercover agents.

I foolishly ask him what happened to the restaurant. His subsequent tirade loudly informs me that he'll spend months filing reports about all the collateral damage. I try to tell him that most of the destruction was done by the competition, but Cyrus shouts, "No excuses! It was a close-quarters urban Job Number. That's why we assigned this to Grey in the first place."

Stealthy, careful, and methodical, an Infiltrator like Grey would be exactly the kind of Level to put into a crowded city restaurant. Not a cocky Interceptor with an outrageously powerful handgun.

As if Cyrus can read my thoughts, he yells, "And where the hell did that sidearm of yours come from, anyway? I know you tested well, Alix, but you're not cleared for custom ordnance." He's right. My small arms skill is 10, so I was issued an LB-502, which has the standard targeting software and fires only 30-caliber ammo. I'm trying to think of what to say besides "Actually, boss, it's the Level 20 weapon I swiped from my dead dad's safe full of classified ExOps bullshit," when Cyrus gets a call on his commmphone.

"Front Desk," he barks. His eyebrows drift apart, then slam back together as he listens to the caller. I expect him to comm silently, but he continues to comm out loud: "Read me the address again . . . Okay, that's what I thought you said. When did you receive this? All right, send this intel to the Info people, prep two Squads ASAP, and find me a Level who can lead a Smash 'n' Grab. No, from my section. Yes, he'll do fine. Put one Squad under Scarlet. Yes, I know. I'll clear her with Chanez." He comms Patrick. "Solomon, meet me in the garage right away." My pulse speeds up, because when Cyrus uses our field handles, it means we're on the clock.

Then he says to me, "Scarlet, there's been an incident at your house."

CHAPTER 5

The front door of my house has been smashed open. Inside it looks like a hurricane blew through. Patrick runs a scan for heat signatures, but it turns up negative. Mom's car is in the driveway, but nobody's home. Nobody warm anyway.

"*CLEO?*" I run around the first floor and shout, "*Mom?* Where are you?" It's such a disaster in here—the inside of my house is almost unrecognizable—that it feels like a different address. Cyrus and I go upstairs to search for clues. Every cabinet, drawer, and closet has been opened and rifled through. They even punched holes in the walls to look for secret hiding places.

Cyrus asks, "Scarlet, did your mother go to work today?"

"No, she was working from home. The water heater crapped out and she needed to be here for the plumber."

Downstairs, Trick examines the house with his scanners. Suddenly he comms, "Oh, shit! Scarlet! Cyrus, sir! Time to go!"

Cyrus and I look at each other. I comm, "Time frame?"

"Right now!" Trick shouts as his footsteps run out the front door.

Cyrus and I each leap out a window and jump off the porch roof. We land halfway across the front lawn. Cyrus drops to the ground and ends up flat on his stomach. I come down on my feet, but I'm immediately knocked off them as the home I've grown up in explodes with a shattering roar. I sail across the street and bash into my neighbor's garage door. The little windows in the door shatter and shower me with glass shards. Trick is there a few moments later, followed by a hailstorm of house chunks and everything they used to contain.

"Alix! I mean . . . Scarlet, are you all right?" It's touching how concerned he is about me. Most people don't have that kind of person in their life, so I consider myself lucky. He's not supposed to call me Alix when we're on a job, but he sometimes loses his composure when I go flying around.

"Yeah . . ." I wheeze. "Wind . . . knocked out of me." I groan as I brush off dust and broken glass. I climb to my feet and stagger out to the street so I can watch what's left of my house burn to the ground while I try to get my breath back. "Trick, you're sure there was . . . nobody in there, right?"

"Absolutely. I checked infrared, spectral, aural, positronic—"

"Okay, okay, I got it. Good. Where was the bomb?"

Trick runs his hand through his hair. "Down in the basement, behind the furnace. I didn't get a chance to examine it, but I heard a mechanical timer ticking."

Cyrus walks around the burning pile of rubble and examines the smoking house bits. "The people who set this device would have given themselves time to get away, but not much more. We aren't far behind them." He walks over to the two of us and says, "The debris pattern is fairly broad, and the individual pieces are relatively small. I'd say this was about twenty ounces of RDX or maybe a pound of HMX." He's been on the job for so long that he can tell what kind of bomb it was simply by looking at the mess it leaves behind.

Cyrus comms back to HQ for some Tech Specialists to scan the area for intel about who did this and where they went. I turn away from the blazing wreckage only to see my family's ruined possessions sprayed all over the neighborhood. Up and down the street my neighbors stand on their front lawns watching the show.

Until I was four years old we moved every six months

or so, but we've lived here for fifteen years now. Even when my dad died, Cleo and I still had the house. Now she's missing, I'm homeless, and all my stuff just got blown to hell. My breath comes in little gulps, and my eyes can't focus. I'm tempted to take some Kalmers, but I'm supposed to use my meds only when I'm in the field. Cyrus finishes delivering his directions and turns around to look at me. His eyebrows move apart, and he walks over and wraps one of his big arms around me. I lean into him, close my eyes, and cry into his shirt.

She's fine, she'll be fine.

I stand in the circle of Cyrus's arm. I decide that I'm in the field and tell my neuroinjector to give me a hit of Kalmers. The Tech Specialists arrive. Patrick takes them around the site before rejoining Cyrus and me.

The three of us drive back to HQ. Patrick zips upstairs to use Info's jackframes, Cyrus heads for his office, and I clatter down to the armory to get heated up and meet with a group of Squad guys. I walk by rows of armored suits, all different shapes and sizes. The really enormous suits are exoskeletal robots used deep underwater or in other hazardous locations like erupting volcanoes.

I don't need a primary gun or communication stuff, but I need everything else. I load up on ammo, grenades, and a full suit of SoftArmor. I keep a small mirror in my locker, and as I dress, I see that I've got dust all over my face and the bandage on my cheek needs to be replaced. On the wall behind me is a rack of mechanical devices that look like body parts. These are the neuroprosthetics for people who have had hunks of themselves blown off. Hands, feet, legs, arms—all the body's parts except heads and chests. There's even a lower torso kit that includes a full set of legs complete with pelvis. I try to imagine how someone who'd lost that much of her body could possibly survive long enough to have this huge prosthetic installed. Nothing pleasant comes to mind.

Trick comms in, "Scarlet, she's okay. They've got your mom in an office park near Quantico." Trick is the fastest jackframe operator in the organization, which I appreciate now more than ever.

"Thanks, T," I comm back.

He tells me, "We'll find her, babe. Then you can give 'em the F.U.C.K.," and comms off. Trick and I have a little in-joke about how many acronyms everybody uses at ExOps. One day at lunch he came up with Freaking Unstoppable Cranium Krusher, and I laughed soda out my nose.

I buckle on my SoftArmor, stop worrying about prosthetics, and listen to the *whop-whop* of the helicopters coming to pick us up. "We'll find her all right," I whisper to myself, "and once we do, craniums won't be the only freaking things I crush."

CHAPTER 6

The Tech Specialists have analyzed a bunch of stuff from the abduction site formerly known as my house. God only knows what they found. I leave that technical crap to the eggheads. Whatever it was, they worked even more frantically than normal because Cleo is one of our people, and nobody fucks with ExOps' people.

Our mission requires three helicopters: one gunship for air cover and two slicks to transport personnel. Each slick carries an eight-man Squad while the Mission Commander rides in the gunship. I get in Slick One with Cyrus, Patrick, and Alpha Squad.

As soon as we're aboard the helicopters, I have Alpha Squad's Med-Tech clean out the cut on my cheek and apply a new bandage. Patrick makes sure my SoftArmor is properly secured, then I recheck my ammo and grenades. Good to go.

While the choppers fly us to Quantico, Cyrus comms his boss to get me promoted from Level 4 to Level 6. He speaks out loud, so I can hear his end of the conversation.

"Yes, Director Chanez, I said Scarlet. Yes, that Level, the Interceptor from yesterday's mission in New York. No, sir, she survived it with only a light bullet wound. I know, sir, but the abductee, Cleopatra Nico, is her mother." Cyrus listens for a moment. "Right, Cleo from Admin. Sir, I want Scarlet on this Smash 'n' Grab, but her clearance is too low to lead one of the Squads." Long pause. "Director Chanez, may I . . . Yes, sir . . . Yes, but sir . . ." He shuts his eyes. "Sir, with all due respect, if we don't involve Scarlet in her own mother's rescue, we'll need a crew of Vindicators to keep her away from it." Cyrus winks at me and continues. "Besides, sir, she fits the mission parameters perfectly, and there will be plenty of oversight." Another pause. "Very good, sir. So I can file this promotion with your approval?" He listens for a long time. Trick, who has been eavesdropping, gives me a smile and two thumbs up. Finally Cyrus signs off with "Yes, sir, as you say. Thank you, sir."

So I'm a Level 6, and Cyrus sternly lectures me about ExOps process and procedure. Like I give a shit about that right now. For all I know, my mom has been tortured or raped or killed. Show me the bad guys and I'll give *them* some process and procedure.

The choppers hurtle in low and land outside a bucolic office park in Virginia, near the marine base at Quantico. We all jump out of the bird before it's even on the ground. Cyrus and Trick run to the gunship and hop on as it lifts off again.

It turns out that the Mission Commander is Raj. He's the last person I want to take orders from, but he's available, he's got the right clearance, and I've heard he's effective in the field. When I ask Cyrus why he doesn't lead this op himself, he says he wants to assess Raj's leadership skills.

I'm about to tell my boss what I think of Raj's leadership skills when Raj comms me from the gunship on my private frequency. "Scarlet, listen up, because I'm only gonna say this once. I don't know how you sweet-talked the Front Desk into promoting you two Levels at once, but if you screw up my mission, I'll have you demoted back down to Training."

Before I can spit out one of my patented smart-ass responses, he switches to the Job Number's group frequency and broadcasts his orders to the teams. Raj directs me to assault the main entrance of the facility with Alpha Squad while Beta Squad surrounds the rest of the building. Rah-Rah will direct the operation from the heavily armed gunship helicopter.

I bring Alpha Squad to the north side of the office park. The guys gather around me and check their gear while I finalize some comm protocols with Patrick. This Squad is all business, no chatter or grab-assing. Squad members are highly trained but nonenhanced soldiers equipped with on-helmet radios that send and receive on the same frequencies as my commphone. Some of them are rejects from Camp A-Go-Go, but anyone who makes it into Initial Training automatically qualifies for Squad duty. Despite the rejection, or maybe because of it, Squaddies tend to have genuine respect for those of us who graduate as Levels. When they're good to go, they radio their Squad number to me, followed by "ready."

Once my guys finish checking in, I comm, "Raj, this is Scarlet. We're prepped and ready to go."

He comms back, "Roger, Scarlet. Proceed to the main entrance and enter the building."

"Roger that." I lead Alpha Squad up to the front door. There's no point in subtlety. We arrived in fully loaded, nonstealthed helicopters. The baddies know we're out here. My troopers lock and load their weapons, then assume a chevron formation behind me to cover our approach.

I comm, "Solomon, this is Scarlet, acknowledge."

"Solomon ready." This is Trick in the command helicopter.

Raj comms for the green light from Cyrus. "Almighty, this is Raj. Permission to proceed with Job Number AB-789."

The comm-handle "Almighty" is reserved for the case officer who bears final responsibility for the job. Normally, the Front Desk doesn't oversee missions directly, but Cyrus knows my mom personally, and he likes to stay connected to the fieldwork.

Cyrus replies to the whole team, "Almighty to Raj,

permission granted." Then, only to me, "Give 'em hell, kiddo."

"Roger that, boss. Hell will be a step up for these motherfuckers."

I've had tons of training for this, but it's my first large operation and my hands are shaking. I release more Kalmers into my bloodstream as I signal my demo guy to blow the north door. He hesitates and says, "Ma'am, we don't even know if it's locked."

I glower at him, jab a finger toward the door, and cry, "Boom!" He scurries up to the door and squishes a blob of C-4 into the doorjamb. Obviously, this guy doesn't understand the psychological aspect of this kind of work. I want these kidnapping assholes totally freaked out so they make all kinds of mistakes.

The demo guy gets the charge wired up, runs back to my position, kneels, and shouts, "Fire in the hole!" We duck our heads, the door blows up, and I charge into the smoke as chunks of door frame and wall land on the grass and front walkway. Alpha Squad crashes in behind me. Trick immediately feeds me directions.

"Scarlet, stay to the right of the security area . . . Turn down this hall . . . Take the second door on the right and go up the stairs."

I open the door by blasting the doorknob with a giant slug from Li'l Bertha.

The .50-caliber bullet rips a grapefruit-size hole through the door and carries away the entire latching mechanism. This is part of our standard assault procedure. It's in case the doors can be remotely secured behind you. When you're on offense, you don't want anything locked.

"Roger, Solomon." I keep it short because I'm sure the baddies are monitoring our comm chatter. Under different circumstances I'd make all snuggly and stuff, but there's not much point since the version of "snuggly" I'm bringing is the kind that results in broken bones and ruptured organs.

We advance to the top of the stairs. I pause to make sure everybody is right behind me. I comm to Trick, "Solomon, advise." Again I keep it short. He knows where we are.

Trick comms back, "Vicinity clear, hard stop 200 left."

I blast the doorknob off and rip the door open. Trick has told me that the area behind the door is clear but that there will be some competition two hundred feet to my left. I use hand signals to direct Squads 7 and 8, my two most junior troopers: *Hold here and cover our rear.* Then I take Squads 1 through 6 to the left.

"Solomon, do we have a fix on the subject?" I figure this is safe to comm since it's such an obvious thing to ask.

"Affirmative, quantum vector 18 down." Patrick and his codes. His cue is "quantum vector," which tells me the actual position is the opposite of whatever he says. Mom is eighteen feet up, so two stories. This means we can fight heavy as long as we don't demolish the whole structure. We pass a row of dark windows that look into a large, dimly lit conference room. I check Li'l Bertha's sensors and see four targets around the corner. Trick is about to comm in, but I cut him off. It's showtime.

"Squads 1 through 6, follow me!" I bang a Madrena-line boost and dash around the corner like a 110-pound demon. Four paramilitary guys are taking cover behind a row of big filing cabinets down the hall. They try to draw a bead on me, but I'm too fast and too small. I zigzag around their shots, waving Li'l Bertha back and forth like a scythe. She lays off the flammable stuff since we don't want to burn the whole facility down. Instead she pukes out a swarm of large-caliber slugs. Her .50-cals punch through the cabinets and leave gaping holes in the guys hiding behind them.

Trick comms, "Scarlet, hold up!" I've already signaled Squads 5 and 6 to move forward and make sure it's clear when the wall of the conference room disintegrates in a roar. Squads 5, 4, and 2 go down immediately. The rest of my Squad hits the deck while I switch to infrared and dive through the crumbling wall, toward the ambush. It's two guys on a crew-served machine-gun. It illuminates the room like a strobe light and makes an incredible racket. Squads 3 and 6 take damage while I bounce a grenade off the ceiling and into the machine gunner's nest.

I put my head down, and the floor bucks under me. This is very close quarters. The grenade was only thirty feet away from me when it went off. Something lands next to me. It's a lower leg, complete with boot. I check Li'l Bertha, but her sensors are dark. All clear. Squads 7 and 8 hustle around the corner, but I had them deployed too far away, and they're too late to help.

"Trick, how'd you miss those fucking guys?" I have to yell this over the frantic chatter of my wounded Squad mates. I run to see how badly they're hit.

"Alix, you're going too fast! My scanners have trouble seeing the middle of the building. That's what I've been trying to tell you."

Raj cuts in. "Solomon, keep the comm in protocol." Oh, right. He's using my real name.

Trick gets back to business, "Scarlet, please report."

"All clear. Five nicks, three heavy and two light," meaning three of my guys are badly wounded and two are just scratched up. Squads 5, 4, and 2 took most of the incoming fire. Their SoftArmor stopped the bullets that hit their torsos but not the ones that hit their arms and legs. Squads 3 and 6 had taken cover to return fire, so the only damage they took was from ricocheting bits of glass. The rest of us whip out field dressings and help the most severely wounded guys first. My hands begin to tremble again. I hold myself together with more Kalmers.

Cyrus comms, "Raj, reinforce Alpha with yourself and Beta's lower four." Cyrus sends Raj to me with Beta Squad's 5, 6, 7, and 8 guys. Squad members are numbered in order of seniority, with 1 the most senior and 8 the least. Cyrus and Patrick will cover the outside with the helicopters and Beta Squad's four most experienced troopers.

Alpha Squad's Med-Tech tends to my injured men while I prowl back and forth watching out for competitors. Raj and Beta Squad's 5 through 8 charge up the stairs. Raj gives me the hairy eyeball, then looks around to take in the situation. He reassigns the Beta guys as part of my Squad, then turns back to me.

"Well, at least you're in one piece," he rumbles,

"Yeah, terrific. You want to take point?" I reload Li'l Bertha while we talk so I don't have to see his face tell me what he thinks of my assault skills.

Raj answers, "No, you're quicker in these tight spaces, but I'll be right behind you."

I slam the ammo pack into my gun and look up at him. "To keep me from fucking up again? Look, why don't you just—"

Cyrus comms in, "Scarlet, cut the crap. Move out!"

Fine. I comm to Trick, "Solomon, this is Scarlet, direction."

"Scarlet, proceed down the hall, past the conference room." And then he adds, "Slowly!"

Slowly. This sucks. My mom is held hostage only two floors away, and Trick has got me in Super Slo-Mo. We ease our way down the hall and across the second floor. I monitor Li'l Bertha's sensors while Raj shoulders his Bitchgun—a savage and unruly beast of a weapon. The 50-mm grenades it fires are just this side of mortar rounds. Only Vindicators like Raj get Bitchguns. They're too big for any other type of Level. The kick would probably tear my whole upper body off. It's the most destructive personal firearm in the world. Rah-Rah must have done really well in his large firearms skill test. The fact that he's cleared to deploy with this game-changing monster lets me see him in a whole new light.

Patrick leads us to another set of stairs. I signal Squads

6 and 7 to wait here and cover our backs, then I take the rest forward.

"Solomon, how's the view?"

"Like glass, Scarlet. Increase speed to the third floor. You've got a clear entrance, with some competition in the middle of the floor." I run up the stairs, shoot open the door's lock, and shove the door open. I peek around the corners to make sure it's clear, and then I scamper through the doorway.

Raj and I lead our guys up the passageway and around the corner to a point directly above where we got ambushed downstairs. I flash my Squad the hold signal so Patrick can thoroughly scan this area.

"Scarlet, two hostiles in the interior space. Same as downstairs." Another ambush. *Gotcha, fuckos.*

Raj hand signals to me and the Squad: *Take cover.* Then he opens fire. His Bitchgun hammers the wall down in flaming six-foot chunks. Big Raj leans forward to counteract the gun's monstrous kick. His feet skid back a few inches every time he fires, and everything in front of him turns into dust and smoke. It's like watching Thor defend Valhalla.

Beyond the roar of Raj's gun, we hear a rapid series of snaps, crackles, and pops as our competitors' ammo catches fire. Raj stops shooting, backs up to my position, and reloads from a big black canvas bag he has slung over his shoulder. We all hunker down while the dust settles. I switch to infrared and see a pile of still-warm body parts off in the far corner of what used to be the third floor conference room.

"Solomon, direction."

"Jesus, Scarlet, everybody all right?" We must have whited out Trick's sensors.

"Fully vertical, Solomon. Not a nick."

"Roger, Scarlet. Keep going. Next stairwell, straight 200."

We duck and cover our way down the demolished hallway. Raj and I are up front while the Squad scans the flanks and rear, watching for surprises. Things are going much better now that we've slowed down a bit. I'm about to comment to Raj on this fact when I remember that we got pounced on downstairs because I was being a cherry dumbass. All this thinking cramps my concentration, so I rip the fifty-fifty mix of Madrenaline and Kalmers I've nicknamed the Scarlet Speedball.

It's hard to balance the uppers and downers. The Madrenaline makes me fast, but if I overdo it, my hands shake like the hips on a belly dancer. The Kalmers help me chill, although in excess they make me dizzy. In the correct proportion they allow me to function at a super-human level, but the combination makes my head hurt, especially my teeth. That's where the Overkaine comes in.

We approach the door to the stairway on the far side of the floor. "Solomon, direction."

"Stand by, Scarlet, very blurry." We stand by, then we hear some noise in the stairway. The door bursts open. It's three of the paramilitary guys! They're as surprised as I am, but they aren't hopped up on synthetic adrenaline, so it's game over for them. I punch the first one in the throat, shoot the second guy in the face, then spin around and kick the third sucker so hard that he flies backward and cracks his skull on the wall. They all hit the ground at the same time while the Squaddies rush by me and pound the shit out of them. ExOps Squad troops are serious about protecting their Levels.

My guys are still giving the baddies a giant tune-up when Trick comms, "Scarlet, retain some of those assets for interrogation."

Oh, right, we're supposed to harvest some intel. But by the time I call off my Squad, it's too late. It might have been too late anyway. Those were some masterful Bruce Lee–style hits I laid out.

"Uhh, roger that, Solomon." I'll break it to Trick later. I look at Raj, who has a funny expression on his face. His eyes are scowling, but the corners of his mouth are twitching like he's trying not to laugh. Maybe he likes kung fu movies, too. I point up the stairs and say to Raj, "Shall we?"

Raj shakes his head and grins despite himself. He says, "We shall."

We creep into the stairwell, then we hear some muted explosions and a long exchange of small-arms fire from outside.

"Solomon, this is Beta 1. Be advised, multiple hostiles exiting from the south side." The sound of gunfire crackles through Beta 1's radio microphone. Some of the rats are trying to jump ship.

Patrick is ready. "Beta, this is Solomon. Suppress hostiles and stand by for support." More noise from outside as our helicopters pitch in. We don't always bring a gunship with us, so this may have caught the kidnappers off guard.

I climb up the stairs slowly because Trick is busy coordinating the activity outside. At least I thought he was.

"Scarlet, this is Solomon. You look clear to the top floor."

"Roger." I launch myself up the stairs with Raj and Alpha Squad right on my six. Rapid movement now counts for more than worrying about our comms being monitored. When we reach the door, I hang back and let Raj bash the lock out with the butt of his Bitchgun.

"Solomon, this is Scarlet, direction."

"Wait one, Scarlet." The noise level outside dies down for a second, and then there's a huge explosion that bounces us around like the BB in a can of spray paint. Patrick must have been evacuating a couple of our people from the blast zone. He's right back with us after the floor stops dancing around under us.

"Scarlet, be advised you have five hostiles coming your way. Another four have exited onto the roof with the subject."

Mom!

"Roger that, Solomon." My jaws are clamped tight. Only my training and the drugs keep the screams inside.

I stand at the door and flash hand signals to my guys: *Five enemies approaching from front.* Raj and the Squad are set up on the steps below my door. I'm on point, at the top of the stairs, monitoring Li'l Bertha's bad guy detector.

When I see movement in the passageway, I pull the door open, uncork a grenade, and toss it out into the hall. They're only a few feet away, much closer than I thought. One of them yells "Grenade!" and winds his leg up to boot it back at me. I slam the door shut and brace myself between it and the stairway's handrail. The door bucks into my back as the bad guys try to kick it open. Then the grenade blows the door completely off its hinges, and my featherweight self catapults down the stairs past Alpha Squad.

I tumble down the steps as Raj opens up with the Bitch. Imagine five Mack trucks crashing into each other at full speed. That's almost how loud a 50-mm grenade blaster sounds in an enclosed concrete stairway. My ears are ringing as I hustle back up the stairs, and Raj steps to the side to let me pass. He needs to reload, and the Squad can mop up whoever survived that boom plate special we just served up. I lead the Squad through the shattered doorway and onto the top floor. We find a seven-hundred-square-foot area completely covered in blood, limbs, heads, and mangled torsos. One of our victims is still alive even though he's lost both arms and his chest is blown open so wide that I can see right through it. He sits on the floor and breathes with shallow gasps. His eyes swing from one blood-gushing shoulder to the other. Then he shudders, coughs, and stops breathing.

Raj finishes reloading his gun and rejoins us. Back to work. "Solomon, this is Scarlet, direction."

"Take a left out of the stairway, go straight to the corner, and up the maintenance stairs to the roof."

"Hostiles?"

"I've got eyes on four hostiles on the roof." A pause.

"Hurry, Scarlet, they've got her with them. We can't risk it with the choppers."

I rocket down the smoking, bloody hallway. Raj and Alpha Squad barrel along after me. They know what this means to me and that I'm done with any kind of strategy. We soar up the stairs. Raj and I hit the roof door simultaneously. The door flies open, and Raj and the Squad troops deploy into a kneeling perimeter around the doorway.

I'm so cranked up that my teeth chatter. Time moves at one-tenth its normal speed, and everything sounds murky, like I'm underwater. The four hostiles are gathered around Cleo behind some giant air conditioners. The two guys in the middle have their guns pointed at my mom. Her eyes go wide when she sees me, but she doesn't move or cry out. ExOps' mandatory training for agents' family members taught her to keep quiet in exactly this situation.

Li'l Bertha goes into Sniper mode: .30-caliber slugs, fired singly, no bursts. Her gyroscopes spin up so I'll be able to hold her steady despite all the natural and artificial chemicals zipping through me. Her sensors label the group as Hostiles 1, 2, 3, 4 and Subject. Hostiles 1 and 4 stand in the open a few feet away from my mother, so I pick them off first with shots to both eyes, both guys. *Ba-bam! Ba-bam!* They're still falling as I charge toward Hostiles 2 and 3 to take away their cover. I'm almost all the way around the ventilators when they instinctively point their guns at me instead of my mom.

Now they die.

I leap in the air to throw off their aim. My jump peaks at about fifteen feet. Li'l Bertha spits out shots for each of the two remaining kidnappers, one at each of their guns. Before these fuckos realize they've been disarmed, I land right in front of them. *Time to F.U.C.K. them up.* I smash Li'l Bertha's barrel into Hostile 2's neck so hard that it slashes his carotid artery open. He screams, and a quart of his blood splatters all over me. I turn to Hostile 3. His eyes are wide open, and his mouth makes a silent little circle. I rear back and smash his chin with a right-handed uppercut that crushes his jawbone into jelly. His teeth shatter, and blood squirts out of his eye sockets. His face turns dark purple, and he tips over like a fallen tree. Something gray spurts out of his nose as he lands flat on his back.

I shut off my neuroinjector's flow of Madrenaline, and my sense of time whooshes back to normal. Mom isn't hurt, so I check myself for wounds. I'm not shot, but my right hand is pointed the wrong way and is throbbing with pain. I'm covered in blood, guts, and eyeball goop. Little bits of bone, shards of teeth, and pieces of skin are stuck to me like glitter.

My stomach churns, I wheeze when I breathe, and suddenly I can see only in black and white. My head and my guts race to see which I do first: pass out or lose my lunch. My legs feel like rubber, so I sit down among what's left of the dead guys and sob so hard that I can't even throw up. My mom says my name, and even though I'm all covered in dirt and gore, she kneels down and throws her arms around me.

I don't know what I'd do if I lost my mother, but I do know she has the best daughter in the whole fucking world.

CORE   PUB-WTH-1090

Washington Times-Herald, May 3, 1980

Residents Mistake Planned Demolition for Gun Battle

QUANTICO, VA—The Quantico police department was flooded with calls from local residents reporting gunshots and explosions at a nearby office park yesterday afternoon. Liam Parrish, a longtime Quantico resident, said, "It sounded like World War III over there."

Apparently, an out-of-state construction crew simply forgot to notify the town of the planned demolition. The police are investigating the incident to ascertain if the crew had the required permits. Police Chief Gary Ren told reporters last night, "We're definitely looking into this. It's not like we just let people come into our town and blow things up."

CHAPTER 7

Overkaine is funny stuff. I normally run it in the middle of a mission, when my pulse is up and its effects are muted by the other drugs sloshing around in my brain. Now, sitting in Director Chanez's sleek and spacious conference room, I can really tell how strong this shit is. I can't feel my broken right hand at all. The painkillers have even affected my taste buds, because the doughnuts I'm noshing on normally seem a lot sweeter than this. I'm on a strong localized dose of Overkaine until I can get into surgery.

My hand is ruined from punching that last kidnapper's head so hard. Dr. Herodotus has me scheduled late tonight for a complete replacement from the wrist down, which I have mixed feelings about. Losing this piece of me feels like I'm dying a little bit. But having a synthetic hand could be a great boost for my career, because the next time I smack some fool in his head, it won't be my hand that breaks.

Meanwhile, my head swims and my right arm is all pins and needles. My undamaged left hand pops a bite of doughnut into my mouth and picks up my third cup of coffee this morning. I slept like crap last night. I've built up so much Post-Stimulant Sleep Disorder over the last two days that it feels like I'll never sleep again. I guess I'll get some rest during my surgery, if that even counts.

The door to the conference room opens, and everyone else streams in: Cyrus, Cleo, Patrick, and Patrick's im-

mediate superior, Information Coordinator William
Harbaugh.

"Oh, *there* you are," Cleo says as she pulls out the
chair next to me.

Patrick sits on my other side. "Look at you, first one
here."

"Yeah," I say, "I thought I'd get a head start on the
doughnuts." Everyone chuckles as they all take their
seats. Levels are notoriously late for meetings, and
greater incentives than free pastries have been employed
to encourage punctuality.

Director Chanez walks in with his arms full of paperwork. He chats with a fiftysomething man I've never
met. The mystery man is medium height and slim, has
salt-and-pepper hair, and wears an expensive-looking
suit. His lined face is very sharp and hard, like it could
split firewood. He's familiar somehow.

Chanez sits at the head of the polished table and lays
his papers down in front of him. Cyrus and Harbaugh
arrange themselves on the opposite side from me. The
fiftysomething man graces the chair at the foot of the
table with his Brooks Brothers butt.

"Welcome, everyone," Chanez says. Then to me,
"How's that hand, Scarlet?"

"Pretty numb, sir."

"Hmm, yes." He nods. "Will you be able to get into
surgery?"

"Yes, sir. Tonight, at twenty-three hundred. It's the
best they could do on such short notice."

"Well, let's get started, then." Chanez holds his hand
toward the man at the foot of the table. "I'll begin by
welcoming our guest, Director Jakob Fredericks of the
Strategic Services Council. He's here to offer us his
broad view of the international clandestine landscape."

That's where I know this guy from. He's one of the
district's biggest brainiacs. Fredericks runs his own think
tank on K Street, but he used to be ExOps. In fact, he
was my dad's Front Desk, the same as Cyrus is for me

now. Except Cyrus isn't a self-centered, conceited son of a bitch. It's been a while, but yeah, I recognize this guy now.

Fredericks briefly flashes a row of perfectly straight teeth. "Hello, everyone," he says. "It's good to be back where the action is."

Next to me, Mom sniffs sharply. She retains a polite expression, but I can tell that she's uncomfortable. There's an awkward pause, then Fredericks says to me, "Alix, you remember me, don't you? Your parents had me over for dinner a few times."

Cleo answers, "I doubt she remembers, Jakob. That was a long time ago."

Fredericks doesn't shift his attention away from me. "Yes." The look in his eyes makes me feel like a prize sow at the county fair. "It was."

The drugs and the situation prevent me from summoning one of my charmingly sarcastic replies, so I simply say, "It's good to see you again, Director Fredericks."

He nods, pauses, then swivels in his chair. "All right, Ed, let's see what you've got."

Director Chanez stands in front of the blabscreen on the wall. "In the last twenty-four hours we've had two major incidents, both involving Scarlet here. Cleo, I know you've already filed your report on your kidnapping, but can you summarize it for us?"

"Yes, Director." Mom leans forward. "They were Russians. The way they handled their weapons told me they were professionals, but there was something strange about how they carried out their mission." She tells us that the team leader had to repeat his instructions to his men and how confused the group behaved after they took her to the unused office park in Quantico. Tasks weren't clearly assigned, and it seemed like they hadn't had time to rehearse.

Mom continues, "Just before the ExOps team arrived, I saw the kidnappers' leader arguing with one of his lieutenants. I didn't catch all of what they said, but I got the impression that they had been abandoned by their handler. The whole operation seemed poorly planned and rushed." She leans back. Under the table, she wraps her fingers around my left hand.

Fredericks has pulled out a fancy silver pen. He slowly twirls it in his right hand. "Cleo," he says, "am I to understand that you've been transferred from Administration to Operations?"

The muscles in Mom's jaws tighten. "No, Jakob, but I've sat through enough meetings like this to know a blown op when I see one."

Fredericks's eyelids lower a little bit. "Of course." He looks at Chanez and gestures for him to continue.

"Thank you, Cleo," says Chanez. He reaches into the papers in front of him, plucks out a dossier, and reads from it. "Our after-action analysis of Cleo's rescue found that all the competitors had been killed during the assault—" He glances at Cyrus, then at me. "—which was unfortunate." Meaning ExOps couldn't interrogate anyone because Raj and I pounded them all into guacamole.

Chanez picks up another sheet of paper. "The analysis of the firefight scene in Manhattan shows that none of the gunmen were captured or killed, but the pilots and crew of the helicopter perished during the event." He flips a page and continues. "The wreckage of the helicopter was sifted, and the aircraft was traced to a military salvage facility in Tucson, Arizona. The records for this helicopter are incomplete, and an inquiry has been filed." He flips the page again. "The remains of the two pilots and crewmen were examined, and their DNA was matched to the DNA records of four retired marines. These men served together as part of the United States First Naval Air Command in Tokyo. All four were dishonorably discharged three years ago for repeated violations regarding the transport of nonmilitary personnel." Chanez raises his eyebrows and looks up from the report. "They were airlifting prostitutes from Tokyo to the USMC base on Okinawa." He returns to the sheets. "Since then, their whereabouts and activities have been unknown."

Chanez lays the reports down on the table and studies me. "That was quite a crew you took on, Scarlet."

My cheeks flush. "Yes, sir."

"Cyrus," Fredericks says as he calmly regards his pen. "I must point out that when I had your job, I never would have assigned that mission to such an incompetent Level."

"Hey!" I blurt. "I'm right fuckin' here, you know." I tap my chest.

Fredericks, unfazed, continues to address Cyrus. "She can't even control herself in a meeting."

I holler, "Well, I'm not some lily-livered desk jockey who falls apart every time the shit hits the fan!"

That gets ol' Jakey's attention. Fredericks swivels toward me like a turret on a battleship. "Scarlet, you blew your cover on a Level 12 *covert operation*! Not at some damned meeting of the Five O'Clock Club!" He slaps the table. "If I were your boss, I'd put you in front of a review board."

My lip curls into a snarl. I lean forward and—

"That'll be all, Scarlet!" Chanez snaps. "Thank you for your input, Director Fredericks. Be assured that Cyrus and I are working with Scarlet to optimize her Development Schedule."

Fredericks locks eyes with Chanez for a moment. "Very well, Ed. Let's get on with this." He smoothes his hair and resumes twirling his pen across his fingers.

"Son of a bitch!" I comm to Trick.

Trick comms back, "Don't let him get to you."

"I am *not* incompetent!"

"Settle down, Hot Stuff. Here's something to consider. Fredericks thinks you were *assigned* to the Hector job."

I try to slow my breathing and comm, "Huh, yeah, I guess he does. Is Chanez gonna tell him that I, um, took the initiative on that one?"

"It doesn't look like it."

Chanez selects another file from his heap and hands it to Harbaugh. "Bill, this is your signals intelligence report. Why don't you walk us through what your people have found."

Harbaugh stands up and takes Chanez's place in front of the blabscreen. He adjusts his tie and clears his throat. "We picked up Hector's comm signal at the airport in Paris, which is how we knew to tail him when he landed in New York." Harbaugh informs us that there was no related comm activity until Hector and I got to the restaurant in Manhattan. Once inside, things picked up speed and the comms started flying.

"The comm calls were very heavily encrypted, and their origins and destinations were spoofed in a maze of routers and proxies. We may never unravel the locations except for the comms we intercepted at their origins. But after twenty-five hours we cracked the encryption."

Ooh, this sounds good. Everyone perks up. Fredericks is especially interested. He sits up straight and stops fiddling with his pen, his mouth hanging slightly open.

Harbaugh says, "The calls were sent without any vox data, so we don't have their voices or inflections."

Fredericks shuts his mouth and glances around the room. I quickly look to the front of the room as Harbaugh uses a small remote control to activate the blabscreen.

"We've assigned labels to the unknown suspects— XSUS One and XSUS Two—and used names for the suspects we do know. Once Hector went into his meeting with the female Protector, we began directly monitoring the restaurant. This is how we nabbed their comms as they were transmitted. Scarlet, you'll appreciate the name we've given the Protector."

He brings up a slide of text. On the screen we see:

Jackie-O to XSUS One: "Our guest says, 'I thought you should know, the report about the Beast is false. He is alive and has been transferred to Carbon.' [pause] I am being watched by an unknown competitor."

Harbaugh comments, "That was the Protector relaying the message she got from Hector. An image file was attached. We think she took a picture of Scarlet with the cameras in her lenses. After the image was forwarded, we have this."

XSUS One to Jackie-O: "Keep the competitor in place. Stand by for further instructions."

Harbaugh pauses to let us read the line, then says, "Thirty minutes later, XSUS One is back." He clicks his remote, and the next line of text appears on the screen.

XSUS One to Jackie-O: "Help is outside. Dismiss guest and terminate competitor."

"And . . . well, we all know what happened next." Harbaugh's eyes dart my way. Everyone looks at me. I gulp down the last of my coffee and try to act like it's no big deal to be the center of this much high-ranking attention. Trick's hand squeezes my thigh under the table and he tries not to smile. I look past Trick's face and see Fredericks pull a handkerchief out of his jacket pocket and pat his forehead with it.

Harbaugh brings up several more lines. "Seven minutes after the firefight, this comm was sent. We were tracking Hector, so we know this is from him. Here we meet our fourth player, whom we've labeled XSUS Two."

Hector to XSUS Two: "Message delivered, but the meeting ended abruptly."

"Now we have a line on XSUS One's comm signal and that of XSUS Two, which is how we picked up this rather heated exchange between the two of them less than a minute later." Harbaugh fills the screen with six lines of text.

One to Two: "I got your message, but the meeting was broken up."

Two: "I heard. We will take care of it."

One: "What have you done to alert the Americans?"

Two: "What makes you think they know anything about this?"

One: "Because it was your organization he—"

Two: "Quiet! Someone may be listening. Why do you think I sent our man?"

Fredericks wipes his forehead with his handkerchief. His face is pale.

"Jakob, are you all right?" Chanez asks. "Do you need some water?"

"No, no," Fredericks insists. He stuffs his handkerchief back in his pocket. "I'm fine, Bill."

Harbaugh gives Fredericks a few more moments. Then he says, "Finally, we have this." The screen displays one last line.

One to Two: "But they didn't send just anyone. They sent his daughter."

Harbaugh and Chanez have already figured out what this final line means, so they don't react. Fredericks turns as white as a ghost. His forehead gleams with sweat, but he remains silent while the rest of us all start jabbering at once.

CHAPTER 8

Cleo covers her mouth with both hands and turns to me. Tears roll down her cheeks and across her fingers. Everyone else is still talking over one another except for me. I'm too busy hyperventilating.

"Mom?" I gasp. "Who is . . ." I can't catch my breath. "Is it really . . ."

She pulls me to her, presses our foreheads together, and whispers, "It's Daddy, honey." She takes a sharp breath, "Oh, my God, it's your father." She sobs, "He's alive, Angel."

Now I'm crying, too. Trick leans over and puts his hands on my shoulders.

Fredericks accepts a glass of water from Chanez while Cyrus peppers Harbaugh with questions.

"Where is he, Bill?"

"We don't know."

Cyrus growls, "What do you *mean* we don't know?"

"Calm down, Cyrus." Harbaugh holds his hands out. "You know our record with Carbon." Harbaugh sits on the edge of the table. "Since we found out Germany had a cloning program in '56, all we've gotten is what little has been in their news."

Mom gently wipes some tears off my face. I grab a napkin and blow my nose. Then I ask Cyrus, "Why are they still calling my dad the Beast?" Cyrus opens his mouth, but the answer comes from the other end of the table.

"Because they're still angry!" It's Fredericks. His colorless face can't seem to decide which expression to wear.

It begins with surprise, slides over to confusion, and then makes a brief stop at terror before starting over again.

He continues, "The German press labeled him the Beast of Berlin because of his foolhardy conduct during the oil embargo crisis."

Cyrus's voice resonates more deeply than normal. "Philip was under *your* supervision at the time, Director."

Fredericks explodes. "I never told him to kidnap women and children, dammit!"

Oh, Christ, not this old argument.

The German oil embargo began as a pissing match between Washington and Berlin. It eventually escalated into one of the worst diplomatic crises of the last forty years. Greater Germany got ticked off about the way American officials were haranguing them for enslaving Europe's Jewish population after the war. So the German Foreign Trade Ministry shut off our supply of petroleum from the German half of the Middle East. The Russians, who own the other half, sure as shit weren't gonna sell us any. The U.S. had to get by on reserves and whatever we could suck out of Texas and Alaska. But that wouldn't last forever.

President Nixon told the CIA to end the embargo by any means necessary. The CIA unleashed ExOps, and it wasn't long before things went crazy. German officials got snatched, and German buildings got bombed. Then the Gestapo retaliated and started doing the same things to us. Not to be outdone, a senior ExOps field agent launched a kidnapping campaign against the families of German politicians and high-ranking civil servants. That ExOps agent was my dad.

One of the abductions was interrupted by the Berlin police, and during the confrontation a young girl was badly hurt. This triggered a huge anti-American protest, which turned into a riot and then became the storming of the American embassy in Berlin. The entire embassy staff was taken hostage. Dad took part in the rescue attempt, which failed, but its spectacular violence shocked the German administration. The situation was spiraling out of control.

The chancellor's office secretly reached out to Washington and hastily negotiated a truce. The CIA withdrew all American agents, including those from ExOps. The kidnapped families were sent home. In exchange for signing a gag order they received financial compensation that was discreetly distributed from a numbered account in Zurich. The American hostages were released. The oil started flowing again, and American politicians stopped crabbing about the enslaved Jews.

Meanwhile that young girl lingered in the hospital for over four years before she died. The German press and public had followed her progress all those years, and her passing sparked a new round of cries for revenge on the Beast. They were still pretty mad.

That happened in an election year, and the resurrected crisis nearly wrecked Nixon's campaign. In the summer, my dad left on a mission. That November, the Germans announced that they had captured and executed the Beast of Berlin. The diplomatic situation settled down and everyone went back to being self-serving dickwads.

But Cleo and I were left devastated. To add insult to injury, some Washington bean counter denied us Dad's death benefits because no one ever actually produced his body. Mom went to see Jakob Fredericks for help, but they got into a big fight instead. Fredericks drummed my mother out of his office, shouting that his career had been ruined by her husband's recklessness and that he wouldn't help us if hell froze over.

Fortunately, Dad's best friend was a Level 18 Vindicator. This best friend paid that narrow-minded bean counter a visit. At midnight. In bed.

We got our first check the next day.

You'd never think someone Cyrus's size would be such a good second-story man. He credits it to the dance lessons he had to take with his five sisters when he was a kid. My dad used to joke that Cyrus could be in the *Guinness Book of World Records* as the world's biggest ninja. Cyrus would lean back from our dining room table and laugh that my dad was already in it for having the world's hollowest leg.

Now Cyrus glares at Fredericks while he stalks around the table to sit next to my mom. She turns from me and wraps her arms around his neck. He holds her while she cries into his shoulder and looks at me with his eyes burning.

He comms to me, "We're getting him back, Alix."

I close my eyes and nod. All I can comm is, "Yes, sir."

Director Chanez returns to the front of the room. "Okay, people, I know this is a big revelation, but let's try to focus on our next step." He turns to Harbaugh and asks, "Bill, we really have no idea where Philip could be?"

"No, sir. Like I said, we've got a lousy batting average with that program." He runs his hand through his hair. "Our deepest contact was when we assisted Germany during the Warsaw Confrontation. We picked up a lot of intel about Carbon, but it's been pretty dry since then."

Harbaugh tells us that while we were helping Germany fend off a Russian invasion, our people were given surprisingly broad access to their classified materials. U.S. Army Intelligence found out about Carbon and hoovered up as much of it as they could. When the crisis ended, so did our classified access.

We didn't hear anything else about Carbon until three years later, when they unveiled the first-ever successful human clone. The U.S. countered a year later with cloned triplets, which absolutely floored the Krauts. Then our stunning cloning program—based on all that intel we swiped—suffered a disastrous scandal and imploded. Congress mired itself in the moral issues that surround cloning like a black swamp. Greater Germany, unconcerned by silly things like human rights, vaulted back into the lead.

"That's our assumption, anyway," Harbaugh concludes. "A research project that big leaves a shadow. We see the shadow sometimes, but that's it. Once we abandoned our own cloning research, tracking Carbon stopped being a priority."

"Well, that's about to change." Chanez looks at Fredericks. "Jakob, what was Philip's last mission again?"

Fredericks presses his handkerchief to his mouth, then holds it in his lap. "He was investigating Russian covert activity in the German sectors of the Middle East."

"That's a pretty broad assignment."

"Philip was a Level 20 Liberator," Fredericks says. "Most of his Job Numbers had flexible parameters."

"Where was his mission centered?"

"It wasn't. He changed location almost every day."

Chanez crosses his arms in front of his chest. "Where was Philip when he was captured?"

"I have no idea."

"Jesus, Jakob." Chanez raises his eyebrows and holds his hands out to his sides. "Give us *something*. Where did he start?"

Fredericks hesitates. Then he looks at the ceiling like he's trying to remember. "Paris," he finally mutters. "His mission started in Paris."

CHAPTER 9

"Here you go, dear," my mother says as she sets a spoon and a bowl of soup in front of me. She arranges the bed pillows behind me so I can sit up straighter, then turns down the volume on the TV before walking back to the kitchen.

"Thanks, Mom." I pick up the spoon and start inhaling the soup.

Mom's voice ricochets from the kitchen: "Ladies don't slurp, Alixandra!"

I sigh and try to eat without making so much noise. One of Cleo's self-appointed titles is etiquette coach, which normally bugs the living shit out of me. For now she can nag all she wants. Friday's craziness completely rewrote my priorities, and I am totally not ready to lose my mother.

I *am* ready to lose this cast on my arm, though. It itches like crazy. The Med-Techs won't give me anything for it because they're worried about how the antihistamines would react with the residual drugs in my body. They were only half joking with me when they said I'd voided my arm's warranty by punching that last guy so hard. Apparently my upgrades are able to withstand only "reasonable force and stress." I told the Med-Techs that we'd see how reasonable *their* behavior was after I'd kidnapped all *their* mothers. I think they're just pissed at me for making them miss their golf games.

I'm quite a sight. My arm is all wrapped up, and there's also the big stupid bandage on my left cheek from that graze I took in New York a few days ago. This is the first time I've had to be rebuilt after a job. When my father was in recovery, he'd gripe nonstop about it, and now I see why. It's only been a couple of days, and I'm *so* fucking bored! I'd be especially grumpy if it weren't for my mom taking care of me.

We're in a two-bedroom suite in the hotel upstairs from Extreme Operations' HQ. The hotel is mostly for VIPs, but it also is used as a hospital and halfway house for homeless recovering Levels and their mothers. It's just as well that we're staying so close to work. The Information Department has spent the entire weekend feverishly plotting a response to the mess I walked into in Manhattan and to Cleo's kidnapping. One guess from Info is that Cleo's kidnappers didn't want my mom so much as they wanted information about my dad. Another guess is that they were supposed to snatch me and got us mixed up.

This has all swirled around me without really sinking in. My father has been dead for eight years, and now we get news that he's turned up alive in Carbon, the Germans' high-profile yet highly classified cloning program. I don't know what to think. I'm so used to how things have been that this feels like it's about someone else. I'd be able to make better sense of it if I weren't so tired from my surgery. I'm also too hungry to think straight.

I hold the bowl in front of my face and chug the last half of the soup. As I bring the bowl down, I see that Cleo has appeared in the kitchen doorway. She puts her hands on her hips and clucks her disapproval. I grin sheepishly, then daintily dab a napkin on my lips with a very prim and proper look on my face. Mom takes the bowl away in a huff. Her mouth makes a thin, straight line not because she's angry but because she's trying not to laugh. My table manners are so hilariously hopeless that she can't stay mad at me about them.

Cleo goes into the kitchen to put the bowl in the sink, and as she walks back into my room, she finally bursts out laughing. She sits next to me on the bed, takes my napkin, and wipes my forehead. I guess the top rim of the bowl got some soup on me when I was drinking it. Now we both start giggling.

"Angel, what will I do with you?" She's still smiling as she takes my face in her hands and looks into my eyes. After a moment, her smile fades and she repeats, more seriously this time, "What *will* I do with you?"

"I'll be fine, Mom. I'll be good at this job. Better even than Daddy was."

After a pause, she says, "I'm not sure how to feel about that, Alix. Your father's work took a terrible toll on him. By the time you were born, he wasn't the man I met and married."

"What was he like when you met?" It's difficult to talk to my mother about my father because she and I had such different relationships with him. The two of them fought a lot, whereas Dad and I got along great on the rare occasions when I saw him.

She gets up and slowly paces around the room. "When we met, he was more . . . balanced. He was strong and capable, but he also had hobbies, interests. He read books about architecture. We'd take walks around the city, and he'd point out different buildings and how they related stylistically. But by the time we had you, all he ever did was that work of his. Of yours." She stops pacing and sits on the bed again. "This—" She waves at all the medical stuff around my bed. "—is the same as it was with your father."

"Not quite the same. You and I aren't fighting all the time."

She looks down at her lap, inhales deeply through her nose, exhales through her mouth, then says, "True. You and I aren't fighting all the time."

We sit quietly for a moment. I ask, "What was all the racket I heard when you guys fought?"

"Oh, my." Another deep breath. "He'd kick the dressers, break the lamps, punch holes in the door. We'd argue about him quitting ExOps and doing something else. He never hit me, but it was still . . . difficult to be around." Cleo looks up at me. "Remember all the shopping you and I used to do together?"

I do remember that. We were always on the lookout for inexpensive furniture at secondhand stores and yard sales. I never thought about what happened to it all, but it sounds like they went through their bedroom sets like other people go through bottles of laundry detergent. I guess I never noticed because when I went into their room, it was always at night. I'd crawl in with my mom after one of my nightmares. When I'd fallen asleep again, she'd carry me back to my room.

"Why would he smash up his own bedroom?" I ask. It seems like a stupid question, but I can't figure it out.

"Oh, God . . . so many reasons. Mostly he needed to vent his anxiety from the field. He'd be alone for months under terrible conditions. Spying isn't like the movies—you know this. There's no room service or fancy cars."

"What was it like?" I talk quietly, the way you do at a funeral.

"He'd be sent to some hellhole to retrieve someone or some item. He'd stake out an obscure little location for weeks, or they'd send him in to do something fast and dreadful. But he'd always do it alone."

"Alone? No Info Operator?"

"Back then Levels didn't have IOs. They did everything by themselves. They'd be inserted alone, and they'd return alone." She looks down at her hands in her lap, "If they came back at all." I reach out with my left hand and wrap my fingers around hers.

Nowadays, all ExOps Job Numbers include a dedicated resource from the Information Department. Exceptions are made for really short jobs, like the one for following Hector around. In those cases, the Level is entrusted with the entire mission, including data acquisition. Most of our missions are big mean mothers, though, and require Info support.

The type of support depends on the job, which means

it mostly depends on the Level's class. Infiltrators typically operate in such deep, long-term cover that they have to get their Info support remotely. Protectors usually work as a security team that includes an Info Operator to synchronize their efforts. Vindicators like Raj tend to act as heavy muscle for larger missions that already include an Info resource.

Then there are Interceptors, like me. We generally don't work as part of a larger group, so we're usually partnered with an Info Operator. Interceptors pull off deep penetrations that result in a lot of intel, but the missions are short, a couple of days to a couple of weeks. Most of the time we only need to maintain a surface cover, which consists of carrying a fake passport and remembering which language to speak. The Info Operator manages the harvested data while the Interceptor does everything else.

I'm not a big rules person, but even I can see where this protocol comes from. I never would have kept my shit together during Mom's rescue if Patrick hadn't been guiding me through it. It hadn't occurred to me that Extreme Operations didn't always work this way.

I ask Cleo, "What made ExOps start requiring Info support?"

She takes a soft breath. "Your father. They'd been thinking about taking that step for a while, but his last mission is what made them finally do it. If he'd had a dedicated Info resource, he probably wouldn't have been captured." She pauses for a minute and almost whispers as she goes on. "He was one of the best they'd ever had. Him and a few others. They created a whole new rating for them. Levels used to only go to 19. They wanted to avoid 20 because it sounds like so much more than 19. But your father and two or three others really were that much better than the other Level 19s."

"What made them so good?"

"They were totally dedicated to the work, and they took the upgrades a lot further than the other Levels.

They were all friends who had entered ExOps around the same time, but it got to be this real macho thing. Who was the toughest? Who could be the most shot up and still finish their missions? Who had modified or enhanced the biggest percentage of their body? They all tried to outdo each other to see who could be the first Level 21."

When I ask her why they did this, she replies, "I think you can answer that for yourself, Alixandra."

She stands up, leaves the room, and returns a moment later with a pack of cigarettes. I've never seen her smoke, so I can only stare as she fluidly pops a cigarette out of the pack and lights it. She inhales deeply and lets out a big cloud of smoke toward the ceiling. She looks fantastic with a cigarette in her hand, and I immediately resolve to take up smoking.

"Alix, after what I saw you do on Friday, I decided to take a good long look at your medical records." She pauses to take another drag on her cigarette. "I suspected that you'd hidden some things from me, but I had no idea you'd gotten so much work done."

"Well, I didn't think you'd let me, so—"

"You're damn right, I wouldn't have! For Christ's sake, you're still a teenager and you've had almost 25 percent of your body modified or enhanced!" She's upset, but I can't blame her. This is my big lie, and I'm totally snagged.

"Cleo, I need them for work."

"Need! What need? Who says you *need* to be a Level 6 already? You're already way ahead of your class, and most field agents don't make Level 6 until they've been in the field for twice as long as you have!" My face must have shown surprise, because she continues, "Yes, I know about your promotion, too, and how Cyrus sold it to Director Chanez." She carries her ashtray over to my bed and sits down next to me again. "Angel, I'll never forget that you came for me, and I love you for it, but I'm also furious that you're turning into your father."

"*Mom*, I'm only—"

"I'm not angry at you, sweetie." She takes my hands. "I'm mad at myself."

Oh, well, okay. As long as I'm off the hook. "How do you mean I'm turning into Daddy?"

"Well, let's go back to why you got all the Mods and Enhances."

"I told you, it's for work. I need them to—"

She gives me the hand. "There's another reason, Alix. Think about how you feel before and after you have these upgrades done."

I think. "Well, before . . . I feel kind of normal, and then after, I feel, I don't know . . ."

"Super?"

Damn, look at the big brain on Mom.

"Well, yeah . . ." I think for a few seconds. "Because I can do things I couldn't do before."

"And how long does that feeling last?"

"It's not like I forget I had them done."

"That's what you think, not what you feel." I'm dimly aware that my mom has a background in behavioral something or other. Here I've thought I've been so sly, hiding things from her. Clearly she's seen a lot more than I thought.

"Cleo, look, I don't know. Like I say, I need them so I can do my work."

Silently, she grinds out her cigarette in the ashtray, then stands up and goes into the kitchen. I think she'll come right back, but she stays in the other room. I switch to infrared and see her leaning against a counter with her arms wrapped around herself. It isn't until she buries her face in her hands that I realize she's crying. I switch off the infrared, suddenly feeling like a Peeping Tom.

Patrick picks this fabulous moment to comm in. "Hey, Alix, got a minute?"

"Uh, not really. I'm in the middle of some intense time with Mom."

"Oh, sorry. I'll comm you later. This can wait."

"Real quick, what is it?"

"We've got a Job Number."

I sit up straight, and my pulse shifts into overdrive. "Where? When?"

"France. As soon as your hand is healed enough for you to travel. We're going to retrace your father's last mission and see what we can turn up while Info looks into Carbon. Chanez wants us to start by talking to our House in Paris."

"Why don't we just call him?" I comm.

"Because the Director wants to keep this job out of CORE. Long-distance comms go through the satellites and are automatically logged. Chanez doesn't want to leave any kind of data trail to tip the other agencies that we're going after Big Bertha."

"How would competitors' agencies read our comm logs?"

"No, *our* agencies," Patrick comms. "He's setting us up with a cover mission. Something we'll have to physically go to Paris for."

What the hell is he talking about? I tilt my head to one side. "Huh?"

"I'll tell you later. You get back to your mom."

Whatever. "Okay. Later."

"Later, *ma cherie*. Hang in there."

CORE   MIS-74-17667A-003

TO: Front Desk, German Section, ExOps
FROM: Office of the Director, ExOps
DATE: May 5, 1980
SUBJECT: Job Number 74-17667A

Cyrus,

You are requested and required to dispatch an Interceptor/IO team to Paris. Their mission is to destroy the operational capabilities of a cell of the Fuerza Libertad.

The FL has become the largest faction of the revived Cuban Liberation Movement, and this group in Paris is channeling money to the Cuban terrorists. Make an example of them. We believe that this movement aims to violently derail next year's twentieth anniversary celebration of Cuba's statehood. They must not be allowed to gain momentum.

Your team will rendezvous with our House in Paris, who will provide additional details.

Good luck,
Eduardo Chanez, Director

Cyrus,
Here's the real one. Based on the signals intelligence from Hector's meeting in Manhattan, we're unofficially reopening the internal investigation into Big Bertha's capture and alleged termination. I've taken to calling it BLOODHOUND.

This is not going into CORE. I share your sense that one of our sister agencies has a mole. Also, we don't need to remind our friends in Langley about one of ExOps' biggest disasters, especially on a long shot like this.

As we discussed, assign this to Scarlet and Solomon. Philip's last mission was controlled from Paris, so have them begin their search there. Remember, if the trail is cold, you're to bring Scarlet and Solomon directly home and we'll see what Info can discover. Speaking of which, Harbaugh is privy to this mission and will provide remote—and very discreet—support.

Good luck,
E.C.

CHAPTER 10

One advantage of being so short is that I'm perfectly comfortable in an economy airplane seat. Trick also fits well since he's only a couple inches taller than I am. I feel bad for those huge guys who have to fold themselves into a pretzel whenever they fly coach.

We drink cherry schnapps and play cribbage on the flight from Washington to Paris. The cribbage board sits on my partner's tray table since he's the one who deals the cards, keeps score, and pours the schnapps into the cans of Coke we got from the waitresses. I'm a terrible card player, but I make it clear that I won't play if I lose. When Patrick points out that it's always *my* idea to play cribbage, I up the ante and tell him I won't sleep with him if I lose. This isn't a very realistic threat. I love him, and he knows it. Fortunately, Trick doesn't care about winning arguments or card games.

It was a busy week for each of us. I spent most of my time with the Med-Techs, learning how to use my new hand. At first I kept overdoing everything. I'd move too fast and knock stuff over, or I'd grip something too hard and bust it. I must have broken an entire crate of wineglasses. I got better when I stopped trying so hard and made myself relax. My synthetic sense of touch will take some getting used to. Everything feels like I'm wearing a thick glove. The Meddies say they can recalibrate my new hand's sensitivity for me after it's more firmly settled into my nervous system. They also grudgingly told me that yes, I'll be able to punch things much harder than before.

Meanwhile, Patrick stuffed his head with intel to prepare for our trip. He's got twice the work he normally does, since we're being sent on two missions at once. After we had our mission brief with Cyrus, I understood what Trick had been trying to tell me. The Fuerza Libertad brief was neatly typed and had been properly entered into CORE. The documents detailed the time frame and the mission goals and parameters and included pictures of our targets and news clippings about their victims. All very official.

Our brief for the Big Bertha job was the exact opposite. It was entirely verbal: no paperwork, no Job Number, nothing. It was like we took extra-strength sneaky pills.

My partner and I haven't had any private time together since I pinched the Hector job. While we waited for our flight, Trick asked me how that evening with my mom went. I told him I had let Cleo cry for a few minutes, and by the time I'd worked up the nerve to go into the kitchen, she'd stopped. She said she was okay in this distant, detached way I hadn't seen since . . . well, in a long time. I gave her a little hug and went back to bed. The next day my mother was already at work by the time I woke up, but she'd left me a note.

Dearest Alixandra, I'm sorry if I seemed upset last night. I'm very proud of you and love you very much. —Mom

For the rest of the week my schedule was totally different from hers. This prevented us from having time for any more serious talks, but that might have been for the best. We both felt bad about hurting the other's feelings, and there wasn't anything else to say, anyway. I kept her note and slipped it in with the rest of my stuff when I packed my bag this morning. I also packed two flasks of 100-proof cherry schnapps.

Covert agents like us travel with an assortment of

guns, ammo, knives, bombs, and other gear. This doesn't cause a problem at domestic airports, where we flash our ExOps ID cards and blow past the security desk. From then on we use our traveling aliases, which are always civilian identities. If we posed as spies from a competitor's agency, we'd be much too memorable. On our return flights we evade security with a variety of acrobatic dodges. My favorite is the ol' ventilator shaft routine.

Our disregard for airport security also enables us to carry on our own booze. I prefer things like flavored schnapps or brandy. I get Coca-Cola from the air waitresses to use as a mixer and let the good times roll.

Sooner or later the Barbies figure out that I've been drinking in their airplane and get on my case. I've learned to break down these busybodies in five stages. Denial: "This girl can't be drunk, she's only had sodas." Anger: "What did she just call me?" Bargaining: "Maybe I can distract her with food." Depression: "I hate my job." And, finally, acceptance: "Oh my God, this girl is a nightmare. Just let her do what she wants."

Trick moves my cribbage pegs for me since my left hand is holding my cards and my right hand is still kind of uncoordinated. It's not my shooting hand, thank goodness, but the lack of fine motor control limits my conversational options. We use a lot of sign language on our missions, and except for simple phrases I need both hands. Patrick invented a system that combines American Sign Language with the tactical hand signals we use in the field. Over time we've embellished his system with so many shortcuts and in-jokes that it's become its own dialect. We showed it to one of the language experts at headquarters, and she couldn't tell what the hell we were signing to each other. We've been taught that it's safe to have quiet conversations on airplanes since there's so much ambient sound, but sometimes we switch to our Patrick Sign Language anyway, just in case.

While Trick and I drink and play cards, we review what the Information Department has learned about the clowns who kidnapped my mom. Even though we didn't harvest any live intel from our recovery mission in Quantico, Info has unearthed some clues by sifting through the bodies and rubble. It doesn't seem to be any of the usual suspects, meaning the German, Chinese, and Russian covert agencies. Although Info accepts Cleo's assessment that her abductors were Russkies, they don't think the kidnappers were acting on behalf of Mother Russia.

But Info is certain about one thing: I was the intended target. Although Cleo's inside knowledge of ExOps would be of moderate value to the competition, it's nothing compared with what they'd gain from snatching me. Also, people like Mom are considered civilians and they're generally left alone, especially since the embargo. Our diplomats work hard enough to maintain the peace. They can't have us running around putting the glom on our rivals' unarmed employees. Besides, most of these regular staffers are affiliated with prominent businessmen and government officials who become *mucho furioso* when international incidents happen to their friends and relatives.

While Trick shuffles the deck he whispers, "And if those kidnappers were our usual competitors, rescuing your mother wouldn't have been so easy."

"Easy?" I blurt. Trick's eyes look from side to side. I'm blurting too loudly. I switch to one-handed sign language and sign, "What do you mean easy? Five of our guys were wounded."

He mumbles, "That's because you were going so fast—"

I let out a low growl.

Trick continues, "—but we didn't pick up a single outside communication to the kidnappers at any point during that op. Which might've been because you were going so fast." He winks at me as he deals the cards.

I smile over my drink and ask, "So you think their handlers abandoned them?"

"Definitely. That operation was a clusterfuck right from the start. I mean, you and your mother *do* look alike, but c'mon. You don't snatch a Level without a major fight. Then to get cornered that way down in Quantico? Normally a snatch team gets their target out of the area as fast as possible."

I pick up my cards and begin to arrange them by suit. "How about the bomb?"

Patrick shakes his head and comms from behind his cards. "I don't know what to think about that. Your father's reappearance makes so many things possible. My boss suspects that the kidnappers' main objective was to acquire intel about your father, first by searching your house and then by abducting you. Maybe they thought your dad stashed something down in his shop, and if they couldn't find it, they were told to destroy it." He lays down a two. "Or maybe they thought he left information with you."

"That can't be it. I don't know squat." I put a four on Trick's two to make six.

"They didn't know that, Alix." Patrick drops a nine and makes fifteen for two points. He moves his peg up two holes and comms, "Besides, you may have picked up more than you think. You've told me that you used to have long conversations with your father after he got home from his jobs."

"'Conversations' isn't quite right. It was more like Dad flushed his stories onto the floor and I'd sit there and listen." I lay down a ten for twenty-five.

"Well, there you go." Patrick discards a six to make thirty-one and moves his peg up another two holes.

I grumble at him, but he doesn't notice. I comm, "Yeah, but he never told me where, or who, or any of that stuff."

"He did tell you *what*, though, didn't he?"

"You mean like how many people he stuffed in a van

before he drove it into a river? That could have happened anywhere!"

"Alix, the fact is it happened *somewhere*. From what you just told me, I'd be able to find out exactly which operation that was."

Meanwhile, I'm not concentrating on our cribbage game and Patrick is clobbering me. He makes points off every card I put down, and then he cleans up with a run of three and two fifteens, all in the same suit. His peg races up the cribbage board and leaves mine in the dust. I grumble louder, but he still doesn't notice. I better see some boneheaded moves from him right quick or he sleeps on the floor tonight.

Maybe Dad did tell me more than he should have, but his adventures were so awesome that I never said no. Children, however, aren't exactly great at informational security. I couldn't resist bringing my father's anecdotes to school. None of my classmates could match my stories.

Their dad: "I went to the office today and leaned on the watercooler."

My dad: "I kicked a guy's ass so hard that the next time he took a dump, it came out shaped like my shoe." When my father told me that one, I laughed so much that I got hiccups. Dad held me upside down by my ankles and had me drink a big glass of water to make them go away.

While I think about my father, Trick starts a new hand and lays down a completely exposed five. He makes this lousy play with no change of expression. I slap down a jack to make fifteen and earn two quick points for myself. He follows with a six—the worst possible card he could drop. I pounce with a king for thirty-one and two more points. He groans like he didn't see it, how could he have been so stupid, and so on. God, I love this person. He's wonderful.

I ask, "Who's our Greeter in Paris?"

"The House himself, Jacques. He'll pick us up at the airport."

"Does he know that the Fuerza Libertad mission is a cover job?"

Trick sips his drink. "Not yet. We'll tell him about our primary mission after we get to his safe house." He puts his glass back on the tray. "I'll be interested to see if Jacques's memories of Big Bertha match what I've read in his dispatches."

I look up from my cards. "You've read my father's dispatches?"

"Sure." He mixes me another schnapps and Coke, which finishes off the first flask. "All of us Info Operators have to read everything related to our current work. Everything I have clearance for. I've read everybody's dispatches."

"Did you find anything about the ExOps inquiry into what happened to my dad?"

Patrick looks at me over his cards and answers, "The Germans' announcement about him came so quickly that the inquiry was called off. The CORE entry states that your father was captured by the Russians in Damascus. Then he was traded to the Germans for some captured Russian assets."

The lagoon of schnapps in my head helps me think about all this like it was someone else's father, but my stomach still clenches. I distract myself by asking Patrick, "Did you notice anything unusual about my dad's reports from his last job?"

"I did." Patrick continues to play incredibly badly, and my peg catches up to his. "In fact, I'm not entirely sure he wrote them." Patrick explains that my father's dispatches all sound like they were from the same efficient and detail-oriented agent, job after job, until the last one. His mission to survey Russian covert activity in the Middle East proceeded in a strangely halfhearted way. This was totally out of character for the hard-charging Big Bertha. The reports were missing specifics about who he was checking out and where he was. They were also all filed at the same time every day.

"I take it my dad wasn't usually so punctual?" I ask.

"Far from it." Patrick puts his cards down for a moment. "His previous Job Numbers are notable for the inconsistent timing of his reports. Morning, evening, nothing for three days, then two in an hour. It was all over the place."

"How about us?"

"What about us?"

"How punctual are we with our reports?"

Patrick holds his cards back up. "*My* reports go out every evening before we rack out."

I'm too busy moving my peg into the lead to snap out a comeback. Trick deals another hand. I ask, "Did my dad find out what the Russians were doing in the Middle East?"

"No, not really. It was strange. He sort of . . . wandered around for a while, until he disappeared."

That *does* sound strange. Dad never wandered anywhere. He either did something with great purpose or he didn't do it at all.

We finish our card game. I win, of course. While Trick shuffles the cards I grab the second flask and pour us another round.

CHAPTER 11

Ah, Paris. The City of Darkness. My father pulled a
bunch of jobs here. He used to tell me stories about how
bright and beautiful this city is, but as far as I can tell,
it's just another dark hole in western Greater Germany.
I've been here twice. Both times it was a midnight landing at the airport, followed by a tinted-window car ride
to some ancient, reeking cellar full of poorly lit spy stuff.

The brightest light I've seen in Paris so far has been the
House, whose name is Jacques. He runs the ExOps safe
house in Paris, which is one of the busiest in Europe.

The House is parked in front of the terminal, waiting
for us. He's in a beat-up old Citroën with "Stairway to
Heaven" blaring at top volume. We woozily hump our
bags up to Jacques's car and lean into his line of sight.
Even in this dim light I can see his long chin, his big
schnoz, and his omnipresent tan. His dark brown eyes
sparkle as he spots us.

"My friends!" Jacques shouts. "It is good to see you
again!"

We both say, "Hi, Jacques." He gets out of the car and
takes our bags from us. They're too heavy for him to
lift, so he drags them around to the rear of his Citroën.
He heaves our bags into the trunk while we pile into the
backseat.

Jacques hops in front, turns the radio up even louder,
and stomps his foot on the gas pedal. The sudden ac-
celeration sloshes my pickled brain around in my head
and makes me dizzy. I can't wait to lie down and sleep
off all those schnapps and Cokes. I hold on to Trick's

forearm as we tear out of the parking lot like we're being chased by Hitler's ghost.

I ask our host if we're being followed, and he says, "*Mais oui!* I am always followed. With a handsome face like zis, how can it not be so?" He laughs as he swerves onto a highway entrance ramp.

Trick and I look at each other. It's not the first time we've wondered if Jacques is actually a Martian.

Jacques pulls onto the highway and zooms toward metro Paris, but his attention is mostly on the rearview mirror. "Hmm," he says, "perhaps tonight my face is especially handsome."

Trick and I spin around in our seats and look back. A white Peugeot noodles along behind us. When Jacques speeds up, they speed up. When he slows down, they slow down.

I pull Li'l Bertha out of her holster. "Jacques, open the sunroof." He flips a switch, and the sunroof slides back. I gingerly climb up to the front seat while my partner stays in the rear and comms with his IC back home. I crouch on the front seat, under the open sunroof. Jacques suddenly floors it and passes a truck. The Peugeot follows suit. It's definitely somebody. We don't want to attract attention, but we can't have anyone following us, either.

"Solomon, any intel on this fucker?" I ask. When we work with other people, I have to use Trick's field name.

He says, "Nothing friendly. He's either a competitor or a joyrider."

"Either way." I stand up through the sunroof, turn off Li'l Bertha's safeties, and point her in the general direction of the car following us. She hones in on the Peugeot's grill and pops three .50-caliber rounds into the engine. Her shots are incredibly loud, but I hope it sounds like a car backfiring. Flashes of yellow light erupt from under the hood as the slugs drill half-inch holes through the engine block. The Peugeot stalls out and shudders to the breakdown lane. Jacques keeps up the speed, and soon we're all by ourselves again.

I plop down into the front passenger seat. "Hah! Score one for the good guys."

"Nice shooting, mademoiselle," Jacques proclaims.

Trick leans forward and tells Jacques, "Okay, all clear."

"*Oui*, M'sieur Solomon." Jacquo stops swerving quite so much, thank God, but doesn't slow down. When my partner asks why he's still going so fast, he says, "We have a unique opportunity to confront ze Fuerza cell you've come to destroy, but only if we hurry."

After a short drive we pull off the highway. A few turns later we glide past the main entrance of an ancient cemetery. Jacques parks a few yards down the street and gets out of the car. I look back at Trick, who shrugs his shoulders.

Jacques leans over the open sunroof and proudly says, "Cimetière du Père-Lachaise!"

I say, "Terrific. What the heck are we doing here?"

"La Fuerza is holding a secret meeting inside. We will . . . how you say? 'Destroy zere organizational capacity with extreme prejudice.' "

"What?" Trick hisses, "Jacques, we *just* got here. We haven't unpacked our gear or anything!"

"M'sieur Solomon, please. A real agent—" He taps his temple. "—keeps his gear up here." He stops whispering and switches to comming. "Besides, Mademoiselle Scarlet has her pistol, and here we have all the Fuerza together and pants down. *Allez*."

My partner sees my unhappy expression and comms to me, "How do you feel?"

"Trick, I'm fuckin' plastered! I can't pull a job right now. How about you?"

"I'm okay, but I had a lot less to drink than you."

I frown. "You did?"

"Yeah. You sort of had that second flask all to yourself . . ."

I did?

". . . but we can't tell Jacques. Even he's not that cool." Trick opens his door. "C'mon."

We get out of the Citroën. I bing some Madrenaline to counteract the alcohol. This makes my tongue feel like a dried-out banana skin, but I have to get myself functional. I take a few deep breaths to help clear my head.

Jacques leads us toward the cemetery's front entrance. We boost ourselves over the wall next to the main gate. Inside the cemetery it's very dark and strangely cold, and suddenly the steady hum of late-night Paris seems much farther away. I switch on my night vision and hold Li'l Bertha in front of me.

"Jacquo, how do we know who the Fuerza guys are?" I comm.

"Zat's simple," Jacques comms back. "Anyone who is dead already is not Fuerza." Through the gloom, I hear Jacques chuckling to himself. Man, he really is the funniest person he's ever met.

"I've got a map loaded up," Trick comms. "We're going straight toward the middle of the cemetery." Both of our visual Mods include an Eyes-Up display that allows us to read virtual documents and monitor our bodies' vital signs. The software for Trick's Eyes-Up display has a global positioning and navigation program. The software in mine is focused on highlighting targets in my immediate vicinity so I can aerate them with Li'l Bertha.

"Well, *this* is a romantic date," I whisper.

We quietly walk up the necropolis's main street. Jacques comms to us about the famous Frenchmen buried in the tombs we pass. Everywhere I look is crammed with crypts and elaborate gravestones. The statues and carvings are creepy as hell. A chill crawls up my spine and I'm about to tell Jacques to shut up, when he switches topics.

"Stop," he comms. We stop. He crouches and shuffles up the path a bit. "Okay, just ahead."

I comm to both my partner and Jacques, "What are the rules of engagement here? Do I just plug 'em all?"

"No," Jacques replies. "We are to capture if possible. If zey fight back and leave us no choice, zen you plug zem all."

I comm, "How many are there?"

Jacques comms back, "Five, maybe six."

Jeez. I comm to Trick, "What the fuck? I'm supposed to capture six guys single-handedly?"

"Well," he comms, "Jacques only said not to shoot them. Besides, we've got surprise going for us. Let's try one of your flying punchfests."

I slide Li'l Bertha back in her holster and zip my jacket. The three of us sneak up the hill until I hear murmuring voices.

I take a deep breath and comm, "Okay, here I go."

"Roger zat."

"Go get 'em, Scarlet."

I have my neuroinjector ramp me up with more Madrenaline, then I charge up the hill. There's a large crypt, or chapel, or something in front of which stands a tight cluster of people. I hit the jets, and by the time they hear me coming, I've already leaped in the air. I smash the back of the first guy's head with my new biorobotic hand as I fly past him. *Clonk!*

I land on the far side of the group and fire my fists into the faces of two more goombahs. The remaining three dudes grab at me. I latch on to two of their arms and yank them into each other so that their skulls clonk together. They drop. The last guy reaches into his coat. I kick him right in the nuts. He exhales sharply and crumples over backward.

As the six men collapse into a groaning heap around me, my enhanced hearing picks up the sound of someone—no, two people—running down the other side of the hill.

"Guys," I comm, "two more targets, moving away from our entrance."

Jacques comms, "They're going for ze back entrance, near Gambetta. Follow zem, Scarlet. We'll pick you up."

Jacques and Patrick gallop back to the car, and I take off after the footsteps. My night vision shows me the way, but not in any great detail. My balance is out of whack because the booze and the uppers are battling for control of my body. I nearly fall down a flight of steps, and then almost wipe out on a patch of damp cobblestones. I slow down a little.

I'm about ten seconds behind the fleeing men as they emerge from the cemetery and jump into a BMW coupe. The car starts and screeches away as I burst out of the back entrance.

"Solomon, where are you guys?"

"We're in the car. Look left. You'll see us coming."

Jacques's Citroën skids around the corner to my left.

"Roger that. I see you." I step off the sidewalk and into the street. "Hey, make sure the passenger-side window is open."

"Way ahead of you. Get ready."

Jacques flies down the street and slams on the brakes. I throw my body into the car's front passenger window as he skids past me. The instant my upper half is inside, he steps on the gas. I fall ass over teakettle onto the passenger seat. My head swims from all this tumbling around. Patrick leans forward from the backseat and helps me wriggle myself upright.

Meanwhile, Jacquo shows us how a Frenchman drives when he really means it. Power slides, e-brake turns, heel and toe, he's got all the moves. I hang on to the Jesus strap as he whips his surprisingly agile Citroën through the nearly empty Paris streets.

"Hey, Jacques," Patrick comms. "Don't we need to keep an eye on the suspects Scarlet trashed at the cemetery?"

Jacques twirls the steering wheel all the way from lock to lock, then centers it again to fling us through a small rotary. Gum wrappers, old lottery tickets, and crumpled receipts skitter back and forth across the dashboard as the car lists from side to side.

"Not a problem," he says. "I've already commed ze police to retrieve zem."

The car's centripetal force has propelled my partner all the way across the rear bench seat and smushed him against the far side door. Patrick comms, "Why didn't you tell them to be there beforehand?"

"Because, my American friend—" Jacques executes a complex zigzag turn, only half of which rumbles over the sidewalk. "—in Greater Germany, it is *plus simple* to ask for forgiveness than for permission." He blows his horn to clear a delivery man out of the way. "Ze red tape, she is much smaller zis way."

We emerge from the tight warren of streets onto a larger, more open boulevard that runs along the Seine. The BMW's taillights are a block ahead, but we're gaining on them. They've got a faster car, but they aren't milking as much out of it.

Jacques switches back to tour guide mode. "On our left, you can see la Cathédrale Notre Dame." We're going so fast, we barely see it before he's on to the next attraction. "Also on our left, we are passing le Pont Neuf, which in English means 'New Bridge.'" The bridge blurs by. "You can see ze famous Louvre museum on your right—" He swerves into the oncoming lane to pass a lumbering produce truck that totally obstructs our view of "—les Tuileries, very beautiful gardens." Very beautiful indeed. In the dark. At eighty miles per hour.

The BMW takes a right onto a street that leads away from the river. Jacques makes up a huge amount of distance by not slowing down at all for the turn. His skid goes on for an entire block. He shouts over the squealing tires, "Here we are passing through la Place de la Concorde, where—whoops!" The last part is Jacques reacting to an unexpected move by the Bimmer. Place de la Concorde is a big roundabout, and the BMW has turned the wrong way, into the flow of traffic. Jacques follows him without a moment's hesitation. We evade a few honking cars and motorcycles and roar onto a wide four-lane street. Now we're only a second or two behind the BMW.

"No trip to Paris is complete without a shopping spree on Avenue des Champs-Elysées." We hammer up the av-

enue. The shriek of our engine battles with the growl of
the Bimmer's. I look up ahead and see—

"L'Arc de Triomphe! Erected to commemorate—"
Jacques cranks the wheel right and left to avoid a police
car. "—ze victory of Napoleon—" He chases the BMW
into the huge traffic circle around the monument. "—at
Austerlitz in 1806." The police car's lights flash and its
siren wails behind us. We chase the Bimmer all the way
around the arch and then some.

Trick is pinned against the right-side rear door by
Jacques's fast cornering. "I think they're lost!"

"Hah!" cries Jacques.

"Can you ram them or something?"

"In my *petite fille*? *Jamais!* Never! But I have an idea.
Scarlet, get ready to jump into their car."

Oh, sure thing, Jacques. No problem. I climb out the
sunroof and squat on top of the car. My hands grasp the
edge of the roof, and my eyes water from the torrent of
wind.

"Hang on!" Jacques yells. He flies up on the BMW's
right side and executes an incredible 360-degree spin
that slings his Citroën completely around the front end
of our competitor's car. I can barely hang on as Jacques's
stunt lands us inches away from the Bimmer's left side.
The wall of tire smoke makes the BMW driver slow
down just enough for me to—

"Jump!" Jacques shouts.

I leap off the Citroën and flop onto the roof of the
BMW. I let myself slide down to the trunk and then ram
my synthetic right fist through the rear window. Jacques
pulls in front and serpentines back and forth. The Bimmer swerves, trying to get around him. I haul myself into
the rear seat in time to slap the passenger's pistol out of
his hand. I karate chop his arm and break it above the
wrist. The passenger screams and scrunches himself
away from me. The driver opens his door, like he's going
to bail out at forty miles per hour.

I grab the driver's hair and yank his head back against

the headrest. My right hand reaches around and clutches his throat. He tries to pull my hand off his neck, but that only makes me crush his larynx even harder. Then I wrap him in a choke hold with my entire arm and drag him bodily into the backseat with me. One big punch and he's out cold.

Suddenly gravity shifts ninety degrees. I'm propelled between the front seats and slam into the dashboard. Then gravity shifts back to normal and ungently deposits me on the center console with the stick shift jammed into my ribs. A loud bang echoes off the arch and the buildings across the plaza.

I'm dizzy, bruised, and hearing things. "Scarlet!" It's Trick's voice. "Hey, you okay?" Wow, he sounds like he's right here in the BMW with me. "Scarlet, up here." I look up. His head is poking in through the shattered driver-side window. Blue and red flashing lights wash across one side of his face.

"Ugh." I struggle to extricate myself from my awkward position. "What happened?"

"The car crashed into a shop."

Oh, right. Nobody was driving.

"C'mon!" Patrick pulls on my arm to help me crawl out of the car. Then he shoves me into Jacques's Citroën and tumbles in on top of me. We leave the scene of the accident at top speed. My partner and I untangle ourselves and sit up.

"Jacques," Patrick comms, "what about the cops?"

"Oh, zey are not after us." He swerves off the boulevard onto a small street. Cobblestones rattle under the tires, and the backseat vibrates against my butt. "Those two officers pulled zat BMW over for a broken taillight and discovered Cuban terrorists inside. It is a big arrest for them."

Trick yells, "Then why are you still driving so fast?"

Jacques looks down at his speedometer and laughs in surprise. "Hah! Sorry, M'sieur Solomon." He slows down. "I am—how you say—all jacked over?"

"Jacked up," I say.

"Jacked up!" he repeats.

Patrick asks our speed demon host how he convinces the police, who are mostly Germans, to work with him. Jacquo explains that it's a function of his official position at the American embassy here in Paris. His title is diplomatic liaison for classified affairs, which requires him to have close ties with, among other people, the area's German covert community. His charismatic nature has led to a useful friendship with Herr Direktor of the regional Abwehr office. The Direktor allows Jacques to run his ops, and when applicable, Jacques lets the Abwehr take the credit. If the collateral damage gets out of hand, the Abwehr puts it on Jacquo's bill and he forwards the bill to the Americans. It is very convenient.

Trick is stunned. "The Germans know you work for American intelligence?"

"*Mais oui*. Every second of my life is spent on their continent. How else would I operate?"

"But, but . . ." Patrick sputters. I think what boggles him the most is that he's never heard of this arrangement.

Jacques continues, "For example, tonight I commed Herr Direktor about ze men we left in ze cemetery, and he was able to seem very efficient and effective when he alerted ze police. I wasn't sure we would catch zat BMW, so I commed him a little earlier than I normally would, just in case."

"Why would the Abwehr help us fight the Fuerza?"

"Because we are allies. It is the same reason ze U.S. works against terrorists of Europe like ze Free French, Dutch Underground, and Circle of Zion."

I brush bits of broken car window off my shirt. "You mean we go after groups that threaten Greater Germany?"

"Not here in Europe. Even in the States, not really. But CIA, FBI, zey stay out of it when someone is careless enough to let ze Gestapo catch zem on American soil."

"Jesus!" My partner exclaims. "What's the *Gestapo* doing in America?"

"Ze same things you are doing here."

Patrick and I take a few moments to absorb all this graduate-level espionage stuff.

"Wait." My partner narrows his eyes. "What about the times we spy on Germany?"

"Well-l-l," Jacques tosses off one of the biggest French shrugs I've ever seen. At its height, his shoulders are practically over his head. "Zen I must lie to my friends in high places. But for me, it is not usually big lies. I mostly help American agents move safely through town and supply zem with whatever zey need. Very quiet, and I need to know very little. Tonight was an exception. The Fuerza are rarely all together in ze open, so to take advantage I had to jump in. But it is not my routine."

"Well, you're very good at it."

"*Merci*, Scarlet. Yes, I do like it very much."

"Do all Frenchmen drive like you do?"

"Hah! *Non, non*. I was a driver with ze Renault racing team. After a race in Italy, I was approached by a film producer who hired me as a stunt driver. Very exciting and glamorous."

"Very dangerous, too, no?"

"Pah!" He waves his hand at me. "Not for Jacques!" He chortles to himself as he turns onto the Rue Saint-Sulpice and pulls into a barely visible alley. He stops in the middle of the alley and pushes a button on his dashboard. The whole car descends below street level, and a thick metal sheet slides across the rectangular hole above us.

The car softly bumps to a halt. Jacques turns to face us and asks, "Okay, *qui a faim*?" Who's hungry?

CHAPTER 12

It's not the same ancient reeking cellar as the last time I was in Paris. Jacques says he had to move the safe house a few months ago. This particular cellar is on Rue Saint-Sulpice on the Right Bank. The poorly lit spy stuff is a typical mix of audio recorders, heat sensors, motion detectors, guns, ammo, a jackframe, a relatively clean bathroom, a few shitty army cots, and the always-excellent chow. It seems that even in the worst circumstances, the French can't bear to have crummy food around.

Patrick talks through a mouthful of bread and cheese. "At wawn't owa reah ob."

Jacques laughs. "Slowly, Solomon. Watch out for your digestion."

It was a long flight, immediately followed by our cover mission. We're starved. Extreme Operations agents never eat airplane food because it's so easy to get poisoned that way. Like all the Houses, Jacques is used to this and has a nice spread of sandwiches and a thermos of coffee waiting for us.

Patrick swallows his food and repeats, "That wasn't our real job."

The House leans back in his battered office chair. "I see." Fluorescent light drags itself across his features and makes his face look even longer. He slurps his coffee from a small bowl and says, "Well, how can Jacques help you?"

I let my partner do the talking while I demolish my second sandwich. Trick takes a smaller bite of food and says, "We're really here to retrace an agent's last mission. It was a few years ago."

"Whose mission?"

"Big Bertha's."

Jacques gasps and accidentally inhales some coffee. He bursts into a long coughing fit. He holds his arms over his head and gradually regains his breath. "Sorry, but I have not heard zat name in a long time."

Patrick drinks from his coffee mug. "He stopped here, didn't he?"

"Oh, yes. Well, not *here*. We've moved several times. But yes, Big Bertha and I worked on many occasions together. Of course I heard what happened to him. Terrible." His eyes pass to me. For the first time tonight, he hesitates before speaking. "I'm very sorry, Scarlet."

I hold off on the giant bite I was about to take. "Thanks, Jacques."

He looks down at his coffee bowl and gently shakes his head. *"C'est la guerre."*

Patrick drains his glass of mineral water. "Can you tell us anything about the last time you saw him?"

"Certainly. His cover story required zat he appear German, not American. I rounded up a selection of men's outfits from a few Paris department stores for him. I remember his shoes were *très difficile*, because he had very wide feet. He already had his identity papers, but I gave him small things to augment his cover—old Metro tickets, a receipt from a movie house, and a card of membership to a popular exercise club. Things like zat."

Patrick thoughtfully chews his food as he listens to Jacques. "Huh. I didn't see anything about that cover story in CORE."

Jacques refills his coffee bowl. "Perhaps it was his idea. An agent like Big Bertha makes many decisions from his own initiative."

"Did he tell you what his assignment was?"

"*Non*, but zat was not necessary. From his preparations I could tell he was infiltrating some kind of organization. When he asked me to get him transportation to Baghdad, I knew who he was going after."

Patrick looks at me with a worried expression. He comms, "This doesn't sound right."

"No," I comm, "it doesn't."

"Jacques," Trick says, "are you sure that this was his *last* job?"

"Yes, M'sieur Solomon. Quite certain."

"What told you he was doing an infiltration job?"

"He did not have his amazing pistol."

I stop chewing my food and make enough room in my mouth to ask, "So?"

"An agent like Big Bertha, when he infiltrates, often he will pose as a sort of security guard for hire. Mercenaries typically have their own weapons, yes, but many organizations will provide weapons for their security personnel to unify ze ammunition and maintenance needs. For him, to bring his weapon on such a job would be like bringing his own pepper to a restaurant."

"That's it?" Trick asks. "That's what told you Big Bertha was on an infiltration job?"

"Yes." He sees our skepticism and spreads his hands apart. "Being in zis game has taught me to stitch ze truth together with very little thread. For example, I knew you were not here just for ze Fuerza."

"How?"

"Because your luggage carries enough ammunition to arm a brigade, and you asked me nothing about Fuerza until we got to ze cemetery."

Hey, Jacquo here is pretty good.

I ask, "Did my father ask you for anything else before he left?"

Jacques looks at the ceiling to help his mind dredge up this old conversation. "He wanted to know where he could get a weapon in Baghdad."

"What did you tell him?"

"We spoke of a man named Ilan who possessed a café in downtown Baghdad. He knew everyone and everyone knew him. I told Big Bertha zat Ilan could make ze proper introductions."

Trick asks, "Who was Big Bertha infiltrating?"

"Ze Blades of Persia. Baghdad was where their leader resided. Zis I guessed before your father left, but after his capture I confirmed it through my Middle Eastern contacts." Jacques tilts his head to one side and asks, "Truly, zis is not in your Catalogue of Records?"

How do we tell Jacques that his version of my dad's final mission contradicts the file in CORE and what we heard from Fredericks? Jacques's version actually makes more sense, given what happened.

My partner deals with the question by pretending it's not there. Patrick asks Jacques, "Who leads the Blades of Persia?"

Jacques shakes his head. "Oh, M'sieur Solomon, do not even consider it. Nobody sees zis man. Even ze fabulous Big Bertha failed to penetrate his group."

Both Patrick and I put our food down and silently glower at Jacques until he shrugs his shoulders and shakes his head. "Very well." Jacquo holds his hands up in front of him like he's surrendering to our stubbornness. "Nobody knows his real name, but ze CIA calls him Winter."

"Do you think this Ilan person in Baghdad knows anything about Winter?"

"Well, Ilan is no longer with us. His oldest son now runs ze family businesses both above and below ze table." Jacques sets his coffee down and opens a bottle of mineral water. He takes a huge swig and wipes his mouth with the back of his hand. "Our presence in Baghdad is very weak, however. I would recommend visiting our House in Beirut and working from zere. I will book you a flight." He burps. "Perhaps a flying carpet?"

We laugh, mostly that our host can be so blasé about things. We eat some more food, and then it's time to sleep. Trick and I share one of the army cots. He spoons behind me and drapes a blanket over the two of us. I'm tempted to get some French-style lovin' from him, but we've been on the move since early yesterday morning, and before I can even start a little fantasy going, I conk out.

My internal clock wakes me up at 6:30 A.M. We gather our gear, meet Jacques outside, and off we go. I see Paris in the daylight for all of five minutes.

CORE   HIS-CUBA-075

The Cuban War
This dossier contains public-facing and classified information. Do not remove this file from ExOps.

Associated Press, January 1, 1959

A New Year, a New Cuba, Briefly

HAVANA, CUBA—Rebels ousted Cuban president General Fulgencio Batista early this morning and declared a provisional Communist government. The island's marinas and docks have been clogged all day with former Batista supporters and American tourists desperate to flee the country. A flotilla of small boats operated by independent activists has worked ceaselessly all morning and afternoon, bringing refugees from this tortured island to Miami and other points in Florida.

The new self-styled president is the charismatic and iconically bearded rebel leader Fidel Castro. He is backed by his brother Raúl and the colorful Ernesto "Che" Guevara. Castro has yet to issue any official proclamations, but his men have already begun rounding up Cuban intellectuals, political activists, and suspected Batista loyalists.

President Eisenhower was quick to condemn the coup, claiming that he would be "damned before I'll allow a Communist country only ninety miles from our shore." This statement from the president confirmed earlier speculation that the United States would invade Cuba. President Eisenhower called on the members of Congress to approve the deployment of U.S. troops "with all haste, that we may expunge this red stain as soon as possible."

———

Associated Press, April 3, 1959.

United States Invades Cuba

HAVANA, CUBA—The United States Marines 1st Recon Battalion hit the beaches here this morning in front of a steel rain as navy battleships pounded Communist defenses. Immediately after the Marines landed, the 272nd Infantry Regiment and the 3rd Army Tank Battalion were put ashore in the largest U.S. amphibian operation since the invasion of Japan in 1943. Air force fighter pilots flew hundreds of sorties in support of the ground troops and devastated the insurgents' efforts to withstand the flood of American men and supplies.

General Anthony McAuliffe, called out of retirement to command the U.S. expeditionary force to Cuba, expressed confidence in the progress of his units. At a frontline press conference, he said, "This shouldn't take long. The rebels don't have the support of the people. They can't be resupplied or reinforced. They are energetically led but terribly equipped." To Russia's charge of America's "cruel and aggressive meddling," General McAuliffe simply replied, "Nuts!"

———

RECEIVED: May 12, 1959

Sir, the Beard has been shaved.—Sheik

———

New York Times, January 1, 1979

Another Deadly New Year's Eve for America's Youngest State

HAVANA, CUBA—Early this morning, Cuba's unique New Year's traditions, which include eating one grape for each month, carrying empty suitcases for good luck, and opening both the front and back doors of one's house, were shattered by a devastating series of blasts that ripped through downtown Havana. Dozens of revelers were killed and thousands more fled for their lives only moments after they finished counting down to midnight. Cuba's New Year's celebrations have been the target of terrorist attacks before, but this morning's bombings—credited to the Cuban Liberation Movement—were unprecedented in their scale.

"We knew it could be a serious attack, and we felt prepared," said Havana's chief of police, Duardo Guerrero, "but the CLM has deceived more people into their ranks than we thought."

When asked if the size of the attack was related to the significant anniversary, he immediately said, "Definitely. It's been exactly twenty years since Castro took power." But Fidel Castro's short-lived reign of terror was crushed only four months later by President Eisenhower's timely intervention.

The Cuban Liberation Movement is actually a loosely knit patchwork of disparate terrorist groups that share the general goal of "liberating" Cuba from the United States, but their lack of coordinated efforts has thus far relegated them to high-profile but unfocused bombings and airplane hijackings.

One of the CLM's largest subgroups calls themselves La Fuerza Libertad, or "The Liberty Force." Backed by a network of wealthy Cuban expatriates, Fuerza is one of the few members of the Cuban Liberation Movement to have a presence outside of Cuba. Although Fuerza did not claim credit for the explosions, Cuban and federal authorities are stepping up their pursuit of this dangerous group's soldiers and supporters.

CHAPTER 13

There's no dark like the dark you're falling through at a hundred-plus miles per hour. My fear is moderated by a delicate balance of uppers combined with some sensory blockers to help me concentrate on what Patrick comms me.

"Scarlet, you're at three thousand feet. Adjust left, five degrees."

I lean a little to correct my aim. We want me to land at a big bus depot on the northwestern side of Baghdad. It's a quiet part of the city, mostly warehouses and empty lots tucked between two dense residential districts. From this height it looks like a dark smudge between two lit-up neighborhoods.

My mission is to drop in, catch a ride with our contact, meet with him at his café in downtown Baghdad, and then get the heck out before sunrise. This is deep inside Germany's half of the Middle East, plus ExOps still hasn't told anyone that we're pulling this job, so I need to be really fast. My time on-site will be minimal—a couple of hours, tops. I move faster when I'm alone, so I'm dropping in while Patrick gives me Info support from our safehouse in Beirut. When I'm done with my meeting I'll swipe a car and light out for the territories. I should be halfway to Beirut before sunrise. Where we go next depends on what I discover tonight.

"Two thousand feet, on target. Confirm, Scarlet."

"Roger, Solomon, two-k feet, on target, confirmed." Night insertions are extra challenging because it's so easy to become disoriented. This is especially true when you don't open your parachute until you're at five hundred feet to avoid radar detection. I dose one more fix of Kalmers and brace myself.

"One thousand feet. Deploy in three, two, one, now!"

I yank the handle and hear a gratifying rush of air and fabric as the parachute's canopy expands. The chute's harness digs into my armpits and crotch as I suddenly brake from 120 miles per hour to just under 10. This is still fast enough to slam my legs out my ass if I screw up the landing, so I focus all my attention on getting on the ground in one piece. Five seconds later I land on the packed dirt of a big empty lot next to the bus depot. Two running steps followed by two dazzling rolls and I'm on terra firma. I unbuckle my skydiving harness and shuck myself out of the straps. Then I gather the chute into a big bundle in my arms while my feet happily reacquaint themselves with solid ground.

Trick comms, "Scarlet, someone's approaching your position from the north. It might be the Greeter."

"You can't tell?" I ask.

"No, he has to run very dark. The Germans in charge of this province don't agree with his views about their occupation of his country," Trick comms back.

"Is he armed?" I ask as I pull Li'l Bertha out of her holster. She can scan Mr. North Guy herself, but Trick's instruments give him a good top-down view.

"Well, yeah," he comms. "Isn't everybody?"

I'm about to make a classic Scarlet-style smart-ass reply when he comms, "Wait a sec. There's two, no, three of them. All different directions."

So much for smart-ass. I tell Trick to find me an exit.

"Maybe they're ours?" I comm.

Unexpectedly, Cyrus comms in. "No, the Greeter would come alone. Solomon, get her the hell out of there."

Oh, Christ, and here I am still lugging my stupid parachute. Li'l Bertha's target sensor displays three amber heat signals in my Eyes-Up display. Amber means she doesn't know if they're good guys or bad guys.

I comm Cyrus while Trick listens in. "Almighty, this is Scarlet. Request permission to engage." This is a complex situation. These may be Germans, Arabic locals, or anybody. Even I know to secure clearance before starting these fireworks. I expect Cyrus will need to call us back.

Instead, Cyrus immediately comms, "Permission granted, Scarlet. Fire at will."

That was fast. A fresh surge of Madrenaline splashes into the Scarlet Speedball I took before the drop and zoots me up.

Patrick comms in, "Targets recognized." Li'l Bertha goes from amber to crimson and gyroscopes onto the closest target, the guy to the north. Trick continues, "Scarlet, exit to the northeast."

I perforate Bad Guy North with some standard .30-caliber rounds. His red dot vanishes from my screen. I turn around and backpedal northeast so I can target the other two bozos. The security lights from the bus depot cast long dim shadows across the ground. The light doesn't reveal much, though, and the glare actually makes the night seem darker.

Li'l Bertha loads up some small stuff to use as suppression because Bad Guys South and West have turned on their heat blockers. I lay down a fog of .12-caliber pellets as I switch to starlight vision. My aim is rotten because I'm still carrying my partially inflated parachute while I run backward across a pitch-dark semipaved lot. Bad Guy South shadows along to my left while Bad Guy West tries to flank around on my right.

That's enough of this nonsense. I throw the chute up in the air and position myself so it floats to the ground between me and Bad Guy West, blocking his view of me. I kneel down and take aim at Bad Guy South. Li'l Bertha senses that my posture is more stable and changes from small-caliber pellets to large-caliber slugs. We blow the top of Bad Guy South's head off with one shot. Strangely, he falls forward. What's left of his brains pukes out of the top of his skull as he hits the ground. I'm glad my night vision shows me light and dark but not color.

Without my chute slowing me down I can really move and maneuver now. Bad Guy West charges and fires his pistol at me. I sidestep his shots as I fly up on him and . . .

"Scarlet! Do not—"

. . . bash his nose halfway into his skull.

"—terminate that asset!"

Bad Guy West flies completely off his feet and lands fifteen feet away from me. He exhales sharply as he lands, but he doesn't budge after that. It's like I turned him into wood.

The drugs have settled in nicely now. I've got exactly the right balance, and an alert but peaceful sense of calm settles over me. "Solomon, what did you say?"

He pauses, then comms, "I was about to remind you of our protocol to interrogate neutralized hostiles."

"Neutralized? I must have dodged fifty bullets from this guy."

"Nine."

"Whatever. If that's neutralized, then I'm Miss Piggy."

Trick pauses again. He's frustrated now. I'm supposed to use a nonlethal takedown for the final member of a hostile group. I know this in training, but out in the field my excitement gets the better of me. There's nothing like winning a round of kill or be killed. I try to mollify him.

"Maybe that first guy is alive," I comm to Trick. I know he's not. His motion signal vanished after I plugged him. Lucky shot, actually. I barely saw him. Given the circumstances, I think this has gone pretty well so far.

Trick still hasn't spoken. I'm sure he's holding his glasses in one hand and rubbing his temple with the other.

"Look, Solomon, pout later, all right? Just get me out of this goddamn area." I gather my parachute again while he gives me directions and coordinates. I stuff the chute in a big Dumpster behind the bus depot.

"What about the meatbags?" I comm to Trick.

"Leave 'em. The Greeter's guys will take care of them."

As I walk past Bad Guy West, I take a good look at him. He's got a blocky head, pale skin, and an ugly, brutish face. I take his picture and save the image for our files.

"Solomon, this guy doesn't look like he's from around here." I send him my picture of Bad Guy West.

"You're right," Trick comms back. "More like he's from KGB central casting."

I approach the bus depot from the rear. A streetlight illuminates a road in front. "What's with all the damned Russians lately?"

"I wish I knew, but it looks like things are even worse than Chanez thought. These guys knew exactly where you were going to land. If they'd been Germans, I'd say they'd simply gotten lucky with their radar, but I'm not sure what to make of this."

"Jesus, Solomon, only three other people know I'm here!" Our pilot tonight knows he dropped someone into Baghdad, but he has no idea who or why. The Greeter knows he's retrieving someone, but he doesn't know who or why, either. That leaves Cyrus, Harbaugh, and Director Chanez. Even Cleo doesn't know where I am.

Trick comms, "From what just happened, I'd say it's more than three."

"Do you think the leak is inside ExOps?" I hate even to think this, but I add, "Could it be Jacques?"

"It *could* be anybody," Trick replies. "But Jacques has been in this game a long time. He'd do a better job of distancing himself from this sort of thing. I mean, we *just* saw him."

I comm, "True, but he is a little crazy."

"I know, Scarlet," Trick comms quietly. "I'll keep working on it. Keep your eyes open."

I run around to the road in front of the bus depot. Headlights are coming up the street.

"Solomon, I have a vehicle on approach."

"That's probably the Greeter," Trick comms back.

"Roger that," I comm. "I see flashing lights behind him. Two cars."

"Hang on." I hang on. Trick continues, "That's the Baghdad police. I've got them on my radio scanner. They're responding to reports of gunshots near the bus depot."

"Then why are they chasing our guy?"

"Oh-h, I don't know. Middle of the night, vehicle speeding toward a gun battle. Seems like something a cop would find interesting."

"What do I do?"

"Do *not* kill those policemen. Russian mercenaries are one thing, but German cops are another." Trick pauses, then says, "You'd better prepare for a hot mount."

Well, la de da. This is doable but I'll need some serious uppers. I let the headlights drive closer. It's a step van like UPS delivery guys drive. When the van is fifty yards away, it slows down a little and edges toward the curb. I turn and run up the road, away from the van. As he pulls up alongside me the van's driver slows down a bit more, but I still need a giant hit of Madrenaline so I can match his speed. I take three sprinting steps and then desperately leap up and grab the handle on the van's sliding door as it flies past me.

The door is open for me, but I still have to fight the wind to swing myself inside. I land on the floor of the van with a loud thud, and my momentum pitches me under the passenger seat. My knees and elbows rattle on the floor as my body reacts to all the Madrenaline. I gulp a few deep breaths and bump a heavy dose of Kalmers to balance out again. All these drugs make my scalp feels like it's on fire.

I look up at the Greeter. He's driving like a maniac but still manages to run his eyes over me and howl, "Whoo-ee! If I knew more girls who could run that fast, I wouldn't be Lonely Rashid anymore!" I don't know what he means, but he must, because he laughs uproariously. It's like I've been picked up by Jacques's Arabian brother. "You'd better hang on," he shouts as he swerves onto a side road.

I slide across the floor like a cat at an ice rink. For a moment the van is up on two wheels, maybe only one. I haul myself up into the passenger seat and look out the back windows. The flashing lights are still behind us. Between the screeching tires, the roaring engines, and the whooping sirens, the noise in here is incredible.

The Greeter is a skinny five feet ten inches and looks like he's in his late twenties. He's got the requisite Middle Eastern skin tone (swarthy), hair (bushy), and beard (closely cropped). He smells spicy, kind of like cinnamon. I lean over to him and yell, "Name's Scarlet. You want any help to ditch the oinkers?"

"I'm Rashid." He looks in his rearview, then back at me, and hollers, "We'll use the Puker. Go to the back of the van, and I'll open the doors from here. Make sure to grab on to something."

Oh, *this* sounds good.

The Puker turns out to be a fifty-five-gallon drum half full of crude oil. The drum is mounted on a platform with hinges that allow it to tilt, and there's a big clear hose leading to the bottom of it. The other end of the clear hose leads to a large air tank bolted to the wall. Next to the air tank is a large green button with the word "Puke" written on it. I pull the lid off the drum and hold on to the air tank's mounting bracket.

Rashid shouts back, "Ready?" I turn and give a thumbs-up to his reflection in the rearview mirror. He pushes a button on the dash, and the rear doors pop open. Dazzling light blazes into the van, and the sirens hammer my eardrums. I tilt the barrel so it's on a forty-five-degree angle out the rear of the van and hit the Puke button. There's a loud *whump!* as pressurized air launches the oil out of the drum, right at the cops. The flying blob of slipperiness splashes all over the cars, and both vehicles slide around until they crash off the side of the road. Very satisfying!

I shut the rear doors and clamber my way to the front of the van. "Hey, that worked great," I congratulate Rashid.

He shrugs and says, "I hate tailgaters," with a smug look on his face. He slows to a less frenetic speed, and we compare notes on our way into central Baghdad.

"How long have you done this kind of work?" I ask.

"Quite a while, Miss Scarlet," he says. "Since before my father died, and that was seven years ago."

"Well, Rashid, you certainly make a good first impression."

Rashid puffs up, obviously flattered. He stays very self-satisfied the whole way into the city.

CORE   PUB-TIME-3492

TIME magazine, June 1, 1972

**Another Day, Another Tragedy
in Greater Germany's Persian Province**

BAGHDAD—Café owner Ilan Al-Nisat has a long memory. He remembers a time when sports dominated the conversations in his coffee shop. "I had posters of our best football players all over the walls," the 65-year-old neighborhood fixture recalls. "My regulars used to sign the pictures of their favorite athletes so they would know which customers to argue with." His animated expression fades as he continues. "But my children and grandchildren, they talk about other things."

Yesterday afternoon, the café hissed with news that German security soldiers had fired into another crowd of protesters. This time, the casualties included 434 wounded and 197 killed, making this last week the province's bloodiest in five years. Almost every native citizen knows someone who has been injured or killed in the recent violence, particularly in the dense downtown area of Baghdad near the Al-Nisat family home.

Taking a quick break from the shop's daily bustle, Mr. Al-Nisat tells of a much different atmosphere than the one he sees now. "People are quieter now. They don't want to attract attention in such a public place. Besides, most of the things that get talked about here aren't happy things."

Mr. Al-Nisat's children have known nothing but Germany's uncompromising "stewardship" of their country. The Germans' thin excuse that they protect their Middle Eastern provinces from Russia's avarice doesn't hold any more water for the natives now than it did back when Ilan was a young man raising his family in the apartments above his café. Across the country—in cafés, at work, and at home—boisterous talk of family and sports has been replaced by hushed, dark conversations of risings and rebellion.

Another day in Baghdad.

CHAPTER 14

Rashid's café is tidy, bustling with activity, and reeks of spicy food. Behind the kitchen is an attached garage for delivery vehicles, which is handy for stashing oil-spewing vans and sneaking nineteen-year-old white chicks into the middle of Baghdad. Despite the late hour, there seem to be a dozen of his relatives here. They're all visiting with one another, and they all talk at once. It's hard to tell the employees from the customers, but Rashid assures me that they can all be trusted never to have seen me in their lives.

He leads me through the kitchen and into a small office. One of his female cousins brings us iced tea and a big plate of flatbread with sauce in a bowl. Rashid tears off a hunk of bread, dunks it in the sauce, and pops it in his mouth. I dunk and pop too, but unlike Rashid I then gasp and grope for the iced tea with my eyes watering.

"Hot?" Rashid asks with a smile.

I'm too busy chugging my tea to answer. Rashid hands me another piece of bread. "Eat some bread. It'll absorb the oils on your tongue." I eat the bread. It helps, a little.

This café has a long history with the international covert community. Rashid's father, Ilan, provided an unofficial safe haven for American, Russian, and Chinese agents in exchange for pieces of intel he could use as leverage with Baghdad's German administrators.

Ilan saw that the *Damen und Herren* posted to the Middle East did not exactly represent the Fatherland's best and brightest. He established an "understanding" with them about the many duty-free items that passed through the café's big garage door. The local Fritzes gladly took his bribes in exchange for seeing nothing and hearing nothing as long as the smuggling didn't get out of control.

Rashid's family has become more actively involved in the black market since Ilan passed away seven years ago. Rashid inherited the café and expanded it from a sleepy neighborhood coffee bar to a chain of five locations all around Baghdad. Five times the space means five times the tax evasion. Some of his many brothers and cousins run the other shops, but Rashid oversees the whole enterprise, especially the under-the-table business. This work gobbles up all his time, hence the "Lonely Rashid" bit. Rashid remains the sole bachelor in his family, but as the oldest he still commands respect among his siblings. I can't imagine having such a complicated family life. It was thorny enough growing up in a family of three.

Still, it's exciting to visit one of the places my father hung around in when he was away from home. I think of the row of stools at the front counter and imagine Dad settling in there for a coffee and quietly trading bits of information with Rashid's father. They probably shared late nights in this very office, like Rashid and I are doing now.

Weird.

My host is just as surprised as Jacques was when I tell him that I'm here to find out what really happened to my dad. Jacques already knew that Big Bertha was my father, but Rashid didn't realize it until this moment. He tilts back in his chair and runs his hand through his hair. Then he stands up and walks to a tall filing cabinet in the corner. There's a thick throw rug under the cabinet. Rashid pulls on the little rug and drags the cabinet out from the corner. He squats down where the rug was and fiddles with something on the floor. He pulls up a square section of flooring and sets it to the side.

Rashid reaches deep into the square hole in the floor. His muffled voice says, "Your father gave my father something to hold." His shoulders shift as he rummages around in his subterranean stash. "Ah hah!" he exclaims. He puts something in his shirt pocket, replaces the flooring, and shoves the cabinet back in place.

Then Lonely Rashid settles back into his chair and slides something across the desk to me. It's a data pod, a small plastic and metal doodad that stores digital files.

My teeth press tightly together. I'm scared to touch it. "What is it?"

Rashid shrugs his shoulders. "My father never looked at what it holds and advised me to do the same." Rashid's expression softens, and he quietly continues, "His advice was always good, so I did as he asked. He said Big Bertha had left it with him for safekeeping and that I should give it to the first trustworthy American who came looking for it."

I stare at the data pod. The last thing I remember about my dad was him leaving for the mission that took him here. The material in this device is from after that, so it almost feels like it's from the future even though it's from eight years in the past.

Rashid misinterprets my hesitation and stands up. "I will give you some privacy, Miss Scarlet." He smiles at me and leaves the office, gently closing the door behind him.

I grab the data pod and slide the top of my pants down to expose the data port built into my hip. I pop in the data pod. A selection of audio files and a stack of text documents appears in my Eyes-Up display. It's my dad's dispatches. They're kind of a mess. The files are only identified by the date they were created, so if I copy them to my Bio-Drive without naming them first they'll all have today's date and they'll be an unholy bitch to work with.

I sort the text stack by date and skip to the end. I open the last entry and see from the header that my father

wrote it eight years ago here in Baghdad. The report
begins with codes and other official crap, the stuff that
Trick does for me. Then I find what I'm looking for: the
Field Action Report.

Big Bertha / Baghdad / Begin 2 November, 04:45

Later this morning I am to accompany Winter to the lab
outside of Riyadh. I've been invited to a meeting with him and
several of his foreign financiers. Most of these contacts are
from Zurich, with a few other Germans and even an American,
according to a memo I was allowed to see.

While my supposed role at this meeting will be security,
I am sure that Winter is testing me. If any of the information
I overhear is reflected back to him from his moles in our
government, he will know where it came from and I will be
eliminated.

It's time to go. All my work has led up to this.

END 2 November, 04:48

Wow, this is already a gold mine for the Information
people. Dad really *was* after Winter and the Blades of
Persia, like Jacques told us. Which means he *wasn't* surveying Russian covert activity in Germany's Middle East
like it says in the official CORE entry for his last Job
Number.

*So who wrote those field reports in CORE? And what
the h-e-double-toothpicks is a-goin' on here?*

I remember that it was summer when Dad left on this
trip and that he hardly packed anything. He only took a
small suitcase to hold his lightest-weight suits, which
could have been for either mission. But he left Li'l Bertha at home, which according to Jacques fits the Blades
mission and not the surveying mission.

I move backward through the documents and find the
beginning of his dispatches from Baghdad.

Big Bertha / Baghdad / Begin 19 July 19:45

Arrived Baghdad earlier today. Uneventful flight, but my taxi was followed from the airport. Two people on a single motorcycle, one adult male in his midthirties, one boy estimated twelve years old. I had the driver drop me off at a coffee house outside the city. The adult followed me inside the café. After ordering a drink, I went to the men's room. While in the men's room, I observed the boy as he loitered outside the window. I climbed out the bathroom window and eliminated the boy. I then reentered the coffee house through the front door. Predictably, the remaining enemy went outside to check on the child.

I followed the adult male outside and eliminated him while he bent over the body of the boy. A search of their papers confirmed them to be, as I suspected, father and son. I rode the motorcycle to a known Blades base and set the vehicle alight. I was two blocks away in a taxi when the motorcycle exploded.

I must make contact with the Greeks and attain their appraisal of the situation here.

END 19 July, 19:58

Whoah! Dad's stories down in the basement never mentioned this kind of shit. I knew that sometimes people got killed on his missions, but I didn't know they were twelve-year-olds! When I entered the field, I was only a few years older than this poor kid. It's pure luck that I never came up against someone like my father.

I look at the dates from his first and his last dispatches. Impressive. In only five months my father went from the new guy in town to meetings at Winter's secret lab. My mother has told me he was very charismatic. Since the report from November was his last, it seems like Winter didn't think my father was as charming as everyone else did.

I close the reports and open a set of audio files. These

are clips my dad recorded to gather evidence. I pick one of the later recordings.

Big Bertha / Baghdad / Recorded 4 October, 14:51

This is a digitally voiced time stamp that gets added automatically to the beginning of official recordings. I don't recognize the first voice I hear, but it's creepy.

"There is no question at sis point."

It's a man's voice, but it sounds weird. The man has a strange accent; I can't place it.

"Do you mean it's inevitable, sir?"

My dad's voice. It's like he's right here. A pair of big, cold teardrops form in my eyes. The drops flow down the sides of my face and soak into my shirt.

"No, not inevitable, Philip, but we know what needs to be done, and we are prepared to do it."

"And what is that?"

A long pause. I hear . . . footsteps? Maybe they're walking together. Finally the other voice says,

"I don't want to demoralize the more senior recruits by accelerating your schedule. You show great promise, Philip, but it is still too early to reveal sat much to you."

There are more footsteps, then a door opens and shuts. Men with different accents speak German, one of them my father. Clinking glass and the sound of pouring liquid. They're having a drink at a restaurant or someone's house.

Recording ends, 4 October, 14:54 hours.

The time stamp ends the recording with a click.

I wipe my eyes with the back of my hands and drop some Kalmers to keep myself together. My father's voice echoes in my head and brings back a flood of memories of the time I spent with him.

Focus, Alix!

I open another unlabeled stack of text documents.

There are two files inside, again labeled only with dates. The first was written after Dad had been on this mission for a month.

Big Bertha / Baghdad / Begin 3 August, 22:47

Jakob,

What's the holdup? I've asked Info repeatedly for an analysis of that sample I sent a week ago. Smuggling it out of here was not trivial, as the facility I took it from has some of the stoutest security in the organization. It *must* be important.

—Big Bertha

End 3 August, 22:49

The second document was created two minutes after Dad's last Field Action Report.

Big Bertha / Baghdad / Begin 2 November, 04:50

To whom it may concern,

If you are reading this, you have spoken with Ilan and received my backed-up data files for this Job Number. It also means I likely did not survive this mission.

I have created this archive because of the strange things that have happened while I've been on this mission. My reports have been barely acknowledged by ExOps, and when I ask for assistance from the Information Department, I'm told that there are no resources available. I fear that something drastic has happened at the agency, and I am not certain what to expect when I return home. Therefore, I will summarize my progress thus far to retain some kind of record.

My assignment to infiltrate the Blades of Persia has gone well so far. I was followed on my arrival from Paris, but after eliminating that inconvenience I was, as far as I know, no longer under surveillance.

My first task was to meet with the Greeks and learn about the general situation here in Baghdad. They told me relations between the Germans and their Middle Eastern subjects are tense, as usual. The same cycle of violence continues, much as it has for the three decades since the war.

Something new are the whispers of a man who is working on a way to eject the Germans and the Russians from the Middle East. The man's plan is never clearly stated, but his name is Winter. The Greeks aren't certain whether this rumor is true or simply something the people cling to out of desperation. I couldn't help but wonder if the Germans themselves started this myth to focus the locals' attention on a baseless fantasy.

But my meetings with Ilan at his café led me to conclude that Winter does indeed exist. Ilan wasn't able to elucidate any further on how Winter intends to achieve his goal, but he did connect me with one of Winter's top lieutenants, Kazim Nazari. I persuaded Nazari to believe that I'm a German security officer who has suffered some minor disgrace. This fictional scandal has forced my early retirement and compelled me to hire myself out as a freelance bodyguard. Nazari expressed interest in having some more experienced personnel around, as many of his local recruits are enthusiastic but largely untrained. Apparently the Blades of Persia employs a fair number of non-Middle Eastern security people, mostly retired Russian Levels.

From there it was simply a matter of working myself into Nazari's good graces. After proving my worth during an attempt on his life, my standing with Nazari improved so much that he decided to introduce me to his reclusive boss and leader of the Blades, Winter himself. This meeting is today. My goal is to make myself so indispensable that I become part of Winter's personal guard. From there I will ascertain what his intentions are.

If I have not survived, tell my wife and daughter that I love them both very much.

—Big Bertha

End 2 November, 05:13

Oh, God, I miss you, Daddy.

A huge sob flies out of my throat and ricochets off the walls of Rashid's office. I yank the data pod out of my hip and clutch it tight while I bury my face in my hands and bawl like a child. I hear the door open behind my chair.

"Miss Scarlet, what's wrong?" It's Rashid.

"Scarlet, what's happening?" It's Trick. He can hear everything I do. "What's the matter?"

Rashid crouches down in front of me. "Are you all right?"

I nod my head and gasp for breath. "Solomon, I'm fine," I comm. "Gimme a minute, okay?"

"Sure thing," Trick comms faster than normal. He's worried.

Rashid closes the door and gets me a cup of water from a cooler opposite the filing cabinet. I drink a little and slowly calm myself down. Rashid sits in his chair behind his desk and stays quiet, letting me recover.

I imagine my father's rapid speech and the way he'd stalk around the room as he told me one of his stories. We'd be down in his shop. I'd watch and listen while he maintained his Mods or reprogrammed his Level 20 handgun and turned her into Li'l Bertha.

He'd keep his drink up on top of his red Snap-on tool cart. Sometimes he was in a cast or wrapped in bandages from all the damage he took on his Job Numbers. He'd tell me stories about what he did to people and what they did to him. By the time he was on his third drink, he'd be telling me how sometimes he hardly felt it when he got shot and how sometimes he could barely think from the pain. It broke my heart to think of my daddy alone in some dark shithole, fighting for his life so he could come back to his little girl and scare the daylights out of her.

His stories gave me terrible nightmares, but never while he was home. The bad dreams would begin the day he left on a mission and stop the day he returned. After his last job, when we realized he wasn't coming back, sleepy time became a nonstop horror show for me. The nightmares got to be less frequent after I joined ExOps.

Rashid sees that I've stopped crying. He leans forward. "I know how you feel, Miss Scarlet. I weep sometimes, thinking of my father."

I sniffle and wipe my eyes again. "Still?"

"Yes." His animated voice has gone flat. "Still." He sits back and stares at the top of his desk. "My mother once told me that growing up isn't learning how to get over loss. It's learning how to carry the pain of loss and keep going."

I inhale a deep rattling breath. "Well . . . that fuckin' sucks." My stoic bluntness brings a smile to Rashid's face, which in turn makes me laugh. He laughs with me.

"Are you hungry, Miss Scarlet? My kitchen is open all night, especially for distinguished guests such as yourself."

"No thanks, Rashid. I need to—"

Suddenly there's a loud rapping at the door. Rashid calls out in Arabic, and the door swings open to reveal a wide-eyed boy. He's about eleven, and I guess that he's one of Rashid's many nephews. The boy stammers something to Rashid, who replies quickly and waves his hands to shoo the boy out of the room.

"Miss Scarlet, my lookouts have seen something they don't like outside." He grabs a set of car keys from his desk. "We must go."

CHAPTER 15

I hate somethings. They're never good. Apparently, the lookout saw two out-of-place-looking men. Out-of-place-looking means competition.

I follow Rashid out to the garage. "Scarlet to Solomon."

Trick's right there, of course. "Go ahead, Scarlet."

"Solomon, the Greeter's people have spotted suspicious activity," I comm. "How's it look outside?"

"Crowded."

Rashid walks past a rack of license plates for the truck and presses a button on the wall. The big garage door clatters open. The parking area beside the café glows in the glare of streetlights overhead. I lurk behind the puker delivery van while Rashid ambles outside and lights a cigarette. He strolls toward the sidewalk and casually looks around.

Trick continues, "You're in an all-night café, and across the street is a movie theater and a jazz club. It's night-owl heaven out there."

Rashid returns from his recon. "We've attracted interest."

"Cops?" I ask.

"No, I know all the police in this area. It's someone else." Rashid rubs his jaw and scowls.

"Lemme guess," I say. "Russian?"

Rashid's eyebrows go up, and he purses his lips. "Hmm. You know, they could be."

"Young or old?"

"Middle-aged. Definitely not young."

"Solomon, did you hear that?" I comm.

"Affirmative."

"Rashid gave me a copy of some of my dad's reports. My father said the Blades of Persia used to hire a lot of retired Russian Levels as security."

"That matches the guys who jumped you at the drop zone earlier tonight," he comms. "We ran the picture you sent through Archives and found a match. That competitor spent fifteen years as a Russian Protector until he left the KGB five years ago."

"Was he working for the Blades?"

"We don't know, but it would explain why he dropped off our radar until tonight. I hadn't even heard of the Blades until all this started."

"Jesus, Solomon, what the hell is going on?"

"We'll figure it out, Scarlet. It could be the Blades, since it seems like that's who your father was after, but it could also be a lot of other people."

"Well, whoever the fuck they are, I think the bastards have found me again. Should I ride out with Rashid?"

"One sec." Patrick mumbles with his Info Coordinator in Washington. Then he comms, "No, the Greeter is being watched too closely. Leave the café on foot and proceed as planned."

"Roger that." I stick my hand out to Rashid. "I'm outta here, Lonely. Nice to meet'cha."

Rashid shakes my hand and says, "Miss Scarlet, are you sure? I can get another car."

"Don't sweat it, Rashid. I'll be fine." I pop outside and turn toward the back wall of the garage. I squat down and then thrust my legs straight. As I fly up to the roof, I glimpse Rashid's mouth dropping open.

I run across the top of the café, crouching low to remain hidden from the street. My boots carry me across the roofs of a few adjoining single-story shops until I get to a side street. I drop down to the sidewalk and walk toward a big parking garage a few blocks away.

I turn on amplified hearing, infrared vision, and starlight vision to keep track of everybody on the street. I call this my Manhattan Radar Mode. After I've traveled a block, I peek back over my shoulder. Two goons have stopped hanging around in front of the café and are jogging after me.

I check with Trick. "Solomon, are you tracking these two?"

"Roger, Scarlet. Two palookas in pursuit."

I'm a few blocks away from the garage. It's got six aboveground levels and I don't know how many underground. I zap some Madrenaline into my blood and break into a full-out sprint. I speed up to thirty-five miles per hour and lean forward to counteract the wind resistance. My arms pump so fast that my jacket sleeves make a clapping sound as they slap back and forth from my biceps to my triceps.

I'm almost inside the garage when a huge Mercedes sedan roars around the corner and skids to a halt across the entrance to the upper levels of the car park. The doors fly open, and a group of men pop out like bread from a toaster. I swerve to the side and disappear down the ramp to the lower levels. The garage is filled down here. Rows of cars are parked among ribbons of concrete barriers set up to direct the flow of traffic. I move into the middle of the floor and crouch next to an old BMW.

"Solomon, I'm hemmed into the lower level by a pack of goons."

"Russians again?"

"Maybe. I don't know. They're not cops." I lean against the car and turn up my hearing. It's one thing to eliminate a group of baddies when they don't know I'm there, like at the cemetery in Paris. When they're all locked and loaded, it's something else entirely. I peek over the hood. "Solomon, I count six competitors."

"Sit tight, Scarlet. Let me see if the Greeter can draw their attention away from you."

I switch off my Manhattan Radar suite except for my

infrared vision. The cars have been here long enough to cool down, so I have a clear look at the pair of over-heated goombahs who huff and puff into the garage. These must be the schmoes who chased me from the café. They pause to catch their breath. One of them is big and muscular, and the other dude is small and wiry, hardly bigger than me. They're only fifty feet away, so I can't count on Rashid getting here before they spot me. I set Li'l Bertha to .45-caliber, chug some Kalmers to steady my aim, then stand up and let 'er rip.

The first slug nails Big Guy right in the forehead. *Fucking perfect.* Small Guy is surprisingly quick and ducks under my second shot. He crawls behind a concrete barrier and calls to his buddy, but I don't think the big fella is feeling very chatty.

Li'l Bertha switches to .12-caliber suppression pellets as I leap out from cover and charge the concrete barrier. I spring across the cars like they're skipping stones, advancing on an angle to take away Small Guy's cover. He's smart, though, and quick crawls about forty feet to my left. He sticks his gun over the barrier and blind fires a flurry of bullets. I have to drop flat to dodge them. My momentum makes me skid off the hood of a car, and I land right on my noggin. My vision goes all white static for a second, and my ears start ringing.

All right, fuck this subtlety bullshit. I switch Li'l Bertha to the biggest thing she's got: .50-caliber Explosives. I stand back up and blast giant holes in all the concrete barriers anywhere near this goddamn guy. Chunks of cement fly around the garage, ping off the cars, and knock out some of the lights. The explosions echo like a freight train falling into a canyon. My infrared vision allows me to see through the smoke and dust. Unless Small Guy has vision Mods, he's effectively blind right now. Even if he has them, all they'll do is let him witness his own demise.

This shithead has done well, but playtime is over. I've got a grenade in my right hand while Li'l Bertha kicks and bucks in my left. Small Guy scrambles to keep away from me, but finally one of my bullets blows his right leg off. I put the grenade away and switch to more reasonable indoor ammunition, standard .30-caliber.

Small Guy is bellowing like a stuck pig. I stand over him, snap his picture with my retinal cameras, then shoot his face until it's goo. Drops of his blood splatter on my forehead and run down my cheek.

Shouts echo from outside as I run back to the BMW. I punch out the driver's-side window, hop in the car, slide the seat all the way forward, and stick my hand under the dash. Being an ExOps field agent makes it certain that once in a while you'll need to steal a car. At Camp A-Go-Go, we learned how to hot-wire everything.

I find the correct wires, yank out the ends from the ignition cylinder, and touch the tips together. The car starts. I put Li'l Bertha in my lap and a couple of grenades on the seat next to me. I stick the car in gear and screech my way around what's left of the concrete barriers to the exit.

I hear more cars arriving outside. The four guys who arrived in the Mercedes run into the garage. More gunmen run up behind them. They stand on the exit ramp and unload their guns at me. Christ, there's too many! I accelerate straight at them and duck under the dashboard. Their shots shatter the car's windows. Safety glass fragments chop into my scalp and bullets pierce my shoulders and upper arms as the Bimmer gets absolutely riddled. Hot streams of blood pour down my back and soak into the leather seat. I keep my head low and my foot on the gas until I feel some goon-size thumps from outside the car. Howls, crunches, gunshots . . . it's like Mardi Gras in hell. Blood splashes onto the dashboard, and ovenlike heat flares from the backseat. Flashes of orange light pulse in time with the heat waves, and I realize that my car is on fire.

I fly out of the garage and into the street. My right hand steers the rolling inferno while my left hand grabs Li'l

Bertha and lays down a suppressive mix of incendiaries and tracer slugs. *Give those fuckers some of their own medicine.* My neuroinjector crams coagulants into my bloodstream to stop the bleeding and dumps in so much Overkaine that I can barely see from dizziness. None of this matters as much as the fact that I've got to ditch this vehicle before it explodes right out from under me.

"*Solomon!* My car's on fire. Get me the fuck out of here!"

"Jesus! Okay, okay, uhh—go straight 300 onto that bridge ahead of you. Then turn right, off the bridge into the Tigris. Don't slow down."

I count to three hundred feet and swerve to the right. I've got the gas pedal floored, and before I know it, my ride flies off the bridge and into the river. The car hits the water like it's crashed into a wall. The steering wheel bashes into my face, and the world goes black as I pass out cold. Patrick has to wake me up with a remotely triggered electric shock.

I'm on my back with my legs over the wheel, totally disoriented. All I see is a gray smudge that turns out to be the inside roof of the car. There's blood on the seats, dashboard, ceiling, everywhere. My mouth hangs open. It's like my lower jaw has seceded from my face. I can barely see because my throbbing eyes have swollen shut. The fire has gone out, but now the car is sinking into the Tigris River. I stuff Li'l Bertha into her holster and wait until the water is even with the windows. Once it is, I gently float myself out of the car. My uncloseable mouth makes loud sobbing gasps because it's full of blood, water, and broken teeth. My neuroinjector has automatically released another shitload of painkillers, but I'm still in agony. The few front teeth I have wobble around like drunken sailors. Oh, yeah, and I'm still stuck in the middle of fucking Baghdad with a gang of motherfucking assholes trying to kill me.

"Scarlet, what's your status?"

I comm, "Oh, God, Trick, I'm all fucked up!" I forget

to use his field name. I forget that I'm an unstoppable badass. I forget everything as I float under the bridge and grope my way to one of the supports. I climb out of the water and lie down on a concrete slab, with the underside of the bridge about six feet above me. I pant, wheeze, and groan as I fight just to stay conscious. A cold puddle forms around me while I use my hands to hold my mouth closed. The world spins and flashes from dark to light even though my eyes have swollen completely shut.

I can hear the anxiety in Trick's comm voice. "Hang on, Alix! He's almost there. Jesus H. Fucking CHRIST—hurry up, Rashid!" He's so freaked out that he forgets to switch comm frequencies. But this is good. Ol' Lonely will come for me, and I'll be okay. He'll take me home and I'll sleep, and then I'll have breakfast with Mom and Dad. Oh, wait, maybe not Dad. Isn't he still on a mission?

The ground starts to shake. A hurricane of noise up on the bridge: screams, gunshots, explosions, the works. Big splash in the water nearby. A pair of spicy-smelling arms lifts me, carries me up to the bridge and into a vehicle. I think it's Rashid's van, but you could tell me it was Apollo's chariot and I'd believe you. There's still a storm of shooting and yelling, but I know I'll be fine. My dad is back from his mission, and he loves me.

"Scarlet! Can you hear me?" Dad sounds and smells like Rashid.

"Sure, Dad, I'm fine. I love you, too." This is what I mean to say, but it comes out more like "Shhthethfo-ouhht." Maybe I'll leave the whole talky thing to everybody else for now.

I'm set down on the floor of the vehicle, which has been carpeted with a rich, thick shag. I watch a TV show of a rabbit in a doctor's outfit sticking a hypodermic into my arm. I don't look so hot. The TV camera zooms in on my face, which is covered in blood. I can't see my eyes, and my mouth is a gaping mess. The camera zooms out as somebody—Dad? Mom? Bugs Bunny?—wraps a blanket around me. We float out of Baghdad on a big red carpet. Then the TV shuts off.

This dossier contains public-facing information.

New York Times, October 20, 1974

Echoes of the Crash and Thunder of WWII

Through all of human history, nothing has exceeded the nobility and the depravity, the brilliance and the ignorance, the colossal production and devastating destruction of World War II. Even thirty years later, the consequences of this history-altering conflict continue to shape our world.

The Blitz of Europe, 1939–1940

In September 1939, Germany launched an invasion of Poland from the west while the Russians invaded Poland from the east. Within a month, the Polish army and government collapsed. In April 1940 the German army quickly occupied Denmark and began their invasion of Norway. In May, the German blitzkrieg rumbled through the Netherlands, Belgium, and Luxembourg. The Wehrmacht took only six weeks to sweep around France's eastern defenses and demolish the once-proud French Army. The Germans then methodically occupied the rest of Europe while they tried to persuade the English to join the German Empire. Great Britain's stubborn resistance sealed her fate.

Germany Invades Great Britain, 1941

In the early morning of June 6, 1941, almost every vessel in the Kriegsmarine crossed the English Channel from Harfleur and Calais to take part in Operation Sea Lion as Germany invaded Great Britain. The deadly effectiveness of Germany's Luftwaffe cleared the skies while her U-boat fleet protected the troop transports. The invasion was brutally effective, and Parliament was forced to surrender. Later that year, Germany surged to victory in Palestine, Syria, and Saudi Arabia. The German Empire now stretched from the Balkans to the Atlantic and from the Arctic Circle to the Persian Gulf.

The End of Hitler's Reign, 1942

Three years of glorious victory had convinced Adolf Hitler that he was unbeatable. He drafted a plan for the invasion of Russia, code-named Operation Barbarossa. His generals were appalled. The vastness of Russia had thwarted every invader since 1249, including Napoleon. All of their simulations yielded the same result: the overextension of Germany's armed forces, a massive Red Army counterattack, and the total defeat of the Fatherland.

On 20 February 1942, a secret coalition of Wehrmacht officers, Abwehr agents, and other German officials—collectively known as the Black Orchestra—carried out the assassination of Adolf Hitler. Three months later, riven by internal conflicts and no longer united by Hitler's hypnotic charisma, the Nazi Party fell apart. Leadership of Germany shifted to somewhat clearer heads, and Operation Barbarossa was scrapped. The Nazi Party's planned extermination of the Jews was modified to a program of noncitizenship and forced labor. One German officer said simply, "We'd rather fill Europe with workers than corpses."

The German attitude in the Middle East, however, was a different story. The best and most disciplined Wehrmacht divisions were needed for the invasion of Great Britain, so the only troops left to capture Syria, Lebanon, Palestine, Egypt, and Iraq were the far less disciplined Einsatzgruppen. These units, sometimes battalions of barely trained police, made no distinction between combatants and civilians. Resistance was both futile and fatal. Cities and towns that fought against the German conquerors were burned to the ground.

Russian Conquest of Southwest Asia, 1940–1943

While the Germans consolidated their hold on Europe, the Mediterranean, and the Middle East, the Russians secured as much of southwestern Asia as possible. The Red Army eventually conquered Afghanistan, Pakistan, and Iran. These campaigns were notable for their wanton disregard for the lives of the civilians in these areas. Some postwar analysts believe that this near extermination was official policy and that Russia planned to relocate some of its huge population to the Middle East.

For the student of current events, the ongoing terrorist activity in the Middle East is a direct response to these murderous campaigns and the draconian occupations that followed. In no other part of the world has the aftermath of World War II been as violent and chaotic. The conquered peoples of Greater Germany resent their occupation to be sure, but Berlin's postwar administration has been positively enlightened compared to the unending crackdown imposed by the Soviet Union on its subjects in the Middle East.

The American War in the Pacific, 1941–1944

Only in the Pacific theater were the invaders successfully pushed back. The Japanese, on the offensive from 1931 to 1942, were decisively defeated by the Chinese and the Americans in mid-1944.

The war in Europe was over before the United States could significantly intervene on behalf of its European allies. This meant that the Americans could respond to the Japanese attack on Pearl Harbor with all their might. All they needed was time to bring that might to bear.

The U.S. Navy bought America that time as they repelled Japanese attacks at faraway places such as Midway Island. America produced more war matériel and more servicemen in less time than any country in history. By the end of 1942 the United States had the largest military the world had ever seen. The president, the Pentagon, and the newly appointed Supreme American Commander, Dwight D. Eisenhower, were ready to dictate the terms of battle in no uncertain terms.

American forces leaped toward Japan with Eisenhower's famous Tsunami invasion strategy. Enemy resistance was met with an unprecedented torrent of American naval artillery, bomber raids, and armored assaults. Hundreds of thousands of Japanese troops were killed while hiding in their bunkers and tunnels. Those who survived were trapped in their underground strongholds until they surrendered or died of thirst. Some of the islands literally changed shape. The bombardment inflicted on one Japanese base was so heavy that it triggered a volcanic eruption.

In 1943 the U.S. Navy gained total control of the Pacific. American merchant marine convoys arrived in China bulging with American vehicles, arms, and supplies for Chiang Kai-shek's Kuomintang army. Navy battleships shelled Japanese positions on the coast of mainland China to support Chinese ground attacks. The Chinese chased the Japanese down the Korean peninsula and pushed them off the Asian mainland.

The U.S. 8th Air Force's strategic bombing campaign reduced Japan's manufacturing capability to smoking rubble. Anything remotely connected with the Japanese war effort was targeted. Some Japanese civilians speculated that the colossal scale of the American bomber raids were manifestations of the wrath of God.

Only thirty months after the attack on Pearl Harbor, U.S. troops invaded Japan's home islands. Starved and surrounded, the Japanese Army fought on until American troops broke down the doors of the emperor's palace in Tokyo. Japan's unwillingness to surrender led GIs to remark that their enemy "must have one heck of an afterlife." The American attacks killed most of the leaders of the Japanese government, although Emperor Hirohito was spared.

Victory and Tension, 1944–1947

Although the United States and China had a common enemy in Japan, they had nothing in common beyond that. Tensions flared immediately after VJ Day in 1944. The Chinese felt that they should be given possession of Japan as a reparation for the destruction caused by the Japanese invasion of their country. The United States already held the islands and planned to maintain Japan as a strategic outpost in Russia's backyard.

The Korean War, 1947–1948

China saw, and still sees, the American presence in Japan as a direct threat to her security. To insulate themselves from a possible American invasion, they declared Korea a permanent part of China and concentrated three armored divisions near Pusan, just across the Korea Strait from Nagasaki. The United States responded to intelligence predicting a Chinese attack by landing American troops from Japan at Inchon, behind the Chinese front. The conflict's first year was characterized by bold flanking maneuvers and a fluid frontline.

The war's second year ground into a bitter, static stalemate. By the middle of 1948, President Truman was under tremendous election-year pressure to resolve the situation in Korea. America had just finished an exhausting war against the Japanese and was ready to vote for whoever could bring a swift end to this new Asian conflict.

With Truman's approval, the U.S. Air Force dropped the world's first atomic bomb on a large Chinese army base at Pyongyang. The effect was as dramatic politically as it was physically. China had no desire to follow Japan's brave but foolish precedent of being obliterated by the Americans. Chinese troops withdrew from Korea and requested an immediate cease-fire.

The United States added Korea to its list of Asian protectorates, and the nuclear age began.

The Shadowstorm, 1948–Present

If the dawn of the nuclear age signaled the end of overt hostilities, it also initiated the Shadowstorm. Each of the four powers launched a multitude of schemes and plots against the others. Germany, Russia, and China were all desperate to obtain the bomb. The United States was just as eager to keep it away from them. The Americans craved the German's rocket and jet propulsion technologies and wireless communications systems. China and Russia were both resentful of the U.S. presence in Japan. Germany and Russia had many border disputes in Europe and the Persian Gulf.

The German-occupied European capitals maintained their cultural identities, if not their political independence. The new owners particularly cherish Paris. Undamaged due to the speed of the German advance, it remains one of the most beautiful cities in Europe. While the French resent *l'occupation* to this day, the white Christians among them have been reasonably well treated by Germany's post-Nazi regime so long as they obey their new masters. The treatment is similar in the Province of Great Britain, although certain regions still erupt in unrest, particularly Scotland. One prominent member of the Reichstag commented that he now sees why the Roman emperor Hadrian simply built a wall to keep the Scots out.

The German Reich Today

Scotland provides an interesting example of the recruitment difficulties faced by anti-German groups. The Reich has kept most of its subjects well fed and reasonably safe. For the common citizen, this is all they want from their government, foreign or otherwise. As a French aphorist once wrote: "The only stomachs that take to the streets are empty ones."

The exception to this unsettled contentment is Europe's indentured Jewish population and those who openly oppose their enslavement. These groups have the greatest potential to launch a serious rebellion. Even German diplomats admit—off the record—that all it would take is the right leader at the right moment.

CHAPTER 16

When I was a kid, one of the things I loved about hanging out with my dad was that he treated me like a grown-up. He'd drink, tell stories, and swear about politicians—especially Nixon. He showed me how to fix stuff and how he maintained his Mods. I even got to help with certain things, like his knees. I'd squirt lubricant into his uncapped knee joints while he held his leg in place. He'd swing his lower leg back and forth to work the grease into the machinery inside. It sounded like two steaks rubbing together and smelled like pizza that's been cooked on a car engine.

Daddy also used to take me to Extreme Operations' firing range. Technically, guests weren't allowed, but he was ExOps' rock star, so they'd look the other way when the two of us walked in. It helped that he held the range's record with a score of 298 out of 300. My initial results were barely over 100, but they zoomed up to 200 after my father taught me how to adjust for wind, elevation, and distance. Then he showed me how to time my breathing, to take a deep breath and hold it while I aimed and fired. Once I'd mastered this, I was up to 250 and qualified as a sharpshooter. As I got better, Dad began challenging me to friendly competitions. If I was shooting well that day, he'd let me win. He always got extra hugs from his Hot Shot when we went to the range.

All this transferred to my attitude at the local public school, which is to say I had a huge one. I knew my daddy could whomp all the other daddies' asses, so I'd pick the biggest kid on the playground and pounce on him: punch, bite, kick. They never expected it because of my size. I barely weighed eighty pounds when I left public school to enter Extreme Operations' youth training facility, AGOGE, commonly known as Camp A-Go-Go.

ExOps recruited me right after my father's memorial service. Some people came to the house to gather his classified materials and equipment. They weren't sure if he'd brought his ExOps-issued LB-505 with him on his last mission. When they asked me about it, I blasted them with enough swear words to make the Devil blush. My father had just died, and here were these clipboard-toting assholes bugging me about the only part of him I had left. They left that part of the form blank.

When Dad was away on his Jobs, I'd putter around in his workshop. He always left his shop a mess, so I'd tidy up for him. I liked to be around all his work things. Meanwhile, my mom would go to her job in ExOps' Administration Department. We'd have our uptight little life together until he got home.

One time, I grumbled to my dad about what a pain Mom had been while he was away. He stopped what he was doing and sat down across from me on the workbench. I could see him collect his thoughts for a minute.

"Alix, honey, I know things are tense around here when I'm gone. You're a big girl now, and I need to ask you for a favor."

My big girl mind raced. *What could it be?* "Yes?" I squeaked.

"You know how your mom and I fight sometimes when I'm home?"

Jesus, did I. So did the neighbors, the cops, and the local newspapers. "Yeah, kind of."

"First off, it's not your fault, okay? It has nothing to do with you. We both love you very much."

"Uh huh."

"Your mother and I fight so much when I come home because she and I are both terribly wound up. She's upset because she doesn't know what happens to me on my trips, and I'm upset because I *do* know. I'd like you to be really good for Mom while I'm away by helping around the house and doing what she asks. Maybe she won't be quite so tense, and I'll try to unwind without making her mad. We'll all have a nicer time while I'm home."

Children helping parents? I'd never heard of this. Kids are supposed to get-get-get, aren't they? Still, that part at the end sounded good. I was always glad when my father came home, but I was also glad the fights stopped when he went away. "Okay, Daddy," I said, "but I want an extra-nice treat."

He chuckled and said, "You got it, sweetheart."

As a typically patient child, I immediately asked, "What will it be?"

"What will what be?"

"My extra-nice treat!" I had my Daddy-slaying charm turned up to eleven. I figured if I played my cards right, I might score a life-size chocolate pony.

He laughed, stood up, and reached down to sweep me into his arms. I held on to his shoulder, right at eye level with him. He said, "Tell you what, Hot Shot. The next time I'm home, I'll teach you to work on Li'l Bertha." I kissed him on the cheek and wrapped my arms around his neck. It wasn't what I'd expected, but my father knew me too well. I'd coveted that gorgeous gun since I'd first laid eyes on it. Some kids get into tennis or chess, but not me. I took to guns the way a senator takes to interns.

Dad had been home for an unusually long time, almost a month. He hadn't had any drinks in a few days, so I could tell he was getting ready to travel again. That night, I lay in bed reading one of my dad's gun magazines from the stash I kept in my closet. I stored my clothes in two-foot-tall heaps all over my room because my closet had become a warehouse of the stuff I scrounged from around the house: piles of magazines, a collection of old tools and electronics, and a few empty liquor bottles with fancy labels.

Most of it was stuff my dad would leave around after he passed out late at night. My mom or I would find him in the morning, asleep in his shop. Sometimes he'd have written things on his bandages. It was usually gibberish, but some things you could make out. Mom would take a big black marker and scribble over it. She didn't want him in trouble for walking around with classified information written all over him.

My parents' room was right next to mine. Government-issue houses have notoriously thin walls, so I could always hear what they said. For once, what I heard wasn't shouts. I didn't hear any crashes, either, since my father had already trashed most of the bedroom furniture. But the fact that they weren't shouting didn't mean they weren't arguing.

"For God's sake," my mother exclaimed, "she's only ten years old."

"Cleo, I know how old our daughter is. She's very mature for her age."

"I don't care! Jesus, Philip. She asks the most awful questions when you're away."

"If she asks, that means she's ready to hear it."

"No, it doesn't! Fourth-grade girls should not ask their mothers about machine guns and strangulation. I can't even look at the drawings she brings home from school!"

"Cleo, I don't talk to Alix about—"

"Well, she sure as hell doesn't hear it from me!" my mom said, her voice rising. "I'm worried she'll turn into a person like, like . . ."

"Who, me? What's wrong with that?" barked my dad. My mother didn't answer. I heard the mattress creak as one of them sat on the bed. My dad inhaled slowly, exhaled all at once, then continued. "Honey, I know my work bothers you, but it's not all as bad as it sounds.

Besides, how many of your friends have a Level 19 Liberator at home?" This is how I learned to handle my mother. She's a real sucker for this kind of charm.

"Philip, stop it."

"Baby, enough for now. We'll talk in the morning before I go to work. Why don't you come here?" The bed creaked again. My dad had successfully lured my mother into bed. They talked for another minute or so, and then it got quiet. After a while I could hear them having sex, moaning and stuff. Maybe my mother wouldn't divorce my father, after all. Once in a while, she would talk about it on the phone to her friends when she thought I couldn't hear her.

I fell asleep and dreamed about being an Extreme Operations agent like my daddy. I'd travel and shoot guns and beat people up, but when I came home I wouldn't drink, and I wouldn't smash up the house.

CORE   INT-AGOGE-004

DATE: February 21, 1968
TO: Office of the Executive Intelligence Chairman
FROM: Office of the Director of Extreme Operations Division
SUBJECT: Project AGOGE

Dear Sir,

Please find attached a detailed proposal for the founding of a special school for the recruitment and training of Extreme Operations field agents. Put simply, this institution will intensify our competitive capacity in the clandestine warspace. This will be achieved by authorizing Extreme Operations to evaluate and indoctrinate potential agents when they are as young as twelve years old. If fully exploited, these young persons' quick reflexes, adaptability to upgrades, and emotional suggestibility will grant our case officers an insurmountable advantage in the field over our competitor's older agents.

We will continue to recruit and train older agents, but my opinion is that the graduates of this school will be so overpowering in the field that older agents will primarily be used as handlers or teachers.

Clearly, employing young people for such dangerous work is a controversial concept. Our public relations people have already generated a series of preapproved talking points and press releases in the event of a public-facing exposure.

Sincerely,
William Colby
Director, ExOps

CHAPTER 17

Considering Camp A-Go-Go's intensity, the first day was pretty soft. It was eight years ago, but I remember it like it was yesterday. My class of recruits was introduced to the rest of the school at the first day ceremony. Some of the instructors and advanced students gave short speeches, and then we plowed through a ton of pizza, hot dogs, and sodas. It was like a birthday party for seventy-five kids all at once.

Camp is actually a well-known secret government training program. Its real name is Authentically Gifted Operatives General Education. Since it's a government institution, it was abbreviated to the annoying-to-pronounce acronym AGOGE. None of us could agree how to say AGOGE, so we called the place Camp A-Go-Go or simply Camp.

There are actually quite a few Camps. The government operates a bunch of these schools to maintain an optimal number of students at each facility and to let the kids live near their families.

Speaking of families, before a recruit is accepted into the AGOGE, all of his or her relatives are dragged through a bureaucratic jungle of prodding, poking, and background checks. The process is so labyrinthine that by the end people are just glad they aren't going to prison for something.

The families are sworn to a secrecy the government knows most of them won't keep, but it establishes a behavior pattern for the family. You see, everybody knows that Camp is where secret agents and other government spooks are trained. But those are the *regular* secret agents and spooks. Those guys stop at Standard Training. Nobody is told about Advanced Training. Nobody is told about the Levels.

If your family members demonstrate that they know how to keep their traps shut, your file is moved to a different filing cabinet with much higher ass-kicking potential. I knew all about Levels already because I'd been raised as a spy brat.

Even so, when I got to Camp, Advanced Training seemed very distant. All of us punks started as Unranked Recruits pending rank testing for physical coordination, interpersonal skills, and reflexes. Most of the other entering students were thirteen or fourteen years old. I was only twelve, but what was painfully obvious was how much smaller I was than the rest of my class.

Fortunately for me, size didn't matter for rank testing. I did well on the coordination sequences where they had us run across beams, climb ropes, quick crawl through a long pipe, and jump from a high board into a swimming pool. I bombed the interpersonal skills section because I hadn't realized you'd ever *talk* your way through anything here. My dad's stories never mentioned talking to his targets.

Then came the reflexes sequence. It was designed to test how quickly you made decisions and acted on them. The instructor called me into an office and guided me to the guest chair in front of a big desk. He walked behind the desk and sat down. He stared at me for a couple of minutes. By this point, I had figured out to sit still and stare back. Fidgeting was sure to lower your scores. The instructor opened a drawer, pulled out a black revolver, and placed it on the desk in front of him. He closed the drawer and said, "I want you to tell me how you would get this weapon from—"

I lunged forward and spit in his face. He squinted his eyes shut and jerked his hand up to wipe my spit away. I nabbed the gun, dropped back into my seat, and pointed the pistol at him. His hand hung in front of his face while he looked at me through his fingers.

After several seconds of silence, he asked, "What if it isn't loaded?"

I cocked the hammer back. *Click.* "Then my grade isn't as high."

They promoted me to the highest rank, Recruit Rank 9, passed me out of Recruit Initiation, and accepted me into Initial Training. Who needs talking? By being the first recruit ever promoted to Initial Training before her thirteenth birthday, I left the rest of my entering class in the dust. I was half the height and weight of the senior student in Initial Training, who had started at Camp A-Go-Go almost three years earlier.

Mornings in Initial Training were like a regular school. We took required classes in history, English, foreign languages, math, and science. I liked history and foreign languages, the others not so much. After lunch was when the difference between Camp and a normal school became obvious. Our afternoons were entirely devoted to physical education classes. We practiced martial arts, competed in team and individual sports, ran for endurance, and trained in gymnastics. I was eager to begin firearms classes, but those are only for recruits in Standard Training and up.

Most of the trainees, including me, liked the martial arts classes best. I'd imagine that I was my dad and fight the bad guys with head kicks and sucker punches in the gut. We would practice our moves as a group, then form up in sparring lines to practice at half speed with minimal contact to avoid injury.

One day our instructor rolled in a cart full of padded gloves, boots, vests, and helmets. He laid them out by size—small, medium, and large—and told us to suit up. When we were all decked out in our fighting apparel, he formed us in sparring lines as usual. This time, however, we were to fight at full speed and full contact until he whistled the fight was over.

We fought hard. Our bodies spun and leaped, glad to fight flat-out and not worry about hurting one another.

All that padding made us feel invulnerable. I wound up across from a much bigger girl (naturally) with a few years of martial arts training under her belt. Her name was Janice. She knocked me around, but I put up a lot more resistance than she expected. Our fight seemed to last longer than the others. By the time the whistle sounded, we were both drenched in sweat and breathing like furnaces. Janice won on points, but given the size difference, she should have blown me right out of the room.

Our instructor had us square off against the same people again and told us we would fight a second round that would count toward our rankings as Initial Trainees. He told us to imagine that we would be kicked out of AGOGE if we lost. This time I fought Janice to a standstill. She had me on technique and hit me with an array of maneuvers and combinations I'd never seen before, but I was faster and blocked everything she threw at me.

I knew I couldn't stay on the defensive forever, though, so I watched her carefully, looking for an opening. Just as I caught a tendency of hers, she faked me out with a great move. I blocked for a kick, but she got me with a punch right in my solar plexus. The whistle blew, and Janice had won again, but by even fewer points than in our first round together.

I was pissed, and I wanted another shot at redemption because I'd figured out her weakness. Once Janice was in her spin, she was too fast and unpredictable for me to go on offense, but I'd seen my chance. To set herself up for that move, she would plant both feet and counterwind her body a bit to spring into the spin. During that counterwind, Janice was wide open.

The rest of the class finished their second-round fights, and the scores were tallied for our rankings. The instructor set us up for a third round. This time we were told to imagine that if we lost, we would be killed. This was a shock to us first-year kids. I don't think it occurred to any of us that we wouldn't live forever. I couldn't wrap my mind around it, so instead I imagined that I was my father on his last mission and that I would fight for my life so I could go back home to see me and Mom again.

I set up opposite Janice. We were both still gassed from our last round, so we faked and feinted for a minute, catching our breath while we looked for an opportunity. Then she planted both of her feet. As she wound herself up, I leaped forward and kicked through the front of her knee. Her leg bent backward and snapped like a celery stick. Janice screamed and tumbled to the floor, both hands on her knee and her eyes squeezed shut. I crouched down and then launched myself over my opponent. I aimed my feet so they'd come down on Janice's neck. Time seemed to slow down. The room fell silent except for the wind whistling past my ears. Suddenly I realized that the sound in my ears wasn't from the wind; it was from my instructor frantically blowing his whistle to signal us to stop fighting. My toes brushed Janice's chin as I spread my feet apart to avoid breaking her neck. Janice's eyes popped open as my foot landed barely an inch from her face.

Time came back to normal speed as the instructor pulled me out of the way and gently picked Janice up. Everyone in the class followed him out of the gym as he carried her to the infirmary. Everyone except me. I stood there, looking down at my feet.

Jesus, was I really about to do that?

After a minute, I joined my classmates at the infirmary to see if Janice was okay. We all hung around outside for a while, but the nurses wouldn't let us in. Eventually, we went back to our rooms, me last of all.

I opened my closet and pulled my clothes out to pack since I was sure I'd be expelled. Half an hour later, there was a knock at my door. It was the same tall woman who'd come to my house the year before. She walked me out of the dorm, but she didn't take me back home.

I had been promoted all the way to Advanced Training.

CHAPTER 18

The pucker factor goes way up in Advanced Training at Camp A-Go-Go. Hollering, cursing, intimidation, all that in-your-face bullshit. The nonstop noisefest is designed to weed out the trainees who can't take it—whatever "it" is. The anxiety level was nothing compared to growing up in my parents' house, but most of the other kids washed out. By this point, a class with an initial enrollment of seventy-five will have graduated fifteen students into Advanced Training. Among those fifteen Advanced trainees, only two or three will become Levels at Extreme Operations. The rest will return to Standard Training, where they can become unenhanced agents, case officers, analysts, or Squad guys. What they can't do is quit. They've seen too much highly classified information. They must work and live within the warm, tender embrace of the federal government. And the families keep quiet since their son or daughter is essentially held hostage.

Advanced Training was constant stress and unrelenting pressure, and it started immediately. The tall woman led me into my new dormitory, took my bags, and shoved me into an elevator by myself. The doors closed and the lights went out, leaving me in total darkness. The tall woman's high heels clicked on the floor as she walked away.

I had overheard one of the older kids in Initial Training talk about how much it cost to develop a recruit into an agent. The training became dramatically more expensive each time you got promoted. It didn't take a genius to know that this was a test to see if I was a potential asset or just some teenage sociopath.

It was pitch black in there, so I had to feel my way around. I pushed all the buttons, tried pulling the doors open, and felt around for loose panels. Nothing. No way out. I leaned on the small handrail that ran around the perimeter of the car and tried to imagine what a grown-up would do. After taking a few deep breaths to calm down, I said to myself aloud, "They'd climb out the roof." But they'd be able to reach the emergency escape hatch in the ceiling. I put both hands on the handrail and pulled as hard as I could. It was firmly bolted to the wall. Perfect.

I hoisted myself onto the rail and leaned my back into the corner. Then I leaped across the car and punched at the center of the ceiling as I sailed past. I felt a panel in the ceiling move. After repeating this sequence a couple of times, I got the panel knocked out of the way. On my next attempt, instead of punching, I slid my fingers along the ceiling and caught the lip of the emergency exit. After I stopped swinging back and forth, I heaved my body though the square hole and clambered out of the car and onto its roof.

Unlike the darkness inside the car, the darkness on top of the car was accompanied by the stink of oil, mildew, and rat shit. I hoped I wouldn't touch anything gross while I blindly groped around. I sighed in relief when I found a maintenance ladder bolted to the wall of the elevator shaft. The ladder ran very close to the elevator car, too close for an adult to fit. I think the ladder was for getting around in the shaft above or below the car but not past it. My small frame allowed me to squish myself down between the greasy shaft wall and the out-side of the dusty, grubby elevator car.

There was one terrifying moment when my shirt got caught on a bolt or something and I almost got stuck. My imagination was very clear about how mangled I'd get if the elevator car moved while I was jammed be-tween it and the ladder. I exhaled as completely as I could, pressed my face and body against the dirt-crusted rungs of the ladder, and slithered past the obstacle, tear-ing a long rip in my shirt. I had never been so filthy. I emerged below the elevator car and quickly climbed down to the bottom of the shaft. Now for a gimmick my father had told me about.

He'd had to pull this kind of shit before. In one of his stories, he was cornered in an office building, so he crawled down the elevator shaft and snuck out the basement. What made it work was how easy it is to open an outer elevator door from inside an elevator shaft. It's just a matter of hauling them open an inch at a time.

This building at AGOGE had the kind of elevator with two doors that meet in the center. I pressed my fingertips into the gap between the doors and slowly pried them apart. Then I slipped both my hands into the gap and pulled until there was enough room for me to squeeze through.

I ran upstairs to the lobby, covered in grease, scrapes, and triumph. I crept up behind the tall woman who had brought me and smugly said, "Excuse me, ma'am."

The woman spun around, her eyes wide open. She gaped at me, looked at the elevator door, then looked back at me.

"That elevator is fucked up," I continued. "You'd better call a mechanic."

She stared at me for a full ten seconds, then finally said, "Let's take the stairs, then." I was grinning like a fox while I followed her upstairs.

I found out later that the elevator is a panic test. They want to see how you control your emotions when you're trapped in a small dark space—if you keep your cool or if you freak. You're not supposed to escape. I heard from Mom that my Houdini act set off a series of phone calls that flashed up the Extreme Operations org chart like flames climbing a pile of napalm. Within half an hour, the Director was told that they might have found themselves another Philip Nico.

CHAPTER 19

It's my Buddhist temple dream. I started having it when I fell asleep on the flying carpet in Baghdad, and I've had it a bunch of times since then. As usual, I sit cross-legged on the floor and watch little puffs of steamy breath come out of my nostrils. The chilly temple is high in the moonlit mountains. It's dark outside. A monk in orange robes sits ten feet away, facing me. The dream is always the same: it never gets light out, and the monk never talks.

This time, though, he says softly but clearly, "The strongest seed pays the price to the jealous gods below."

Then we're silent again while the sun comes up.

Every morning the sun blasts through the goddamn window and shines right in my face. I've been able to ignore it until now, but today it's especially insistent. I open my eyes for the first time since I got pulled out of Baghdad, which feels like a hundred years ago. There's a short, chubby woman sitting on a chair at the foot of my bed, doing a crossword puzzle. I try to talk, but it comes out as a scratchy hiss. She looks up.

"Oh, thank God," she proclaims. She gets up and bends over me, looks in my eyes, then looks over my head. She's dressed like a nurse. "Sit tight. I'll call the doctor."

I'm like, oh, okay, because I was about to jump up and go to my fucking tennis lesson. I look to see what's so interesting above my head. It's a video monitor with lines and numbers on it. Attached to my temples and chest are a half dozen sticky pads with wires coming out of them. I try to sit up, but my muscles are as limp as boiled lettuce, and I just flop back on the pillow.

The nurse returns with a tall middle-aged man wearing a sport coat and black pants. "So our little phoenix has risen from her ashes. Let's have a look at you." It takes me a moment to recognize that it's Dr. Herodotus. He looks in my eyes, then at the monitor over my head. It would seem that "me" has been reduced to my eyeballs and whatever is on that stupid screen.

"Harriet," Dr. H says as he studies the monitor, "let's get her loop before it overwrites itself."

"Yes, Doctor." Harriet the nurse grabs a data pod from the side table and walks to my side. She slides the data pod into the port in my hip.

Dr. H shifts his attention from the monitor to me. "Alix," he says, "can you do something for me?"

I nod my head.

"I want you to copy your Day Loop to your Bio-Drive right now."

My doctor needs me to initiate this because only I can access my Day Loop. I grapple through my physical soreness and mental disorientation to do as I'm told. Quicker than I can say Autonomous Single Day Memory Recall Loop it's backed up to my Biotic Data Drive. Now whatever's in my loop won't be lost during the next twenty-four hours.

"Done," I whisper.

Dr. H punches some buttons on the keyboard under the monitor. My Eyes-Up display shows him copying my archived Day Loop file from my Bio-Drive to Harriet's data pod.

Harriet says, "I've got it." She pulls the data pod out of my hip and gives it to Dr. H.

"Okay," he says, "we'll take a look at this and see what survived."

"Doc," I croak. "What happened?"

He answers, "I was told that you took on a platoon of Arab terrorists and Russian mercenaries and then drove a flaming car into a river. When you arrived here three months ago, you were quite a sight, let me tell you." Dr. H has that annoying doctor's black humor where he gets all peppy describing his smashed-up patients.

There's a bendy straw in a glass of water on the table next to my bed. I lean over and drink from it, then try to growl while I say, "Just tell me what the fuck happened to me." It comes out more as a rattle than a growl, but it gets their attention.

"Ah, yes." Dr. Herodotus sighs. "Wonderful vocabulary." He pulls a clipboard off the foot of my bed. "Well, you came in here with twenty-three wounds from bullets and shards of glass. You also had second- and third-degree burns on about 20 percent of your body, mostly your neck and back . . ." He reads on and adds, "Also, your legs were badly broken . . ."

I remember now. The bullets. The fire. How the car hit the river. I gingerly move my hands over my face.

The doctor glances up from his clipboard and finishes his carnage countdown with ". . . and your face required extensive reconstruction as well. Both your upper and lower jaws were shattered, and you lost most of your front teeth." I run my tongue around the front of my mouth. It feels normal to me. Dr. Herodotus notices me checking myself out and says, "You're all healed now. We patched up your wounds, set your broken bones, replaced the burned skin on your shoulders and neck with Exoskin, bolted your jaw back together, and replaced your missing teeth. You'd almost never know what a mess you were when you came to us."

I'm *really* glad I slept through all this. I wouldn't have wanted to be awake when they bolted my jaw back together. I gently run my hands over my face. It feels normal. A bit tender in front, right under the nose. I move my hands down my body to my legs. They feel straight. I hope they look all right. My legs have been shaping up nicely, and I'd hate to ruin them.

The doctor blathers on. "Some of our best work, wouldn't you say, Harriet?"

Harriet replies, "Yes, Doctor, especially since all these

wounds were floating around in a filthy river." They continue to discuss in minute detail what a great job they did. These two will be the death of me.

"When can I bust out of this nuthouse?" I ask.

"You'll have to do a lot of rehab, then it's up to your boss," Dr. Herodotus states as he places the clipboard back at the foot of my bed. "We've told him you're awake. He should be right up." The doctor gives Harriet some instructions before he leaves my room.

That tells me I'm in Washington, in the ExOps hotel. This also tells me that Cleo is around here somewhere.

"Where's my mom?" I ask Harriet. Talking hurts. I drink some more water.

Harriet says, "Right now she's over in the main building, but I know she's still living upstairs. She had plans to move into another house when you got back from your mission, but she decided to stay put when she found out what happened to you. Your mom and I have talked quite a bit while you've been recovering."

"Is she mad at me?" I don't know why I ask Harriet this. It just pops out.

Harriet's eyebrows move up, then she smiles and gently shakes her head. "Sweetie, I've seen a lot of parents at their children's bedside, but your mother absolutely broke my heart. She slept on the floor next to your bed for a week. We offered to bring in a cot for her, but she thought it would make too much noise, so she unrolled a sleeping bag, like she was camping. The night nurses kept stepping on her by accident. Once you stabilized, we were able to talk her into sleeping upstairs."

Warm tears run down the sides of my head and into my ears. Maybe Harriet the nurse isn't so bad, after all. Her head turns toward the door as it opens, revealing an unexpected visitor.

It's Raj. He nods hello to Harriet and comes in. Harriet excuses herself, thinking we're friends. I quickly wipe my eyes dry while Raj looks around, scoping out my room.

He walks over to my bed. I stare straight up at the ceiling and grouse, "Come to gloat, Rah-Rah?"

He doesn't say anything. I keep staring, and he keeps not saying anything. Finally I look at him and demand, "Well?"

His low voice rumbles, "I just wanted to see how you were, Shortcake."

Shortcake?

I ask, "You aren't here to tell me how much I cost ExOps by fucking up my Job Number?" Raj sits down in the guest chair, next to the bed. I continue, "And since when do you call me anything but my field name?"

"Scarlet," Raj says, "I read the reports from Rashid and Patrick. It sounds like you did a great job getting yourself out of there in one piece."

"The doctor makes it sound like it was more than one piece."

"Well, whatever. All the pieces are still alive. Look, I know we haven't gotten along since the day you blundered into ExOps, but you showed me some real potential when we rescued your mother. And now this impressive escape. It's made me think we have more similarities than differences."

I move my eyes up and down his giant limbs and torso. "I don't know, Raj. It seems like you could eat me for dinner and still have plenty of room for dessert." Raj looks at me for a moment, then bursts into one of those big deep-voiced guffaws where you can't help but join in. It hurts my throat to laugh, but it feels good to have this giant on *my* side for a change.

"Yeah, Scarlet, I could, but all your metal and plastic wouldn't be so good for my digestion." In spite of myself, I laugh again.

I'm not sure what's happened to Raj. It's like aliens came down and upgraded him while I was out. My voice rasps, "So what are we, friends now?"

Raj leans forward with a smile. "How about colleagues first? We're both Levels on our way up, and it could just as easily be me recovering in that bed right now instead of you. There's plenty of work to go around, and I figure we'll both do better if we watch each other's back. What do you say?"

"Can I still call you Rah-Rah?"

His eyes narrow, and he thinks for a second. Then he smiles a little and answers, "Only if you don't tell anyone I said it was okay."

I grin. "Deal!" We shake on it. His giant paw envelops my tiny hand. We talk shop for a few more minutes, then he gets up to go to a meeting.

As he opens the door I ask, "Hey, Rah-Rah, now that we're all colleagued up, what's your real name?"

Raj stands in the open doorway and considers. "Nah, not yet, Shortcake." Then he ducks out to the hall and calls back, "Maybe if you save my life someday."

"*Maybe?*" I shout at the closing door. Yelling so loudly strains my throat and triggers a giant coughing fit.

Just as I catch my breath, I hear footsteps racing up the hall outside. The door bursts open, and Cleo sails into the room. She flies all the way from the hallway to my bedside in one running step. "*Alix?* Oh, Angel, it's true. You're awake!" She smothers me in hugs and kisses while she cycles through, in no particular order: "Honey," "Angel," "Baby," "I missed you," and "Are you okay?"

I say back to her: "Oh, Mom," "I missed you, too," and "I'm fine," also in no particular order.

We wallow in each other's arms for a few minutes. Both of us cry and look at the other's face, memorizing what her features look like.

"Alix, I've felt so terrible about us ending on a fight like that before you left."

"I know, Mom. Me too. I didn't mean to make you sad that night."

She sits on the side of my bed and reaches out to smooth my hair. "I've got your birthday present upstairs. I'll bring it down to you at dinnertime."

My birthday? Cleo sees the confused look on my face. "Yes, Angel, you're twenty now."

I missed my birthday! Well, that sucks. "What did you get me?"

Cleo smirks. "Something nice. You'll see." She puts her hand on my cheek, takes a breath, and says, "I've read the reports of your mission. I'm horrified by what you went through, but it's clear to me why Cyrus needs you for this work. I've never seen such high scores assigned to a Level who came home in the condition you did."

"Why would I get high scores? I almost got killed."

"Well, that's exactly it. You *didn't* get killed. The Information Department has concluded that your odds of surviving that ambush were one in three thousand."

"So I'm lucky?"

"Alixandra, you're more than lucky. Cyrus thinks you may be the fastest, toughest, most talented Level that ExOps has ever had." She pulls my covers up to my shoulders and says, "You rest, baby. We'll talk more tonight. I have to get back to my meeting with the head of Administration. I ran out on him the second I heard you were awake. My pen is probably still hovering in midair."

This cartoony image makes me laugh and almost start coughing again. Cleo kisses my forehead and leaves, taking a good look at me before closing the door behind her.

Later, Patrick and Cyrus visit me. They stand on either side of the bed until I make them move to the same side so I don't have to keep swiveling my head back and forth.

Cyrus is glad I'm awake for a couple of reasons. He's happy that his most sensational field agent is back, of course, but there's another, more pressing reason. My Johnny Blaze trip into the Tigris broke more than my jaw and my legs. It also trashed the data pod I got from Rashid.

"Oh, crap," I groan after Cyrus tells me this. "I'm

sorry, sir." I brace myself for one of his roof-shaking scoldings.

Cyrus shrugs, and his eyes flick away from my face. "It happens."

Uh oh.

I keep my eyes pointed at my boss while I comm to Trick, "Why isn't Cyrus yelling at me? What's wrong with him?"

Patrick holds his expression steady. "Nothing's wrong with him."

"He *is* pissed, though, right?"

"Oh-h, yeah."

"About me losing that firefight?"

"No, not that."

"What, then?"

"You know how Levels are supposed to comm intel to their Info Operator the moment they receive it?"

"Oh." *Damn.* "That."

"Yeah, that." Patrick shifts his feet so he's behind our boss. "Cyrus gave me a loud earful when he realized we'd dropped that ball, but he cooled off when we realized how badly hurt you were."

I sit up straighter. "Sir, I'm sorry I forgot to comm my intel to Solomon. Couldn't the Med-Techs access my Bio-Drive?"

"They could—" he sighs "—but you didn't copy the files off the data pod."

Double damn.

"And your partner didn't remind you." Cyrus turns and briefly roasts Trick with a scorching glare. Trick's jaw tightens, but otherwise he stands still.

I look down at the bedcovers. "Boss, I'm really sorry. It was . . . I . . ."

Shit, that data was the whole reason I went to Baghdad.

He sighs. "It's all right, Alix." His hand pats my leg through the blanket. His fingernails are very smooth, and he has unusually long fingers. "Rashid got a sense of what was on the data pod from your reaction to it. Hearing your father's voice after so long can't have been easy." He pulls a chair up to my bedside and sits down. "It's been a long three months, though. We've only been able to work with the intel you got from Jacques, which isn't much. The sole copy of Rashid's intel is in your organic memory, and maybe in your Day Loop."

Three months lost. "Oh, crap," I groan. "Boss, I—"

Sharply, Cyrus says, "You've already apologized, Scarlet, but I want you to remember this. We never know what's going to happen out there. The moment you harvest intel, you send it in. Understood?"

"Yes, sir." I say quietly. "Do you want my report now?"

"Not yet. Chanez is on his way. Let's wait for him so you only have to say it once." He softens his voice. "There were two positives to the delay. We had time to research the Blades of Persia, and things had a chance to cool down a bit."

It seems my high-visibility adventures in Baghdad forced Director Chanez to account for why his agents were shooting up someone else's city. The Director tacked our Middle East trip onto the Fuerza Libertad mission, backdated the entry, and talked his way past his superiors.

"I didn't know the dates in CORE could be faked," I comm to Patrick.

"They can't, supposedly," he comms back. "Chanez's clearance must give him a work-around."

Cyrus tells me that—based on the evidence Patrick and I gathered in Paris—the ExOps brass is questioning whether my father was genuinely assigned to investigate the Blades of Persia or if he just made it up and went rogue.

Well, my report will certainly have something to say about *that.*

"Okay, and one more." Harriet hands me another pill.

"Jesus, Harriet," I grouse, "this one's as big as a base-ball!"

"Oh, that's nothing." She's totally imperturbable. "You should see how we get the really gigantic pills into people."

"Hmph." I cram the pill into my mouth, sip some water, and choke it down. "Glagh! It *tastes* like a base-ball, too."

Harriet cheerfully ignores me and chirps, "All righty, sweetheart, you're done."

She could give a shit what the pills taste like.

"Now then, gentlemen," Harriet purrs to Cyrus and Director Chanez. "I'm sure the world is about to end, but if you wear out my patient"—she flashes a big smile—"I will kick both your honky asses off my floor." Harriet bustles herself out of the room, followed by my bosses' stunned stares.

Patrick presses his lips together to keep from laughing. "You tell 'em, Harriet," he comms to me.

"Now we know who wears the pants around here," I comm back.

Director Chanez shifts his eyes back and forth a couple of times, like he's trying to figure out if that was in-subordination or not. He shakes his head a little, shifts in his chair, and clears his throat. "Scarlet, let's begin with the files Rashid gave you. I've got Info recovering what they can from your Day Loop, but I'm not sure there's much left."

I comm to Trick, "What happened to my loop?"

"It didn't like the electric shock I used to wake you up after you crashed into the river."

"How about me being in a coma?"

"It didn't like that either."

Meanwhile, Chanez is saying, "I'll hear what you can tell me now. They were your father's reports from his last mission, correct?"

"Yes, Director." I summarize the written reports as best as I can. I vividly recall my dad's recorded conversation, and I'm able to recite most of it from memory. Chanez remains keenly focused on everything I say. Only when I'm finished does he ask questions.

"Scarlet, you're sure about the name of the man your father worked for in Baghdad?"

"Kazim Nazari? Yes, sir."

"And your father's reports were clear that a man called Winter was running the Blades of Persia?"

"Yes, sir."

"Well," Chanez says to Cyrus, "it sounds like this man Winter is real, after all. One moment, please." The Director stops talking, and his eyes seem to lose focus. He's comming. His expression shifts as he concentrates on his comm conversation. After a minute, his eyes clear and he looks at me again. "Okay, I've forwarded what you just said to Information Coordinator Harbaugh. He'll run it through the jackframes and see what he turns up."

I shift my position in bed. "Do we know anything about Winter, sir?"

"Only that Winter, or a group writing as Winter, periodically releases statements and manifestos to the press. He writes about freeing his people from the oppression of the West, that sort of thing. But the Blades have never claimed responsibility for a terrorist attack, and Winter has never appeared in public. He's been more myth than man."

"Except now he has a known associate," Cyrus adds.

"Yes, he does." Chanez stands up and gets himself a cup of water from the cooler in the corner. "And myths do not have associates." Chanez and Cyrus discuss what they've heard about Winter. What little there is tends to contradict itself. Winter has done a good job of masking himself.

The door opens, and a stoutly built middle-aged woman clomps into the room, hands Chanez a sheaf of papers, and stomps back out again. Seems like Chanez prefers his secretaries to be the taciturn Brunhilde type.

I ask, "Do we know who Kazim is, sir?"

"We do now." Chanez reads from a printed sheet. "Kazim Nazari, originally from Damascus, is a microbiologist and former biology teacher. He received his PhD at New York University, and his tuition and board were paid for by a charitable fund called the Darius Covenant. His current location is unknown."

"Is that scholarship fund part of all this, sir?" Patrick asks.

"I would say so. It's existed for almost ten years now. We've already got a file on it." Chanez flips to another page and tells us that the Darius Covenant pays for selected people to go to college. Science degrees, mostly. Middle Eastern people, always. The administrators of the Darius Covenant have spotless records, but where the money comes from is still unknown. Our traces have only gotten lost in a web of shell corporations and affiliated organizations, most of which are barely more than a post office box and a disconnected phone number.

"Darius Covenant," I mumble. "That's a pretty dramatic name for a scholarship fund. Do we think it's dirty?"

"Definitely." Chanez nods. "Why else would its corporate structure be so convoluted?" He sets his printed pages aside and says to Trick, "Solomon, sit next to Scarlet, please, so I can brief you two at the same time."

I scoot over to make room for my partner. He sits on

the corner of the bed. Chanez leans forward with his elbows on his knees.

"Scarlet, your report indicates that your father was pursuing what he believed to be a genuine ExOps Job Number. It links Kazim Nazari with our mystery man, Winter, and his Blades of Persia. That link may even connect the Blades of Persia with the Darius Covenant. This is a significant breakthrough, because we finally have someone to go after. Good work, both of you."

"Thank you, sir!" Through the covers, I poke my finger into my partner's leg. Patrick smiles.

Cyrus says to me, "We also have a possible explanation for all the Russian Levels you've been encountering. First Hector in New York, then your mother's kidnappers, and finally those three competitors who were waiting for you when you dropped into Baghdad." He rubs his chin and looks at his boss. "None of these confrontations have fit the KGB's normal methods."

"Agreed," the Director says, "Our Soviet cousins are much more discreet." Chanez glances at me. "More effective, too." He flips through his paperwork. "We haven't heard a whisper from our sources in the Kremlin, and we definitely would have picked up *something* about three blown ops." Chanez sets his papers on his lap and rubs his eyes. "No, these missions are being run by someone with extensive tactical resources but without the operational apparatus of a state-run covert agency."

Cyrus's eyebrows move up. "We've stumbled into a private war."

"Exactly." Director Chanez leans back in his chair and inhales deeply. "Our next step is to track down Kazim Nazari. He can lead us to Winter, the Blades, and the mystery behind Big Bertha's last mission. I intensely dislike that we know so little about this. But what needs our immediate attention is how you two keep getting ambushed everywhere you go. Your trip to Baghdad didn't officially happen until you were already back here." Chanez thoughtfully taps his pen on his pile of paperwork. "We either have a mole, or someone has tapped into ExOps."

Chanez says that he's run a full security scan on everyone at ExOps. He didn't find anything, but he admits that doesn't mean there isn't a mole. In fact, he's pretty certain there's been one for a while.

ExOps suffered a major security breach soon after my father was captured. The evidence indicated that there were three moles—an astonishing number in such a small agency. They ferreted out two of them, but the third mole either escaped or just never got caught. This third mole, nicknamed Scorpio, has haunted ExOps for eight years. These ambushes may be renewed activity on Scorpio's part.

"Your last cover mission was based where you actually went." Chanez jots down a note on one of his printouts. "This time, I'll set up something that masks not only what you're doing but also where you're going. If you still get jumped, it'll be because of where you physically are, not what the paperwork says."

"Sir," Patrick asks Chanez, "how could it be someone on the outside?"

Chanez answers, "It's not probable, but anything is possible. Tapping into ExOps would be difficult. They'd need full access to multiple jackframe systems, one of which is only intermittently connected to the network. Unless . . ." He considers for a moment. "If someone had root access to your commmphones, they could trace your locations through your No-Jack modules. But I don't think anyone has that kind of clearance. I certainly don't."

Chanez writes another note to himself, then says, "Our friend Kazim Nazari left his teaching job ten years ago. He hasn't appeared in our records since then, except for his apparent engagement with Big Bertha." The Director puts his pen down and looks at me and Patrick. "Which brings us to your next Job Number. Scarlet and

Solomon, I want you to interview a CIA stringer who may lead us to Kazim."

"What's the stringer's name, sir?" Patrick asks.

"I don't know." Chanez's expression reveals not a trace of irony. "But I know who does." He tells us that the CIA maintains a Very Important Asset in the Middle East. The Director knows the case officer who runs him. This officer is based in—

"—Manhattan." Chanez pauses dramatically and lowers his eyebrows at me. "Scarlet, I do *not* want another Wild West show. Is that clear?"

"Yes, Director."

"I also don't want to explain why we need this intel. If the CIA finds out about Big Bertha's lost mission and our evident security problems, they'll bury us with an Office of Security probe. We need to acquire this information without asking for it."

I expect the Director to say something else, but instead he silently regards me and my partner. There's a pregnant pause.

I comm to Trick, "Did I hear that right?"

"A-yup," he comms back. "We're gonna black bag the CIA."

"Wow," I comm.

Chanez makes some more notes, then says, "An Infiltrator will perform the actual acquisition. Cyrus, you can assign whoever you like. Scarlet, you and Solomon will provide backup and Info support."

"Yes, sir," we both say.

The Director turns to Cyrus. "Meanwhile, you and I will dig into CORE and find out where the hell the reports for Big Bertha's last mission came from."

"Yes, sir," Cyrus says.

I ask, "Director, the nurse will need my schedule. When is the official briefing for this mission?"

Chanez stands up. "We just had it."

TO: Director Chanez
FROM: Cyrus El-Sarim, Front Desk
SUBJECT: Advancement of Scarlet-A59 to Level 8

Dear Sir,

Attached please find the after-action reports, Information Department analyses, and field team testimonials from Scarlet's latest mission in Baghdad. I strongly recommend that we promote this outstanding field agent from Level 6 to Level 8.

She has survived, yet again, a situation that probably would have killed any of our other Junior Levels. Her performance demonstrated stunning physical talents, ferocious combat instincts, and a bottomless pain threshold.

Her skill set will be a major factor in helping us achieve our goals regarding Big Bertha's lost mission and the Blades of Persia. Please feel free to contact me with any questions you may have regarding this matter.

Respectfully,
Cyrus El-Sarim

CHAPTER 21

Every day I spend in rehab, I find another reason to hate being in rehab. The first day it was all I could do to have Cleo help me walk down to the end of the hall, and that was with a goddamn walker. My legs were as floppy as cooked spaghetti, and my forehead was slick with sweat from the effort. The second day Harriet removed my catheter and helped me use a bedpan to pee. I'd never used a bedpan before, and after that one time I vowed that I'd get to the bathroom if I had to drag myself there by my fingernails. A twenty-year-old woman deserves *some* dignity.

While I was on my twelve-week holiday in Comaville, Harriet shifted the position of my body so I wouldn't get bedsores and Dr. Herodotus used some mild electrotherapy to keep my muscles active, but even with my Mods and physical conditioning I have to learn how to walk all over again. My legs have been incredibly stubborn about this. At first, I couldn't even get myself out of bed without falling down in a cloud of swear words. After a week I could lurch myself into the bathroom with my stupid walker. Thank God my arms still have some strength, because they had to do most of the work. It's been two weeks since I woke up, and now I can get around fairly well. It's been really humbling to be so completely dependent on other people.

I've done a lot of reading. Patrick brought me tons of files and dossiers from the ExOps Archive, including a long *New York Times* article with information about the European campaigns in World War II. I've only read stories about the American fight against Japan, so it's interesting to read about what happened in "the other war."

I've also been grinding my language skill by taking an advanced course in German. Every morning a nurse wheels me to class, where I learn amazing words like *Geschwindigkeitsbegrenzung,* which simply means "speed limit." My classmates and I have found that the easiest way to memorize these monsters is to shout them at one another while we pound our fists on our desks.

After class I have lunch, then more physical therapy, then dinner. In the early evenings I either meet with Cyrus or attend a tedious Info briefing about the Blades of Persia or the Middle East. All this activity keeps my mind off how much I hate rehab, but eventually I wind up back in my goddamn bed, trapped and lonely.

Last week I was so miserable that Cyrus wheeled me outside to the park across the street from the Bethesda for our meeting. He set me on the grass under a tree and sat next to me. I helped him unload a bag of lunch he'd brought from a deli down the street. Subs! Sodas! Bags of potato chips! That morning, Dr. Herodotus had finally cleared me for regular food. I tore into my sandwich like a Tasmanian devil. After a week of being on hospital chow, it tasted like heaven. Cyrus and I ate and went over some things that the Information Department had figured out.

Cyrus didn't waste much time on small talk. "We think someone has taken out a contract on you and hired the Blades of Persia to carry it out." He cracked open a can of soda.

I reeled in shock. My mouth hung open for a moment until I remembered it was still full of potato chips. I crunched them down. "Who the hell would take out a hit on me? I'm only a Level 6—I mean, Level 8."

"I'd say it's whoever we'll find at the end of this investigation."

"Don't you have any guesses?"

"Of course."

I waited for him to go on. Finally, I prompted him. "Well?"

"They're too speculative for me to say out loud."

"Oh, c'mon!"

Cyrus shifted onto his side so he could see me better. "Drop it, Scarlet. Leave this to us grizzled old geezers to figure out. There are a lot of angles to consider, and it could be a lot of different people." He rolled onto his back again. "I am sure of one thing. It's related to the mission we're doing."

"Then why aren't they after you, too? You're the Front Desk."

"I'd say it's because you scare them more than I do." Cyrus propped himself up on his elbow and sipped his soda. "Don't forget, I'm only an expendable bureaucratic cog. You're the superspy."

I waved my hands in frustration. "Why are you so freaking relaxed about this?"

Cyrus looked up at the sky. "Alix, sooner or later this happens to practically everyone in our business." He stifled a small belch, then said, "The Cuban Liberation Movement has had a price on my head since 1959. During the embargo, the Germans found out your father was the American agent who'd been kidnapping all the Reich officials. They put out a huge bounty on him. When he tried to rescue the hostages in '67, their reward for delivering Big Bertha went through the roof." Cyrus picked up his bag of chips and regarded it thoughtfully. "It's actually quite a compliment."

I didn't know whether to hide under my wheelchair or chuck my soda can at his head. "Cyrus, are you *nuts*?" I looked over both my shoulders again. "How is *this* a compliment?"

"It means you're kicking ass." Cyrus winked at me. "Which we knew, anyway." He explained that going after a Level is one of the most expensive things a competitor can attempt. "Honestly, Alix, don't worry about it. I've planned dozens of these things, and they're much harder than you'd think, especially when the target is a Level. For example, what's happened to the people who have come after you?"

"I've mangled the shit out of them."

"My point exactly."

I eyeballed him for a few seconds. He *really* didn't look concerned, like he was only talking about a parking ticket. "Okay, Cyrus." I shrugged and took a huge bite of my sub. "If foo fay fo."

Cyrus looked over at me, grinned a little, and shook his head, "Alix, don't take such big bites. You're gonna choke on that."

We chatted for a while longer as we finished eating our lunch. I asked if they'd gotten anything out of my Day Loop, but they hadn't. The data had been too badly corrupted by the bullet circus that happened to me in Baghdad. It sounded like my verbal report still gave the Info people a lot to go on, but Cyrus made sure to drive home the importance of intel transmission. The whole time he lectured me about it I was gradually airing out a giant burp, so I just kept nodding until we both ran out of air.

Eventually Cyrus had to get ready for a meeting. He picked me up, put me in my wheelchair, and pushed me back to the Bethesda. As we rode the elevator up to my floor, I took one of his hands in mine and held it until the doors opened. When we got back to my room, he plucked me out of my chair and gently laid me back in my bed. He smoothed my hair with his hand and said, "All right, I'll see you later. Keep up the good work with your rehab and you'll be back in the field before you know it."

"Okay," I said. He began to walk out of my room. I called out, "Hey, Cyrus?" He turned and looked back at me. I had a little lump in my throat. After a few heartbeats I said, "Thanks for taking me to the park."

He smiled. "You're welcome, kiddo."

The Oil Embargo and Hostage Crisis

This dossier contains public-facing and classified information. Do not remove this file from the ExOps' Archive.

New York Times, January 21, 1965

President Vows to End Segregation by Christmas

WASHINGTON—President Richard M. Nixon began his second term yesterday by declaring war on racism in the United States. His administration has spent much political capital getting the Civil Rights Act pushed through Congress, and now he intends to give it the teeth it needs to be effective.

"My fellow Americans," said the president during his inauguration speech, "to quote the brave and brilliant Dr. King, 'None of us truly have freedom until all of us have freedom.' We must join hands and finish the work that our Great Emancipator started one hundred years ago." After extolling the courage of those who participated in last year's freedom rides, President Nixon leveled a challenge to our biggest ally, Greater Germany.

"We have an opportunity to end our past hypocrisies, to achieve our true potential, and to send a message to the world. Oppression, hatred, and bigotry are not American ideals, and 1965 will be the year they are no longer American realities."

Over 70 percent of black children in southern states attend all-black public schools. Most of these facilities are in deplorable condition, despite postwar legislation requiring equal facilities for all publicly funded schools. While this is nowhere near the human rights violations committed by the Reich, this tragic situation has always undercut American diplomats' attempts to persuade German officials to end Jewish slavery in their territories. "Why should we listen to the Americans?" quipped a spokesman for the German embassy here in Washington. "They still lynch their Negroes."

The president certainly has his work cut out for him. Jim Crow laws are deeply embedded in the cultures of the former Confederate states. Said one southern Democrat representative, "I'll do everything in my power to preserve segregation, even if it means I have to stand in the school doorway myself."

————

From the Voice of America broadcast of May 3, 1965

Germany Responds to Nixon's Call for Human Rights with Oil Embargo

"The Greater German Foreign Trade Ministry today announced that it will cease exports of petroleum to the United States, effective immediately. The announcement makes it clear that President Nixon's continuing charges of German human rights violations have infuriated both Chancellor Adenauer and the Reichstag. A U.S. embassy spokesman here in Berlin said: 'If we shared a land border with them, they might have declared war instead.'

"This oil embargo will affect Americans from all walks of life. Gasoline may quadruple in price, when it's available at all. The higher cost of transportation and energy will impact all American industries and businesses. Increased domestic oil exploration will eventually bring some relief, but that may be years away."

————

Der Tagesspiegel [translated] 31 July 1965

Minister's Wife Kidnapped at Gunpoint!

BERLIN—Marlene Höhler, wife of Foreign Trade Minister Johann Höhler, was abducted from her home this morning as she prepared to take her two children to school. The children were not taken or harmed, and their account of the event makes it clear that the operation was professionally planned and executed. This is the fifth family member of a public official to be kidnapped since the beginning of the oil embargo against the United States.

The U.S. embassy in Berlin has issued brief statements officially condemning the abductions. Minister Höhler fired back that American agents were clearly behind the kidnapping of his wife and vowed that his ministry's policy would never be dictated to him by terrorists.

————

DATE: August 5, 1965
TO: Front Desk, Extreme Operations Division
FROM: Room 88, Hotel Zoo Berlin, Kurfürstendamm 25, Berlin.
SUBJECT: Operation GEMSNARE

Sir,

Gemsnare-6 has been plucked from her nest. Per your standing order, the Gemlets were not touched.

—Big Bertha

————

New York Times, April 3, 1966

U.S. Ambassador to Greater Germany Taken Hostage

BERLIN—An anti-U.S. political rally staged in front of the American embassy here spiraled out of control yesterday when German terrorists stormed the building and captured the ambassador and his entire staff. A report on casualties was not immediately available.

The rally was held to protest the alleged American kidnapping of several prominent German officials and their family members. Fueled by hours of passionate speeches and heavy drinking, the crowd became violent and began pelting the embassy with bottles and rocks.

At 8:05 P.M. local time, a group of paramilitary radicals led by the infamous Gudrun Ennslin broke through the embassy's front gate and occupied the building.

German Chancellor Konrad Adenauer refused to censure the violation of diplomatic immunity. "Now we will see if the Americans can take it as well as they dish it out," he said, adding that he would do what he could to ensure the safety of the captives. "We are not monsters, after all."

Denounced in the U.S., Ennslin and her followers in the Red Army Faction have been praised by German conservatives for demonstrating "the consequences of clashing with Germany." The headline of this morning's edition of the far-right German tabloid *Bild-Zeitung* screamed *"Nehman Dass!"* which approximately translates to "Take That!"

President Nixon condemned the act and vowed that he would see the situation resolved. "American citizens have inalienable rights no matter where they are," the president declared, "and I will bring our people home safe if it's the last thing I do."

———

Washington Post, March 29, 1967

Failed U.S. Hostage Rescue Attempt Kills 70

BERLIN—The German newspaper *Der Tagesspiegel* reported this morning that the spectacular shootout here yesterday was a failed attempt to rescue the hostages being held in the American embassy. According to the report, the embassy hostage takers came under attack from eight U.S. agents who inflicted an enormous amount of damage before they were routed by Wehrmacht helicopter gunships. Seven American agents were killed along with forty-eight Berlin policemen, three German Army helicopter pilots, and thirteen members of the Red Army Faction. One of the American agents was wounded and captured but later escaped. He apparently remains at large.

This open violence could signal a breaking point in the Shadowstorm, which has thus far been a relatively discreet battle between the clandestine communities of the Big Four. The combined pressures of the embargo, the kidnappings, and the hostage situation have resulted in the worst diplomatic crisis since World War Two. Vice President Lodge, formerly the U.S. ambassador to Germany, had a long phone call with his friend the chancellor to head off a general mobilization. The vice president then had an equally long meeting in the Oval Office with the president and his cabinet.

Although details of this meeting are unknown at the time of this writing, one thing is certain. Yesterday's street battle may have been an operational disaster, but domestically it was necessary for the White House to display a show of strength before the one-year anniversary of the storming of the U.S. embassy in Berlin. Despite the mission's lack of success, it still sends a message to the American people that President Nixon is doing all he can to resolve the hostage crisis.

———

Washington Post, April 4, 1967

Greater Germany Warns of Impending Soviet Invasion

BERLIN—A spokesman for the Abwehr alerted the German media yesterday that his agency has collected clear evidence of a Soviet buildup all along Germany's eastern borders. He went on to say that the KGB has increased their presence in Berlin to the point where there may be more Soviet agents in the city than German ones. Citizens were warned to report any suspicious activity immediately.

This dire news comes less than a week after Berlin was rocked by a bloody street battle around the American embassy. This event marked a new low in German-

American relations and no doubt served as the impetus for Russia's latest aggressive maneuvers. Despite the charged anti-American rhetoric flying around the Reich, the chancellor and the Reichstag have so far decided to maintain their alliance with the U.S. while Germany faces such an immediate threat from the Soviet Union.

———

DATE: April 7, 1967
TO: Office of the Director, Extreme Operations Division
FROM: Front Desk, German Section, Extreme Operations Division
SUBJECT: **Disciplinary recommendation for Big Bertha**

Sir,

As you are no doubt aware, Big Bertha walked into ExOps headquarters this morning. This agent went missing in the aftermath of our failed hostage rescue attempt last week. He was smuggled out of Europe by members of an underground organization that fights for the release of Germany's Jewish slaves. It seems that Big Bertha had already established ties with this group, the Circle of Zion, during his missions in Greater Germany.

I strongly recommend an official review of Big Bertha's conduct during this ongoing crisis. His recklessness has only strained our deteriorating relationship with Greater Germany. He has been acting on his own initiative, and I feel that he has been found sorely lacking in proper judgment.

—Jakob Fredericks
Front Desk, German Section

———

DATE: April 7, 1967
TO: Front Desk, German Section, Extreme Operations Division

FROM: Office of the Director, Extreme Operations
Division
SUBJECT: **RE: Disciplinary recommendation for Big
Bertha**

Fredericks,

We need an official review of one of our agents like we
need a third tit. We're on the bubble, Jakob, and we must
present a successful face. You will award Big Bertha the
enclosed commendation for valor and promote him to
Level 18.

You will also select a senior field team to send to Germany's eastern frontier, where they will be attached to a
special Gestapo force that is infiltrating Russia to under-
mine the alleged impending invasion. This will provide us
with intelligence about the situation in that region, plus it
will act as a good faith gesture toward our understandably
upset cousins across the pond.

—William Colby
Director, ExOps

PS: Make a big deal about this. I want to hear the members
of the Covert Affairs Committee applauding Big Bertha
from my desk.

————

DATE: June 18, 1967
TO: Senator Goldwater
FROM: The Office of the President of the United States

Subject: **Third term as president**

Barry,

The reversal of the 22nd Amendment is a crucial step
toward maintaining steady leadership for our nation during
this time of crisis. This critical piece of legislation would
not have passed without your enthusiastic assistance.

I hope I can rely on your continued support while I

begin the campaign for my third term, and when I'm re-elected in 1968, you can be sure that there will be a place for you in my cabinet. If we are still suffering from the Germans' oil embargo and the hostage crisis, I will need your help to teach those "supermen" a lesson.

—Dick Nixon

———

New York Times, November 4, 1968

Hostages Released, Oil Embargo Finally Ends

WASHINGTON—White House Press Secretary George Christian reported yesterday that German Chancellor Adenauer has convinced the Red Army Faction to release the American hostages held in Berlin since April of 1966. Mr. Christian also revealed that the German Foreign Trade Ministry will lift their four-year embargo on petroleum shipments to the United States.

The embargo and hostage crisis strained Pan-Atlantic diplomatic relations to—and sometimes beyond—the breaking point. Although the situation seemed intractable, both governments repeatedly stated that they did not want war. The drain on resources and political capital was considerable, especially with the perception that Russia and China were waiting to claim whatever was left after the United States and Germany finished wearing each other down.

Mr. Christian spoke to this idea when he said, "The Germans have gotten as weary of all this as we have." Since the embargo began four years ago, a brutal undercover war has raged between German and American intelligence agents. Bombings, kidnappings, and shootouts have shattered the peace of Berlin, Paris, London, New York, Washington, and many other German and American cities.

The hostage situation at the American embassy in Berlin led to one of the most high-profile moments of the Shadowstorm when eight U.S. commandos attempted to rescue the hostages by force. Over seventy people lost their lives, including seven of the assailants. The eighth commando escaped and returned to the United States.

The timing of this announcement couldn't be worse for the Democratic nominee, Lyndon Johnson. The election is only four days away, and the president's approval ratings will certainly get a significant boost. With the repeal of the 22nd Amendment it would seem that nothing can keep President Nixon from a third term in the White House.

CHAPTER 22

The rabble on Bleecker Street is the usual bubbling stew of hornswogglers and desperadoes, but today there's an extra pinch of menace. After you've been in the field for a while, you can feel when you're being followed. It's sort of a tingling sensation I get. Patrick feels it, too. He comms with his Information Coordinator to confirm that whoever is shadowing us isn't a friendly.

I try to look backward by examining the reflections in the store windows. I can't see who's following, but I do see the two of us. Trick is dressed in white Chuck Taylor sneakers, blue jeans, and a dark blue windbreaker. I'm wearing black Jack Purcell sneakers, black cargo pants, and my birthday present from Cleo: a baby-soft maroon leather jacket with black and white stripes down the sleeves. It's the best present ever, and I've worn it every day since she gave it to me a month ago.

The Front Desk has sent us to Greenwich Village to assist Grey as he sneaks into a CIA office to swipe the name of their Middle East stringer. Trick and I got our final orders at 9 o'clock this morning in Cyrus's office. We stood behind his guest chairs while he paced back and forth across the floor. He was very brusque and clear that he wanted there to be absolutely—

"No bullshit this time, Scarlet. The last time you were on a Job Number in New York, it was almost my head on a plate."

"Sure, Cyrus," I said.

"Don't you 'Sure, Cyrus' me! You say, 'Yes, sir!'"

I gave a little laugh, "You're kidding, right?"

"No, I'm NOT kidding," he boomed, "and neither is the Director! Look, Alix, I've always gone easy on you because of our history together. As a result, your mission discipline has suffered, which has nearly wrecked your last two Job Numbers." Cyrus's eyebrows bump together. "I've sweated through a very uncomfortable series of meetings about you, and now is when you learn that shit rolls downhill. You're a Level 8 Interceptor now, and it's my job to make sure you act like it!"

"Yes, sir!" I shouted as Trick and I snapped to attention. Technically, we're supposed to be all spit and polish, but that hardly ever gets enforced because ExOps is such a small agency and we all work so closely together. He must have gotten a ton of flak from upstairs about my promotion.

Cyrus glowered at us for a minute, then finally said, "You'll go to Manhattan. Grey will do the black bag work. You two will wait at the Hotel Luther next door. If something goes wrong and Grey needs help, you'll provide security and Info."

"Yes, sir!" Trick and I both yelled.

"He's one of my best Infiltrators, so hopefully he won't need your help at all." Infiltrators are undercover agents who specialize in stealthiness and other sneaky, non-Alix things. Cyrus sat down, looked at me, and said, "Let's see if you can do a quiet assignment." Then he turned his attention to some paperwork on his desk.

I'd already started to leave when Trick commed, "Wait!"

"What?" I commed back.

"He's testing us, dummy. We haven't been dismissed. Stand still." I stood still.

Cyrus looked up, pressed his eyebrows together, and bellowed, "Dismissed! Scram, before I put my foot in your asses!" Trick and I bolted out of Cyrus's office, cabbed it to Washington National Airport, and hopped a shuttle flight to Idlewild Airport in New York.

Now we're on Bleecker Street, walking east. Patrick

comms with his IC while I try to catch suspicious reflections in storefront windows. My enhanced hearing is turned up, but there's so much ambient noise, it doesn't really help. The evening rush hour is in full swing as all the suburban assholes run their daily race for the commuter train.

"Man, how do they stand it?" I ask Trick.

"Stand what?" he replies distractedly.

"Such predictability!"

Trick isn't sure what I mean, so he has to look around. "Oh, they'd rather be safe than happy."

I grunt, and we keep walking. I don't know how safe these people are. The Russians and the Chinese constantly assault our way of life. They blackmail Washington policy makers, rig elections, create stock market panics, plant fake news stories about pandemics, and kill our covert agents. And this is just from our enemies.

Each pair of allies has some major sticking point they can't agree on. For the Russians and the Chinese, it's Mongolia. They've been arguing—and sometimes shooting—over it since the war. For the U.S. and the Germans, it's Europe's Jews. The talking heads on television insist that institutionalized slavery is un-American. When Cleo hears this, she grumbles at the TV, "Of course it is! But what's really un-American is that if the German economy weren't trouncing ours, you jackasses wouldn't give a shit." Then she storms out to the kitchen to cool off.

We're almost to the Bowery. Trick is still looking over his shoulder. "Got her! That chick who just ducked down Mulberry Street." I tune in as he comms to his IC. "Sir, I saw her. White female, late teens, five foot five, a hundred and ten pounds. She's got dark hair, dark clothes and big dark sunglasses."

Clothes can be changed, or simply removed, in only a few seconds. The sunglasses are peculiar. The sky today is blanketed by heavy cloud cover.

Patrick's boss, Info Coordinator Harbaugh, comms back. "Solomon, be advised that we do not have any friendlies in the area matching this description. Proceed as though hostile."

Trick replies, "Yes, sir," and comms off.

I ask him, "Sunglasses?"

"Yeah, that's what they looked like." He tilts his head and purses his lips for a moment the way he does when he's thinking about something. Then he says, "You know, they might have been bug eyes."

Bug eyes are really obvious lenses that Protectors use for their optical enhancements. They aren't trying to fool anyone, so external lenses work fine for them. I pretend to bump into someone so I can glance back over my shoulder. She's not there. I ask Trick, "Who the fuck tails someone using bug eyes?"

"Someone with really lousy tradecraft," he says.

We arrive at the Hotel Luther on the Bowery. It's over some shithole bar called CBGB that stinks like piss and beer from a block away. I've read that the neighborhood has tried to close it down, but nobody else would rent a space that's soaked up almost ten years of puke, so the club keeps reopening in the same spot. We like this area because cops hardly ever patrol here, which allows us to operate pretty freely.

We check in as Mr. and Mrs. Chowder. Patrick is so stupid sometimes. He's always got to use these asinine names instead of a simple name like Smith. We take the elevator up to the fifteenth floor and our room, number 1517.

We leave the lights out and the shades drawn while we set up our gear. Patrick snoops around and looks for hidden microphones. He's got a small handheld gadget he points into the corners, at the lights, at the bed. It's a long shot that the room would be bugged, but Trick is convinced the hotel's people could be bribed to assign us a particular room. He finishes his sweep and gives me a thumbs-up: "All clear."

"Any word from Grey?"

Trick shakes his head. "He'll comm us when he's finished."

"Then we go back to D.C.?" I ask.

"Then we see if anything else comes our way." Trick peeks around the window shade to look across the street.

"You mean Little Miss Bug Eyes out there?"

Trick nods.

After a few moments I ask, "See anyone?"

"Not yet."

Levels and Info Operators are always the same rank. The IOs don't have a rank of their own. They inherit the rank of their Level, so there is no real boss. Our decisions are made by consensus. In practice, the IO thinks while the Level acts or, in my case, acts out.

I toss myself on the bed and murmur to Trick, "I know what we can do while we wait." I turn on a small light next to the bed.

Trick glances over at me. I'm fully clothed, but my pants are snug enough to give him a good view of my ass. He takes a long look and finally tells me, "C'mon, Scarlet, I've got to keep an eye out here."

Hmph. Using my ExOps handle is his way of saying we can't fool around on the job.

"Okay, okay." I turn the light back off. "Should I monitor the hallway?"

"Yeah. I'll keep an eye out the window." Patrick puts on his starlight goggles. His modified eyes can record video, like mine, but to see in the dark he needs external equipment. I lie on the bed with my eyes closed and my hearing turned up so I can pick out every sound on the entire hotel floor. I hear the floor above, too: people coughing, crapping, snoring. Very sexy, dynamic work. I zing myself a little Madrenaline to help me stay focused.

After a couple of hours I get up to use the bathroom. When I come out, I'm ready to start bitching about where the heck is Grey, but Trick has his hand in the air. Something's cooking. I tiptoe over to him.

He leans back from the window and comms, "Grey is in the office."

I peek around the window shade and turn on my night vision. Next to our hotel is a seven-story turn-of-the-century office building. There are lots of carved stone knobbies and blobbies all up and down the thing. A CIA team works out of there, including the case officer who runs the Middle Eastern stringer Chanez wants us to meet.

We watch to see if we can catch a glimpse of Grey. I've never met the sneaky bugger, but that's not uncommon at ExOps. Infiltrator missions can take years, and even when they're between assignments most Infiltrators prefer to stay away from the office. They like to maintain as much anonymity as possible. Sounds pretty lonely if you ask me.

We peer through the gloomy New York night. We can't see Grey, but Patrick spots something else. "What's that, on the roof across the alley?"

The ornately facaded roof is a half story lower than our room. I see a huddled shape over there. I switch to infrared. Bingo! It's warm and person-sized.

I lean over to Trick. "Should I go nab 'em?"

Trick comms, "No, not until we get the all-clear from—"

Just then Grey comms in to both of us. "Grey to Scarlet and Solomon. I got it. Thanks. Out."

Trick comms back to Grey, "Roger that. Out." Then to me, "Well, that's done. Let's see who our secret admirer is over there."

I nod and give him a peck on the cheek. I pull down the window shades while he goes to the bed and pulls off the covers. He stands in front of the door to the room and holds the blanket up as high as he can while I open the door and slip out. The idea is to try to block the light from the hallway. It can tip people off that someone has entered, or in this case exited, the room.

I gently shut the door and sneak down the hallway. A

winding set of stairs wraps itself around the elevator shaft like an affectionate snake. I assume the stairs are being monitored, but it's probably only below this floor. I silently move upstairs until I run out of building. I shove open the door to the roof. I'm hidden from my target's view since this roof is three stories higher than the top of the offices across from my hotel room. I stay low, anyway. You never know who else is watching.

I move to the back side of the roof, away from the office building, and look over the edge. There's a shorter structure over here; it's a five-story drop. I jump down, land with a thud, and feel a sharp stabbing pain in both knees. I suck in my breath and stifle a curse. *Fuckin' hell!* My neuroinjector sends in some Overkaine so I can stay mobile.

Rather than jump five more stories to the street and completely ruin my knees, I clamber down a fire escape. Then I circle two blocks around until can I approach the office building from the side opposite our hotel. I look up and notice an elaborate patio garden just below the roof with a cluster of tall plants and one good-size tree. I leap to the fire escape and climb up as quietly as possible. As I slither onto the patio, I check out the tree. The top of it is higher than the office building's roof.

Oh, this is perfect.

I scan the area with my infrared and night vision.

All clear.

CHAPTER 23

I scale the tree in a flash, sway back and forth for a moment, then leap to the roof of the office building and silently land on all fours. My infrared vision shows my target around the other side of a big air vent. I take a deep breath and sneak around the vent. There she is, pointing a microphone gun at our room across the street. It's the chick Patrick spotted on Bleecker Street—dark hair, dark clothes, and giant-sunglasses-looking bug eyes.

I sneak up behind her, clamp my left hand over her mouth, and stab my upgraded right hand through her jacket, shirt, skin, and muscle. I wrap three fingers around one of her ribs and snarl, "One move and I rip your fucking spine out."

She grunts into my hand, twitches in pain, and manages a quick nod.

I hiss in her ear, "Who sent you?"

She shakes her head under my left hand. I squeeze my right hand around her rib a little more and ask again. Same result. Then her body relaxes. I must have tripped a pain-numbing module. Dammit, now she's useless.

"Say good night, shithead."

I'm about to tear her skeleton apart when I hear Trick in my comm channel. "Scarlet, do not terminate that asset!"

I comm, "Asset, my butt. We won't learn anything from this one."

"Let me try. Bring her here."

Fine, Trick, have it your way. I slide my right hand out of the chick's back and whack her in the neck to knock her unconscious. I throw her body over my shoulders and carry her to the middle of the roof to give myself room for a running start. Then I sprint at the roof's edge and leap across the street to the ledge outside our hotel room window.

Back in our room, we bind our captive hand and foot, then set her on a chair. I bandage her back while Trick attaches some electrodes to her skin and shoots her up with a chemical cocktail. After I tape up the wound on her back, he gives the girl one last injection and she regains consciousness. Her bug eyes retract into her brow when she wakes up.

Patrick takes her face in his hands and looks into her eyes. It's almost tender how he does it, sort of like when we're alone.

"You know what comes now," he begins, "but we don't have to do this. I can file an easily intercepted report that states you withstood hours of chemotorture before you talked."

She spits in his face. I lunge toward her, but Trick holds up a hand to me. I can't believe how calm he can be at times like this.

He wipes his face with the back of his hand. "Okay, fine," he says to the girl. "Let's start with who sent you."

"Let's start with this, Xerox," she snarls. "Your girlfriend's father went rogue to buy himself a bottle of Thunderbird."

Gun. Point. Bang! Her right shoulder bursts open, and a jet of blood sprays out.

"Godammit, Scarlet!" Trick shouts while he dives into his bag of tricks for a pressure bandage. "It's a dodge. She *wants* you to kill her before we get any intel out of her!" The bitch falls off the chair and thumps onto the floor. Her dark lenses slide down and hide her eyes. Her shoulder pulses red liquid all over the chair, the floor, and Trick. Looks like I hit an artery. Trick tries to stick a bandage on her before she bleeds to death while her blood splashes all over his white sneakers. She twists and turns so he can't patch her up until her blood flow slows and she stops moving.

"Fuck! Damn it, damn it!" Trick yells as he gives up on saving her. He reaches into his bag and pulls out two long needles with red handles connected by springy red wires to a brick-sized battery pack. For some reason, it occurs to me that the wires are the same color as my family's old telephone from when I was a kid.

He stabs one needle into her lower back and the other through her left lens and eyeball. This interrogation technique is called the Thackery Procedure. My training has taught me to stand back because this stunt sprays biojuice all over the place. Patrick won't try to keep her alive anymore. He'll extract what info he can in the next few seconds before she croaks on us. He flips a switch on one of the needle handles, and she comes off the floor and wails like a banshee. Only now does it occur to me to worry about the neighbors.

The Thackery bypasses every possible pain inhibitor and cooks the brain's cortex. It's very effective in the short term, but it's always lethal. I knew I should have done this chick on the roof. I'm not sure if I can actually tear someone's spine out, and I really wanted to give it a shot.

"Give me a name!" Patrick shouts at the girl to drown out her howls. "WHO SENT YOU? A name and I let you go!"

She stops bawling long enough to hiss at us, either "Sss" or "Fff" or "Shh." It's hard to tell. Then she's silent and her body falls slack. She's gone. We don't use the Thackery Procedure very often, mostly because it's so fucking gross. The smell is especially nasty.

The company that makes this device claims that if you don't procure the intel you want, it absolutely means the subject didn't know. In practice, the results are a little less predictable. Except the lethal part. That's always the same.

Trick quickly packs up his bag, bloody bits and all. I

shovel my clothes back into my backpack, and we're outta there. One quick look around and all I see is blood, a dead smoking girl, and more blood. Mr. and Mrs. Chowder will not be welcome at this hotel again, that's for sure.

If Miss Deadbitch has any friends around here, they're probably down in the lobby or out in the street. We run up the hall, away from the elevator and stairs. The hallway turns left onto another side of the hotel. I use my infrared vision to scan the rooms for warm bodies. When we find one that reads cold, Trick picks the lock. We enter, close the door behind us, and listen for a moment.

The elevator doors grind open, and loud footsteps echo in the hallway. Then we hear curses and shrieked commands. "Move, dammit! Fan out. Find them!" Whoever it is has an American accent.

Patrick has already opened the window. He waves me over to him and points at a fire escape across the alley. It's only a couple yards away. The alley isn't even wide enough for a car. I climb out the window and jump to the fire escape as silently as possible. Trick jumps next, and I half catch him to help him land quietly. We scuttle down the fire escape and walk out into the street. Down the block we find a parking garage. I hot-wire a small pickup truck with Jersey plates, and we're a block away when we hear the first sirens.

Later that night, Trick and I are in Chelsea, on the terrace outside one of our safe house apartments. We quietly drink beer. I can tell he's frustrated with me, and I take a guess that talking might help. Sometimes that seems to work.

"Sorry about earlier . . ." I begin.

Trick exhales very slowly, looks out at the city, and mutters, "It's my fault. I should have had you leave the room."

"I just didn't think. She made me so mad. It was like my gun leaped into my hand all by itself."

"I know, Alix, I know." I can tell I screwed up because

Trick is so quiet about it, which makes me feel worse. He continues. "But that's the problem: you don't think. Sometimes it makes it hard to work with you."

Whoah. Code Red. "What does that mean? Hard to work with? You want a new partner?" This sounds stupid even as I say it, but I can't stop myself. "And how do you know I didn't think?"

Trick sips from his beer bottle and replies, "Because *I* didn't have time to think, which means neither did you."

"Oh, you're so fucking smart now?"

Trick turns to me and finally raises his voice, "Yes, Alix, I *am* so fucking smart! That's why we're partners. I'm the brains, and you're the . . . you're . . ." He sputters, grasping for words.

"What? I'm what?"

He thinks. For someone who's so fucking smart, he takes a long time to think of something obvious like "fabulous," or "awesome," or "amazing."

"You're the hotheaded ass kicker who saves our butts all the time."

Well, it's not "fabulous," but I'll take it—especially the ass kicker part. "That's right!" I say as I throw my arm around his shoulders and clink my beer bottle into his. We watch a homeless guy stagger up the street and into a subway station. I think about what the girl said. My dad never drank Thunderbird, but she knew way more about me and him than she should have.

I rest my head on my partner's shoulder. "Trick, who the hell *were* those people at the hotel?"

My partner swigs his beer. "Considering what we were doing, the most likely explanation is that they were CIA."

Patrick must be kidding. I slide my arm from around his shoulders and turn to face him. He's not kidding.

Oh, man, did we just torture and kill an agent from a sister U.S. agency?

"How could they possibly have known we were there?"

"I'd say Grey tripped a silent alarm, except that we

were being followed before he was anywhere near the place."

I lower my face into my hand and rub my temples. All this thinking hurts my head despite the four beers I've had.

Trick continues, "Harbaugh commed me half an hour ago, while you were at the liquor store. After we left for New York this morning, he picked up a familiar-looking burst of encrypted comm chatter in D.C. I told him about the girl on Bleecker Street, how you apprehended her, that she knew about your father, and how we evaded her backup team." Patrick pauses, then says, "He thinks it might be XSUS One again."

My eyes bug out. "XSUS One is CIA?"

"Harbaugh said 'might.' The encryption on these new comms was an order of magnitude more secure than the last batch, so it may not be possible to crack them. The depth of the encryption is what first caught his eye. Then, hours later, you and I have another adventure in Manhattan. We'd say it was the Blades of Persia again, but our competitors at the hotel all had American accents. That doesn't fit what we know about the Blades." Patrick runs his hand through his hair.

I lean against him, and he puts his arm around my shoulder. I ask, "Why would the CIA follow us?"

"Well, *if* they were CIA people, it'd be because we sneak around behind their backs, break into their offices, and steal their shit."

"Yeah, *now* we're doing that." I wave my hand in a circle. "But what about the Hector job?"

"That damn Hector job . . ." Patrick mutters. He regards the dark city's skyline. "Harbaugh and I talked about that. What happened on that job was so out of nowhere that it keeps breaking our theories." Trick's boss is certain that our investigation into my father's last mission is clearly the right course. The deeper we dig, the wilder it gets. Harbaugh says the degree of interference we've met indicates that our XSUS One is way up the food chain somewhere.

Flash! Corruption in high offices of government. Dozens stunned, film at eleven.

What nobody has figured out is the obvious security breach at ExOps. Keeping our activities out of CORE should seal them within our small circle. So far, though, we might as well be publishing our mission briefs in the *Washington Post* classifieds. Chanez, Cyrus, and Harbaugh are all sniffing around the agency, looking for a mole. They've carefully reviewed the CORE files about my dad's last mission. They appear to be legit except for the fact that they don't jibe at all with what my father thought he was doing.

I sigh. "Have you talked to Cyrus about this?"

"I left him a message while you drove us here. He and Chanez are in their monthly Executive Meeting."

Executive Meeting means President Reagan. Cyrus will be stuck there for hours. He always grumbles about how much our current president likes to talk. Cyrus refers to him as "our current president" because after all those years with Nixon, he likes to imply that this country's highest elected official is some kind of temp.

My partner tilts his bottle up and finishes his beer. "We need more intel. Whatever happened to your dad is out there, no matter how mysterious it seems right now."

Mysteries. I hate mysteries.

We watch the city rot for a while. Eventually, sleepiness drapes over me. "All right, Tricky-Trick, let's go to bed. I need to relax."

My partner smirks. "It's my turn to relax first." He runs inside and leaps onto the bed so energetically that he bounces off and crashes into the nightstand. The lamp on the stand falls over and breaks, pitching the room into complete darkness. I burst out laughing, and I have to hold on to the terrace's railing to stay on my feet.

When I catch my breath, I call, "Trick! You okay?"

He doesn't answer, but I can hear him on the floor, alternately groaning and giggling into the carpet.

Later, we're curled up together in bed. Trick has his arm across my chest, sleeping like a baby, while I lie on my back staring at the ceiling. Damned Post-Stimulant Sleep Disorder. I finally fall asleep a couple of hours later, thinking how lucky I am to have someone who loves me because I'm a hotheaded ass kicker.

CHAPTER 24

NEXT DAY, THURSDAY, SEPTEMBER 18, 8:00 A.M. EST
MANHATTAN'S CHELSEA AREA, NEW YORK CITY, USA.

The next morning I find a whole new way to be freaky
with people. I'm in line at a coffee shop down the street
from our safe house in Chelsea. Some dickhead right
behind me tries to strike up a conversation, like this is a
good place to pick up women. I finally turn around,
look this fool in the eye, turn on my infrared vision, and
unleash a barrage of my dad's favorite expletives. Dickhead drops his charming smile, spins on his heel, and
runs away. I guess he's never been confronted by a foul-
mouthed red-eyed devil chick. The Med-Techs didn't tell
me that my IR vision would make my eyes turn red, but
it's a nice side effect to use on people who talk to me
before I've had my coffee.

While I wait, I inhale the fresh-baked, fresh-brewed
coffee shop smells. A small TV on the counter runs a
news story about the brutal murder of a young woman
in the East Village last night. She'd been tied up and then
tortured to death in her hotel room. We see pictures of
cops milling around, pictures of paramedics milling
around, and pictures of neighbors milling around. The
suspects are three Cuban terrorists, each with a prior
criminal record. Their angry-looking mug shots are dis-
played so New Yorkers know who to be afraid of.

I finally get to the counter. "Two large coffees with
cream and extra sugar and a half dozen of your chocolate glazed." Mmm, doughnuts. I carry the breakfast
loot back to the room we stayed in last night. Patrick
glances over as I open the door. He wiggles his eyebrows

up and down to acknowledge my successful doughnut safari.

I put our coffees on the nightstand. Neither of us is a big talker in the morning, especially when we're on a job. He's sprawled across the bed, conference comming with his Information Coordinator and Director Chanez about what happened last night with the bug-eye girl. I sit on the edge of the bed with my coffee and turn on the TV news. Maybe the cops have already caught those three dangerous Cuban dudes.

I click around the channels until I find a semicircle of suits blowing hot air out their asses. It's a discussion panel about current affairs, and the covert community's point of view is being presented by none other than Jakob Fredericks. He's in the middle of a long and pompous harangue about the importance of maintaining good relations with Greater Germany. After he runs out of breath, the camera angle switches to a wide view of the group. Fredericks's seat is on the far right. As the show's host talks about what else is on the agenda, Fredericks turns and beckons to someone from off camera. The person walks into the edge of the picture. She's a young female, about my age. The girl leans down to hear what Fredericks says, like she's his assistant. She's got big bug-eye lenses.

Well, look at that.

I reach across the bed and tug on Trick's sleeve. He turns his head, and I point at the screen. He squints at the TV, then shrugs at me with one of his eyebrows up.

"Look at that!" I hiss.

He looks again, and this time he sees what I mean. He presses his mouth into an upside-down crescent and nods his head. He holds up one index finger and whispers, "Hang on, I'm almost done."

I tune in to Trick's conversation.

Trick is comming, "Yes, sir, the competitor's gear and Mods indicated that she was a Protector. Very much like the Hector job, sir."

"And Scarlet captured her alive, Solomon?" It's Chanez.

"Yes, she did, Director, but the Protector expired before we got any intel out of her. As we left the hotel, we heard her backup team coming to check on her."

"And these were Americans?"

"They sure sounded like it, sir."

Harbaugh comms, "Stand by, Solomon," and mutes his commphone. Most Info Operators are young, like Patrick. If you remain unkilled, like Bill Harbaugh did, you eventually come out of the field and work as an Info Coordinator.

Harbaugh returns to the call. "Solomon, be advised that all intel related to this Job Number shall be classified at Level 12 and your submissions must be approved by Director Chanez."

Chanez had Cyrus put us on this mission, and so the Director himself will oversee our progress and review all the intel we gather. That's the only reason a puny Level 8 like me can work anywhere near this job, which keeps getting bigger and bigger. The classifications aren't meant to prevent junior agents from harvesting supersensitive material. They're meant to dictate how much oversight we need while we're doing it.

"Roger that, sir," confirms Trick. Their discussion shifts to a special shorthand the Info people speak, so I tune out. I'm eating my third doughnut when the ache in my knees reminds me it's been a couple days since I did any maintenance on my joints.

I pull my travel tool kit out of my backpack, then take off my pants and open up my kneecaps. Oh, yeah, definitely some abrasions. That five-story drop I made last night was not a good idea. I rub oil into my knees to lubricate the mechanized joints and synthetic fibers. While that soaks in, I field strip Li'l Bertha. As I work, I wonder how much time my father spent doing exactly the same thing in some crappy room somewhere all by himself. I'm glad I have Trick with me.

It sounds like Patrick is soft-pedaling my impulsiveness last night. If Cyrus finds out why we didn't get any intel out of that chick, he'll clobber me. I rewind my Day Loop to what the bug-eyed girl said last night.

"Your girlfriend's father went rogue to buy himself a bottle of Thunderbird."

Going rogue, switching sides, and anything else colloquially known as leaving the reservation are among the few cardinal sins in this game. I can't imagine my dad doing that. He was always so dedicated and used to go on about how lucky we were to live in the United States.

Trick taps my shoulder and says, "Grey hit the jackpot. My boss is setting up a meeting with the CIA stringer, and we're gonna do the interview. Let's get packed."

"What's the stringer's name?"

"Imad Badr. He's an Arab businessman and philanthropist." Trick tells me that like a lot of self-made businessmen, Badr used to be a smuggler. He's been legit for a long time now and has built up the largest Arab-owned group of businesses in Greater Germany. Rumor has it that Badr is also a buddy of our man Winter.

"What's his angle?" I ask.

"You mean why does he pass intel to people like us?"

"Yeah."

Trick starts packing up his stuff. "Basically, he rats out his business competitors to the Americans and Germans."

I stuff another bite of doughnut in my mouth. "Why does the CIA listen to him, then?"

"Well, a lot of the people Badr competes against spend their spare time running terrorist cells."

"But not all of them do."

"Nope." Trick shakes his head as he carefully arranges his gear back into his bag of tricks. It's a black leather doctor's bag he found in a used-clothes shop here in New York. I've never understood how he can fit so much stuff in it. I swear the thing is bottomless. After he bought it, we added a long black leather strap so he can sling it over his shoulder. He's cleaned most of Bug Eye's blood off of it, although there are still some stains near the bottom.

"All right." Patrick zips his bag shut. "Here's what we've got." He holds his hands in front of himself, palms up, like they're supporting a big open book. "Our competitors have been female Protectors or they've been groups of Russian mercenaries. The comms we intercepted in Manhattan show that XSUS One was running Jackie-O and her backup team, so that accounts for the Protectors you've faced. They also revealed that XSUS One knows XSUS Two, who we've tentatively identified as Kazim Nazari based on the stuff you got from Rashid. Your dad discovered that—at the time—the Blades employed a lot of former KGB Levels who reported to Kazim. So Kazim's possible involvement could account for the Russian mercs you've faced."

Trick pauses and purses his lips. "Fortunately, neither One nor Two seems to possess sufficient resources to overcome your performance index."

"Huh?"

"I mean you kick their asses every time they jump you."

"Right! Yes." I bounce off the bed. "Ass. Kick!" I punt my empty backpack across the room and hold my arms over my head. "Score!"

Trick smiles and says, "Did you notice that the Thackery girl last night had an American accent?"

This reminds me. "Oh, hey! That chick on the TV. Did you see her?"

"Chick? I thought you were pointing at Director Fredericks."

"No, his assistant. She looked like Jackie-O and Thackery Girl."

Trick tilts his head to the side. "So?"

"So maybe Fredericks is XSUS One."

Patrick cracks up.

"What's so funny?" I throw a pillow at him. "I'm serious!"

He blocks my fluffy missile and exclaims, "Oh, *come on*, Alix! Do you expect anyone to believe that the pussiest Front Desk in ExOps history would take out a murder contract on an agent from his own country?"

"Why not?" I put my hands on my hips. "You saw that girl."

"Oh, my God, Alix. Fredericks could barely stand to order hits when it was his *job*." My partner grabs his toothbrush and heads for the bathroom. "Besides, everybody at his pay grade gets a security detail. Washington is crawling with Protectors." His voice echoes from the tiled bathroom. Water runs in the sink, and then I hear him brushing his teeth.

I'm not ready to give up. I stomp over to the bathroom door. "How many of those Protectors are young women?"

"Well, yeah, that'sh a funny coincidensh, I guesh." He spits out his toothpaste and wipes his mouth. "Most officials get jumbo-size Protectors to soak up their bullets for them. You ever see those two hulks that drive Director Chanez's car for him?" He kisses me as he walks back into the bedroom. "But who knows? Maybe ol' Jakob has a thing for the ladies."

"Especially ladies named Alixandra Nico!"

"Hey. Enough." Patrick gives me a long look. "We are not gonna charge the Director of the Strategic Services Council with high treason."

I frown and cross my arms across my chest.

"At least," he says quietly, "not until we have a lot more to go on."

"Hah!" I bark. "You think I'm right."

My partner holds his hands up. "Whoa, there. Fredericks *could* be XSUS One. But it could be a lot of other people too. If we jump the gun on something like this, we'll spend the rest of our careers shoveling shit in Crapville, USA."

Patrick figures XSUS One is either an official in another country's covert community or he's a mole in one of our many intelligence agencies. Obviously, he's one shady goat planker, but beyond that we're stumped.

I drop the Perry Mason bit and get myself packed up. I dump my tools into my backpack, then scoop my clothes off the floor and cram them in on top of the tools.

We walk downstairs and catch a cab to the airport. Once we're under way, I take one of Trick's hands in mine and lean against his shoulder. He tilts his head so his cheek presses lightly on my hair. I hold his hand up and slowly kiss his fingers, imagining that we're an old married couple going home from a Broadway show. I wonder if Trick will want kids. I'm not sure if I do, but that's okay; there's plenty of time.

We ride quietly for a while, and then I comm to Trick, "Thanks for talking last night. I'm really sorry about icing that girl."

Trick comms back, "That's all right, Alix. We'll get to the bottom of all this one way or another."

The way to a man's heart may be through his stomach, but the way to my heart is through unconditional forgiveness. I snuggle against my partner and whisper, "I love you, Tricky-Trick."

He squeezes his arm around me. "I love you too, Hot Stuff."

We cuddle and make out until we arrive at the airport. Patrick looks up our flight's departure gate, and we haul our asses to the VIP line at security. The guard looks at our ExOps IDs, checks us against his Do Not Hassle list, and waves us around. This is best for everyone because although Patrick could pass through the metal detector with no problems, I'd probably melt the stupid thing.

As we board the plane, all the waitresses say "*Bonjour*" and "*Guten Tag*" to me. I turn to Trick and ask, "Where the hell are we going, anyway?"

"Paris, your favorite."

"Do I see it in daylight this time?"

Trick answers, "*Peut-être*."

Maybe. *Hmph.*

CORE   TEC-EO-026

Enhanced Optics: External Lenses

External lenses provide a flexible optics platform to which the user can add, upgrade, or remove optical effects as needed. When not in use, the lenses retract to a recess carved in the agent's brow bone and are detectable only on very close inspection. While these lenses are in use, they are clearly visible as shallow domes over the eye sockets (hence their common nickname, bug eyes). This high visibility restricts their suitability for undercover operations, but they are a natural fit for assignments where an obvious security presence is desired.

CHAPTER 25

Two days later,
Saturday, September 20, 8:50 a.m. CST
Montparnasse, Paris, Province of France, GG

Paris in the daytime is brighter and prettier, but it's also much noisier. Trick and I sit in cute wicker cane chairs at a sidewalk café on Boulevard Montparnasse. Our red-and-white-striped tablecloth flutters in the wind from the trucks, cars, and scooters roaring up and down the street. The incessant din reverberates against the fronts of the handsome eight-story buildings that line the boulevard. The buildings' ground floors are occupied by colorful cafés, paneled tobacco shops, and chic little clothing stores. Above the commercial spaces are row after row of tall two-panel windows looking out at the neighborhood. I watch as a white-robed woman on the fourth floor across the street pulls her window open and peeks up at the sky to see what the weather is doing. Inside her apartment I see a fancy chandelier on the ceiling. On her wall I glimpse the top half of a large painting with a man in a green hat.

The sun shines down on the bustling street and illuminates why people love this city so much. It's as though the whole town were designed by one superbly tasteful person. It's amazingly pleasant to just sit here, sip delicious coffee, and watch the stylish French and German people glide by. What's not so pleasant is the pounding in my skull.

"Fuck me, that traffic is loud," I gripe.

Trick is reading a newspaper, *Le Monde*. Without looking up, he asks, "How's your head?"

"Killing me."

"You drank too much on the flight."

I glower at him, but his nose is still in the paper. "And whose fault is that?"

He looks up. "It sure as hell isn't mine."

"You're supposed to keep an eye on me."

"Jesus, Alix. I'm not your mother."

"Thank God for that," I groan. A truck horn blasts. My skull switches from punched by gorilla to stomped by elephant. I could make my headache go away, but the Med-Techs tell me not to use my painkillers unless I really need them. They're worried I'll get hooked. I said I thought they were nonaddictive, and they blathered on about the difference between physical and psychological addictions. I tuned out most of it. What do I know about biology?

I'm still thinking about Overkaine when Trick puts his paper down and taps my arm. He nods toward a man approaching our table. The man is six feet tall, is well dressed, and has dark hair that's gone white at the temples. His skin color makes him look like a really tan European or a somewhat pale Middle Easterner. He's a bit older, about fiftysomething.

Mr. White Temple sits down, doesn't introduce himself, and lights up the stinkiest goddamn cigarette I've ever smelled. He's polite enough to move the cigarette below the table and blow his smoke off to the side after I make a face that delicately says: *That piece of shit smells like a dead mongoose.*

Trick inquires, "Herr Badr?"

The man nods. "M'sieur Badr."

"Nice to meet you, m'sieur. I'm Solomon, and this is Scarlet."

"Is very good to meet you, M'sieur Solomon." He nods toward me and says, "And you, Mademoiselle Scarlet." Imad Badr looks us over. He's in good shape for an older dude. He keeps his beard trimmed very short, which emphasizes the angularity of his face.

"If you will forgive me for saying so, you are bose quite young." He cocks one eyebrow up and takes another drag on his stinky stick. His cigarette's dead rodent stench includes a hint of rotted citrus and makes my headache worse.

Maybe smoking isn't so cool, after all.

Patrick responds, "Yes, sir. We're junior agents doing some research. We're hoping you can help us find someone."

Badr looks at his watch. "And who would sat be?"

"Winter."

Badr's eyes flick from his watch to Trick's face. "Ahh, more Americans searching for se enigmatic Winter." He shifts in his seat. "Perhaps it would be best if you told me what you know already so your valuable time is not taken with sese sings."

His accent, while not too strong, is really weird. Its foundation is the Arabic and German speech patterns he grew up with in the Middle East. The English he layers over this has a strange formality that takes me a minute to place. I finally figure out that it's because he doesn't speak English like an American. He speaks it like an Englishman.

Patrick tells Badr that we know Winter runs the Blades of Persia and he's rumored to be working to reclaim the Middle East from the Germans and the Russians. My partner says nothing about my dad, Lonely Rashid, or how many times we've gotten ambushed by Winter's goon squads.

"It is interesting to me," Badr comments, "how one man can be so differently perceived. My friends in se West fear Winter as some kind of terrorist mastermind, while se people of se Middle East hail him as a peace-loving humanitarian."

An idea springs into my mind. If I had to explain my train of thought, it would be something like this: terrorist mastermind + peace-loving humanitarian = shadowy scholarship fund. Naturally, I don't consciously process this. I just blurt, "Is that because of his Darius Covenant?"

Badr's eyes narrow slightly. "Yes." The end of his cigarette glows red as he takes a drag.

Winter runs the Darius Covenant.

I try to comm "Score!" to Trick, but he's already comming this intelligence bombshell to his boss back in Washington.

Badr launches a big cloud of smoke over our heads. It hovers there like a miniature storm cloud. He continues, "Perhaps *les Amis* have finally found agents who do sere homework." Badr tells us that Darius has sent a steady stream of Middle Eastern students to U.S. colleges to learn about the wealth floating under their countries. He declares, "*Here* is se reason Winter is regarded as he is both in se West and se Middle East." He looks at his watch again. "But you are bright people. I'm sure you see se hypocrisy in demonizing someone who simply aspires to a fairer world." He finishes his cigarette and stabs the butt into the ashtray on the table.

He's about to continue when someone's shriek is cut off with a loud thump. My natural adrenaline triggers a quick Madrenaline boost, so I've got plenty of time to spot a big Mercedes sedan as it plows up the sidewalk, straight at our table. Fast people dodge out of the way, and the not-so-fast people go under the tires. The total sluggards fly over the top. I don't have time to admire this beef fountain since the car is really cruising. Badr has great reflexes and whirls out of the way. I wrap my arms around Trick and jump us over the car as it bashes through our table.

We land right where the table used to be. I slam myself into psycho killer mode and race after the car. A flood of Madrenaline gushes into my bloodstream, and I burst up to thirty-five miles per hour. I yank out Li'l Bertha. It's a good bet this deathmobile is armored, so she loads up her big Explosive ammo. Crashing into so much stuff has slowed the car down, and I see my chance. I leap at the Mercedes and land on the trunk.

My rebuilt right hand crushes a grip into the trunk's lid while my left hand tries to aim Li'l Bertha. Even her gyroscopes can't counteract all the swerves. I fire a few rounds at the driver, but he steers so wildly that I can't draw a bead on him. The car rips through a small park and up an embankment. He floors it across a flat little plaza and aims for a flight of steps down to a big fountain across from the Eiffel Tower. I hang on for dear life when the car flies off the top of the stairs, tips forward with its trunk pointing at the sky, and bounces down the steps on its grille. Jesus, this maniac is a really lousy driver!

The car begins to flip over onto its roof. I let go and jump over the skidding two-ton wreck to be. I tumble down the steps to keep away from this giant Alix squisher until it finally crunches into a wall at the bottom of the stairs.

There are people all over the place, so I don't have a clear shot at Lousy Driver as he climbs out the far-side window and runs off toward the tower. I jump over the car and punch my way through the crowd. *I've got to nail this fucker!* He's fast, though, and is already across the street by the time I've extracted myself from the rubberneckers.

The killer is wearing khaki pants and a stylish blue blazer, so it's easy to spot him among all the terribly dressed tourists. He dashes into the nearest leg of the tower and begins to run up the stairs. I look up as I run under the Eiffel Tower. This is one tall fucking . . . whatever it is. I hyperventilate to pump more oxygen into my blood, then charge up the stairs.

I'd try shooting him, but he's too fast. In fact, I can barely keep up with him. My best chance is that he seems a lot older than me. I think I can outlast him. He must have Mods. No normal person can take so many steps at a time.

I comm my progress to Trick. "Hostile has ascended the east leg of the Eiffel Tower. We're past the first tier."

"Go get him, Scarlet!" Trick comms in. It's like cowboys and Indians. I let out a war whoop and pound up the stairway. The tower's second tier comes and goes. We enter the upper tower. I can't imagine where this blockhead thinks he's going. The last time I checked, this thing *does* have a top. It's not like it goes straight up to heaven.

I'm only a dozen steps behind Lousy Driver as we near the summit. I'm so close, I can hear him gasp for breath in time with his steps. I'm drenched in sweat, and my Eyes-Up display shows my pulse at 240 beats per minute. In the few minutes since our café table got smashed into kindling I must have burned a zillion calories.

Lousy Driver reaches the top with me hot on his heels. All the sightseers turn and gawk as we barge out of the stairway like we've been belched out of hell. My opponent runs along the observation deck with Le View on the left and Le Gift Shop on the right. Past the shop, he screeches to a halt in front of a narrow metal door marked *seulement employé*. It's a service closet or something. He rips the door open, tears his blazer off, then reaches into the closet and hauls out a big backpack.

I'm glad comming doesn't take any breath. "Trick, our hostile's got a bag. I think he's going for a weapon."

I expect the jackass to turn and face me, but he doesn't. He runs the other way and pulls the backpack on. I bolt after him. He fiddles with the straps of his pack and accelerates straight for the edge of the deck. Finally it dawns on me what he's up to. He gathers his body like a spring and jumps over the safety fence into thin air.

"Trick, he's got a parachute!"

"Let him go. We'll catch him when he lands."

But before I can process what Patrick says, I leap over the fence and hurl myself into the cool Paris morning. I'm so hopped up on speed I have time to flash a V for victory sign to some camera-firing tourists on my way over the fence. They'll have a great time with that snapshot back home: "Here's a picture of us at lunch. Oh, and here's a picture of a crazy French girl who chased her boyfriend right off the top of the Eiffel Tower."

We are *really* high. For some reason it feels higher than when I've jumped out of airplanes. The enemy operative arches his back to control his speed, but I do not. I dive-bomb straight at him. He's about to pull his parachute release when I catch him from behind.

I shriek *"Gotcha!"* as I wrap my legs around his waist and claw my way underneath his body so that I'm in front of him. My left hand pulls the D-shaped handle on the front of his skydiving rig. His chute bursts out of the pack while I grab his shoulder straps. The canopy pops open, and we decelerate from 130 miles per hour to less than 20 in only two seconds. My legs slip off Lousy Driver's waist, and my hands lose their grip on his straps. I stab the fingers of my right hand in behind his collarbone to hang on. The agent lets out a monster scream. I swing my legs back around my ride's waist as his blood flows around my fingers.

The poor slob can't knock me off him because he's so exhausted from the run up the tower. He's also in shock. Nobody expects someone to reach right into his body and manhandle his skeleton.

Since the two of us are using the same parachute, we sail down quickly, headed for a small park. He still hollers in pain, but with less oomph, like he's about to pass out. Before we land, I hoist myself up so he'll take all the impact with his legs. There's a chorus of crunches and snaps as his legs turn into calcium kindling. I land on top of him while the chute settles around us like a bedsheet. I slither out from under it. Trick runs up while I souse my bloodstream with Kalmers to bring my pulse down: 240 beats per minute is dangerous, even for me.

"Oh, Jeez, Scarlet, is he dead?"

"No, he's passed out. But you'd better make like a medic. I kinda tore him open."

"Crap," Patrick mutters as he opens up his bag of tricks. "He's probably gonna bleed to death."

"Hey!" I yell at him. "How about a 'Good job'? I just apprehended a modified competitor in mid-fucking-air!"

Trick pulls bandages out of his bag. After a moment he grins. "That really was terrific." He looks up at me. "Great job, Hot Stuff."

"That's better," I say. "Let's get out of here."

Patrick looks around, "I've got a ride on the way." An ambulance barrels up the street and turns into the park. Two burly guys jump out, pick up the unconscious hit man, and stuff him into the back of the ambulance. Trick and I hop in with him. There's a Med-Tech in the back. She nods at the two of us as she straps my victim to a gurney. The burlies return to the front of the ambulance, turn the vehicle around, and roar back down the street. This all happens very quickly. By the time the local cops arrive, we've disappeared into the Left Bank's warren of side streets.

Our prisoner is still zonked. Patrick and the medic both pull on surgical gloves and begin to check him out. The Med-Tech cuts the enemy agent's pant legs off while Trick looks for booby traps and weapons. He finds a pair of pistols, three small throwing knives, four sets of ID, and a plastic box full of different colored pills.

The Med-Tech can't help but notice the pile of stuff Trick has found. She comments, "Your friend travels heavy."

Patrick keeps searching. "Yeah. It's like he works for us." This gets a grin from the Med-Tech while she sets splints on Lousy Driver's legs. We hear a nasty, crunchy squishing sound as she straightens them out. Our special guest groans but doesn't wake up. Trick rummages around in the dude's mouth and feels for suicide capsules, secret messages, whatever. The Med-Tech reaches into a little cabinet and pulls out a device that looks like a space-age plastic clothes iron. She plugs the gadget into a monitor on the wall of the ambulance and hovers it over the assassin's body. A black-and-white image on the screen displays strange blobs and shapes, some of them moving.

I notice the ambulance has stopped. Since nobody gets out, I assume we're waiting to see if anyone has followed us. For the first time I notice how bad our captive smells. He must have let loose in his pants from all the excitement. I wish we could open a door, but I know we need to be ready to move at any moment.

"Hey," I ask Patrick, "what happened to Badr?"

"He vanished." My partner shrugs. "I watched you run after the car, and when I looked back for Badr, he was already gone." Trick gently bites his lower lip as he works. "I guess he didn't like the café's service."

As we talk, the Madrenaline fades out of my bloodstream and my hangover returns with a vengeance. The flock of stinkobirds flying from this putz's pants is accompanied by the return of the head-pounding gorillas. Suddenly the ambulance feels very hot and stuffy. My stomach heaves, and I groan. That horrible prepuke taste leaps to the top of my throat. I hold one hand over my belly and the other over my mouth while I peek out the back windows. I don't see anyone outside. My gut clenches like it's caught in a vise. *Fuck it.* I push one of the back doors open, lean out, and ralph what's left of my coffee and croissant onto the street. *Splat!* I slam the door shut. Then I drop down to a squat on the floor and hold my hands to the sides of my head.

I hear the Meddie say, "Scarlet, are you okay?"

I moan but don't say anything as I rub my temples and dredge up one of the prayers they made me memorize at St. Bony's.

O my God, I am heartily sorry for having overdone it last night, and I detest all the booze I drank because I dread the loss of my lunch and the pain of puking my guts out. I firmly resolve with the help of Thy grace to avoid the cheap stuff, to never again mix grain and grape, and to make sure I eat something beforehand. Amen.

Trick's voice says, "She's probably motion sick from that jump off the tower." Count on my partner to cover for me even though he knows I'm hung over.

To hell with it. If the Good Lord wanted me to suffer like this, he wouldn't have given me painkillers. I dose some Overkaine and immediately feel better. Even though the drugs make my fingertips and toes a bit numb, it's worth it. My stomach is still jumpy, but the gorillas hammering on my head have vanished. I stand up and lean against the wall to watch the Med-Tech wave her sensor device around the rival agent's body. The monitor displays more strange shapes. Dense things like bones show up brighter than soft things like muscles and organs, which are rendered in varying shades of gray. The Meddie moves her sensor over the guy's midsection, and we see a small white hard-edged shape with a suspiciously manufactured look to it.

"Ah hahh," she exclaims.

"Found something?" Trick asks.

The Meddie answers, "Yeah, under his rectus abdominis. It's his No-Jack." A No-Jack module is a locator beacon and distress signal transmitter. It can be triggered manually or, if you get knocked out, it'll activate by itself. Nowadays everybody in the field has one of these, including me and Patrick.

The Med-Tech pulls out a scalpel. She slices the skin below Lousy Driver's chest while Patrick uses wads of gauze to soak up the blood. She carefully cuts her way through the muscle until we can see into the competitor's guts. It's fascinating. I've examined the insides of people before, but not while they were still alive. How cool!

There's all kinds of activity: blood vessels pulsate, muscles twitch with each breath. But my unhappy tummy heaves again. It's not in the mood for this grisly view. I look up at the ceiling for a moment and take some slow breaths to help my stomach settle down.

The Med-Tech tells Patrick, "Spread that for me, will

you?" Trick places one of his gloved hands on the incision and uses his thumb and forefinger to hold it open. The gross flesh-squishing sound makes my stomach start grumping again, so I turn my hearing down. The Med-Tech peers around inside the enemy with a little flashlight.

Patrick spots it first. "There it is, near the fifth rib."

"I see it." The Med-Tech uses a forceps to reach under our patient's abdominal muscles and snare the module. She lifts out an inch-long lozenge. It's about the size of the first joint of my thumb.

"It looks like a big gnocchi," I say as the Meddie deposits it into a tray. "What are we gonna do with it?" Trick tells me we'll have one of Jacques's agents carry the locator beacon out of town. They'll transport it someplace quiet and wait to see who shows up. Meanwhile we'll pump our captive for info right here in Paris.

Or I should say Patrick will do it. He doesn't trust me around prisoners anymore, so he keeps Lousy Driver under sedation until we return to ExOps' Paris headquarters. I start bitching at my partner. Who says I'm a hotheaded kid who can't control herself? As we ride across town, I review some of my old Job Numbers and realize that sometimes I am hotheaded and that I'm not always very good at controlling myself. Okay, fine, Patrick. You do the interrogation. I'll take myself out shopping. I could use the fresh air anyway.

CHAPTER 26

Now this is more like it. Paris is gorgeous! It's a trip just to stroll the broad tree-lined boulevards, weave past the sidewalk art dealers, and peek into the shops. And the food! I've never had such good bread. The French complain that things have gone downhill since the war, but I don't know what they're talking about. This is great.

The baking sun is directly overhead, so I pop into an air-conditioned department store called La Samaritaine to get a quick break from the midday heat. The store bustles with well-dressed weekend euroshoppers. Two women are at the register, paying for their stuff. One woman writes a check while the other holds a half dozen shopping bags. They turn and walk toward the door, but the woman with the bags doesn't get any help from her companion. Some friend, I think to myself. The empty-handed woman gets to the door and waits for her overburdened pal to hold it open for her. Jesus! I've got half a mind to—

The woman with the bags turns and backs into the door to open it. When she does, I see her face. There's a big Star of David tattooed around her left eye. They're not friends out shopping together. It's a well-off German woman and her Jewish slave. The slave woman drops one of the bags, which gets her a slap in the face and a sharp rebuke from her mistress. The Jewish woman's face remains neutral, like she's trying to be invisible. I grit my teeth and make myself continue into the store, but I feel hotter now than I did outside.

I wander into the women's section and let the cool air wash over me. I see a couple shopping across the main aisle in the men's clothing area. The woman is piling things onto the man's outstretched arms. I can see from here that the pants she's choosing are way too big in the waist for the skinny guy she's with. She leads him off to another department, and he turns his head to the side so he can see where he's going. Around his eye is another star.

"*Guten Tag.*"

I jump at the sound of a man's voice. It's a nicely dressed older fella. His name tag reads "Pierre."

"*Bonjour,*" I reply.

He instantly switches to perfect French and indicates the display of scarves I happen to be standing next to. "*Pour vous, mademoiselle?*" For you, miss?

I say, "*Non, m'sieur, pour ma mère.*" No, sir, for my mother.

The man helps me check out some scarves for Cleo. Washington, D.C., gets pretty windy, and Mom likes to wear something to keep her hair from blowing around. I find a turquoise scarf with thin white stripes for only ten marks. Cleo loves any piece of clothing from somewhere else, and this color will complement her dark red hair. Pierre rings up the sale and folds the scarf into a small shopping bag.

We both say "*Merci, au revoir*" as he hands me the bag. I leave the store with my eyes down and think about all the Jewish people trapped in Europe. I'm not used to feeling so helpless about something. Once I'm outside, I try to distract myself by reading the signs and posters.

Getting around Paris requires you to read two languages. Trick warned me about this on the flight. Most cultural communications are in French: things like billboards, concert posters, and restaurant menus. You see German written on anything official like road signs, news bulletins, and government vehicles. The Germans run the large institutions, but the small stuff is still *très français*. Of course, politically speaking, France doesn't exist anymore. It's all Greater Germany now, although the cities and towns have retained their French names and most of the genuine Frenchies still speak French. The only government-run part of Paris still in the original language is the famous Metro subway system. All the train directions and fares are listed in French. Maybe the *Übermenschen* are more romantic than we give them credit for.

One thing the Germans are *not* romantic about is Europe's population of Jewish people. The Krauts have kept them as slaves since the mid-1940s. I've read that the Jews are mostly used for heavy labor in factories and on farms, but the few slaves I've seen here in Paris seem to work as domestic servants for rich people too important to wipe their own asses.

As I tour around the neighborhoods, I overhear a few old French dudes gripe about how their kids use slang that combines German and French. They talk about it like someone pissed in their soup. Being an American, I could give a damn. We don't even bother to have our own language. We just mangle the one we got from England.

You can sense the tension around here if you listen for it. The French are still pissed off, or maybe embarrassed and frustrated is more like it. I've heard the war referred to as "The Disgrace." They blew it pretty bad. How many other countries have lost a major war in only six weeks? Trick told me that all hope for the United States to save their *derrières* got wiped out when the Germans invaded Great Britain. Without a nearby base, we were never gonna bounce the Krauts out of Western Europe.

So we did what powerful states have always done. We signed a fistful of toilet paper, shook hands, and smiled for the cameras. Then we waited. Decades later, Europe still simmers with resentment and suffers the occasional minor rebellion because the Germans didn't have the foresight to exterminate the native populations like us Americans did.

The French, therefore, are still here. They still cook great and they still dress well. They also still gripe about their occupiers or, as they say, *les Boches*. Except for the whole sovereignty thing, I'm not sure what the Froggies have to complain about. Due to the lightning speed of the Wehrmacht invasion, France came through World War II relatively unscathed, unlike England, Wales, and Scotland, who all got the shit bombed out of them. If you're going to lose to the Fritzes, it's better to do it fast.

I mull over the history I learned at school while I relax in a café overlooking the Seine. They have plenty of seats outside, but after nearly getting run over earlier today, I prefer to sit indoors. I watch an older French guy glower at a couple of German businessmen who are flirting with their young French waitress. The older guy leaves in a huff. A minute later, a girl about my age takes his seat. She picks up a menu, but I can tell she doesn't read it. Her eyes move around the café. My spy senses kick in. *Get ready.* The chick looks my way and blinks at me with a pair of big dark lenses that cover her eyes and then retract back into her brow.

I leap out of my seat, knock my table over, and send my coffee flying. I'm halfway across the café before the girl even starts to react. Li'l Bertha loads up with little bullets—we are indoors, after all. I'm right on top of Mystery Girl when she disappears—poof!—like someone turned off a TV. There's a trail of tipped-over furniture and pissed-off café patrons that leads directly from my chair to where I stand in front of an empty table with a big gun in my hand. The waitress shrieks. It's time to skadoodle.

I zip back to my table, grab my La Samaritaine bag, and run out into the street with my vision and audio Mods at full strength. I try to see and hear everyone around me, searching for threats. There isn't anything unusual. Well, except for me. The regular citizens on the street are understandably alarmed at the sight of a hopped-up girl brandishing a big-ass firearm in broad daylight. I put Li'l Bertha in her holster and make myself walk normally so I'm not so conspicuous.

What the fuck was that? Am I imagining things? That couldn't be my hangover. Have I done too many drugs? Maybe I hit my head extra hard and don't remember it. I should see a Med-Tech, but I remember my father used to tell me that if they thought you were slipping, they'd take you out of the field. With all the biotic shit I've had installed on my person, I can't do a desk job, cooped up in some crappy office all day. My Nerve Jet glides some Kalmers into me, then Patrick comms in.

"Hey, Scarlet, where are ya?"

"Oh, hey, Trick," I try not to sound freaked out. I do *not* want to tell Patrick that I'm seeing things. "I'm near the Louvre. What's up?"

"Our bird has sung quite a tune. Come on back here. I'll tell you about it as you go." I jog along the Seine toward our Paris HQ while Trick fills me in. The assassin I caught at the Eiffel Tower is named Pavel Grigorevich Tarasov. He's got other handles, but this is the one Extreme Operations calls him. As we thought, Tarasov is a pro, despite his panicked driving.

He's one of the retired Russian Levels who freelance for the Blades of Persia. Once you've become a Level, you're not suited for any other work, and the Levels who hit retirement without enough money saved up enter the private market. There are more Russians in these positions than other nationalities because the Russkies don't pay their agents squat. Tarasov revealed that the KGB lets him be a freelancer as long as he sends them any intel related to Russian security. He's also forbidden to pull any jobs in Russian territory.

Tarasov started blabbing as soon as he woke up in Jacques's ancient reeking cellar. He'd already been shot at, wrecked his car, BASE jumped off the Eiffel Tower, a maniac girl tried to tear his collarbone off, and he'd undergone stomach surgery in the back of an ambulance. Resisting interrogation was the last thing on the poor guy's mind.

Our captive is familiar with Winter, although he's never actually spoken with the man. Tarasov said that Winter speaks only with a few lieutenants. It seems that the reclusive leader has trust issues with foreigners, perhaps because so many of them have tried to kill him. Tarasov received his assignment through one of those lieutenants, Kazim Nazari, but he knows that the contract on me came from Winter himself.

I comm to Trick, "So this confirms that the Blades of Persia is mixed up in all this."

"Right," he answers. "It links your mother's kidnapping and the attacks in Baghdad directly to Winter."

"Wow." I cross the street in front of Jacques's safe house and walk down the alley to Jacques's hidden car elevator. "Do we know why Winter is after me?"

Trick comms back, "Not yet, but we've got our next step. Tarasov gave us Kazim's location, his comm code, even a picture of him."

"Where is he?" I check that nobody can see me, then I open the bulkhead door to Jacques's safe house.

"He's in Riyadh. But check this out. I jumped on the jackframe and plugged Kazim's comm code into our signals-tracing program. I cross-referenced Kazim's code against the two unknown subjects in the comm calls we decrypted in May."

Jesus, next he'll tell me about the fucking algorithms.

I comm, "Can we skip to the good part, please?"

"Kazim's comm code came back positive as the person who sent Hector to New York." Trick pauses. "Kazim Nazari is definitely XSUS Two."

CHAPTER 27

Our mission to trace my father's last assignment has been expanded to include harvesting intel about the Blades of Persia, their leader Winter, and the Darius Covenant. All three of these mysteries run through our one concrete lead, Kazim Nazari. We've received clearance for this high-level mission because the Front Desk has signed on as the principal agent. He'll personally monitor everything we do. He's really stuck his neck out. If I screw up, he's toast. No pressure, though. Just the fate of me, my partner, my boss, and whatever ghosts of my father we find along the way.

Patrick and I are traveling into Riyadh to meet our Greeters. Our ride is one of those fucked-up ancient buses crammed full of sweaty villagers sweating their sweaty asses off. Yelping kids, grunting goats, clucking chickens, the works. You'd think it was a ride at Disneyland if it weren't for the stench.

The Germans don't ride buses. They drive like jerks in their gigantic Krautmobiles with the AC cranked and their horns blaring. One of them cuts us off, and our driver has to lock the brakes to avoid a collision. We all slide off our seats and land on the floor like a bunch of pumpkins. A few chickens tumble all the way down the aisle and make a squawking feather pile next to the driver.

We pick ourselves back up, and I mutter, "Asshole," to Trick.

"True, but our driver did the right thing, avoiding that car."

"He should've pushed that Düsseldork off the road."

"He probably knows better than to mess around with the Germans," Trick whispers. The Germans' rules for this region are transparently biased. If there's a traffic accident involving a German person and a local person, it's never the German's fault.

I'm dripping sweat. One of the side effects of the drugs I use is that my body constantly tries to flush itself out. My abundant quantity of Exoskin doesn't help. I'd kill for some air-conditioning right now. I've killed for a lot less.

"Christ, this must be the hottest place in the world."

"Actually, it *is* the hottest place in the world," proclaims Trick. "Well, it's the hottest city. Next is Baghdad, then Phoenix."

"Arizona?"

"Yeah, we have the third-hottest city in the world. How about that?" Trick is such a nerd sometimes. Like I give a shit about Phoenix. But even when I'm a sweaty, pissed-off mess, Trick can make me laugh, because he knows so much more crap than he needs to.

He sees my grin and reaches over to take my hand. It breaks my heart how nice he is to me despite what a Bitchzilla I can be. I don't deserve this person. I wrap my arms around him and give him a kiss on the mouth. He leans against me with a big smile on his face as I rest my forehead against his cheek. We stay snuggled up as a cloud of chicken feathers and body odor chases our bus into the city center.

As soon as we arrive in the main plaza, half the people on the bus try to force their way off first. This sparks a raucous storm of shouted threats and universally intelligible hand gestures. After a minute the knives come out. We decide we've had enough of this rolling circus and exit the bus by jumping out a window. Another advantage of our under-tall statures.

We walk around the plaza and look for our Greeters. They'll be two men, we assume, but they might be gals. The Germans brought relatively equal rights for women. The old-timer locals hate it, but the Fritzes have made it abundantly clear that if their subjects don't like the new rules, they can go fuck themselves.

Patrick scans the faces while I scope the vicinity. It's a generally rectangular space, about half a city block, surrounded by shops, garages, and houses. The buildings are short, three stories at the most, but they all have lots of windows and doors. Plenty of places to hide. Lots of people scurrying to and fro. Buses groan their way in and out of the plaza while a few German policemen try to keep everyone in line by pushing them around. There's a permanent cloud of dust settling on everything. The people wind up the same sandy color as the buildings. You can tell them apart because the people are sweatier.

I spot two big men across the plaza. They sit at a small table and sip out of little espresso cups. Behind them is a large garage door, and over their heads is a sign with a picture of a car being pulled by a tow truck. Besides the fact that they aren't scurrying anywhere, these two stand out because one of them is wearing a Pittsburgh Pirates baseball cap, the kind with a flat top. They've got to be our Greeters. They were told that we'd approach them, so it's natural that they ignore us for now. I nudge Trick and tilt my head in the direction of the garage. He glances at the guys, then looks back at me and nods. We dodge traffic across the plaza in their direction.

We approach our Greeters. They're setting coasters on top of their espresso cups between sips to keep the dust out. They watch us as we walk up to their table. The Pirates fan is about fifty with gray hair; the other guy is a dark-haired twentysomething. They're both stocky, rugged guys.

Trick opens the conversation. "We're from the University of California. Are you the men we're supposed to meet?"

"You're the journalists?" asks the older one. The younger one eyeballs us keenly.

"That's us," I pipe in. Patrick and I are supposed to alternate answers, back and forth.

"The soccer match is already over," counters Young Guy.

"We'll cover the next soccer match." Trick gets his lines right.

Old Guy states, "It's not until next year."

I finish our coded introduction. "Then I guess we'll write a longer story."

The Old Guy laughs and stands up. Young Guy gets up, too, and the two of them walk into the garage. We follow them inside.

Compared to the dust storm outside, the inside of the garage is spotless. Several shiny, high-end German sedans are parked in a row, and each wall is occupied by racks of tools and carts of fancy-looking equipment. The guys get into the front seats of a big white Mercedes, and Trick and I pile into the back. Young Guy drives us out of the city center. All the windows are tinted to keep the sun out. The air-conditioning is deliciously frosty. I relax in the back and hold my damp shirt away from my skin.

Trick leans forward. "What should we call you?" he asks Old Guy.

"I'm Domicles," declares the older man, "and this is my son, Graccus." He indicates the younger guy behind the wheel.

"Hi, Domicles. Hi, Graccus. I'm Solomon, and this is Scarlet."

Domicles scrutinizes me, then Patrick. "Which one of you is the Interceptor?"

"She is. Level 8."

Graccus inspects me in the rearview mirror. I wink at him. He looks back at the road with no change of expression. Tough guy.

"So what have you got for us?" Trick asks.

Domicles shifts around in his seat so he can see us better. He tilts his Pirates cap back and explains what he and Graccus have learned about our target.

Kazim Nazari is the founder of a bioresearch facility

outside Riyadh. It's called White Stone Research Institute. The rambling facility is lavishly endowed with high-end equipment and well-decked-out personnel.

Domicles has three contacts in the lab's maintenance department. These informers say that although some members of White Stone's science team are Middle Easterners, many of the researchers are European. Graccus snooped around and found that every one of the Middle Eastern scientists at White Stone had their educations paid for by the Darius Covenant. When my partner asks how much oversight the local German authorities impose, Domicles gives us a crash course in how things work on Greater Germany's sandy frontier.

When Berlin parcels out the cushy government jobs, the best and brightest administrators are sent to glamorous places like Paris, Madrid, and London. The rest are dumped in the Teutonic equivalent of Bumfuck, Nowhere, which includes Riyadh.

So not only are the local German authorities from the bottom of the barrel, they've been publicly humiliated in direct proportion to their postings' distance from the Fatherland. The ever-savvy and enterprising locals see how much these barrel scrapers resent their superiors for banishing them here. This resentment has been monumentally exploited with a dazzling matrix of bribes and payoffs that would make Vito Corleone proud. A thriving black market has sprung up, fed by the despair of the cast-out bureaucrats and the avarice of human beings everywhere.

The black market's starting line is the Mediterranean ports, where all the dockworkers are native Middle Easterners. The only Germans working the docks are the overseers, who receive kickbacks proportionate to the quantity of goods that make it into their shipping ledgers as "breakage." From there the "duty-free" goods travel the width and breadth of Middle Eastern Greater Germany.

As long as this illegal traffic remains discreet, there's minimal interference from the Reich's regional representatives. They rationalize their laissez-faire attitude as a good way to give the Middle Eastern *Üntermenschen* the illusion of putting it over on *der Mensch*.

Not all the area's German officials are on the take, but they still keep their mouths shut. The quickest way to scuttle a career as a bureaucrat is to expose the corrupt behavior of one's fellow bureaucrats. Everyone in the organization will assume they're the next to be ratted out. Their defensive response will be to collectively scorn and slander the whistle-blower until that person resigns or dies.

All this results in a lively black market, and here's where Imad Badr comes in. Much of the information he passes to the Abwehr and the CIA results in the arrest of one of the underworld's prominent crime figures. Often these figures use legitimate businesses as a front. The way Rashid hides his black market operations behind his cafés is a good example. Unlike Rashid's cafés, however, some of these criminal facades compete with part of Badr Enterprises, which becomes their undoing. Badr finks them out to the Western powers and absorbs their share of the market.

This has had twin effects. Legitimate local markets have been gradually delivered to a handful of native-run corporations, especially Badr's, and the black market has for the most part been taken over by a few big Middle Eastern cartels, one of which is the Blades of Persia.

The CIA maintains files on both the Blades and Badr Enterprises, but they're very thin files. We know the names of these two organizations but not much else. An underground group like the Blades is naturally wrapped in secrecy and has no written records anywhere. Badr Enterprises is an inscrutable multilayered company within a company. Badr has his hands in a lot of businesses, but it's very difficult to pin down if he actually runs any of them.

What's also hard to pin down is whether Imad Badr's shady business practices are relevant to our Job Number. It's certainly good data, and Trick files it all away before he brings Domicles back to our task at hand: harvesting intel about Kazim Nazari.

"Good timing," Domicles says. He points out the car window. "There is White Stone's front gate."

We've traveled into the desert, west of Riyadh. If you look up "middle of nowhere" in the dictionary it'll be a picture of here. Except for the occasional small house and vegetable stand, there's nothing out here but sand. Well, except for the ominous installation we're approaching.

Graccus slows down as we pass a tall heavy-duty chain-link fence with a gate in the middle. The fence is topped with a coil of razor wire. An unassuming sign has the facility's name in Arabic and German. The German part reads "*Weisser Stein Forschung Institut*" for White Stone Research Institute. A one-story sheet-metal guardhouse sits inside the perimeter. It's big enough to provide shelter for half a dozen guards or so. Opposite the metal shelter is a skinny twenty-foot-tall guard tower. A grim trio of well-armed men glare at us as we pass by. The net effect is serious enough to repel the riffraff but not so zealously defended that it attracts undue attention. Which of course attracts our attention.

Graccus accelerates, and the surly guards dwindle in our rear window.

Domicles turns to face us. "So now you have seen the entrance to Kazim's facility."

"Yes, thank you," says Patrick. "Can you get us some flexible transport, Domicles?"

"Most certainly."

Trick nods to our Greeter and comms to me, "Okay, we've completed our recon. Now we begin the next phase of our mission."

I comm back, "You mean where we bust in and see what's cookin' in there?"

Trick winks at me. "You got it, Hot Stuff."

CHAPTER 28

Now I'm frozen! What's with this fucking place? It's roasting hot during the day and icy cold at night.

"I hate deserts!" I yell to Trick, who doesn't respond. He's busy comming with his Info Coordinator while I drive our all-terrain vehicle across the dunes. It's one of those three-wheeled jobs with fat, knobby tires. It's not very fast, but it's quiet because it's got so much muffling on the exhaust. Patrick sits behind me with his arms around my waist. He has to hold on tight because the ATV squirms around like a greased iguana while I struggle to keep us from flipping over. Who knew that you could stack sand so steeply?

Trick leans forward and puts his mouth right next to my ear. I feel a little thrill from the contact as he says, "Turn left about ten degrees." He can't comm to me because he's still on with his Info team back in Washington.

I turn to the left. Even with my starlight vision and the compass in my Eyes-Up display, it's no picnic to stay on course. We're in the middle of an unfamiliar, featureless desert in the middle of the night. "How's that?" I ask over my shoulder.

"A little more." I turn a little more left. "Perfect." Trick goes back to his comm call.

There's a glow ahead, but it's obscured and hard to see clearly. The desert air isn't as clean as I would have expected. It's surprisingly foggy or smoky. Patrick finishes his comm call and sniffs the air.

"Trick, what is this fog?"

"It's sulfur and hydrogen sulfide. They're by-products

of petroleum refining. It's unusual to see a whole fog of this stuff."

"Whew! It stinks! Is this shit bad for us?"

"Not nearly as bad as our jobs at ExOps."

The chemical fog gets thicker as we drive closer to our destination, the White Stone Research Institute. The glow turns out to be security lights from a long, low building set in a small valley.

I ease off the throttle and stop between a couple of tall sand dunes. Trick and I hop off the ATV and crawl to the top of the dune closest to the facility. We've successfully placed ourselves at the back side of the installation, as far from the front gate as possible. The place is a series of large rectangular blocks, all stuck together. It's lightly covered in dust. The painted beige metal walls and roof are rust-free, I assume because of the dry climate. The huge building is a string of prefab boxes that snakes along the valley floor, with an occasional box stuck to the side as though someone needed another room in the middle. Security lights illuminate the corners and several spots along the walls' length. The whole place is ringed with a tall fence that's topped with coils of razor wire.

I lean over to Trick. "Think that fence is electrified?"

"Oh, most definitely." He pulls out his handheld millimeter-wave radar device, points it toward the fence, and slowly waves it back and forth. "The radar shows a line of hidden pits and moats in front of the fence."

"Can we go around them?" Trick doesn't answer but continues to scan the area. I mutter, "I'll take that as a no."

He says, "Hang on, I'm still surveying the ground. They've got it dug up pretty good."

Something catches my eye along the shadowy walls. Inside the perimeter, off to my left, two men come into view. They walk together near the building, each cradling an assault rifle. I silently wait for them to pass on to my right while my partner quietly works his gadgets. The two men turn the corner and disappear.

I comm, "How wide are the moats?"

"About ten feet. Got a plan?"

"Yeah. Is there any surveillance equipment?"

Patrick stows his radar gun and takes out a pair of binoculars. "I don't see any. Maybe cameras don't survive the sandstorms."

"Good. I think we can jump that fence."

"What do you mean 'we,' Kemo Sabe? I don't have your physical enhancements."

"I'll carry you."

Patrick takes his binoculars away from his eyes and stares at me. "Scarlet, I weigh twenty pounds more than you. You think you can vault over a fence this high with that much extra mass?"

"Of course! It'll be like in New York when I jumped over the alley with that chick on my back. C'mon, let's go. These mugs will never expect this move." I pull Trick to his feet and lead him down into the valley. He puts his sensor gear in his bag of tricks, and we creep up as close to the fence as we dare.

I have Trick stand with his back to the fence. I face him, then we put our arms around each other. Trick wraps his legs around my waist so I carry all his weight. I bend my knees down into a squat. I have my neuroinjector spritz me a splash of Madrenaline.

"Ready?" I ask.

"I think so." Trick is nervous, and with good reason. If we land on the fence, we're fucked. I take a deep breath and launch us up and forward. My left knee gives a pop, and my arms strain to keep Trick with me. His body tenses as we fly over the top of the razor wire.

Made it! I let go of him on the way down. He spins around, and I push him away from me so we don't land on top of each other. We both hit the ground on all fours and roll onto our backs. We pick ourselves up and brush the sand off our clothes. Trick gives me a thumbs-up and a wink. He pulls out his heat and motion scanner, plus the millimeter-wave radar again.

While he gets them booted up, I rub my knee. It stings, but there's no time to repair it. I dose some Overkaine and hope I didn't screw it up. Getting an operation done on your knees really sucks. It can take a week to recover from the surgery, and the Med-Techs make sure it's as long a week as possible.

I follow Patrick toward the factory. My hand holds Li'l Bertha out in front of me so I can see her target sensor. This mission is a Creep 'n' Peep, so we stay quiet and keep our eyes and ears wide open.

There aren't any guards in sight. They must think the fence and an occasional patrol is sufficient for keeping people out. A cluster of communications antennas on the roof nestle against a row of radar dishes that all point in different directions.

We tuck up against a wall. Both of our sensors show activity inside but no movement outside. We slink along the structure's perimeter, looking for an entrance we can sneak through. The idea is to be so foxy that they'll never know we were here. We tiptoe around a corner, then run to get through a spotlit area as quickly as possible. Trick is in front with his handheld sensor gear, and I cover our rear with Li'l Bertha's sensors. I wrap my fingers around one of the belt loops on my partner's pants so I can follow him while I walk backward. I notice that the ground here has been packed down so hard that we don't leave any footprints. Suddenly Trick stops and kneels. We hear male voices arguing.

He whispers, "There's an entrance up ahead."

"The main entrance?"

"No, it's more like a shipping entrance. There's a truck and three guys with rifles." Patrick surveys the situation for a moment and says, "I have an idea." He tells me his plan. *Ooh, it's a good one.* Trick takes a pair of thin disks out of his bag. They're the size of nickels; one is black, and the other is white. He slings his bag's strap over my shoulder and sneaks into the shadows away from the lights.

I pussyfoot back around the corner. Then I crank some Madrenaline, face the building, and sprint straight at it. My feet *clang-clang-clang* on the sheet metal as I use my momentum to run up the side of the structure. I grab the lip of the roof and haul myself on top of the facility.

The guards' loud conversation stops. They run around the corner, stand directly under me, and peer into the darkness away from the structure. It always amazes me how easy it is to hide above people. The jamokes snoop around a little before returning to the shipping entrance. Maybe they think it was the metal popping as it relaxed from the day's heat. After a minute or two, Trick returns. I swing myself off the roof, hang from the lip for a moment, and drop to the ground. I favor my right leg as I land.

"How'd we do?" I ask as we sneak back to within sight of the shipping entrance.

"Good. I got the acid patch planted."

"How long till it goes off?"

"Any moment now," Trick answers as he takes his bag back. We crouch near the corner. I visualize the two scrunched-together disks as they chemically react with each other and transform from a pair of boring nothings into an excitingly corrosive blob of acid. We hear a loud pop sound. One of the truck's tires has just suffered an attack of instant manufacturing defect. The guards move to the front of the truck as we scuttle down the length of the wall, pass through the doors, and get inside the building.

We've entered a storage room filled with rows and rows of big steel containers and wooden boxes. We duck behind a stack of crates to the left. I scan the room for people and security devices while Patrick checks out the containers. The ceiling is just an unfinished roof held up by steel trusses. Plain metal lighting fixtures cast a yellow glow onto the room's contents. It's all very sparse and functional.

In situations like this we've been trained to have the IO investigate material evidence while the Interceptor provides security. Trick is about to walk into the main passageway between the containers when we hear steps outside approaching the shipping door we came though. He jumps back behind the crates with me, and we both stand still, holding our breath.

One of the gorillas from outside clomps in, shambles down the center aisle between the crates, and exits through a set of double doors on the far side of the room. He returns momentarily with a toolbox and a couple of canteens. The dude moseys back outside.

I turn to Trick and use our sign language. "Let's go."

We sneak down the row of crates and through the double doors. We enter a long corridor with four doors along each wooden wall and another set of double doors at the far end. Our heat and motion sensors are at full sensitivity as we ease our way down the hallway. My heat sensor picks up a group of warm, motionless blobs in the rooms to our right. The blobs are in stacks of three, and the stacks are arranged in long rows. They're people sleeping in bunks. We must be passing through a barracks area. It's the middle of the night watch, so these guys in bed are the day watch.

We creep through the next set of double doors and enter a high-ceilinged open room with a couple of fork-lifts, a pair of pickup trucks, and a huge Mercedes oil tanker truck. We've found the garage. There are six large windows, but instead of facing outside, they reveal brightly lit rooms full of computers, tables full of micro-scopes and glass vials, a group of big round tanks, lots of pipes, and rows of machinery. A handful of fair-skinned Europeans busily mill around all this equipment, along with a dozen or so swarthy Middle Easterners. All these people carry clipboards and wear white scientist coats. Some of the white coats are vigorously discussing something. Their debate is accompanied by a lot of animated hand gestures.

"Labs," Trick whispers. "We've got to move closer."

We sneak behind a forklift and look around the garage. It's surrounded on two sides by the windows looking into the laboratories. We're on the side that leads to the barracks. The last side is dominated by three truck-size garage doors and a few more guards armed with pistols. The guards noisily joke and laugh with a big hairy guy wearing a sweat-stained wife-beater shirt. Hairy Guy shouts something to the guards as he connects one of his tanker truck's big hoses to a pipe that runs from the unfinished ceiling into one of the labs.

I look around. We're too conspicuous. "We can't stay here."

"I know. Let's find some lab clothes."

We double back to the barracks area. The stacks of warm sleeping blobs are now to our left, so we gingerly open the first door on the right. It's a storage room for office supplies, boxes of paper, file folders, that kind of crap. We try the next door and discover a locker room with a long row of open closets like professional athletes get, except these are for the scientists and technicians. Trick stashes his doctor's bag in one of the closets, and we shrug ourselves into the smallest lab coats we can find.

As we exit the locker room, a big bearded guard with an assault rifle slung over his shoulder walks out of the garage and nearly bumps into us. None of our spy gear is visible, which saves our mission. Nobody would believe that any of the white coats would skulk around with military-grade weapons and targeting equipment.

Patrick, without missing a beat, speaks to the guard in Arabic. I have no idea what he says, but his tone is quiet and polite. The guard grunts and gestures for us to follow him down the hallway, toward the warehouse we originally entered. Trick follows, and I tag along. The guard opens the last door on the right for us.

We walk into an office. Three big desks, each holding a computer terminal, fill the room. No one is in there. The guard gestures to the computers, chuckles to himself, and leaves us alone.

I comm to Trick, "What did you tell him?"

Patrick is already at the first terminal. "I said my lazy, overpaid, bourgeois boss wants me to run some calculations for him." He cracks his way past the security screen and accesses a long list of data that scrolls up the display. He sits still and memorizes the information as it zips by. A series of engineering drawings flash up the screen. One of them catches my eye.

"Well, *that's* suspicious-looking," I comm.

"What?" Trick asks.

"That schematic. It's for a device the size of a briefcase."

"Yeah, I noticed that, too." Trick types some more, and a long series of chemical formulas fills the screen.

"Huh," my partner mutters. I wait. He continues. "They're developing some kind of organic compound and a device for transporting it. But . . . the compound isn't an explosive." He reads some more. "Christ, I think it's alive."

I tiptoe to the doorway and peek up and down the hallway. Empty. I return to my partner.

"Okay," he whispers. "I've got all this." His fingers rattle across the keyboard. The screen flashes like a strobe light for a second and then pops up with a normal screen saver. He's erased his activity.

He stands up from the terminal. "I'll take a better look at this stuff later. For now let's see if we can find more about whatever it is they're making here."

We walk back toward the garage and try to look like we belong here as we pass through the big double doors.

Trick whispers from the corner of his mouth, "Let's get near those labs."

"Okay."

We stroll across the garage. Trick hisses, "We should have an argument."

"Huh?"

"Look around. If we walk along quietly, we'll stand out."

Trick's right. All the guys we've seen have been practically screaming at one another. I see a couple of arguments right now. Hairy Guy hollers at the guards, who laugh. He must be funny. In one of the labs, several white coats gesticulate while their mouths move. The European-looking white coats aren't as furiously animated as their Middle Eastern counterparts, but they seem to be catching on.

Trick comms, "It'll be best if the guards can understand us."

"I don't speak any Arabic," I comm back, "but they probably know some German."

"You're right. At the very least they probably know German words like this." Trick takes a deep breath and calls me a shithead by shouting *"Scheisskopf!"*

I try not to laugh as I holler *"Halts Maul, du Affe!"* Shut up, you ape!

Trick suppresses a grin and leads us out into the open as he launches into a percussive tirade. Every few seconds I punctuate his filibuster with *"Nein!"* or *"Idiot!"* When he pauses for breath, I blast out a good one like *"Du bist ja ein Schlappschwanz!"* You're such a limp dick!

The guards and Hairy Guy look in our direction. Trick stamps his foot in time with the rhythm of his harangue. I wave my hands around and shout *"Schwein!"* four or five times in a row. Trick crosses his arms, then turns his back on me and pretends to ignore me. I smack him in the back of the head. He spins around and bellows so loudly that I have to turn my hearing down. The guards laugh and point at us. Then, already bored with the common everyday spectacle we present, they return to their exchange with the truck driver. Times like this are why Trick is so much fun to work with.

We argue our way toward the laboratory and stand in front of one of the big windows. Patrick slowly passes his gaze across the entire lab. He's stopped talking while he memorizes what he sees for his Info Coordinator. To pick up the slack, I yell *"Scheiss!"* and *"Fick!"* I throw in a bunch of French curse words like *Encullez* along with some grunts and shrieks, all accompanied by a whirlwind of hand waving and foot stamping. Anyone watching us will focus on me instead of Patrick as he carefully studies the lab.

Meanwhile, across the room, Hairy Truck Driver Guy disconnects his truck's hose from the lab's plumbing. As he coils it onto a big spool on his tanker, the hose drips a thin stream of brown liquid on the concrete floor.

Finally Trick finishes his scan and resumes our verbal brouhaha. Thank God, I'd run out of breath. While my partner rages, he notices the dark liquid on the floor.

He comms, "Let's get a sample of that glop."

I loudly question Patrick's intellect, calling him *"Dumkopf!"* while I comm, "Time for the ol' razzle-dazzle?"

"Yah," he comms back, "I'll be razzle, you be dazzle."

Still shouting in German, my partner leads me across the garage. Hairy Guy stops his argument with the guards to watch our performance.

Trick lines himself up so he's in front of the small puddle of brown liquid on the floor. He yells his way to an earsplitting Teutonic crescendo, then comms, "Now, knock me over."

I tell my partner he's as stupid as they come by screeching, *"Du dümmer als die Polizei erlaubt!"* and shove his chest. He falls over backward, howls in indignation, and rubs his coat into the puddle as much as possible. The guards laugh hysterically while the truck driver helps my partner up. Hairy Guy is even hairier-looking up close, and do I detect a hint of last week's cabbage on his breath?

Trick grabs me, and we start to wrestle with each other. After a few moments of grapples and curses, Trick comms, "Now, run away from me." I break his wrestling hold and slap his face. We dash around the room, scamper back through the double doors, and run to the locker room where we found the lab coats. I swear I heard a round of applause from the garage as we left.

I laugh. "That was awesome!" I shuck out of my coat and put it back in the locker where I found it.

"Yeah, great job." Trick grabs his doctor's bag. "Everyone thinks we're just a pair of pissed-off research assistants working for one of the European scientists." He reaches into his bag and pulls out a pocketknife and a small, clear plastic Baggie. Patrick takes off his lab coat and spreads it across a bench so he can see the big blotch from the stain on the garage floor. He scrapes the goop with his knife and then rubs the knife inside the Baggie. After he repeats this several times, a small pool of brown glop collects in the little plastic bag.

I ask, "Any idea what that shit is?"

"I think it's the runoff of whatever those scientists are trying to invent." Trick stuffs his stained lab coat in a laundry hamper in the corner. "This sample and the data we've got should help us figure out what this place is really for." He puts his knife and the Baggie back in his bag of tricks. "Let's get out of here."

We're about to sneak out when we hear footsteps in the hallway. We lurk behind the door and watch a heavyset, dark-skinned man walk past our locker room, open a door across the hall, and step inside. He turns to shut the door behind him. I catch a sliver of his face just before the door closes.

Trick looks at me and raises his eyebrows a couple of times.

I comm, "That who I think it was?"

"Yep," Trick comms back. "That was White Stone Research Institute's founder, formerly known as XSUS Two."

I access my Bio-Drive and rifle through my mission files until I find the image we got from Pavel Tarasov back in Paris. I look at the picture of Kazim in my Eyes-Up display. It's him.

I've finally laid eyes on Kazim Nazari. This is one of the last people who saw my father before he got captured. In fact, he was almost certainly in on it. My pulse speeds up and my breath gets shallow and faster as a wave of blood-warm anger washes over me. *That door looks like I could break it down no problem. Then I'll grab that motherfucker and—*

Trick shakes my arm and hisses, "Scarlet, we'll deal with him later, okay? We've got what we came for, and we need to see what Cyrus wants us to do next."

I can't speak for a moment. Finally I grumble, "Fine, later. But not too much later." My hands shake, and I have to grit my teeth to keep them from chattering. I have my Nerve Jet hit me with some Kalmers.

Trick lets me pull myself together and whispers, "Let's go."

CORE   TEC-RAD-012

Rapid Access Database (RAD)
Developer codes in ROM allow root-level access.

Every digital equipment manufacturer leaves a back door access code hidden in its devices' ROM chips. This code is initialized to grant engineers root-level access to its prototypes for testing and tuning. During production, the device's back door is preserved to permit firmware updates and emergency access on installed units.

The existence of these access codes is not made public, and the codes themselves are a tightly guarded secret. The back door codes are typically held by the organization's chief technology officer. This individual is not permitted to reveal the codes to anyone—not the company's president, not the board of directors, not even law enforcement officers.

Through the painstaking work and the fine tradecraft of our Infiltrators, ExOps acquires these codes and maintains the Rapid Access Database. This priceless asset allows us to rapidly crack almost any digital device and represents one of our largest advantages over our competitors.

Carrying RAD into the field presents a significant security risk. Thus, RAD is placed on the lowest sector of an agent's Bio-Drive, which falls behind the device's Direwall. All data within the Direwall is automatically erased in the event of unauthorized access or upon the agent's demise.

CHAPTER 29

We're back in Riyadh at ExOps' local safe house. It's a refreshing change from the ancient reeking cellar full of poorly lit spy stuff we visited in Paris. Here in Riyadh we have space in a new and well-lit three-story office building that's the same beige color as every other structure in this neighborhood of tinted-window office parks, apartment buildings, and covered parking lots. I was surprised at first by all the green grass, plants, and trees I see here, considering that we're in a desert. Then I realized that the lawn spritzers spray water on the manicured landscaping all day long. It must cost them half their water to have so many shrubs and trees here.

Patrick and I are in the vault, meeting with Info Coordinator Harbaugh. All of our safe houses have secure conference rooms equipped with long-range communication gear and jackframe uplinks. This vault has a new blabscreen and a top-notch satellite feed. We can't use them, though, because this whole mission is still under the table. Chanez sent Harbaugh here on some false pretense so he can debrief us in person.

Harbaugh's expression and demeanor do not exude happiness. He's not angry, either. He's just very, very tense. He and Trick review the intelligence we collected. After a few minutes, he's got a question for me.

"How did you withdraw from the compound?"

"The same way we got in. I carried Solomon and jumped the fence."

"Sounds like quite a jump," he says. "How did your Mods and Enhances handle it?"

"Fine, sir, although I may have strained my left knee." This is not a lie so much as a modified truth. My knee hurts like crazy, but I don't want to be pulled off this Job Number.

Harbaugh says, "Okay, Scarlet, very good. I want you to get that knee checked out right away. Solomon, you stay here and we'll examine your intel in more detail."

"Yes, sir." I stand up to leave.

Trick hands me a data pod. "This has all the files I got from White Stone. You can rummage through them while you have your knee looked at."

I tug the waist of my pants down a little, plug the pod into the port on my hip, and copy the files to my Bio-Drive. It's a lot of stuff. When it's done copying, I give the pod back to Patrick and leave the two brainiacs to their data banquet.

I walk down the hall and up a flight of stairs to the medical ward. The ward has the usual herd of highly polished roll-cart-mounted gadgets that go ping when they're happy and honk when they're sad. In a small office behind all the pinging and honking doodads, I find a Med-Tech hunched over her desk, filling out some paperwork. The only furniture aside from her desk is an examination table and the chair her butt is in.

"What's up, Doc?" I joke. She's an older woman I haven't worked with before.

"Good morning, Scarlet. What can I do for you?" Med-Techs always refer to Levels by their field names.

"My knee is a mess. Can't you Meddies install gear that doesn't break all the time?" I love to tease these people.

This Med-Tech is sassy and tosses back, "Can't you glory-hound Levels stop busting everything we give you?"

"Think of it as job security." I laugh. "What's your name?"

"My friends call me Chico."

"Did someone give you that as a nickname?" I take my pants off and hop up on her exam table.

"Yep." She gathers a double handful of instruments from a desk drawer and brings them over to the table. I watch her and wait for her to continue about her name. Instead, she slides out a small shelf from the table and sets her instruments on it before pulling up her chair so she can sit with my knees at her eye level. "Do you need anesthesia?" she asks.

"Aren't you going to tell me who gave you that name?"

She grins. "Nope."

"Why not?"

"Because it'll give you something to think about while I work."

"What do I need that for?"

"You need it because I don't want to be distracted." She lifts my kneecap off and pokes around in the joint with a metal probe shaped like a very thin pencil. It hurts, and I flinch. She says, "Let me anesthetize you. This will be quite a bit more uncomfortable than that."

"I can use my Nerve Jet."

"I'd rather do it myself. That way I know exactly how much you've got in your system." Chico takes a dope rag out of a small plastic pouch in one of her pockets. These are small circular cloths soaked with specific doses of painkillers. I lift my head up, and she gently sticks it to my throat. The chemicals will soak right into my bloodstream.

"Will this make me sleep?"

"No, you'll be awake, but your pain receptors will be disabled. It can make your legs a little rubbery, and until it wears off you may have some trouble talking."

"More thoe than nermal? Heh heh." My speech is already slurred.

Chico smiles and takes my pulse. I lie down, close my eyes, and begin to skim through Trick's files on my Eyes-Up display.

At first I think Chico's anesthesia has suppressed my ability to read. Even after I adjust to the fact that the files are all written in German, it's still page after page of unintelligible scientific gibberish. After a minute I give up randomly rummaging and decide to see if I can find out how many of the White Stone researchers got their educations paid for by the Darius Covenant. I run a search for "Darius."

I get about a zillion matches, but none of these documents are about scholarships or colleges. They're about some kind of research. I skim through them and see the word *Öl* over and over.

Oil?

I run a frequency-filter, excluding common words like pronouns and articles. Near the top of the list is *Bakterien*. This word appears in the Darius Covenant documents almost as many times as *Öl*. Oil and bacteria.

What the hell do oil and bacteria have to do with each other?

I open my ExOps-issued onboard reference library—for the first time, I think—and query how often oil and bacteria appear together. The list of relevant articles fills my Eyes-Up display.

I find an article that's written for laypeople and discover that a certain kind of bacteria is used for cleaning up oil spills. Apparently the microscopic buggers can eat petroleum. I can only imagine what they crap out afterward.

I switch back to the White Stone files. One of the Darius hits is a calendar. I bring it up. There's something happening this weekend. I expand the entry. It's an itinerary for Kazim Nazari, who will be traveling to Zurich for an event of some kind. It's not a conference, or a symposium, or one of those other snooty soirées academics use to justify sucking down buckets of alcohol.

Finally I figure out that it's a fund-raiser at the University of Zurich. The guest list is packed with megarich whales who can write checks for more than the net worth of some small countries. Listed among the glitteringly notorious pillars of society are two Middle Eastern men. One is Kazim Nazari. The other is Imad Badr.

Well, la-de-da.

The search also turns up a list of the researchers who work at White Stone. All of them received scholarships from the Darius Covenant—except the Europeans. I check the bios of a couple of the Euros, and it turns out they were all recruited away from the Carbon Program. Now they work together at White Stone, along with their Middle Eastern counterparts. All these eggheads are supposedly exploring new ways to have fun with petroleum. We hope this info-plunder from our Creep 'n' Peep will tell us what they're really hatching in there.

I have the search engine look for Big Bertha. There's one hit. The file opens in my Eyes-Up display. It's a . . . receipt? It's from the Abwehr, Germany's version of the CIA. I read the page so quickly that I can't understand it. When I try again, I translate the first line as "In gratitude for delivering an enemy of Greater Germany." The document grants a special security clearance that permits unlimited access to one thing: the Carbon Program.

Even through Chico's numbing anesthetic, I feel my temperature rising. Someone traded my father for access to Carbon. That someone is in the Blades of Persia. When I find that someone, I am going to kill the shit out of him.

A voice calls out fuzzily, like it's behind a wall of wool blankets. "Okay! Time to wake up!"

A cotton ball bats against my cheek. The voice passes through the wall of blankets and becomes Chico's voice. "Scarlet, you're all done. C'mon, honey, time to wake up!"

I open my eyes. Chico's face looms over me, and she stops patting my cheek with her hand. "Guess I gave you a little too much. Try to stay awake, okay? But don't move around yet."

My eyes are damp as the sedation begins to wear off. Chico cleans her tools and instruments while I shake off

the effects of the anesthetic. She sees that I've been crying, brings me a tissue, and dabs my eyes with it. Then
she holds the tissue under my nose. Oh, God, I haven't
had this done for me since I was three years old. I blow
my nose, and Chico gives me a smile. She walks out of
my line of vision and bustles around. I can't really sit up
yet, but I can talk fine.

"How'd it go?" I ask.

"Great. You'll have some tenderness in the natural tissue around the modified areas for a day or two, but
otherwise you shouldn't feel anything different."

"When can I use them?"

"You can walk today, but I don't want you doing anything crazy for a couple days or as long as they still feel
tender."

"Crazy?" I exclaim as I slowly sit up. My head is
swirling, and my mind's current inability to focus helps
me transition from . . . whatever I was just thinking
about . . . to doing my drunken sailor impression. I ex-
aggerate my leftover slurred speech. "Who the fush you
callin' crazhy?"

Chico laughs and continues to put her stuff away.

"C'mon, Chee-sho, I'll fush you up." I feign a fighter's
stance, my fists held out in front of me. I try to stand,
but my legs have gone on strike and refuse to hold me
up. As I fall, Chico runs over and catches me.

"Wait, wait!" she exclaims. "You need to sit for a little while. I gave you a larger dose once I realized how
much damage you did to your knees." She guides me
back to the examination table. I begin to lie down again,
feeling dizzy.

Then I see her. She peeks around from behind Chico.
Her big bug-eye lenses are down and reflect two tiny
pictures of my face back at me. I reach for my gun, but
it's with my pants across the room. Someone holds me
down, and the bug-eyed girl reaches into her pocket.
No, not her pocket. She reaches into her chest, right into
herself.

"Scarlet!" someone yells at me. "Scarlet! Oh, Jesus." It's Chico. She's upset.

"What? What's the matter?" The bug-eyed girl has vanished. Chico looks totally freaked out as I lie back on the table. She reaches over to her desk, opens a drawer, and fetches a handheld scanner shaped like a clothes iron. It's the same kind the Med-Tech used on Pavel Tarasov in Paris.

I ask, "Did you see her, too?"

Chico freezes.

Oops. I shouldn't have said that.

"Did I see who?" Chico asks slowly. She hovers her scanner all over me, especially around my head. "Christ, you've taken so much damage."

"Yeah, I'm a good little Intersheptor," I brag, glad to change the subject.

"Obviously not, or you wouldn't be so badly beaten up."

That hurts. "How the fush would you know? Maybe I've worked shum tough Job Numbers!" I shout, although I only mean to yell, and I can't seem to turn off my drunken sailor bit.

Chico steps back for a moment and looks at me. She resumes waving her scanner around me and murmurs, "I'm sorry, Scarlet. You're right, that isn't for me to say. It's just that I hate to see someone so young take on so much."

"It's not *that* much damage." I pout.

"Well, actually it *is* that much damage, but mostly I mean taking on so much responsibility. You're still a Junior Level." She puts her scanner down, takes out a small notebook and ballpoint pen, and jots down some notes. "Your Exoskin coverage is 20 percent, which is close to the limit. I'll bet you sweat a lot." She closes the notebook and returns the scanner paddle to her Med-Tech toolbox. "I want you to rest here until the anesthesia completely wears off," Chico orders gently.

"All right," I say. "Is it okay if I comm my IO?"

"Sure, sweetie, but stay on the table." Chico looks in my eyes, gives my shoulder a squeeze, and walks out of the room, dimming the lights on her way out.

I hope she's forgotten about my hallucination. I may need to talk to someone about that. God forbid it happened on a mission. It looked so real! I freak myself out and take a good look around the room. Nope, no dead bug-eye girls in here. Get a grip, Alix! I'll see if Trick is busy. He always makes me feel better.

"Hey!" I comm. I keep it simple. He'll know it's me. If he doesn't respond, it means he's busy.

He comms right back. "Hey! How's the knee?"

"Make that 'knees.' I screwed 'em both up."

"They'll be okay, though, right?" Trick sounds concerned.

"Oh, yeah, yeah. They hurt now, but I'll be ready for action in a day or so."

"That's perfect. You can heal on the way."

"Where are we going?"

"Switzerland, Hot Stuff," Trick comms. "We're gonna follow Kazim."

"I was just reading his itinerary. University of Zurich, right?"

"Wow, look at you." Trick sounds impressed. "Yeah, Harbaugh and I found his calendar after you left."

"Is something going to happen at the fund-raiser?"

"We're not sure, but this isn't the first time my boss has encountered intel that includes this university. The U of Z hosts more than an annual charity gala. It also hosts a research lab for Carbon."

Oh, that is *really* weird. "Trick, did you guys find the letter from the Abwehr about Big Bertha?"

"Not yet, we spent most of our time on those briefcase schematics." He pauses. "How many times is your dad mentioned?"

"Once." My comm voice darkens. "But it's enough."

German Cloning Research: Carbon Program (aka *Kohlenstoff Programm*)

By the end of World War II, the German Wehrmacht had seized vast wealth, engulfed a huge population, and conquered an empire stretching from the Arctic Circle to the Persian Gulf. The Reichstag moved quickly to pacify the Third Reich's half billion new citizens. The Geheime Staatspolizei, aka the Gestapo, conspired to inflict a climate of fear and obedience. Many other government bureaus followed suit. The Ministry of Agriculture, however, chose a different strategy to introduce the new *Volk* to the joys of being German.

The Reichsminister of Agriculture reasoned that people are more likely to accept new leadership if they are well fed. To this end he launched a research project to enhance Greater Germany's harvest by cloning the hardiest variants of crop seeds. This well-funded initiative was named the Carbon Program and attracted the finest scientific talent from all over Greater Germany. Within four years these scientists succeeded in the mass replication of a blightproof strain of wheat germ. The story of this achievement was proudly touted by the Ministry of Propaganda and received heavy coverage from news sources around the world.

Kept from the press was the fact that the Wehrmacht and the Gestapo had secretly commandeered Carbon. The program's new goal became the asexual reproduction of humans. The subjects were to be persons gifted with fearless martial talent and the proper mental aptitude for ruthless decision making. These parentless supermen would be exploited for military purposes.

This quest required at first hundreds, then thousands of research personnel. The Carbon Program grew to become history's most ambitious scientific enterprise and the Shadowstorm's worst-kept secret. By the late 1950s, our intelligence agencies had provided scientists here in

America with enough data about Carbon to begin our own domestic cloning research program.

Germany stunned the world when it presented the world's first human clone in 1959. Carbon's director of research read a prepared statement to the press. Gen-2, their second generation of cloning experiments, had already begun. After the media event, Carbon withdrew once again from public view.

Our efforts to penetrate Carbon have not been robust. Much about Carbon is unknown to us. The contents of our thin case file were harvested primarily from our brief access during the Warsaw Confrontation and by passively observing known Carbon facilities.

CORE Entry Update: A recent spike in visits from high-ranking government officials indicates that something significant may be happening inside Carbon. Perhaps Gen-2 has been a success.

CHAPTER 30

"Three fifteens for six, a pair royal for six more, and eight from my crib," Trick announces. I harrumph and toss down my cards. He's dangerously close to beating me in our traditional in-flight game of cribbage. I catch my partner's eye and wink at him as I slowly glide my tongue across my lips. My hair is too short to toss around seductively, but I still primp it a little and flutter my eyelashes at him while he grins and gathers up the cards.

"Don't worry, Hot Stuff. I'm sure your luck will change soon." Trick winks as he deals out the next hand.

"It better." I pick up my cards and arrange them by suit.

We're lucky I remembered to grab the cribbage set. We had only three minutes to pack because our orders gave us practically no time to make this flight. Info Coordinator Harbaugh briefed us and then offhandedly told us we had to leave for Switzerland immediately.

Our mission is to track Kazim Nazari while he visits the University of Zurich. He's been invited to attend a fund-raiser on behalf of the Darius Covenant. That's not why he's going, though.

The Info Department already knows the school hosts part of Carbon, the program Winter was granted special access to for capturing my dad. There's no way it's a coincidence Kazim's visiting this place; we think he's here to get something for his boss. The Blades of Persia have sunk their talons into Carbon and tailing Kazim is our best chance to find out why.

Despite Kazim's connection to both Carbon and the

Blades of Persia, the agendas don't seem related. In fact, they seem to be at cross-purposes. Carbon is about furthering German dominance, whereas Winter and his Blades are about ending it.

ExOps allocated us to this Job Number because we fit the cover and our capabilities match the mission parameters. We're also the only living ExOps agents who have seen Kazim Nazari in the flesh. Our cover story will be that we're newly arrived American students. This gives us a built-in excuse for "accidentally" being in high-security areas while we shadow Kazim, explore the college, and hoover up all the intel we can.

Today has flown by like a whirlwind: get debriefed, visit Chico the Med-Tech, receive the assignment, sprint up to our room, pack as quickly as possible, race to the airport, gallop through the terminal, and dash onto the plane. We motorvated so fast that anyone trying to follow us would have needed Acme Rocket Skates to keep up.

Now that we have nothing to do but drink and play cards, I can have Patrick catch me up on the details of our mission.

I quietly ask him what's up with all the science and research I saw associated with the Darius Covenant. "I thought it was a scholarship fund."

He lays down a five of hearts and glances around. "It is, but it's more than that."

"So the kids going to college is a front?" I pounce on my partner's five with a ten, making fifteen for two points.

"No," he comms, "not exactly." When I give him a confused look, he sets his cards down and spells it all out for me.

Patrick whispers that according to the intel we swagged from the lab, the scientists working for Kazim at White Stone Research are engineering an oil-eating bacteria that can thrive in an airless environment. Normally this bacteria has to have air or it dies. White Stone calls this project the Darius Covenant, the same name as the scholarship fund. The Darius files include those suspicious-looking briefcase schematics, which are for some kind of portable bacteria factory. That brown liquid I pushed Trick into contained a unique strain of bacteria. Our Med-Techs found that it can survive without air.

Trick says that all this research is ostensibly to clean up oil spills more efficiently. Info Coordinator Harbaugh believes that the Darius Covenant is related to Winter's notorious statement, "If the infidels think it will be a cold day in Hades before we reclaim our birthright, then I shall give them a winter they will never forget." This is, not coincidentally, why the CIA calls him Winter.

The college scholarships, the bacteria research, even Hector's trip to New York, are all connected to Kazim Nazari and, through him, to Winter. And Winter has got the ExOps brass losing a lot of sleep. Anybody who can protect a secret identity from both the CIA and the Abwehr is trying pretty hard. Winter's Blades certainly don't want us getting anywhere near the end of this riddle. Add in that we have no idea how Winter's people managed to deliver a Level 20 Liberator—alive—to a competitor and you have one secretive, dangerous motherfucker.

"Wait," I say. "The college fund still sounds like a front."

Patrick takes a sip of the coffee brandy we brought for ourselves. "No, it's a legitimate scholarship fund."

"Except all the scholarship recipients wind up at White Stone."

"Right." Trick nods.

"I bet I can guess what they work on."

"Right." Trick nods again. "Oil-eating bacteria."

"How come the Germans haven't looked into this?"

"Ha!" My partner tops off my drink. "That's the best part. The Germans are paying for it." He tells me that Kazim won a grant from the German government to improve emergency responses to oil spills. The Krauts had three bad spills a while ago, one right after the other. The Germans suspected terrorists, but nobody stepped forward to claim responsibility. The investigators' report was inconclusive, and the matter was pushed to the back burner. New safety procedures were dictated for the tankers, and a call went out for better cleanup techniques.

Enter Kazim Nazari with his state-of-the-art microbiology research facility. His pitch wowed the German parliamentary committee so much that they gave him more than he asked for. Not that money is a problem for White Stone Research. The place is swimming in so much cash that you could make a money lake and race porpoises in it. Except for the grant from Germany, all that dough is from private sources. And all of those are anonymous. Of course.

We finish our cribbage round, and I deal out our next hand. While I sort my cards, I ask, "You saw that Imad Badr is on the list, too?"

"Yeah, I did." Patrick smiles at me in surprise. "You're getting a lot better at research. Pretty soon you won't need me at all."

I reach over and take his hand in mine. "Tricky-Trick, if I ever thought it would come to that, I'd stop reading altogether."

He smiles again and leans over to give me a kiss. I resist the urge to peek at his cards and instead concentrate on how good his mouth feels.

As we play through our round, we get back to Imad Badr. My partner figures that high-society events like this are part of how Badr maintains his steady supply of intel for his handlers.

I ask, "Do you think Badr and Kazim know each other?"

"It's likely," Patrick comms. "Heck, Badr probably knows Winter."

"Why hasn't Badr ratted him out?" I throw down a six.

"Maybe he's waiting for the most profitable time." Patrick drops a nine and makes fifteen for two points.

"What a slimeball." I drop a two for seventeen and ask, "Isn't it a big problem that the Darius Covenant bacteria can destroy oil?"

"What do you mean?"

"I mean, what if they decide to clean up *all* the oil, not just what spills out of ships?"

"Oh my God Alix, there's way too much oil for that." Patrick drops a four for twenty-one.

"How much is there?" I slam a king down for thirty-one and two points.

"In the world?"

I nod my head as I scoop up the crib.

"Twelve hundred billion barrels, give or take." He tallies his score and moves his peg up the board.

"So it would take awhile for that bacteria to eat it all." I add up my take and slide my peg past Trick's.

"Forever, essentially." He shuffles the deck and deals out the next hand.

I arrange my cards and ask, "What do we have on Carbon?"

"A whole lot of nothing. It's been off the CIA's to-spy list since our own cloning program collapsed." Patrick quickly orders his cards. "We're on the first Job Number aimed at Carbon in almost twenty years." We quietly trade discards for a minute, then he says, "I'm pretty excited, actually. I've always wanted to know more about clones."

I earn eighteen points and win the hand. I'm really clobbering Patrick now. He must be distracted by how great my hair looks. He shuffles the cards while I debate how to tell him about my hallucinations. The rule is I have to tell my IO *everything*.

As Patrick distributes our cards, I take a deep breath and ask, "So, on a different topic, is it possible that someone's vision Mods would make them see things that aren't there?"

Trick stops laying cards down. "You're seeing things?"

"I'm not talking about *me*. I'm only asking."

"Well, I *am* talking about you. If you have a problem, you have to tell me." He's still frozen in middeal.

I mutter, "Keep dealing, will you." He deals, puts the pack down, doesn't pick up his cards, and looks at me. I try to talk, but my voice shakes too much.

Trick takes my left hand, gives it a little squeeze. "Hey, it's okay. What's going on? You can tell me."

Another deep breath. "I've seen that bug-eyed girl, but I don't want anyone to know. Because if they take me out of the field, you'll get reassigned to another Level and I won't see you anymore." *So much for the cool, unflappable seductress.*

Trick blinks a couple times and asks, "Bug-eyed girl?"

"The one in New York, remember? I nearly blew her arm off. Then she bled all over the place. Then we—"

"Yes, yes, I remember. But what about her?"

"I don't know. I've seen her a couple of times." I tell him how I thought I saw the girl at the café in Paris and at Chico's office in Riyadh. He sits back for a moment, still holding my hand.

"You know, your father had stuff like this."

"He saw things?"

"It was more like nightmares, but they were pretty debilitating."

I remember the nightmares. We'd all be asleep, and I'd spring awake as he shouted at the top of his lungs, "Motherfucker! I'll kill you! You stay away from them!" I'd listen to my mother try to calm him down. Sometimes it worked, and other times it didn't. When it didn't, I'd hear Dad stomp down to his shop. We'd find him in the morning, passed out on his ratty old couch with a few empty bottles on the floor. My mother would silently gather them and throw them out.

I'd climb on the couch and curl up next to him. He'd wake up after a while and run his fingers through my hair. I'd be careful not to put my weight on his stomach.

My father got grouchy when I did that, especially after he'd been in his shop all night.

Patrick ponders what I've told him. Finally he says, "We'll need to take care of this, but I've heard much worse."

"Do we have to tell Cyrus?"

"Oh, yeah. Alix, this rule is for you as much as anyone else. You need treatment."

I groan and take his hand again. *Christ, I've only been doing this for five years and I already need to see a shrink about my job?* "What's wrong with me?"

"It's post-traumatic stress disorder. It happens after someone has been under a severe strain, especially over an extended time period."

"Does this happen to the other Levels?"

"Totally." Now it's my turn to blink a couple of times. I ask Trick to tell me what he knows about this. It turns out he knows a lot. Most Levels have some kind of reaction to the work—typically substance abuse problems and nightmares. Sometimes it's paranoia or schizophrenia. Every once in a while a Level dive-bombs into flat-out delusional insanity.

All Levels are monitored for this stuff as well as secondary issues like hallucinations and potential suicide. Some Levels have taken their own lives, and it's thought that some other field personnel have stopped caring and purposely let themselves be killed.

"Jesus," I whisper. "Do Levels ever get old?"

"Sure. Your father was in his forties when he disappeared."

"Forty? Trick, that's not old!"

Patrick looks down at the cards and mumbles, "It is for a Level."

CHAPTER 31

She's faster than me this time. I stand to return fire, but Jackie-O's shot blasts through my heart and kills me. Everything suddenly goes silently black. I vividly experience the absolute emptiness of my own death.

Eventually, the light fades back up. I'm in the temple again.

The monk's orange robe flutters as a cold wind blows in from the mountains outside the temple. He stands up, plucks his head off his shoulders, and sets it on a low table in front of me. While the headless body returns to its seat, the head looks at me and says, "The caterpillar's bloom reveals a winged flower with dragon's teeth."

I stand up and walk outside to see the mountains. A frightened voice echoes from the valley below.

Alix!

I jolt awake, covered in sweat, and gasp in a mouthful of air. Another nightmare. But I heard someone call out to me—a voice I know but can't quite place. Now the room is quiet. I switch my vision to infrared. We're in our student apartment at the University of Zurich: tiled bathroom, efficiency kitchen, two desks, two closets, and two twin beds that we pushed together when we got here three days ago. I don't see any heat signatures except for Trick in bed next to me.

Wait, that's not true. I look back at my pillow. Behind the warmth from my head there's another heat source. I reach under the pillow for Li'l Bertha and check her status indicator. It says "ready," meaning she's turned on. I always power her down when I'm in bed. She boots up so quickly that it's not worth the risk of having a live firearm only an inch from my head while I sleep.

Weird. She's never booted herself up before. I'll have to take a good look at her in the morning. I turn her off, lie back on my pillow, and wait for my pulse to slow down. I'd like to use some Kalmers, but I'm trying not to rely on them so much.

I turn off my infrared and switch to starlight vision. Tree-filtered light from the main quad creates a pattern like a flock of birds on the ceiling. A light wind brushes the trees, and the birds look like they're flying. I've still got Li'l Bertha in my hand. I hold her up in front of my face and slowly turn her from side to side. The spiraled neural interface connector built in to her pistol grip is magnetic. I click it in and out of the WeaponSynch pad installed in my left hand's palm while I think.

Who called to me? It was familiar, but it wasn't my mom. I don't remember my father ever calling to me. He didn't have to. When he was home, I constantly shadowed him to make the most of him being around. I switch off my starlight vision and put Li'l Bertha back under the pillow. I'm drifting back to sleep when I hear it again.

Alix!

My body freezes, and my eyes pop open. I activate my visual enhancements again and reach for Li'l Bertha under the pillow. My thumb feels for the "on" switch, but she's already on. Dammit! What's wrong with her? I fret and mull for a minute, then I have an idea. I rewind my Day Loop a couple of minutes and listen to the playback until it catches up to the present. The only thing audible was my breathing. I don't know what to think now. The voice didn't actually make any sound.

I carry my gun into the bathroom, splash some water on my face, and look in the mirror. My reflection seems to stare right through me, like I'm the one made of glass instead of the other way around. I turn away from the mirror and dry my face with a towel. I won't be able to sleep anymore tonight, so I field strip Li'l Bertha on the bathroom counter. I might as well figure out what the fuck is wrong with my sidearm.

I had trouble sleeping when I was younger, but it's been awhile and I've forgotten how frustrating it is. Once the staff at my grade school figured out that my home life was why I was so spacey, they took it easier on me. They'd gently suggest that I visit the nurse's office to lie down on her sofa. There I was in third grade and I still needed nap time, like I was in preschool.

The kids never made fun of me, though, because of what I did to Bobby Houseman at recess one day. You need to scare the shit out of people only once. The secret is to make it so frightening that they'll never forget it. I was the smallest kid in class, I had an alcoholic semiabsent father, and a misspelled boy's name. Yet nobody ever teased me. My daddy would have been proud of his little Hot Shot.

I've got Li'l Bertha completely apart when Trick knocks on the bathroom door. When I answer his knock with a grunt, he opens the door and pokes his head in. His hair is mussed up, and his eyes squint in the light.

"You okay?"

"Yeah. I can't sleep."

"What's up?" He rubs his eyes, then leans on the door frame. I don't say anything. "Alix." He's a lot more awake all of a sudden. "What is it?"

I take a deep breath and blurt, "A fucking voice called my name." Patrick doesn't respond, so I tell him how I rewound my Day Loop and there was no actual sound.

"Trick, please don't say anything to Cyrus. He'll bench me for sure, and then I'll never find my dad." That last part surprises both of us. I've never said that out loud before. I'm not sure I've even consciously thought it before. He crosses the room, wraps his arms around me, and gives me a nice squoosh. Then he sits on the counter.

We both fall silent for a moment. I whisper, "I guess we have to tell Cyrus?"

"Are you kidding?" Trick says, "A field agent hears a nonacoustic aural signal? It might be some kind of psyop."

That hadn't occurred to me. "Could my hallucinations be the same thing?"

"Could be. I don't have them, but you take a lot more stress than I do." He yawns and rubs his eyes again. "How about nightmares? Did you have the same one you had last night?"

"Yeah." I sigh. "Jackie-O killed me, and then I was in that temple again."

"She killed you in the Hungarian restaurant?"

"Yeah," I say.

"Was anything different?"

"Nope. Same room, same waitresses, same Jackie-O and Hector." I stretch my arms over my head. "I was wearing the same clothes and hiding under the same Redskins hat."

Patrick looks at the floor and thinks for a few moments. Then he slowly raises his head and locks his eyes on to mine. "You mean," he scowls, "*my* Redskins hat."

Oh, dammit!

"Alix," he gripes, "I looked all over for that thing!"

I'm snagged and I'm tired, so I take his hand and put myself at his mercy. "Trick, I'm sorry. I lost it in the firefight, and I keep forgetting to get you another one."

"Wait." Patrick is still scowling. "Was my Redskins hat supposed to be your *disguise*?"

"Okay, okay. Jesus!" I throw my hands in the air. "The Front Desk already reamed me for this."

"Yeah, but Cyrus didn't know you were wearing . . ." He stops in midsentence, and his eyes drift off to Massive Brainstorm Land. He mumbles, "Oh, my God."

"What?" I ask, desperate to change the subject. "Are they gonna win the Super Bowl this year?"

"No, no." He shakes his head and says, "The Five O'Clock Club!"

I tilt my head. "What?"

"The Five O'Clock Club," he repeats. "Fredericks, at our meeting, after we rescued your mom."

"Trick, do you need to see a shrink, too?"

"Sorry, I'm not saying this straight." He starts over. When Fredericks berated me about my conduct on the Hector job, he said that it was a covert op, not a meeting of the Five O'Clock Club. As any good Redskins fan knows, the Five O'Clock Club is an informal postpractice gathering of players in an old equipment shed near the stadium. The guys hang out, drink some beer, and blow off steam. The sports writers found out about it, and the club became an open secret. The coaches figure it's a good bonding experience for the players, so they pretend not to notice.

The reason Patrick has latched on to this is that there were only three people who knew I was wearing a Skins hat on that mission: Jackie-O, Hector, and XSUS One, who received a picture of me from Jackie-O before I blew her into little Protector meatballs.

Trick pensively holds his hand up to his mouth. "My God, Alix, you may have been right all along. Fredericks *could* be XSUS One. Which would mean . . . holy crap!"

It would mean that the Director of the Strategic Services Council is in bed with a terrorist organization, that he betrayed his own agent to the enemy, and that he took out a murder contract on that agent's daughter to cover it up. If Fredericks is capable of all this, God knows what else he's up to!

"Ho-o-oly crap," I echo. "Should we tell somebody?"

"Well . . . Jeez." Patrick rubs his chin. "Not yet. It's still a guess. I need to run a trace on Fredericks's comm code to see if it comes back positive for XSUS One." He leans on the counter. "I'll need a terminal. We'll find one later this morning, when the school's buildings are open."

Fatigue sneaks up on me like a ninja kitten. Even with these stunning revelations, my head droops onto my chest. Patrick takes my hand and leads me back to bed.

The two of us curl up together, with Trick spooned behind me. We face the window, so I see it's slowly getting light outside. I'm tired, but I'm afraid to shut my eyes.

Trick doesn't fall asleep right away like he usually does. He's probably figuring out some fucked-up unsolvable math formula in his head. I'm convinced I won't sleep at all, so of course two minutes later I'm out like a light.

CORE   PER-A59-627

DATE: August 27
TO: Office of the Front Desk, Extreme Operations Division
FROM: Dr. Thomas Herodotus, Medical Director, Extreme Operations Division
SUBJECT: Psych-Eval for Scarlet

Cyrus,

As requested I've compiled a psychiatric evaluation for your Level 8 Interceptor, Scarlet. While physically and mentally quite capable of performing her job, I have grave doubts about Scarlet's emotional ability to positively assimilate her experiences as she matures.

Her family history is not encouraging on this count. Philip suffered from alcoholism, depression, and anxiety. Cleo clearly struggles with codependence and self-esteem issues.

I'm aware of Scarlet's outstanding record, but I would be remiss in my duty if I did not alert you to my conclusions. Extreme Operations is getting tremendous field value from this young woman, but at her current pace of promotion we won't be getting it from her for long.

Respectfully and sincerely,
Tom

CHAPTER 32

*I return to the temple. No Jackie-O this time. The monk's
head is still on the table, but the headless body has left the
meditation room. After I sit on the floor, the head recites:
"Spring's tender flirtation, cut short by summer's wrath."*

I wake up to full daylight outside. I pat my hand
around on Trick's side of the bed, but he's not there. I
turn over and see him in the bathroom, brushing his
teeth. He's already dressed in his white Chucks, blue
jeans, and a gray long-sleeved shirt with a big yin-yang
symbol on the back. His sneakers still have some dark
brown smudges on them from the bloody mess we made
at the Hotel Luther.

I flop back toward the window while I build up the
energy to get out of bed. I'm exhausted from missing so
much sleep last night. Madrenaline would help, but I
worry it's contributing to my hallucinations. I drag myself out of bed and get dressed. I pull on a gray T-shirt
printed on the front with some unexplainably popular
blue-skinned German cartoon character wearing a floppy
white hat. I complete my outfit with my jeans, black Pur-
cells, shoulder holster, and dark red leather jacket.

Our cover is that we're chemistry students from New
York University, so we want to look like everyone else.
The fad in student fashion lately is peace and unity. This
is symbolized by wearing iconography and fashions
from all the major powers. We don't have anything Russian on, but this is German territory, so that's a good
thing to leave out. Those two countries have always had
tense relations.

Patrick and I shuffle downstairs to the school's main

quad. Our time here has been spent scouting around, looking for clues about Kazim and Carbon. We've seen some of the labs but not all of them. Naturally, the ones we can't get into are the ones we're most interested in. We keep getting stonewalled by the university staff. The Swiss are graciously consistent about politely refusing access to restricted areas.

We walk to the cafeteria for breakfast. Trick takes two pancakes, and I snag everything else: eggs, potatoes, waffles, bacon, toast, and a big mug of coffee. We sit next to each other with our backs to a wall and dig in.

This is a swanky university, so they've got a luxo eatery with a high ceiling, large picture windows, and real china plates. The big room is full of overachieving international students, all chowing down and jabbering about how smart they are.

Two big, muscle-bound guys sit a few tables away. I notice that they're twins. I nudge Trick and nod my head in their direction while I comm, "Hey, look at those bruiser twins." Trick sneaks a peek at them and glances away. Then he turns his eyes back to them and takes a good, long look.

"I don't think those are twins," he says under his breath.

"What are you, blind? They look just like each other."

Patrick doesn't respond. He keeps studying the twins. They're both tall dudes with blond hair. One has a close buzz cut, and the other wears his hair in a ponytail. Now that I really pay attention, I notice that their table manners are terrible. When they pick up hash browns with their forks, it's like they're stabbing a dead animal. They talk with so much toast in their mouths that some of it falls out. They keep stealing bacon off each other's plates. Buzz Cut protests one such theft, and his mouthful of orange juice splooshes into his lap, earning Ponytail a punch in the shoulder.

Trick continues. "I mean, they look exactly like each other."

BLADES OF WINTER 255

"Well, duh. They're identical twins."

"Yeah, but they're too old to be *that* identical."

My mission brief included notes about how our genes dictate most of what we look like but not everything. For example, our ears typically don't line up with each other because our genes don't carry specific instructions for that. The little bio–worker bees that assemble us just wing it. Our uniqueness compounds as we age, too. By the time identical siblings are old enough to go to college, they've manifested minor physical differences from things like diet, sun exposure, and health issues. The identical twins we see now look like they've lived identical lives, which would be mighty unusual.

I steal another look at the bickering brothers over my coffee cup. "What, you think they're clones?"

"Well, we *are* looking for Carbon."

I let Patrick look. I know he'll want us to follow them, so I wolf down the rest of my breakfast. Buzz and Ponytail finish eating and stand up to leave. Buzz mops orange juice off his pants with a napkin. They carry their cafeteria trays to the kitchen's dirty plate conveyor belt and head for the door. We drop our trays off at the kitchen and follow the twins outside.

I switch on my infrared to memorize their heat signatures. I only need one, though. Their heat sigs are an exact match. That *is* weird. Normally everybody's heat signature is as unique as his or her fingerprint.

The twins mosey around the left side of the library, so we swing right. Patrick uses his handheld millimeter-wave radar screen, which allows us to "see" the two guys through the library. Any passersby will think we're geeky engineering students testing a class project. We follow the twins all the way across campus, primarily tracking them through solid objects. Twice we're following closely enough that we've got our quarry under direct observation, but the risk of detection is minimal since we blend in so well with all the students.

We might just have clones on the brain. Maybe it's

because we've been here for three days and we're a little desperate. But somehow I can't escape the feeling that as my grandfather would have said, "There ees something fishlike going on here."

The twins walk through the front doors of a tall, imposing building labeled "The Chemistry Institute at Zurich University." We enter the chemistry building in time to see Buzz and Ponytail get on an elevator at the far end of the otherwise vacant marble-floored lobby. After the doors slide shut, we hustle over to see where they go. Trick hands me his radar device, which I use to watch the twins ride down while Trick reads the numbers over the door. "Basement 1, Basement 2 . . . still on Basement 2 . . . I think that's as low as the floor numbers go."

"Hang on," I say, "they're still going down." I barely see them on the radar screen, but I can tell they stop moving a few seconds later. The twins walk under us, about five floors below. I finally lose them as they walk back under the center of the structure. Trick has already hit the down button. When the elevator returns, we hop in and look for secret panels or hidden buttons. I switch my infrared vision back on while Trick takes back his millimeter-wave radar device and sweeps it over the walls of the car. We can't find anything out of place. The buttons only show ten floors above us and two basements: B1 and B2.

Patrick reaches into his bag of tricks and pulls out one of his toys. The small device is shaped like a TV remote except for the metallic, bulgy snout on the end. He presses a red button on the doohickey and gets a reading right away.

"Ah hah!" he says. He adjusts some of the dials on his little scanner device. He presses and holds the B2 button with one hand and waves his contraption over the buttons with the other. He rapidly presses the B2 button. Then he presses it a few times slowly, then fast again, all while keeping his eyes on his gadget. He takes his finger off the button for a moment, then presses it three times fast and three times slow. Then he keeps the button pressed for about four or five seconds, and suddenly the elevator begins to descend. He turns to me with a broad grin.

I smile back at him and shake my head. "I'm not even gonna ask."

He returns his magic button scanner to his bag. "Amazing, huh?" He preens.

I give him a quick kiss. "Amazing."

The doors open, revealing the secret sub-sub-sub-subbasement. I'm tempted to pull Li'l Bertha out from under my jacket, but that'll kind of blow the whole student thing. I pat her under my right armpit and mentally practice quick drawing her.

We face a brightly lit hallway that stretches away for about two hundred feet back under the chemistry building. Two gray doors are spaced evenly along each side. The floor is white linoleum, the walls are painted a light beige, and the high ceiling is a sheet of white acoustic tiles interrupted by rectangular fluorescent lighting fixtures. Huge ventilation pipes, two feet in diameter, poke through the ceiling tiles here and there. They give the place a very industrial look. The air-conditioning is cranked, and the skin on my legs gets goose bumps. We try to appear casual as we walk off the elevator and stroll down the hall.

A loud discussion emanates from the first door on the right. Actually, it's just one woman's voice, but the tone in her voice is unmistakable. Someone is getting chewed out big time. It sounds like Cyrus does when he dresses me down for something, except this is even scarier because it's in German.

I'm still using my infrared vision, which shows me three warm blobs about to enter the hallway from the chew-out chamber. There's nowhere to hide, so we keep going. I peek behind us as the door opens. The angry woman pushes Buzz and Ponytail into the hallway. The twins hang their heads and stare at the floor passing beneath them while the woman propels them ahead of her.

Angry Lady lowers her voice to a pissed-off, hissing whisper. She warns her sulking charges, "If either one of you ever sneak out like that again, I'll personally stuff you back in the tanks." Patrick and I stand to the side. They tramp past us, march down the corridor, and turn right at the hallway's far end.

One of the classes I took at Camp A-Go-Go was called Overt Stealth Techniques, which was taught by an ancient little man named Dr. Charles. His nickname was the Chameleon because he was the CIA agent who attended Stalin's funeral as an honored guest of the Soviets. He was even in the official pictures of the event, and naturally he sent marked-up copies of them back to his handlers showing who all the major Russian players were.

Dr. Charles was a master of hiding in plain sight, and something he taught us comes back to me. He said, "The tighter the outside, the looser the inside," meaning that the harder it is to access a location, the more the people inside tend to relax on security. Clearly, no one in this secret facility thinks it's possible for a competitor to crack that elevator code, because we don't get so much as a glance as we resume walking down this hallway.

We come to a big open area on our left. There are six rows of desks, and the room is lined with books and computer terminals. It's a library. We duck in and sit next to each other at a couple of terminals.

Patrick cracks into the network in nothing flat. His fingers come up to full speed and blur into a rattling haze above his keyboard.

My fingers rest on my terminal's space bar while my eyes recon the room. A man who looks just like Ponytail works a few terminals away. But his hair is different, more of a crew cut. Wait, there's another one over there! Now I pick out more twins, triplets, and quadruplets, but some of them are from a different family. They don't look like Buzz and Ponytail, but they do look like one another. There are some non-twins in here, too, but half the people I can see are identically related to someone else in this library.

Trick comms, "This is interesting." I lean over to see what it is. "It's a residence schedule," he continues. "Kazim is already here." Patrick continues to type with blazing speed. His eyes are glued to the screen, and he doesn't even glance at the keyboard. For someone with only minor Mods and no Enhances at all, he can type like a motherfucker.

He suddenly stops typing and reads the screen with his mouth open. Trick can memorize upward of a zillion words a minute, so something must have caught his eye to halt him in his tracks like this.

"The Germans have finished their second generation of cloning research," he comms. "They called it Gen-2."

"What'd they figure out?"

"They figured out how to mass-produce clones." He reads some more. "Accelerated growth from infancy to adulthood." More reading. "Oh, no way. This timeline can't be right." He hisses, "Jeez-us," then he comms, "Gen-2 can grow a clone from infancy to adulthood in only two years."

While he works, I notice that the computer equipment in here doesn't look like anything I've ever seen before. It's all smaller than what we have at ExOps, yet something about the design of it exudes incredible processing power. Maybe it's the giant vent slots on all the cases. They look like fire-breathing dragons. I've been told that Carbon is the best-funded government project on earth. The gear I see here reinforces that in my mind. This stuff seems awesome.

"Ah, here it is," Trick comms. "Gen-3." He scans the screen. His eyes open wide, and the color drains out of his face. He whispers, "Dear God."

I've never heard my partner say that. "What?" I comm. "What is it?"

"A Gen-2 clone is an adult in body only. Its mind is still the mind of a child."

That would explain Buzz and Ponytail's atrocious table manners back at the cafeteria.

"So, giant kids?"

"Basically, yeah. But Gen-3 aims to fix that by . . . by . . ." He stops.

I wait as long as I can, about one second. "How?" I comm.

"Carbon's Gen-3 is going to try to map the consciousness of an Original into the minds of Gen-2 clones. If that works, Carbon will be able to generate exact duplicates of people in only two years. The duplicates would be twenty-year-olds no matter how old the Original had been." He turns to me and comms, "They could make copies of some famous person, like Werner Herzog or somebody. If they kept on doing this, he'd never die."

"What on earth," I comm, "are these guys smoking?"

"I know, I know. It sounds insane. But so was Gen-2." He pauses. "If this next step worked . . . it would change everything about being human."

A group of half a dozen people walk into the library. They have to hunt around for terminals to use. It's getting full in here.

I pretend to work on my terminal and comm, "Somebody's going to notice us if we stay here much longer."

"Right," Patrick comms back. He shakes his head a bit to clear his blown mind. "I'll run that comm trace on Fredericks, and we'll relocate." He types like crazy for a minute, then comms, "Damn, I can't tunnel into our comm-tracing program from here. C'mon, I think I know where we can get better access." Trick logs out from his terminal, stands up, and walks out of the library. I follow him. He takes a left, deeper into the facility. He's going somewhere specific. Our purposeful stride helps us fit in, since everybody here seems very Type A.

Trick takes a right into a smaller, coldly lit hallway. We climb a flight of stairs and stop at the last gray door on the right. Trick reaches into his bag for his lock pick, and I put myself into Manhattan Radar Mode—fully amped hearing and vision—to give myself advance notice if anyone walks up the hall. Footsteps echo from the main hallway, but no one comes into sight. Patrick works on the lock for about a minute and then pops open the door. We slide inside, shut the door, and turn on the lights.

I comm, "Where are we?"

"Kazim's office."

"He has an office here?"

"Yeah. He shares it with other visiting investor big shots. I figure the terminal in here will have better outside access." The office's primary occupant is a desk on which sit a lamp, a computer terminal, a square cup full of pens, and two telephones. One phone is white, and the other is black. In front of the desk are two visitor's chairs, and behind the desk is a wall of filing cabinets. There are no windows. Air flows in from a big vent in the wall up near the ceiling. There's another vent on the opposite wall. I figure one vent is in and the other vent is out so the air can circulate through the subterranean room.

Patrick sits at the desk and uses the computer terminal. After a minute he says, "Ah hah, here we go." His fingers flash across the keyboard, and then he sits back to wait for a result.

I ask, "Do you think Gen-3 has anything to do with my dad?"

"Hey, you know what?" Patrick hunches over the keyboard again. "It might." More furious typing, and then he stares at the screen as page after page of data shuttles past.

I tiptoe to the door and listen to the hallway outside. We do *not* want anyone to catch us in here.

Patrick is in his glory. While he makes like a big data sponge, he mutters, mostly to himself, "This might be the most intel we've gotten from Germany since the Warsaw Confrontation."

I look around the room. Nowhere to hide unless you count the vents. Trick and I have crawled through ventilation systems in airports, but not on a mission. None of our previous Job Numbers required nearly the amount of sneakiness we're attempting now.

Suddenly Trick sits up straight, "Oh!" he exclaims. I wait for him to finish. He reads some more. "Yes! He's here!" He looks up at me. "Big Bertha is being used as a test Original for Gen-3." Back to the screen. "Christ, they're trying to make copies of your father."

I can't respond or react. Dozens of questions splash into my mind, but I'm too stunned to ask any of them. Finally, I just point at the computer screen. "Where did you find that?"

Patrick says, "It's an inventory of the Carbon Program. Big Bertha was transferred to Gen-3 in April, only a few days before you pulled the Hector job." He looks at a different part of the screen. "Ah, the trace is done." He types a brief sequence, takes one look at the screen, and lurches back in his chair with his hands on his temples. He stares at me with eyes as wide as saucers.

"It's him!" He moves his hands over his mouth. "Fredericks is XSUS One! Oh, my God, Scarlet, Jakob Fredericks has been rogue for at least eight years." Trick counts the puzzle pieces on his fingers. "He's the one who panicked when he realized that the ExOps agent following Hector was Big Bertha's daughter. He falsified your father's last job in CORE—and probably wrote all those out-of-character reports. Those two Protectors *were* his." Patrick looks at his hands while he puts it all together. "He must have a tap into ExOps, and he's been passing that info to Kazim Nazari." He looks at me again. "Shit, he might know we're in Zurich. We have to get out of here. Right now."

My swirling thoughts are interrupted by footsteps in the hall. "Oh, fuck! Solomon, somebody's coming!" Trick logs out of the computer while I jump up to the vents and yank each of the big covers off. After he shuts down the terminal, Trick throws his bag into the In ventilation shaft and then turns to me.

We've practiced this next move in our agility classes. It always reminds me of a sequence I've seen cheerleaders perform. I get down on one knee and hold my arms over my head. Trick puts his hands on mine, steps onto my knee, and climbs onto my shoulders. Then I stand up and guide him headfirst into the ventilation pipe. I grab one of the vent covers and pop it back in place.

A key clicks in the lock. I grab the other cover and leap toward the Out vent. While I sail across the office, I adjust my body's orientation and slide feet first into the pipe. The office door opens before I can properly snap the vent cover back in place. I hold the cover in front of my ventilation shaft and try to breathe as quietly as possible.

CHAPTER 33

Kazim Nazari enters the room and shuts the door. He looks up at the lights.

"Damn!" I comm to Patrick. "I left the lights on."

"Maybe he'll think it was one of the other guests."

Kazim crosses the room to the desk. The desk's chair creaks as it takes his weight. My hand that grasps the vent cover is only a few inches from my face and blocks most of my view. I peer between my fingers and watch Kazim's hand reach across his desk, pick up the black telephone's receiver, and rapidly punch in a number.

After a few moments he says, *"Sind Sie fertig? Gut. Ich auch."* Ready? Good. Me too. He turns on the computer terminal. I say a quick prayer that Trick covered his tracks correctly. Kazim logs in and opens a complicated-looking spreadsheet.

I hear the office's door open. Through my fingers, I see two pairs of men's feet walk in and stand to either side as a third man strides in. Then the first two men step back into the hallway and shut the door.

Kazim stands up and obediently offers his seat to his visitor. I can't see the visitor's face as he takes the seat behind the desk, but Kazim's head and legs move into my striped field of vision as he relocates himself to one of the guest chairs. I tilt my head to try to see who sits behind the desk, but all I can see are his elegantly mani-cured hands poking out from the sleeves of his dark gray suit jacket.

"Solomon," I comm, "can you see these guys?"

"No, I'm on my back, so all I see is the ceiling. What's happening?"

"Some big shot and his bodyguards just walked in. The goons went back out to the hall, and the big shot took Kazim's seat behind the desk."

"What does the big shot look like?"

"I can't see his face from here."

Mr. Big Shot speaks to Kazim in rapid and authoritative Arabic. I can't follow a word of it, but my commphone's recorder is capturing the conversation so it can be translated later. Trick's commphone is also recording everything, and he knows enough Arabic to comm me snippets like

". . . finally acquired the completed Gen-2 formulas . . ."

". . . will work much faster on such small organisms . . ."

". . . Darius Covenant . . . can now move forward again . . ."

". . . make sure no one links the calamity to the Blades, even after it's done . . ."

Then Mr. Big Shot recites a list of words I can understand. They're the names of places in the Middle East, the Caucasus, the United States, and others all over the world. Kazim makes a note of each place on a little pad.

Trick comms, "He's laying out a specific sequence of locations." Mr. Big Shot reels off a few more places, and my partner comms, "Jesus, they're all major oil fields."

Mr. Big Shot finishes his list. The desk chair creaks as he leans back. Kazim whips out a Zippo and holds it across the desk, out of my view. I hear the distinctive click of the lighter opening, the sharp rasp of Kazim sparking it up, and then the metallic note as he flips the lighter's lid back into place.

Mr. Big Shot mutters, *"Danke."* A thin stream of smoke issues from his side of the desk.

Kazim sits back down. He says, *"Bitte schön, Herr Winter,"* which draws a low chortle from both men.

Winter?

I comm, "Solomon, did you hear that?"

"You mean *'Herr Winter'*?"

"Yes!"

"I sure did. Can you get a picture?"

"No, he's too far to the side." As I try to slide my eyes around my fingers, the smoke from Herr Winter's cigarette wafts in through the ventilation cover in my hand. I stifle a cough. The cigarette smells incredibly bad, like it's made of dead rodent—

Wait a minute . . .

—and rotten fruit.

. . . The sidewalk café in Paris. That shit smells like a dead mongoose. Tell me what you already know. Darius Covenant? Score.

Winter exhales another mouthful of smoke and ominously comments, in English, "As sey say in America, 'Sey will never know what hit sem.'" His accent is a singular blend of Arabic, German, and British English. I've only ever heard one person talk that way.

Oh, my God, I know who Winter is!

"Solomon, you know how Imad Badr is so well informed about Winter?"

"Yeah, why?" Then it dawns on him, "Oh, no way."

"They're the *same fucking guy*!"

More cigarette fumes drift into my vent.

"Solomon, the smoke is gonna make me cough!"

"Hold your breath or something."

I press my mouth against my sleeve and try to use my jacket as a filter, but the leather isn't porous enough. I stop breathing as long as I can. When I finally take a breath, the smoke jams in my throat like a lump of hot coal. My eyes water, and my lungs burn.

"Shit! Solomon, I—"

Cough!

The conversation in the office screeches to a halt. Kazim jumps out of his chair. He stares right at my vent and shouts a sharp command. The door bursts open, and the two bodyguards charge inside. They follow Kazim's eyes to my position. At first I think it's Buzz and Ponytail, but these two have different hair. One has a crew cut, and the other has long hair. Crew Cut growls and reaches for something on his hip.

I blast my bloodstream with Madrenaline and drop the vent cover. My modified arms launch me out of the ventilation shaft like a missile. I smash Crew Cut with a flying head butt and ride him to the floor. I jump to my feet, block Long Hair's punch, and grab his wrist and arm. I'm so hopped up that I barely hear it as I wrench his elbow ninety degrees the wrong way. I pop Long Hair in the nuts with my knee, and I'm about to pick him up and throw him at Badr when the door behind me flies open and all hell breaks loose.

It's more guards. There must be six of them. They all look like Buzz and Ponytail, except they each wear their hair differently. I'm about to carve a death tunnel out of there when I remember that I've got to bust Patrick out, too. *Dammit!* Fortunately, the office is so small that they can't all grab me at once. I need to deal with only two or three at a time. As I bash and smash these fools, Trick comms in, "Scarlet, I just heard an automatic being cocked."

I turn toward Badr/Winter as he takes a point-blank shot at me. I duck under the bullet, but the concussion still stuns me. I'm blind and deaf for a second, and that's all these guys need.

The next thing I know, each of my limbs is in the grip of a twin and Winter has a pistol stuck in my face. Bodies sprawl all over the floor. Some are draped across the furniture, and there's even a couple out in the hallway. Man, I must have really hammered them to send them flying way out there.

I'm about to demolish all these dumbasses when Winter points his gun away from me and up at Trick's vent. Trick is smart and has stayed in the vent while I've taken care of the fighting. My system is at full speed, so I've actually got some time to think. Winter's mouth moves in slow motion. He obviously knows how we do deep-penetration work at ExOps, that we work in teams of one Interceptor and one Info Operator. If I didn't have all these fucking guys galhandling me, I could easily disarm him before he got a shot off.

"Solomon," I comm, "you still in the vent?"

"Don't worry about me, toots. I'm sliding toward another office down the hall."

I comm, "Keep going!" Then I extend my limbs as much as possible, breathing in. I exhale sharply and snap my body into a ball. The goons' heads all clack into one another like coconuts. Winter fires into the vent as I jump to my feet, push up as hard as I can, and slam two of the twins into the ceiling. The flash and boom of Winter's gunshots fill the room as I leap into the air and kick a full circle around me. Another twin goes down.

Winter looks up into the vent he's fired into. He sees there's no one in there and barks an order at Kazim, who hurries out the door. There are only two twins left between me and the Blades' leader, but they've both got giant semiautomatics loaded up and pointed at my head.

Winter swings his pistol around and aims at me, too. Three guns in my face and Li'l Bertha in her holster. This situation doesn't have too many positive outcomes for me. I'm sure I can take down two of these jackasses, but the third buttsmoker will almost certainly shoot me before I get him.

"Solomon, what's your status?"

"Kazim's grabbed one of my arms! I was climbing out the vent in the next office, and he ran in."

"He's got you?"

"Yeah. You'd better take off."

"Solomon, you must be crazy if you think I'll leave you here!"

"Scarlet, you have to." He quotes from the ExOps field manual: "'In the event that an IO is captured—'"

"Fuck that shit, Solomon!" Our objective here was to gather intel, which we've done. I'd love to smash Badr/

Winter into his component organic pieces, but it's time to get the hell out of here. I jack even more Madrenaline, which makes my teeth taste like copper and the hair on the back of my neck stand up, but I've got plenty of time simply to turn and run out of the office. The three guns fire, but all they hit is air and wall. I sprint down the hallway and burst into the next room.

Kazim Nazari is dragging Trick out of the vent. My partner is trying to crawl back in, but Kazim has his hands clamped around Trick's wrist. As I charge into the office, the big man lets go of Patrick and pulls a revolver on me. I whip out Li'l Bertha and splatter Kazim's brains onto the wall. His body collapses to the floor.

Trick slides himself out of the vent and lands on Kazim's chest. He drags his bag out of the vent by the shoulder strap. We dash back into the hallway. Twins in both directions, but Winter and his molls are to our right. We run left. I keep Li'l Bertha in front of me and spray a light fog of small-caliber suppression fire to keep them all hiding in their rooms or offices while we get the fuck out of Dodge.

Trick has his infrared goggles on and helps me identify targets. He hardly needs to; there's someone to shoot everywhere we go. We fight our way past the elevator to a door labeled *notausgang* at the end of the hallway. Perfect, because this is an emergency and we need an exit.

Li'l Bertha changes to .50-cal, and I blast away the door's latching mechanism. The shot also shoves the door open, which triggers a piercingly loud *whoop-whoop* from a wall-mounted speaker with the word FEUERALARM stenciled beneath it. We run up the gray metal stairs, illuminated by naked light bulbs in the ceiling, with me up front and Trick in the back. For the moment we're alone in here as we pound our way up one flight after another.

I comm, "Who the fuck *are* all these guys?"

Trick comms back, "I think they're the mass-produced Gen-2 clones."

"There's a shitload of 'em!"

We've ascended to the ground floor. Patrick has pulled out his little millimeter-wave radar device and points it through the door to the lobby.

He comms, "Dammit, there's a bunch of people out there."

I ask, "Are they more goons or just students?"

"It doesn't matter. We can't risk a firefight in a room full of civilians."

An idea pops into my head. I comm to Trick, "Let's go all the way to the top. They won't expect that."

"What do we do from up there?"

"I'll carry you down the outside. They won't expect that either."

Trick thinks for a second and comms, "Roger, let's do it." We race back to the stairs. This building has five stories belowground and ten stories above, so by the time we reach the top, we should be able to build a huge separation between us and our pursuers.

We soar up the stairs. Trick gasps for breath, but he keeps going. I may have to pay for all this frantic activity with another visit to Chico or Dr. Herodotus, but for now I feel fine. We can't hear the posse chasing us over the wail of the fire alarm, but it's a safe bet that *someone* is coming after us.

We reach the door to the roof. I kick it open and we emerge into the Swiss sunshine. Trick reaches into his bag and pulls out the high-stress line we'll use for our external descent. I scan the area while he gets the line secured. Most of the people down on the ground have moved away from this facility because of the fire alarm. A group of determined-looking men run toward it, but I don't think these fellas are here to douse any blazes. That is, unless Swiss firemen carry assault rifles.

As Trick hands me the line, I spot something coming from the roof of a neighboring building. It's hot, fast, and headed right for us.

I shout, "RPG! Solomon, get down!"

He doesn't get down.

He pushes me off the building.

I turn as I fall and watch the rocket-propelled grenade explode right next to Trick's position and blow him to bits.

"PATRICK!!!"

The grenade's blast wave wallops me, and I streak toward the ground. My synthetic right hand grabs the rappelling line as tightly as possible. The line burns into the metal and plastic of my right palm as I arc toward the wall. I hit a window and crash through in a shower of shrieks and shattered glass. For a moment I watch all this action from outside myself, like I'm someone else. I land at the end of a hallway, skid all the way down the long linoleum floor, and bash through a door into a broom closet.

I look behind me, toward the window I smashed through. Flaming bits of crap tumble from the roof above. Tracer bullets ram orange streaks into the walls outside. The floor shakes, and the ceiling rumbles. I wonder if the architect planned for rocket-propelled grenades and a storm of gunfire.

"Almighty, Almighty, this is Scarlet, over," I comm directly to the Front Desk, the last resort of an ExOps field agent on a fucked-up mission. This long-distance comm call will definitely get picked up by the CIA, and they'll know ExOps pulled some crazy job without telling them. Chanez will probably fire me, but I've got no choice. I'm surrounded, and I just watched my Patrick—

"Scarlet, this is Almighty, report." Cyrus comms very quickly. It's all so fast right now.

"Almighty, my cover is blown, I've lost my IO, and I anticipate a heavy assault. Request emergency evac."

"Roger, Scarlet, please confirm: your IO is terminated?"

—oh, God, he's gone he's gone he's GONE—

"Scarlet! Confirm!"

"HE'S FUCKING DEAD!" This can't happen, not to

Trick, not to me and Trick. I sob hysterically. I can feel my neuroinjector gushing Kalmers into me, but they barely help.

"Scarlet, hang tight. Help is on the way. Are you mobile?"

"Roger, Almighty, I am mobile." Thank God for comming. I'd never be able to actually talk right now.

"Stand by for extraction, Scarlet."

Booted feet clomp into the far end of the hallway. A group of silhouetted figures walk to the broken window and trace the path of blood and broken glass that leads to my dark little closet. I can't move. I can't do anything. My life has ended, and it's only a matter of seconds until these assholes make it official. I'm sure they can hear me. I can't stop bawling. I don't even *want* to stop. I'll never see Trick again, and I'll never stop crying again.

Alix!

Oh, my God, it's happened. The voice talks to me when I'm awake now. I've been driven insane.

C'mon, Alix, get up!

"Why? I've failed my mission, Trick's dead, and it's all my fault."

You've got to get up! Your mother and I love you very much. We want to see you again.

Two flashlight beams land on me. Big guys with big feet and big guns arrive and clear all the broom closet junk off me. My eyes are so wet that everything looks blurry, but I still see that these men all look exactly alike.

If you get up, I'll tell you a secret.

"Daddy, please, not now."

The twins, or quadruplets, or zillionuplets, whatever the fuck they are, have spotted me. One of them steps into the closet. At that moment, even I'm not aware that it's the last step he'll ever take.

Alixandra, I need your help.

My dad was always totally honest with me.

I can hear a little. But I can't see. It's so dark here.

He never lied, even when he should have.

I've missed you terribly, honey.

This can't be happening. It must be the drugs.

No, baby, it's real. But I'm so cold. I need you to find me.

"What do I do? How do I find you?"

First, you've got to get yourself out of there. Go, now.

Somehow, from wherever he is, my father has found a way to talk to me. He's really alive!

Alix, go!

He's alive he's alive he's—

GO, HOT SHOT!

All the willpower I've cried out rushes back into me like a hurricane, and I burst out of the closet howling like a deranged tiger. My fingers gash through stomachs, lungs, and intestines. Torsos explode into crimson fountains. There's so much blood in the air that it looks like a gore blender. Once I clear a small perimeter around me, I haul out Li'l Bertha. She's turned herself on again, and she immediately perforates the rest of the goons while I watch their faces flash bright and dark as my gun illuminates the hallway like a strobe light. The gorillas I shredded on my way out of the closet hit the floor as the dudes I just shot begin their graceless flops. I'm so cranked up that I can watch individual drops of blood hang suspended in midair, floating like helium balloons. My gunshot victims collapse to the ground as I race back up the long hallway, leap through the shattered window, and land in the main quad.

There are dozens of men with assault weapons out here. I sight on the closest one and decapitate him with a huge bullet from Li'l Bertha. The priceless look on this shitfuck's face as his head tumbles to the ground without his body makes me burst out laughing. I pick up the head with both hands and give it a big kiss, right on the mouth. Then I hold it up by the hair and bellow, "Who wants to get *fucked* like a dog tonight?"

274 G. T. ALMASI

I think that's what I say. I don't really know. Whatever it is, all the goons in sight look at each other, turn, and run away, just like that. This might be the most fucked-up thing they've ever seen. I'm a living nightmare that terrifies everyone who lays eyes on me. I drop-kick the head across the quad and hold my hands up like I've scored a point in soccer. "Goooooooaaal-l-l-l-l!"

"Scarlet, this is Almighty. Evac inbound on your present position." A chopper soars in fast and low. It's good that he told me it's friendly because I don't feel very discriminating right now. This is the new worst moment of my life, and I'll fuckin' take on anybody.

Some detached, well-trained part of me comms, "Roger, Almighty. The LZ is clear. Scarlet standing by," while I hunt around the quad. I may have lost him, but I won't leave him behind.

I find what's left of my Trick under a pile of rubble at the base of the Chemistry Institute building. His legs aren't connected, but I scoop them up along with the rest of him as a big helicopter hovers into the quad and lands. The helicopter has a Zurich TV station's logo painted on its side. Six heavily armed Squaddies in civilian clothing hop off and form a circle around the aircraft, facing out. I carry Patrick past them and climb into the evac.

I put Trick on the floor of the chopper and take a seat. I sit facing forward while the Squad members jump back on board. Two guys station themselves on the door guns, three of them take the seats opposite me, and one guy sits next to me. Nobody talks. One trooper stares at me. I'm about to ask him for a date when he leans over and pukes out the door. I guess I'm not his type. The Squaddie sitting next to me has pulled out a first-aid kit. His hand wears a ring with a red cross on it. He's the Squad's Med-Tech.

He looks me over and asks, "How much of this is you, Interceptor?" with a very serious expression on his face.

I look at him and intelligently reply, "Huh?"

He looks into my eyes for a second. His face softens, and he says, "Scarlet, you're covered in blood and . . . stuff. Have you been wounded, or is this from everyone you left down there?"

I look at my hands. They're slippery with dark red goo. My synthetic right hand is shredded and scorched from the rappelling line. Li'l Bertha droops in my left hand. The glop oozes down my arm, flows across the pistol grip, drips off the end of the barrel, and forms a puddle on the deck. I look down at my feet. My sneakers and pants are covered with gore. It's like I punched my way out of a cow.

"I might have s-screwed up m-m-my knees again," I stutter. My voice shakes terribly. Must be from the helicopter. As I look up from my feet, I notice that Trick's legs are rocking back and forth with the motion of the chopper. His torso is facedown, but I can see his profile. Suddenly I can't breathe, and my vision goes from full color to black and white. I try to scream, but only air bubbles come out of my mouth. Everything sounds like it's underwater as my vision fades out entirely.

A fish shouts, "She's going into shock!" and then—

The roof of the temple rattles from the rain outside. The monk has reunited his body with his head, but now his head is a fleshless skull. Naturally, he can still talk, and he says, "Father Sun takes flight and leaves darkness at sunrise. The Children of Light pass on to make room for their tragically mortal offspring."

CORE   HIS-WC-058

The Warsaw Confrontation

This dossier contains public-facing and classified information. Do not remove this file from the ExOps Archive.

―――

New York Daily News, April 8, 1956

America Answers the Call to Defend Europe from Aggression!

WASHINGTON—Congress has authorized the Joint Chiefs of Staff to send the U.S. Army's 1st Infantry Division to Europe in response to Russia's surprise invasion of Greater Germany in the territory formerly known as western Poland. The Soviet Union's unprovoked attack on April 6 broke their nonaggression pact with Germany and enraged the international community. Yesterday, President Eisenhower pledged to assist our ally and this morning reiterated his stance that "the enemy of our friend is our enemy, and he will be met with maximum resolve and determination." In Berlin, U.S. Ambassador Henry Cabot Lodge Jr. called the situation in the east "dire" and declared that help "can't come soon enough."

The Big Red One will deploy under the command of Lt. General Creighton Abrams. Details are still coming into focus, but military spokesmen anticipate the troops' arrival in Greater Germany by the end of May. What remains unknown is whether our boys will be bringing the Bomb with them. General Abrams refused to divulge if American forces would again use atomic weapons, limiting his response to, "Ask the Chinese troops we left in Korea."

―――

DATE: April 9, 1956
TO: All Intelligence Supervisors
FROM: Office of the Director of Central Intelligence
SUBJECT: Opportunity knocks in Berlin

Ladies and Gentlemen,
　As you no doubt know, the U.S. 1st Infantry Division is

going to Germany. The crisis in Poland has created a huge opportunity for gathering data about German technology and industry. The mission to collect this intelligence has been code-named GR/LIBRARY. We will be working closely with Army Intelligence personnel to make the most of this situation. Feel free to contact my office with any initiatives or questions.

Sincerely,
Allen Dulles, DCI

————

DATE: June 2, 1956
TO: Office of President Eisenhower
FROM: Office of the Director of Central Intelligence
SUBJECT: Compiled GR/LIBRARY intelligence.

Mr. President,
   Now that the Russians have backed down in Poland, we anticipate that the Abwehr will withdraw our access to classified German materials by tomorrow. It's a shame the Russians were so easily cowed, since the Army Intelligence agents are providing us with very high-level intelligence product every day. Each of these men and women have performed their duties brilliantly and are a credit to their service.
   In forty-five days of classified-approved status, we have acquired information about many German technological breakthroughs and initiatives. I have attached full-length reports, but to summarize:

   • **Wireless communications.** Telephones you can use anywhere. System of networks link small send/receive devices, either handheld or headset.
   • **Physical modifications to humans.** Upgraded joints and skeletal elements wired into the user's nervous system allow greatly enhanced field performance. This confirms

our field reports of German agents effecting nearly impossible feats of strength and agility.

• **Cloning**. Also known as "Carbon." This technology was invented to enhance agriculture before being shifted to the replication of humans. The Carbon Program has achieved steady progress and overcome many obstacles.

• **Supersonic flight.** A predictable but still impressive extension of the jet aircraft developed just after WWII.

• **Space travel**. Very close to launching *Bahnbrecher*, their experimental satellite. They plan to follow this up with a manned orbital mission.

As you can see, the Germans are even further ahead of us than the Russians, with many important advancements. This recent intelligence windfall will aid us greatly as we strive to catch up. Several improvements have been discussed already. One that would be particularly useful is an in-body installation of a wireless communications device.

Please feel free to contact me with any questions, especially as much of this material is quite technical in nature.

Sincerely,
Allen Dulles, DCI

CHAPTER 34

They come for me again. The hulking dark beasts seem to be all mouth, topped by eyes that glow like dying coals. Leisurely, they begin to feast on me. Hard, moist jaws snap off my feet and then my legs. My bones crunch in their gullets, and boiling saliva pours onto my stomach. They eat their way up my body until the daggers in their mouths pierce my face and banish my screams.

A brief period of darkness. They come for me again.

SIX DAYS LATER,
FRIDAY, OCTOBER 3, 11:55 P.M. EST
EXOPS HEADQUARTERS, HOTEL BETHESDA,
WASHINGTON, D.C., USA

I don't wake up in heaven, but it's not hell, either. I'm in a bed. It's quiet. I turn my head to look around. Cleo is asleep in a chair to my left. A huge stack of books, magazines, and dossiers from the ExOps Archives sits on a table next to her. I use my visual enhancements to zoom in on my mom's watch. It's 23:45. Since when does she keep her watch on military time?

She stirs and half opens her eyes. When she sees that I'm awake, her eyes pop open completely and she springs out of her chair like a mom-in-the-box.

"Oh, baby, you're awake!" She takes my left hand in hers. "Oh, thank God."

"Mom, what happened? Are you dead, too?"

She freezes for a moment, then laughs. A big long laugh, like she's held it in for a while. "No, Alixandra, we're okay. I'm not dead, and neither are you." She runs her hand through my hair and lays her palm against my cheek.

I sit up. "Where are we?"

"We're in Washington, honey. At the hotel."

It's not the same room as last time. "Again?"

"Yes," she answers, her face darkening. "Again."

"Oh." I look down at myself. All the usual lumps are under the covers. Legs, feet, nothing's missing. I hold up my artificial right hand. It looks fine. You'd never know that I scorched the hell out of my plastic palm sliding down that rope in Zurich.

"How long have I been here?"

"You've been unconscious for almost a week."

No wonder I'm mostly healed. While I was out, they must have taken care of everything and gotten me all fixed up . . . *Oh, shit, they've taken care of everything!*

"Where's Patrick?"

She's very brave and tells me that they wanted to wait for me to wake up. After a few days the Med-Techs admitted that they didn't know how long I'd be out, so they cremated him and held his memorial service. I look at the ceiling as tears spring from my eyes and run down my cheeks.

Oh, my God, Trick!

Cleo's eyes well up, too. "We had to have his service in the main auditorium, so many people came. Cyrus told me Patrick's family was there, but I didn't get a chance to meet them. I'm so sorry you missed it, Angel. I know how much he meant to you."

A big sob escapes my throat. I cover my mouth with my hand to hold the next one in. Tears run across my fingers. "Mom, it's my fault. I got him killed! I was supposed to leave him once he got caught."

Extreme Operations' policy is that a Level will do whatever is necessary to remain at large, even if it means abandoning his or her Info Operator to capture. Arrested IOs don't usually suffer much abuse. All the sensitive data on Trick's Bio-Drive would have erased itself, and everybody in our business knows that IOs are hardwired to expire if you torture them. They're so useful for prisoner exchanges that they almost never get executed. He'd have spent some time in a stinky prison being interrogated, but he'd still be alive and we'd get him back eventually.

Levels, in contrast, are almost never exchanged. Once a Level gets snatched, he or she is gone forever. Mods and Enhances are worth their weight in gold, plus they provide excellent intel about how the other side works. The captive is given the opportunity to switch sides. If a Level remains loyal, it's torture time. Exactly what this torture is supposed to achieve has never been clear to me. Sometimes I think people just like to hurt things.

This doesn't come up very often, since we're rarely apprehended in the first place. We win, escape, or fight to the death. Levels are tough to snatch. Those goon clones in Zurich didn't kill me when they found me in the broom closet because I must have looked like easy pickings.

Cleo hands me a box of tissues from beside her chair. I take one and blow my nose. I toss the tissue in the wastebasket next to the bed. I notice that there's already a pile of tissues in it. Between that and the books, I figure my mom has camped out in my hospital room again.

My crying slows down. I wave my hand at the pile of books and her chair. "Did you camp out with Dad, too?"

She takes a second to figure out what I mean. "Oh, when he was hurt? Yes, I did—until we had you. Then I stayed home."

"Doesn't it make you crazy to wait here?"

"Not as crazy as waiting at home."

We're quiet for a few moments. Then I lie back and ask, "How did Dad wind up in ExOps?"

She turns her head with a far-off look in her eyes. She moves from her chair to the bed next to me. "Your father was in Army Intelligence when we met twenty-two years ago. He'd had successful missions in Germany and Southeast Asia but was being transferred to an administrative post. 'Goddamn desk job' he called it." She tells me he lasted only a month before he began to ask around about assignments with more excitement. Someone mentioned a new agency called Extreme Operations, and that caught his interest.

He applied to be a field agent, and because of his reputation they signed him without even interviewing him. He didn't tell my mom until the day he was accepted. This was not good news to my mother. She'd been around Washington and knew enough about covert work to know what kind of life they were in for: long separations, too many secrets, and the strain of dangerous work hanging over their relationship like a sword on a thread. Even if an agent survived the missions, the marriage almost never did.

Dad's decision made Mom furious, and they had a huge argument. I wasn't around yet, but I've heard about this particular fight many times. I hadn't known what caused it until now. Between the two of them, most of the stuff in the house got trashed. Neighbors called the cops, and that cooled them both off. They both had government jobs, and if you're busted, you're fired. The government is supposedly about preserving the peace, not disturbing it.

"He couldn't stand to be bored," Mom grumbles. "He'd get all antsy, and he'd start with his drinking." She sits quietly for a minute, then she reaches out and takes my hand. "That's why I'm so anxious about your work, Alix. I've seen what it does to people."

I almost say that Patrick will keep an eye on me. Instead I respond, "Don't worry, Mom. Cyrus will keep me in line."

She sighs. As if on cue, someone knocks on the door.

Mom calls out, "Come in." Not loud enough. Nothing happens.

I shout, "Come I-I-I-NNN!"

The door opens. Speak of the devil; it's Cyrus. He wears a dark suit and carries a big file folder.

"I heard she was awake." Of course he knows I'm awake. This hotel is one giant listening device. "How is she?" he asks my mom as he sets the folder on the floor by my bed.

Cleo gives a little laugh, "Cyrus, she hasn't lost her power of speech. You can ask her. I'm going to take a shower and lie down for a while." She leans over and kisses my forehead. She gives Cyrus a hug on the way out. Cyrus watches the door close behind her, then turns to me.

The polite, encouraging smile drops off Cyrus's face like a sparrow bouncing off a plate-glass window. He sets his jaw, frowns, and pulls at his chin. He takes a deep breath and says, "Winter has found a way to end the world."

This must be red hot. My boss is never that dramatic.

Cyrus sits down. "Scarlet, I've never seen a single mission harvest so much intel so quickly. I'm very proud of you." A glimmer of affection peeks through the anxiety in his face. "Fredericks, Winter, the Blades, the Darius Covenant, those schematics you brought us, what happened to your father—all of it has come together because of what you and your partner retrieved in Riyadh and Zurich."

Cyrus opens his file folder and pulls out a sheaf of reports from the Info Department. He reads sections of them out loud and unloads so much processed analysis on me that it makes my head spin.

The Carbon Program's success with its Gen-2 research had two important consequences. The first was that Winter now had access to a critical piece of technology for his Darius Covenant: rapid-growth cloning. The schematics Patrick found at White Stone Research are indeed plans for a briefcase-size bacteria factory. This device will combine Gen-2's rapid-growth cloning with White Stone's special strain of oil-eating, no-oxygen bacteria. Cyrus tells me this bacteria is called *Geobacillus thermodenirificans*. When delivered into a petroleum deposit, the device will flood the reservoir with anaerobic *Geobacillus thermodenirificans* and transform the oil into the useless glop I pushed Patrick into at White Stone. ExOps has taken to calling the device a "petron bomb" and estimates that one of these suckers can devour an oil reservoir the size of Lake Ontario in a single day. The White House did not receive this news with equanimity.

The second consequence of Gen-2's success was that the notoriously dead Big Bertha appeared in Carbon's inventory as a Gen-3 test subject. Winter obviously felt that Fredericks should know about it, and he had Kazim Nazari dispatch Hector to bring a message to Fredericks without leaving a comm trace. My appearance at his Protector's meeting with Hector panicked Fredericks into making his ill-advised comm call to Kazim.

Combined with the falsified Job Number, this comm call implicates Jakob Fredericks in a conspiracy to abandon my father to capture by a foreign government and an attempt to block the investigation into my father's fate with a second conspiracy to have me murdered. Cyrus says that Chanez has reported this to the Justice Department, which is seriously considering opening a case about it.

"Considering?" I bark. "Cyrus, it's *treason*!"

"True," he replies, "but Justice has a case against Chanez, too. ExOps isn't supposed to pull missions without telling anyone, and Chanez has had us off the books for months. The Executive Intelligence Chairman is furious. So is the White House and the Covert Affairs Committee. Justice needs to confirm that Chanez isn't trying to distract them from what ExOps has been doing."

My Almighty comm call from Zurich triggered the CIA Office of Security probe our Director tried so hard to avoid. A lot of bureaushit is flying around, and the Justice Department wants to resolve this situation with ExOps before it looks into our evidence against Fredericks.

"Don't even tell me," I growl, "that Fredericks might get away with this."

My boss shakes his head and frowns gravely. "He won't." He points his scowl at the ceiling and rubs his chin. "I should have seen it," he whispers. "Philip and Jakob shouldn't have been working together anymore.

Their relationship went down the toilet after that failed rescue. But my God, I never thought Fredericks would terminate his best agent and cover it up with an entirely fictional Job Number." He closes his eyes and rests his forehead against his fingertips. "The security people are going to lose their minds."

I twist my fingers into the bedcovers. "Sir, I'm sorry I had to comm you for help. I knew the CIA would find out about everything, but I didn't know what else to do."

"Don't worry about it, Scarlet. You did the right thing, and this would have happened anyway." Cyrus tells me that the Darius Covenant's clear and present danger would have compelled our boss to report it no matter what the ramifications were. "Director Chanez might bend the rules sometimes, but he's not crazy."

Cyrus shifts his paperwork and selects a new file folder. "All right," he says. "Back to work. Fredericks and Chanez can face the music later. For now we have bigger fish to fry."

My Front Desk hands me the new dossier. It's labeled "Darius Covenant," and what's inside makes grim reading.

The ultimate goal of the Darius Covenant is to drive foreign influence out of the Middle East by removing their reason for being there. No oil, no foreigners. Although it might be enough to destroy only the oil under the Middle East, Winter doesn't want to leave the developed powers any chance of giving him his comeuppance. The global havoc unleashed by his Darius Covenant will ensure that the developed world will be too busy starving to death to consider any reprisals. Hardly any citizens of the Big Four live near their food supply anymore. Once the local supermarkets run out of goodies, everyone goes on a permanent diet of water and air.

Without fuel for trucks to transport food to the large population centers, it's possible that only a tiny fraction of the earth's residents will survive. At best, we lose all the big cities and life reverts to the early Industrial Revolution. Unless everybody gets sick, which is what usually happens during a famine. If a pandemic broke out, it could be more devastating than the Black Death. This near extinction could rewind the human experience back to 3000 B.C., when the moon was a god and writing was some newfangled thing only the kids could do.

Even if we figure out a way to relocate people to food-producing areas before they all turn into toothpicks, the global economy will implode. Everything will have to be run on far less powerful energy sources such as coal, wind, and solar. Maybe even steam. Locomotives would be a decent solution, but the United States, like the rest of the Big Four, has put so much into our interstate highway system that we don't have much of a rail network anymore.

Air travel will vanish until engines that run on electricity or biofuels can generate enough power to get an airplane off the ground. Trucks and cars can eventually be switched over to electric motors, but by the time that happens, modern civilization as we know it will have ceased to exist. If it weren't for the fact that we'll be dead, we'd still be able to live and work in our giant buildings since most of the power for them is generated by electric plants that run on coal, nuclear energy, or natural gas. Communications can still be instantaneous, so we can all share the apocalypse together in real time.

Transport is really the main problem, but given the way our society has spread out and specialized, it's the worst possible problem. Winter's mad scheme is absolutely brilliant because it doesn't try to untangle the knots his people are bound in. It slashes right through them.

Of course, his people won't fare particularly well, either. Our analysts presume Winter's feeling to be that his people are doomed anyway, so what's the difference? Starvation, disease, and revolution will blaze through the Middle East like an ocean-size forest fire. Anyone currently wielding power there does so through the rev-enue they generate selling oil. These regimes will be swiftly swept aside and replaced. We might be able to watch it unfold on TV, but we won't be able to do a damn thing about it.

Once I'm done reading, Cyrus concludes, "There's nothing as plentiful and powerful as oil. We've got to save it and control it as best as we can. This has received top priority from the president, the Pentagon, fucking *everyone* who knows about it. It may be the greatest threat to civilization since the Mongols."

I remember those assholes from history class. They stormed out of Mongolia about 850 years ago and demolished most of Asia and Europe. Russia's notorious xenophobia dates from this event because of the Mongols' spectacular brutality.

Cyrus looks up at the ceiling and inhales deeply. "The White House has authorized the Pentagon to use any means necessary to destroy the Darius Covenant." He looks out the window for a moment. "If anything will exonerate ExOps, it'll be how hard the Information Department has been working. They've been hammering their jackframes since you got back from Zurich."

I ask, "Speaking of which, how did I get back, sir?" It's like when a drunk wakes up after a big party and can't find his pants. Cyrus lays it out for me. The "TV News" helicopter that extracted me and Patrick from the university flew us to the TV station that acts as an ExOps front. From there, a car with diplomatic plates drove us to the U.S. consulate in Zurich. The consulate is seething with spooks, so they occasionally need to smuggle people out of the country. The office keeps a few fictional employees on the books who conveniently "pass away" at exactly the right moment. The official story of my extraction was that a heavyset clerk had died of a heart attack and his body had to be flown home to the States. What really happened is that Trick and I were packed into a big-ass coffin and flown from Zurich to Washington. They hooked me up to an oxygen supply and a chemical stasis feed to make sure I didn't wake up in transit. Trick made the trip in a body bag at the other end of the coffin.

After we got home, I remained unconscious for the better part of a week. The Med-Techs attributed it to stress-induced shock and severe exhaustion from using so many doses of Madrenaline, Kalmers, and Overkaine. On the bright side, I wasn't nearly as beaten up as last time.

They retrieved most of my partner's intel from his Bio-Drive. I choke up a little as I think about them removing pieces of hardware from Trick's dead body. Then I remember the way his legs rolled around in the helicopter, and I almost pass out.

I hold my hand out and ask Cyrus to stop.

He says, "Alix, is this too much?"

"No, I just need a second." I try to blink the tears back. Totally doesn't work. *Fuck it, I'll cry a little. I'm sure Cyrus has seen worse.*

My boss sits back while I quietly weep. I take a tissue and blow my nose. After a minute I look over at him. "Cyrus, why did Patrick push me off that roof?"

Cyrus raises his eyebrows a little. "I think he was completely drained from running up fifteen flights of stairs. You'd already shown him that you weren't willing to leave him behind. If you had hesitated for even an instant, the rocket that killed him would have killed you too. Patrick did what he did to make sure that at least one of you got out of there."

This does *not* make me feel better. I put my hands over my face and really start bawling. "What a fuckup I am!"

Cyrus says, "No, this was a tough mission, and you're still learning."

Between sobs I choke out, "But Uncle Cy, I've been doing this for five years already!"

"Alix, you have *not* been doing this for five years." Cyrus leans forward and puts his hand on my shoulder. "Look, you only got promoted a few months ago. There's a big difference between Level 4 and Level 8. One thing that's much stricter is following field protocols like leaving a captured IO to his own devices. Patrick knew that, and you showed him you didn't."

"So I blew it."

Cyrus takes one of my hands and holds it in both of his. "Kiddo . . . it's true you made a mistake, but Patrick bailed you out."

I look up at Cyrus. My face is wet, and my nose is running. "Bailed me out how?"

"We got the intel he gathered, and you returned intact. Although you were badly injured." Cyrus takes one of his hands from mine and gently brushes a few stray hairs off my face.

My crying slows down a little. I sniff really loudly. "It was mostly my right hand. It's synthetic anyway, so—"

"Not physical injuries so much as emotional ones. The nurses and your mother have told me you've been having severe nightmares." Apparently I've been moaning and thrashing around in my bed. This is common for field agents who have undergone significant trauma and usually lasts two or three days. What worries them is that it's been going on for a whole week. Now that I've come out of my little coma, they intend to keep an eye on me to see if it goes away.

I take another wad of tissues and blow my nose, which makes a big honk that I'd think was funny if life didn't suck so much. I inhale deeply, then slowly exhale and close my eyes. After a few more breaths I ask, "Boss, what happened after I fell off the roof?"

"You were engaged by about eight clones inside and we don't know how many outside. They disengaged when they heard our helicopter approaching."

"I'm not sure it was the chopper that scared them off." I look at Cyrus again. "It might have been me."

"I can certainly understand why," Cyrus says with a little sparkle in his eyes. "We tested the DNA samples you brought back. Their genetic uniformity suggests that

Carbon has greatly enhanced the efficiency of its production techniques."

"I brought back DNA samples?"

Cyrus lifts one eyebrow. "Your clothes were soaked with biomatter."

That's right. I was covered with goon guts when I got on the helicopter. No wonder that Squad trooper threw up. Now I remember the voice I heard in the closet. It sounded just like Dad, and it seemed so real.

I'm so cold. I need you to find me.

I ask Cyrus, "What happens to the people who get cloned?" Cyrus tells me that we still don't know much about the Originals, but the intel that Trick and I retrieved gives us a pretty good picture of how the Germans are doing it.

Gen-2 was a huge advance. They figured out how to speed-grow clones. What keeps the Germans from cranking out thousands and thousands of clone troops is that the Gen-2 clones are so emotionally immature. As impossible as Gen-3 sounds, our science teams admit that they used to say the same thing about human cloning in general. Greater Germany's vast wealth and record of incredible scientific breakthroughs makes gainsaying them a dicey proposition. Winter certainly has faith in them.

I ask, "What happened to Winter, sir?"

"He escaped. By the time we got there, the school's grounds were in absolute bedlam. The priority was to get our people out of there. It was good that you commed me."

Swell, I can abort a mission like a seasoned pro. "Do we know where Winter is?"

"As a matter of fact, we do," Cyrus states. "He's back in Riyadh, at that damn lab of his, White Stone Research."

"Are we gonna have the Germans go and get him?" I ask.

Cyrus snorts. "And have them ask us how we know all about an underground operation in *their* territory?

No, our betters will deal with it and then cover it up." My boss reaches into his file folder and pulls out a thin manila folder. He drops it on my bed and says, "This is the plan from the Pentagon. They want to wipe out the Darius Covenant by staging a discreetly targeted event at Winter's lab. Once the dust settles, our local stringers will confirm that Winter was under the bomb and the mission will be considered a success."

A chill runs down my spine. "Are we gonna nuke it?"

"No, no. We'd never be able to cover that. The plan is to fire a thermobaric cruise missile from the Arabian Sea." He glares at the Pentagon's plan. "Eight hundred miles. It's the extreme range for our longest-range missile."

"When does this go down?"

"As soon as one of our submarines with the proper ordnance can get on station." Cyrus checks his watch. "About forty-two hours." He takes a very deep breath, bumps his eyebrows together, and rubs his chin. He even purses his lips. He's deliberating something.

"Sir?" I say.

My boss thinks for a few more moments. Then he nods his head and reaches into his file folder one more time. He pulls out a memo typed on a sheet of ExOps letterhead.

"Director Chanez and I talked about this when we heard the Pentagon's plan. We've been advised by Justice that if we want to make sure we nail Fredericks, they'll need stronger evidence than what we've presented so far." He curls the memo into a cylinder and holds it between his big hands. Jeepers, he's really nervous!

"Chanez knows he's probably going to lose his job after this is over. He's got one last mission he wants to run. He used up all his favors in Langley to get approval for this." Another hesitation. It's making *me* nervous, and I don't even know what's going on.

Finally he spits it out. "ExOps is going to snatch Winter before the missile hits. He'd be a star witness against Fredericks. We think we can persuade Winter to testify in return for certain legal protections. This way they'll both be neutralized. Only a few people at Justice and the CIA know about this."

I think to myself: *This must be way-y-y above my clearance.*

"Alix, there's an additional motive behind our desire to acquire this man."

There's only one reason Cyrus would be telling me all this stuff.

My boss sweeps the manila file back into his briefcase, "Your father was ExOps' highest-ranked Level. The best of our best. And he was captured alive. Ever since then there's been talk that our agency is unreliable, that we're too far removed from traditional covert methods. Some say we need more oversight or even that ExOps should be dissolved."

The reason is that he's sending me.

"Fredericks seems to know everything about our day-to-day operations, to the point where *he* puts out contracts on *us*. This role reversal has been a blight on the, ah . . . notoriety . . . our agency has enjoyed since our founding."

He's sending me back to snatch Winter.

Cyrus stands up, sticks out his chin, and begins to pace the room with his hands clasped behind his back. "I'm sending two Levels—an Interceptor and a Vindicator. The Interceptor will penetrate the lab to pull the snatch while the Vindicator provides backup. I'm going to keep the mission's Info Operator here where he can work from a jackframe and have the entire Info Department at his fingertips."

When I catch Winter, that bastard . . .

"Plus, I am *not* losing another Info Operator. I couldn't send one if I wanted to, actually. This mission has such a high Estimated Violence Index that I've been ordered to manage our risk by only dispatching the absolute minimum number of assets. They also need to be Level 10 or lower."

. . . when I catch him, he'll wish he'd never been born.

Cyrus stops pacing and faces me, "You're my only Level that has actually seen this man in the flesh. You've got more personal motivation to snatch him than anyone. Besides, you're becoming a specialist in surviving impossible missions."

I've got to get back there.

"Scarlet, I can't order you to do this." He pauses, seemingly forever.

I grit my teeth so hard it feels like I could chew steel and crap Tiffany cuff links.

Finally he asks, "Do you want this Job Number?"

"Yes, sir!" My voice trembles not because I'm scared but because I'm trying not to shout. "That motherfucker will never know what hit him."

The Front Desk raises one eyebrow. "We want that motherfucker *alive*, Scarlet."

"Fine." I roll my eyes. "But he still won't know what hit him. When do I leave?"

CHAPTER 36

I look good in a fascist uniform. Its lines make me look taller, and Trick would have loved to see me in these black boots. I'm the newest member of Gruppe 775 of a quasi-military program called The German Youth, or *Der Deutsche Jugend*.

My American accent is part of my cover story. I'm a German national who was raised in New York City. When I was fourteen, my family relocated to Munich, where I joined a Gruppe. My family has recently moved again, this time to Riyadh. I've transferred to Gruppe 775 just in time for this field trip to White Stone Research Institute.

The cover has to last only through today, and I've found that the fifty or so kids in my group have no trouble accepting me as a genuine German Youth as long as I'm pushy and obnoxious.

Der Jugend is to the Boy Scouts what grizzlies are to teddy bears. In addition to military training and political indoctrination, this institution gives German kids a head start on their arrogant sense of entitlement. One of the ways this happens is that The German Youth are allowed to visit almost any business, school, or government facility.

This includes microbiology research laboratories like White Stone Research, which it turns out is *not* owned by the late Kazim Nazari. It's part of a science conglomerate called Research Associates, SA, which is a wholly owned subsidiary of Eastern Innovations, AG, whose voting stock is held in trust by a consortium of private investors, which is chaired by the CEO of General Equipment International, AG. Controlling interest in General Equipment is owned by none other than Badr Enterprises, which is not owned, held in trust, or controlled by anyone except Winter. When I saw this crap all mapped out on Bill Harbaugh's whiteboard, it almost gave me vertigo.

White Stone was administered by Winter's pal Kazim Nazari until ol' Kazim got himself killed in Zurich last week. Domicles's men inside the lab have tipped us off that Winter is running things himself now. They also let us know that they had just unpacked a pallet of boxes that were chock-full of briefcase-size doodads. The science teams have been working overtime getting these things ready. Domicles's contacts also found out about a mandatory meeting for the entire research staff. All nonessential personnel have been given the rest of that day off.

That day is today. The meeting is at noon. Our thermobaric missile will arrive ten minutes later. It's being launched from 800 miles away, and it travels at 550 miles per hour. That's a flight time of 87 minutes, so Mr. Sub will launch his rocket hoagie at 10:43 A.M. It's 9 A.M. now.

When I asked Cyrus why Winter would allow a bunch of kids to visit the day he unleashed the Darius Covenant, I got a one-word answer.

"Cover."

Winter wants his involvement in the coming calamity to remain a secret. What better way to prove his innocence than having fifty ironclad alibis? Fifty know-it-all brats will see that White Stone Research was innocently building a better oil sponge. Not plotting the end of the world. No-ho, not us.

Der Jugend is providing a great way to get me into the lab, but they also pose a problem. The collateral damage at the lab will be bad enough without blowing away a platoon of German kids. That would definitely bring significant repercussions from our ally across the Atlantic.

The Gruppe's itinerary has them leaving the lab at 11:45 A.M. to get back to Riyadh in time for an afternoon of insensitivity training. The attack is timed to miss the kids and hit Winter and his damned petron bombs. As this unfolds, everybody who's anybody in Washington will be glued to a live feed from the White House Situation Room. What most of them won't know is that I'll be grabbing the main target out from under their long-distance blam-o-gram.

We ride to the lab in a big air-conditioned Mercedes tour bus. My skull pounds like a blacksmith at his anvil. I may have had too much to drink on the flight from Washington. The wheels of the bus jolt through a small crater in the road. I goose some Overkaine into my bloodstream and take a swig of water from my canteen as the bus continues to bounce across the desert. I look out the window and think about riding out here with Trick. *I still can't believe he's gone. Trick, I . . .*

I blink a few times to hide that my eyes are wet and try to think about anything else. I discreetly recheck my gear. Li'l Bertha snoozes in her holster, hidden under the right side of my jacket. Next to my gun's holster is a short-range signal jammer the size of a deck of cards. Under the left side of my jacket is my combat knife in its holster, plus a dangling grid of what look like half-inch-thick drink coasters. These are my grenades.

We couldn't figure out how to hide regular pineapples in my outfit, so the Tech people made these flat, disk-shaped grenades for me. The way they line the inside of my jacket makes me feel like one of those shylocks who sell phony jewelry. *Hey, buddy, wanna buy a bomb?*

Normally it would have taken over a week to get this Job Number set up and then a few days to get myself and another Level into Riyadh. The time taken to prep for this mission has been compressed from days into hours. Everything has been thrown together while all the pieces were in motion. Money is absolutely no object, so I got to fly first class. Ohh, that was nice. I even got a free back rub in between the six or seven glasses of wine I drank.

The Vindicator took a different flight. When Cyrus told me who it was, I grinned and said, "Tell him to bring his Bitchgun."

Now Raj follows my bus in a beat-up-looking produce truck. His forged papers say that he's transporting food to the cafeteria at White Stone Research Institute. Once I'm inside, his truck will overheat and stall just outside the compound so he can be nearby in case I need help.

I comm to Raj, "Still there Rah-rah?"

"Still here, Shortcake."

We're on comm-silence, but that's for the long-range network and the satellites. We can comm peer-to-peer as long as we're not too far away from each other.

The plan is that I'll sneak into the lab, spirit Winter out the back door, a helicopter will pick us up, and away we go. Then the lab gets blown into the next century. That's the plan, but none of us maniacs who volunteered for this mission expect things to go exactly as planned. If Winter were that easy to snatch, my father would have captured him a long time ago.

My stomach is in knots, and my hands are shaking. I ball my hands into fists to hold them still and juice some Kalmers. I stop trembling, but the butterflies in my stomach still swoop around like Snoopy chasing the Red Baron. I close my eyes and try to think about something happy, and my mind lands on how much I liked going to the shooting range with Dad.

He looked so great in his firing stance: feet apart, shoulders relaxed, the weapon in his hands like an extension of his body. His confidence rubbed off on me and helped my concentration when it was my turn. We didn't talk too much at the range. I knew it was serious grown-up time. Afterward he'd take me to Dairy Queen for grilled cheese sandwiches and ice cream, and we'd talk while we ate.

Jesus, I'm starting to cry again. *Are we there yet?*

I turn my head toward the window so nobody can see my face. The desert slides past and stretches forward. I think about the meeting I had with Cyrus early yesterday morning. I was six minutes ahead of schedule, so I sat on the couch in his little waiting area and pulled an apple out of my backpack. I'd taken only two bites when Cyrus poked his head out of his office and waved me inside. I sat in his guest chair while he shut the door behind me. He sat down at his desk and didn't waste any time. "Our colleagues in Central agree that Fredericks has been involved in crimes against the state."

That's a big one, I thought. *They could put Fredericks in front of a firing squad.*

Cyrus leaned back and slowly passed his fingers through his hair. The relaxed movement of his hands contrasted with the intense expression on his face. He said, "We're monitoring Fredericks's commmphone twenty-four hours a day. He's boosted his encryption into the stratosphere, so we can't tell what's being said. But we can track when a call happens, especially when there are a lot of them."

"Is Fredericks still in Washington?"

"Yes." Cyrus nods. "As head of the SSC, he's planning our response to the Darius Covenant. I heard that the cruise missile was his idea."

"He has no idea that I'm going after Winter, right?"

"Right. We've initiated a new encryption code for your commmphone, which should lock Fredericks out while Justice builds a case against him. He's been passing your movements to the Blades or sending his Protectors after you." They've decided that if Fredericks has a tap, it isn't into ExOps. It's into me.

Info feels that the only way he could have traced my location so often is to have monitored my No-Jack module through my commmphone. This is certainly not how these components are supposed to work, so Fredericks has found some kind of hack.

The rest of our meeting was about my mission to snatch Winter and how important it is for me to fit in with my Gruppe. Something that definitely won't help me maintain my cover is crying on the bus. Part of being a German Youth is making all the other people cry.

I touch my cheek, but it's already dry. That's one advantage of working in this giant toaster oven of a country. The climate is so arid that teardrops evaporate before they even get to your chin. I turn back to face the front of the bus, smile to my seat mate, and remind myself—again—to *not* kill Winter.

CHAPTER 37

We finally arrive at the lab. Since we're The German Youth, we blow right by the security gate and guardhouse. The driver parks in the shade of an outbuilding. Gruppe 775 files off the bus and lines up in formation. If my day as a German Youth has taught me anything, it's that lining up in formation is a big deal to these people. Of course, not all German kids join Der Jugend. Based on the few kids I've met, this organization doesn't attract too many young German artists, musicians, writers, liberals, or intellectuals.

Our tour guide turns out to be Winter himself, Imad Badr. He wears a light tan suit and a dark brown tie. He welcomes us with open arms and effusive German. I stand near the back of the group and pull my hat low over my brow. This is a problem. I can't exactly abduct someone while he gives a tour to a troop of rules-crazed German kids.

Winter leads us inside and jabbers away about what they supposedly do there. The overhead lighting throws his sharp features into high relief. This gives him a sinister appearance, but his manner with us is very warm and inviting.

Ol' Imad has charm, I'll give him that. He's also got an intense way of looking at people as he talks to them. When one of the German kids in my group asks him a question, Badr looks him or her straight in the eye and delivers an intelligent, patient, and complete answer without any hint of condescension.

Our tour slithers past rows of small laboratories and

offices filled with earnest-looking scientists. Badr tells us the White Stone Research Institute's founding goals are to explore ideas to minimize the environmental impact of oil spills, streamline the methods used in oil refineries, and find new uses for the by-products of the refining processes.

Ka-snore.

We pass a large hallway, and Badr waves us past it. "This corridor leads to the main garage, our warehouse, and the barracks for my security personnel. Trucks, crates, and cots—nothing of interest to intelligent *Volk* like yourselves. Please follow me."

I cast my peepers down the hall as we pass. At the far end, a set of double doors opens into the garage Trick and I discovered. The edge of the big glassed-in laboratory we scoped out peeks around the edge of the doorway.

I guess the secret doomsday lab isn't on the tour.

It's 10:04 when our tour guide leads us into a lecture hall. We fill up the first three rows of seats. Winter sits in the front row, next to our Gruppe Leader.

A strapping twentysomething lab coat bounds onto the stage. The man exudes enthusiasm and raises my hopes for something interesting to listen to while I wait for my chance to snatch Winter. That hope is crushed like a Jack Fisher fastball as our speaker jauntily launches into an interminably detailed account of the sex life of bacteria. Short version: they don't have one.

At 10:43 an alert blinks in the corner of my Eyes-Up display. The missile is on its way. Somewhere over the Province of Arabia a jet-powered bomb the size of a Chevy Impala is hurtling toward this building. By the time it gets here eighty-seven minutes from now, it may find a room full of kids who have already died of boredom.

My attention drifts, and I think about how crazy my last two days have been. I have a new Info Operator partner. His field name is Darwin-5015. Normally he'd have dropped with me, but the EVI for this mission is so high that Cyrus couldn't risk sending anyone who didn't absolutely have to go. Darwin has been closely monitoring my mission from his jackframe in Washington.

We've got a quick airlift planned, but my timing needs to be perfect because the lab has fairly robust air defense capabilities. This will work if I can snatch Winter without setting off any alarms. If I trigger an alert, I may not make it to the landing zone before the local airspace is choked with armor-piercing bullets, rocket-propelled grenades, and antiaircraft missiles.

To spice up the challenge, we're sure Winter is equipped with a No-Jack module. If he gets knocked unconscious, the module will send a distress signal and bring his goon squad. My first option is to convince Winter into coming along quietly. Since I don't have a partner here to be all diplomatic and shit, this gentle request will basically consist of me pistol-whipping him into submission. If that doesn't work, I'll just have to knock him out and haul him away as fast as I can.

11:30. Boom minus 40 minutes. We're finally released from science hell. Another few minutes and I was going to have to risk simply grabbing Winter by the hair and dragging him outside. The bunch of us youngsters troop off to use the bathroom before we get back on the bus. I hang back for a moment. Winter beckons one of his security guards over and confers with him in hushed tones.

It seems like forever before everyone is finished in the bathroom. Winter is nowhere to be seen. The security guard Winter spoke with leads us out the way we came. I drift to the rear of the noisy, chatty pack. As we pass the hallway to the garage, I slip off to the side.

I hear Winter before I see him, giving orders to someone. He's in that big garage where I pushed Trick into the puddle of glop. Winter stands in the doorway of the glassed-in labs while he directs a group of the research assistants inside. They busily arrange bottles of champagne and several dozen glasses on one of the long metal tables.

I press myself against the wall and check the hall behind me. Empty.

Boom minus 25. The German Youth kids should have left by now. As for the missing new member, Der Jugend's habit is to leave lollygaggers behind as an example of how to act like a jag-off when you're older.

Boom minus 23. Winter's minions continue to fuss around in the lab. It's pretty crowded in there, but nobody is looking out here. I slip into the garage and crouch behind a tarp-covered stack of stuff. I lift the back corner of the covering to see if I can hide under there and keep watch at the same time.

Lurking under the tarp are four neat stacks of black rectangular boxes. Each box is the size of a briefcase. They all have a small panel on one side. The panels have a readout screen and a row of three buttons labeled in Arabic. The readouts each display a single red dot that ominously crawls across their dark screens. The dot oozes off the screen's left edge and slinks back on from the right.

A cold bead of sweat trickles between my shoulder blades. I recognize these things from the schematics we found here. They're the petron bombs. I'm tempted to stick a grenade between these stacks of the Apocalypse, but I refrain because an explosion might attract a bit more attention than I can afford right now.

I drop the tarp back in place and survey the garage. A group of wooden shipping pallets catches my eye, especially one that's propped on an angle against the wall. I check that nobody's looking, scuttle across the garage, and quickly insert myself into the triangular space under the inclined pallet.

I carefully peek out from my hiding place and nearly jump out of my skin when my commmphone suddenly receives a call.

"Scarlet, your pizza is getting cold." It's my ride, Lovebird. He's lurking out there in the desert, close enough for short-range comming. Him and his pet helicopter.

"That's all right," I comm back. "It's better that way."
Meaning, stay put.

"Roger that."

Boom minus 12. The missile is 110 miles away. Every
minute brings it 9.2 miles closer.

The lab assistants have poured out glasses of champagne. Winter mingles through the room with a big Mr.
Roarke smile on his face. I can't hear through the glass
windows, but I see him shaking hands, patting backs,
and sharing some little in-jokes with people. It's quite a
party.

Boom minus 10. Ninety-two miles away. I start to
wonder if I'm gonna have to barge in there and snatch
him right the fuck out of his own party. Winter assem-
bles everyone in front of him and makes a short speech.
The lab coats all smile and nod to one another in self-
congratulation.

*Good job, everyone! By this time tomorrow, the world
will be absolutely fucked!*

Winter takes one of the champagne glasses and invites
the others to do the same. While I try to figure out how
Winter found such a dedicated group of supersmart socio-
paths, he raises his glass to the room and says, *"Prost!"*
Cheers! He brings his glass toward his mouth. Everyone
chimes in, *"Prost!"* and takes a swig of champagne. They
all nod appreciatively about how good it tastes.

Winter holds his glass in front of his lips. He lowers
his untouched champagne and places it on the table in
front of him. He walks out of the lab and locks the door
behind him. He stalks across the garage wearing an expression as dark as ebony lightning and passes through
the double doors toward the barracks and shipping entrance.

Boom minus 8. I'm about to follow Winter when the
scientists notice their boss's unexpected exit. Many of
the faces look out into the garage, freezing me in my
angled hideout. An animated discussion begins. One of
the researchers, a younger blond-haired man, tries the

door handle. Nothing happens. He tries it more forcefully, but the door remains shut. I can almost see the question marks appear above everyone's head.

Suddenly all the people in the glassed-in laboratory drop their wine and clutch at their throats. Each mouth splits open and expels an ear-shattering scream. Everyone's eyes seem to bulge from their sockets, and their faces flush from light pink to a florid red. Gasping and choking, some of them rush the door. The door frame lurches from their combined weight but still holds them trapped inside their antiseptic charnel house.

They drop like epileptic rag dolls, shrieking and twitching onto the broken wineglass-covered floor. Middle Easterners, Europeans, men, women. All of them. The smallest victims stop moving first, then the largest wretches lie still.

One of my eyelids starts fluttering so badly that I have to hold my fingers on it to keep it still. My other eye watches a group of six guards march in from the main facility, where we had our tour. They wear white hazmat suits with black rubber boots and gloves. The leader unlocks the door, and the rest file inside the lab of death.

"Scarlet." It's Raj. "You all right in there?"

I wipe tears off my cheeks. I hadn't realized I was crying, but at least my eyelid has stopped pulsing. "Yeah, Rah-Rah. I'm good. Standby, I've almost got him." I suck in a breath of cold air. The guards are all bending over the dead scientists, so I sneak out from beneath my pallet, bolt across the garage, and follow Winter's steps through the double doors.

Boom minus 5. This is cutting it close even for me. I pull out my pistol and run down the wide hallway with Li'l Bertha leading the way. Our heat scanners show dark, empty rooms until we get to the last door on the left. It's directly across from the office where Trick and I hacked into the lab's data server.

I gingerly try the doorknob to the occupied room. It's locked, naturally. Crap. My lock-picking skill kind of sucks, so by the time I pick this fucker, we'll all be blown to hell. So much for sneakiness.

I crouch in the doorway opposite Winter's room, slam some Madrenaline, and launch myself across the hallway. I flip over in midair so my feet strike first. The door smashes apart like it was hit by a cannonball. Splinters of wood shatter in every direction. I bounce back onto my feet with Li'l Bertha ready for some serious intimidation.

Winter stands in the middle of the room. He recognizes me instantly. "You!" he exclaims.

I ball my right hand into a fist and slam it into Winter's stomach. He exhales sharply, doubles over, and falls to his knees. While he gasps for breath, I take a plastic zip-tie out of my pocket and cinch his hands together with it.

Boom minus 4. Okay, I've got him. We'll walk out the back, hop on Lovebird's chopper, and away we go. Plenty of time.

"Lovebird, this is Scarlet. Target acquired."

"Roger that, Scarlet. On my way."

I bend down to lift Winter to his feet—

Wham!

My vision turns to static, and I topple across Winter. I push myself off him and try to get back on my feet, but I can barely see and my sense of up and down is totally whacked. A powerful pair of hands grabs me by my jacket and hurls me into the air. I catapult across the room and skid across the top of a desk, scattering papers and shit onto the floor.

I scramble to my hands and knees in time to see a blurry pair of shoes approaching. I pivot away from a zealous field goal attempt and lash out with a kick of my own. My foot connects with an ankle, I think. Whatever it is, my strike staggers my assailant enough for me to back off and stand up.

I know this guy. It's Hector! He recovers his balance and comes at me, growling in Russian. I fend off his first flurry of karate attacks, but my head is still reestablishing its connection to my body, and Hector's whirling hands knock my defenses aside. He grabs my shoulder and spins me around with my left arm bent up behind my back.

Meanwhile Winter fishes around under the desk with his bound hands. He recovers what he's looking for and points it at me. It's Li'l Bertha.

Hah, good luck with that, limpdick.

Winter comes over and presses my pistol against my temple. I stomp my heel down on Hector's toes. He grunts and lifts my arm up further. Just before my shoulder dislocates, Winter pulls the trigger.

Click.

I snarl. "Surprise, asshole."

My vision has cleared and my sense of balance has returned enough for me to go on the offensive. I leap in the air and kick Winter in the knee. He bends over. I lash out with my free arm and punch him in the head. He drops like a rock.

Hector wraps one of his arms around my chest and the other around my neck. My elbows are pinned to my sides. I wriggle back and forth, but Hector's grip gets tighter and tighter until I can't breathe. My pulse throbs in my ears.

I'm twelve. My dad drives the two of us home from the shooting range. I sit on his lap and steer while his feet work the pedals.

Everything begins to lose its color. My lungs blaze. My mouth gasps.

I'm nine. I compete in my first gymnastics nationals. Cleo is there, shouting encouragement to me as usual. Dad is there, too. It's the first time he's come to one of my meets, and I can see his stunned expression from across the arena.

I flex my arms to try to break free. My synthetic right hand brushes against the front of Hector's pants. With the last of my strength, I grab his thigh and crush his flesh between my fingers.

I'm seven. A huge snowstorm wipes out three days of school and prevents Daddy from taking his trip. The first night we all huddle around the portable radio and play cards.

I gouge five wet gorges out of his quadriceps. My fingertips meet at his femur. I rotate my arm and rip a slippery hunk of flesh out of Hector's leg.

Hector screams and shoves me away from him. I land on all fours and spin around to fend off his next attack. But there is no next attack. Hector has dropped to the floor. His leg squirts blood all over the place, and he's desperately trying to stanch the bleeding.

I gasp to regain my breath. My commphone activates. "Scarlet, I'm on station but I don't see you." The air-chopping thrum of a helicopter rotor reverberates from outside.

I'm twenty. I've got less than two minutes to avoid a terminal cruise missile overdose for myself and the only person who knows what really happened to my father.

"Sorry, Lovebird, I was unavoidably detained." I retrieve my pistol from Winter's limp grasp. I say to Winter's unhearing ears, "Too bad, jerkoff. My little girl doesn't put out for just anyone." I snap her grip into the WeaponSynch pad on my left palm. Li'l Bertha wakes up and jacks back into my Eyes-Up display.

Lovebird asks, "What's your status now?"

"I'm on my way, but my target is nonmobile."

The deep rhythm of Lovebird's engine is joined by the sharp rattling of automatic gunfire. My pilot comms, "Hurry it up."

I squat down and hoist Winter across my shoulders. Then I stand up and drag him toward the door. Time to break long-range comm-silence.

"Darwin, this is Scarlet. How are we doing for time?"

Darwin comms, "You've got ninety seconds until missile impact, Scarlet." I don't even know what Darwin looks like, but so far he's been perfectly competent. It's weird to work with a new partner. Whenever Darwin comms me, I think I hear Trick's voice in my head.

I haul Winter through the shattered doorway. He's so much taller than me that his knees scrape the ground. I lurch down the hallway and into the warehouse. Someone runs up behind me, but I keep going. Someone gets in front of me. Someone gets a biomechanically enhanced kick in the nuts from one of my German Youth jackboots. Someone effectively vanishes from the gene pool and goes down in a howling heap.

Boom minus 75 seconds. C'mon, feet! Move it! I turbo-schlep Winter to the shipping entrance where Patrick and I originally entered this place. Winter's head rams the door open with a shuddering *bonk*, and we emerge into the scorching desert heat. There's no one out here. The shipping area is deserted. Fast-moving footsteps sound from back inside the warehouse. I shrug Winter off my shoulders, and he thuds to the ground. Li'l Bertha loads herself up with some big-ass bullets. A guard pops out of the door and promptly sails back inside with a gaping hole in his chest. He leaves a long red smear on the door frame. Li'l Bertha's sensors display four remaining heat signatures. They hang back inside the entrance, no doubt stunned by their colleague's sudden transformation into a smoking wad of meat.

I holster my gun and pull three of my disk-shaped grenades from under my uniform jacket. I twist the arming knobs and shovel the frags through the doorway. Voices shout and feet clomp away from my triple helping of shrapnel strudel. I grab Winter by the collar and drag him away. The explosion is awesome. All three grenades detonate at once, and the entire shipping entrance vanishes in a cloud of fire and smoke.

My ears are ringing, but I still hear my helicopter on the way. When it gets close, the pilot radios to me.

"Scarlet, this is Lovebird. Everything all right down there?"

"Affirmative, Lovebird. Table is set for a dust-off."

"Negative on evac, Scarlet. I've been locked on. Stand by for a vehicle drop."

"Roger, Lovebird. Standing by." That sucks. He's my fastest way out from under what's about to happen here, but there's no point getting in a helicopter if the baddies have already fired missiles at it.

The chopper flies in very low, barely higher than the roof of the lab. I don't need to signal. He knows where I am by my No-Jack signal and the smoke from the ruined shipping entrance. Lovebird's helicopter zooms over the perimeter fence and momentarily slows down. A custom hatch in the bottom of the chopper opens like a pair of bomb bay doors. A machine drops out of the hatch and hits the ground about thirty feet away. It bounces off the packed sand, lands again, and settles onto its wheels. Lovebird swoops away, over the warehouse.

Boom minus 35 seconds. I swear I can hear the missile coming. The machine is a sand rail dune buggy. The vehicle's steel-tube frame holds four open wheels, two racing seats, and a big mother engine. They're fast as hell, and they're tiny so they fit me just right. I drag Winter over to the passenger side and stuff him in the seat. He mumbles like he's coming around, so I give him another knock in the head. Gunfire clatters from the other side of the lab as Lovebird makes his escape.

My new Info Operator comms, "Scarlet, impact in twenty-five seconds."

"Roger, Darwin."

"You'd better shake your ass out of there."

"Yeah, yeah. I'm shakin', I'm shakin'!" Hop-in-seat-start-engine-stomp-gas. The exhaust belches a low, throaty roar, and the vehicle launches us past the smashed shipping entrance like a frog leaping off a lily pad. I slide around the warehouse's corner and accelerate straight for the main gate. I hold the steering wheel with my right hand and aim Li'l Bertha with my left. I dial up an all-out bullet blitz. This is going to happen all at once. No point in holding back.

Darwin comms, "Fifteen seconds, Scarlet!"

There is no past or future. There's only now, this precious instant of clarity when I know I'm about to die and the important things are thrown into sharp relief.

I take my right hand off the wheel to shift up to third gear, steadying the wheel with my left knee. I rapidly comm to Raj, "Rah-Rah, I'm on my way out. Can you clear the main gate for me?"

Raj comms back, "Roger that, Scarlet. I'll be right there."

I comm to Darwin, "Hey, D! Where's my goddamned air support?"

Darwin answers, "Lovebird has to stay clear of the blast zone, but you'll have gunship cover after the air strike. For now, just get the hell out of there!"

The small guardhouse next to the main entrance has puked out four of the men who patrol the front gate. Li'l Bertha unleashes a minihell of flames, explosions, smoke, and sparks. If it's terrible, it happens to the little sheet-metal structure and the jamokes around it. Li'l Bertha demolishes the gatehouse so quickly that some guards can't even get out of the way before it collapses on them.

Raj makes a dramatic entrance by smashing his produce truck straight through the gate. He keeps the engine at full throttle as he cranks the steering wheel over to the right. A half-moon of sand sprays out from under the rear wheels of his truck as it slides through a 180-degree skid and kicks up a billowing cloud of dust. The shattered gate bashes into the guard tower and breaks one of its legs. The tall structure falls over and dumps its occupants into Raj's maelstrom. We've created such intense chaos that the two guards who have evaded the collapsing guardhouse and the toppling tower come completely unglued, drop their guns, and dive for cover.

I flash past Raj's truck and roar out of the compound. Both of my feet jam down on the gas pedal, and the buggy bucks like a racehorse in heat. We hurtle toward the horizon, hammering our way to Riyadh over a sand-strewn two-lane highway. Scattered one-story houses and shops blur by.

"Darwin, we're out!" I comm. "Where to?"

"Proceed to this location, Scarlet. And hang on to something!" Darwin comms me a set of coordinates. They point to the middle of Riyadh. He continues, "Impact in three, two, one—"

Suddenly my sand rail buggy hops up and down even though the road is smooth. My car casts an unnaturally sharp, short-lived shadow straight ahead. Then a long, shattering explosion erupts from behind me, back at the lab. The concussion is so big, it feels like an earthquake. The buggy bounces off the road into someone's vegetable garden and stalls out on me. The locals squeal and point back the way I came, where a colossal mushroom cloud of dust and fire rises from the desert. Dark spots in the debris fountain indicate large objects that weren't instantly incinerated. It's quite a sight, but I can't stay to admire it. I start the buggy back up. An old man sees me plow my way out of the garden, and he shakes his fist at me. His mouth moves, but my roaring engine drowns out his voice. The man's inability to make himself heard reminds me to switch on my signal jammer.

Moments later a massive dust storm rushes past, covers the sun, and brings instant dusk to the whole area. The explosion continues to echo in my ears as sand chisels into my skin. Visibility drops to about ten feet. I slow down a little while I drive around all the rubbernecking bozos who gawk at the source of the noise and smoke. Everyone is so distracted by the DTET—short for Discreetly Targeted Event: Thermobaric—that I make it all the way to the outer neighborhoods of the city proper without anyone paying the slightest attention to me.

A column of German police charges past me, going the other way. I have to pull over to allow a row of fire trucks to go wailing by, toward the blast site. The DTET is sucking every Kraut city official toward it like a colossal lager whirlpool. Excellent! This will help clear my path into and out of the city.

Mixed with the swirling sandstorm is a cloud of gray flakes. It almost looks like snow as the flakes cover the road and buildings with a light gray blanket. The sky is slowly getting lighter. Visibility still sucks, but this fall-out fog does a great job of hiding me and Winter as we drive into and through downtown Riyadh. I could be dressed like Bozo the Clown right now and not get a single glance from people.

I turn off the main street into a crowded residential neighborhood of twisty little streets that all look alike. My coordinates lead me to a narrow three-story tan house sandwiched into a dense row of two- and three-story houses. Red shutters cover the windows, and the ground floor is a garage. I screech to a stop in front of the house, jump out, open the wooden garage door, hop back in the buggy, and then drive inside. I slam the door shut, then hoist Winter out of his seat, and lug him up to the second floor of the house.

It's the kitchen. The place is clean, but the old appliances, chipped counters, and exposed electrical wiring show how long it's been since the interior was updated. Although the room would never get the Good Housekeeping Seal of Approval, the age of the decor is convenient because I need something to restrain Winter. I rip two lengths of wire off the wall and use them to tie him to a chair.

So far, so good. Now we wait for the DTET-induced dust storm to die down so Lovebird can come pick us up.

CHAPTER 38

The only way we could think of to prevent the Blades of Persia from finding Winter was to jam his No-Jack signal. I could try to remove his No-Jack like we did to Pavel Tarasov in Paris, but that's pretty serious surgery and I'm no Med-Tech. Carving this turkey up with my combat knife and no anesthetic would be quite satisfying, but my mission is to capture this fuckhead, not kill him.

Good Scarlet, not kill.

The jammer is a heavy little box I've got in my jacket pocket. It works only at very short range, but that's all I need for this mission. Jamming Winter's No-Jack also blocks my commphone, so I'm on my own for now. My instructions are to wait here until Lovebird picks us up. If Lovebird doesn't show by 1:15 p.m. local time, I'll have to stop jamming long enough to check in with Darwin.

I'm searching Winter for weapons when he finally wakes up. I back off for a minute in case he's feeling heroic. After taking a moment to get his bearings, he looks at me, and then he tilts his head back in despair. He barks a couple of words in Arabic and then lets his head slump forward onto his chest.

I say, "Welcome to the first day of the rest of your life, pal."

"After a failure like sis, sere is no life," he groans. "My people will never believe in me now."

"Oh, I wouldn't say that." I resume patting him down. "They'll believe all kinds of shit about you. They'll believe you're a two-faced crook. They'll believe that you ratted out fellow Arabs to the West." I lean into his view. "They'll believe that Winter was a self-serving lunatic who wanted to end civilization."

"Civilization." He shakes his head. "If sis is civiliza-tion, sen perhaps it is just as well I am finished," he de-clares.

"Oh ho, no. You're not finished." I haven't found any weapons or suicide agents in his clothes, but I'm not done yet. "You've been recruited by the United States Justice Department to help combat government corrup-tion." I stand behind him and slide my hands down the back of his sweaty shirt, my fingers pressing through his back hair, looking for anything irregular. Then I do the same for his chest and stomach. Yuck.

He tenses up, clearly uncomfortable at being groped like this. He grumbles like he's about to say something, but he changes his mind.

The only surface of Winter's body I haven't explored is up between his legs. I'm just going to presume that he doesn't have anything in his ass. He's a busy guy, after all, and I'm sure someone of his social standing is not going to yank a derringer out of his butt every time he has to take a shit. I unbutton his pants and tug them down to his knees. The things I do for my work.

Out in the street, there's a lot of bustling activity and noisy conversation. It sounds like the local citizens are still freaked out by the huge explosion in the desert. I peek out the window and see that the dust has mostly settled down now. The ground and rooftops are covered in those gray flakes mixed with sand. It's almost normal daylight again. I walk back to Winter while he looks toward the window and listens to the noise from out-side. He spins his head back to me as I slide my hands up between his thighs.

It's more awful, sweaty hairiness, but finally I find something. Under the skin of his left thigh is what feels like a large button that squirms around as my fingers try to get hold of it. Ah hah! I stand up and draw my combat knife out of its holster under my left armpit.

Winter declares, "You do not look like your father."

"Oh, yeah? When was the last time you saw him?"

"Much more recently san you, little one." He grins as he says this.

I keep my eyes on Winter's face as I hold my knife. I step away from him.

This would be so easy.

Winter sees me hesitate and says, "Go ahead. It will be poetic. You can finish what your father started."

So easy to end it all.

Winter grits his teeth and growls, "Go on, Alix! Finish it!"

He knows my real name! Did Fredericks tell him everything about ExOps?

"I *am* finishing what he started." I stalk back to his chair and squeeze the fingers of my right hand around the suspicious object under the skin of his thigh.

He squirms and says, "Ah, but your kind is only satisfied with one finish."

"What the fuck would you know about 'my' kind?" I slice the knife though the skin over the hard object and squeeze a pudgy little plastic disk out of his leg while Winter grits his teeth and makes noises like "Ach!" and "Ow!" I hold up the blood-smeared disk. "Tell me what this is."

"No." Winter shoots little sabers from his eyes. "And do not waste your time with threats. If you were an assassin, I would already be dead."

I spin my knife over in my palm and jab it into the seat of the chair between his legs. The knife's edge takes a tiny bite out of his scrotum. Winter presses his eyes shut and groans into the back of his teeth, but he still doesn't answer me.

"You're right, tough guy. You would be dead. But you're useless as a corpse. You will, however, be perfectly useful as a falsetto." I bring my arm up over my head and clearly aim a giant stab right at the center of his party zone.

"Wait!" he cries. "It is a suicide tab. The poison is released when se device is firmly pressed for five seconds. It is a manual version of what your Infiltrators have."

I lower my knife, drop the disk on the floor, and crush it under my boot. Then I wrap a hand towel from one of the kitchen drawers around his thigh and begin to pull his pants up. I can smell coffee on his breath.

I ask, "That was you who kidnapped my mother, wasn't it?"

"It was supposed to be you, but yes, sose were my men."

"Why the hell did you blow up my house?"

Winter says, "A regrettable misunderstanding. In my haste I hired men I had not worked with before. I found sem lacking in . . . refinement, which is why I abandoned sem to Extreme Operations' vengeance."

I hoist his pants past his knees. "How do you know so much about us?"

He grimaces as I jostle him around, getting his pants back on. "I know so much about you because I employ many people like you."

"You don't employ anyone now, asshole."

He looks up at me. The sun is coming back out. It glows through the shutters onto his face and casts his features into sharp shadow. "No, not anymore," he says. "But after what you have shown me today, I'd never be satisfied with sem again."

I finish getting his pants back up and sneer. "Flattery will get you nowhere."

"It is true. I have spent most of my adult life recruiting talent. I think that even your father did not have the raw ability I see in you."

I lean in close to Winter and bark, "Stop. Talking. About. My. Father."

I check the time. It's 1:21 P.M. and no Lovebird yet. I

turn my back to Winter so he can't see my face. I reach in my jacket and shut off the signal jammer.

"Darwin, my taxi is late."

Darwin was waiting for me and instantly replies. "Scarlet, be advised we cannot get an evac to your current location. There are too many competitive units in the area. I'm sure they're searching for the subject. You'll need to relocate to the following position ASAP." He sends me new coordinates to a location outside the city. Damn. I wondered how they'd land a helicopter in this rat's nest, and it turns out they won't. Darwin continues, "I'll send these to Raj, too. He'll rendezvous with you en route."

"Roger," I comm. "Out." I switch the jammer back on. Then I untie Winter from the chair, leaving his hands bound and his ankles tied to the ends of a twenty-inch-long piece of wire. He can walk but not run. I lead him down the stairs and into the garage.

I shove him into the dune buggy's passenger seat. Through the garage door, I hear the sound of a car approaching with its engine revving wildly. I turn up my modified hearing. Make that several cars approaching.

There's no way they triangulated Winter's No-Jack signal in the few seconds I had the jammer turned off. The only way they'd find us so fast is if Winter gave them directions to this exact house. But that's impossible. He was out cold until we were inside the house.

"Who's that outside?" I yell at him, and grab his shirt-front. The bastard smirks at me like he's pulled a fast one. Suddenly I know what happened. He *wasn't* out cold. Winter woke up in the buggy and played possum. He watched where I took him and commed the address to his cronies the moment my jammer was off.

I holler, "You fucker!"

I should have guessed how sneaky this douche bag can be. Now I'm about to be ass deep in bad guys. Clearly Winter needs a lesson in kidnapping etiquette, so I punch him in the head again. While I buckle his nearly unconscious butt into the seat, the cars roar up the street and stop right outside.

I switch off the jammer. "Darwin, I've got a situation."

"Roger that, Scarlet. Multiple hostiles are outside your current position. Raj is thirty seconds away. Stay on comm and get out of there!"

"Roger, Darwin. Exiting stage left."

Time for some serious driving. I jump in the driver's seat and fire up the ignition. The engine is deafeningly loud inside the garage. I set Li'l Bertha on my lap and shift into reverse. I do a brake stand to build up the revs as high as I can, then release the brakes. The buggy fires backward right through the wooden garage door and into the street. I slam the shifter into first gear and leave five thousand miles' worth of rubber howling on the white-flake-covered cobblestones. There are hostiles out here, all right, but they're all still in their cars. I take off down the street. Four big sedans full of Winter's guys take off after me.

"Darwin, get me some cover and find me an exit!" My feet do the Detroit polka across the pedals while my left hand steers and my right hand chucks a grenade behind us. My Madrenaline is flowing freely, so time slows down. Crap, I threw my grenade too soon. Three bad-guy cars drive over it before it explodes under the last vehicle and detonates the gas tank. The disintegrating automobile flies up in the air and crashes through the front wall of a house, which bursts into flames.

Wow, that was one hell of a grenade.

"Scarlet, take your next left. Air cover inbound." Darwin leads me through the twisty little streets. I sling the buggy into the next left. "Okay, straight through this big plaza."

He can't see that the plaza is crammed with big, heavy carts and wagons selling produce and shit. It must be market day. I slam on the brakes and slide between two screaming women. The lead chase car crashes into my rear bumper, jolting me and Winter in our seats. I race around the cobblestone square. It's big but almost completely hemmed in by houses and stores. One of Winter's drivers has blocked the way I got in. I'm trapped, but since all the shoppers have simultaneously decided to take their business elsewhere, I've got some room to maneuver.

A dark shadow passes across the plaza, accompanied by a roaring clatter. "Scarlet, this is Lovebird. How can I provide excellent service for you today?"

"Lovebird! Take these fuckers out!" His helicopter has black smoke coming out of the engine. He must have taken a hit after dropping off my buggy.

"Roger that, Scarlet. You'll need to create some separation first. The targets are too close to you."

You want separation? Fine, I'll give you separation. There's one other exit from the plaza, but it's jammed with crates, barrels, and escaping pedestrians. I see room for motorbikes and people on foot to pass through but not enough for a four-wheeled vehicle. At least not for a four-wheeled vehicle that's actually *on* all four of its wheels. I execute a screeching e-brake turn to get us lined up with this little exit, floor it, and head for the crowded passage, honking my horn as fast as I can.

I glance over at Winter. He's awake. His eyes are wide open, and his mouth is stuck in an O shape. I run the driver-side tires up a small staircase and crank the steering wheel so the buggy tilts up onto the two passenger-side wheels. Winter looks down at the ground whipping past his seat, then up at me. He's so petrified with fear that he can't even speak.

I laugh down at him and, over the roar of the buggy's engine, holler my best Deep South war cry. "Whooohoooo!" He takes his eyes off mine as we bounce between the two rows of containers. People scatter wildly. Many leap on top of the crates, their eyes as bright as little moons in the shade of the arched passageway. My buggy knocks over the last wagon on the right, and veggies fly everywhere. A big tomato bounces off Winter's nose. I cackle at how his expression shifts from terror, to indignation at being hit by a tomato, and then back to terror again. The buggy drops down onto all four tires after we soar out of the plaza.

Lovebird uncorks a sparkling bottle of ass blaster on all the penned-in pursuit vehicles. His 20-mm cannon fire hoses down the bad guys and makes a loud ripping-fabric sound that harmonizes wonderfully with the screaming victims, crunching metal, and shattering glass.

"Yeah, Lovebird! Smoke those jackasses!" *Trick would have loved this.*

Speaking of Trick, Darwin is just as fast as he was. "Scarlet, right 90!"

Ninety feet later we career onto another single-lane road on the right. It's a slightly wider street, meaning the houses don't scrape my buggy as I roar by them. We're really cookin' now. I haven't felt this good on a job since I chased Pavel Tarasov up the Eiffel Tower. Three more dark sedans slide around a corner and take position behind us.

"C'mon, Darwin, what's next? There's more of these fuckin' assholes behind me!"

"Scarlet, straight 2,000. Let 'er rip!" Darwin is in the groove, too. I crush the gas pedal, the buggy accelerates to eightysomething miles per hour, and we flash down the one-lane road. Some of the bumps launch us a few inches off the ground. When we're in the air, the engine snorts to its redline and the unencumbered wheels spin even faster. Then we land, and our seats kick us in the ass. *You must be this tall to ride the Jolt-a-Butt.*

The pursuit cars are still right on my tail. Their engines wail, and their tires thunder across the ancient pavement. I grab my pistol and blindly lay down some suppression fire behind me. The chase cars don't back off. Winter's people aren't wimps; they won't discourage that easily.

I put Li'l Bertha back in her holster and grab another grenade. This time I'll cook it for a couple of seconds so any close pursuit will be caught in the blast. I pull the pin with my teeth and hold the grenade under Winter's nose so he can see me pop off the safety handle.

He yells, "Throw it! Crazy demon bitch! Throw the grenade!"

I toss it behind us as Lovebird comms in, "Scarlet, be advised that three—"

The grenade explodes under the first car, kills the driver, and slams the blazing mess into a wall.

"—make that two—"

The second car plows into the now-exploding lead vehicle.

"—okay, one! One vehicle in pursuit." The third sedan swerves around the two wrecks and barrels after me.

I begin to comm, "Lovebird, can you take care of—"

The chopper pilot answers my unfinished question by nearly sawing the third vehicle in half with his automatic cannons. The car catches fire and crashes into the back of someone's house.

Darwin comms in again. "Scarlet, left 150." I face front, put both hands back on the wheel, and slow down a little. This job has gone well so far, no need to fuck it up. I take the left after 150 feet and keep an eye out for more bad guys. A cloud of black smoke billows from the street I just exited.

"Darwin, can you advise regarding pursuit?"

"Negative, Scarlet. There's too much smoke. Lovebird, do you have eyes on any competition?"

"Negative, Darwin. We're lookin' good."

I keep driving. Still there's nobody back there. I think we got 'em all. I'm about to appoint myself mayor of Smugville when a huge truck pulls across the intersection up ahead and stops, blocking the street. Guys pile out of the back of the truck. Lots of guys, with lots of guns.

"Fuckin' A, Imad. How many floyds do you have?" I shout at Winter while I comm, "Lovebird, smoke that truck! Darwin, roadblock 200, get me an exit."

A heartbeat later, Darwin comms, "Turn right!" I turn right, and the buggy bounces over the curb. Straight at a house. It's got a first-floor garage like the safe house had. I hit the brakes, but since the buggy isn't on the ground, we don't slow down at all. Winter and I both duck our heads as we crash through the garage door. There's nothing parked inside, so we fly completely through what turns out to be more of a carport than a garage. We blast into someone's backyard and get stuck in their garden, which backs on to an alley. Goddamn gardens! I slam the buggy back and forth from reverse to first as I try to rock us out of the soft dark brown dirt.

A loud screech on the street behind us makes me look in the rearview mirror. Another dark sedan stops in the street, and the door pops open. I'm reaching for Li'l Bertha when I see Raj's giant head emerge from the car, followed by his giant body. While he opens the back door of his car, he looks at me with a grin and comms, "Darwin, please tell Scarlet that her team driving skills need some more work."

Meanwhile, Lovebird hammers the guys near the truck. They shoot back at him and make a terrific racket of it. Lovebird's helicopter flies over the alley, followed by a storm of tracer fire. The black cloud coming out of his engine is much heavier than before. Lovebird comms, "Darwin, my engine just took a critical hit. I've got to get on the ground ASAP."

I look away from the helicopter to glance back at Raj. He hauls his Bitchgun out of his car's backseat and props it against his side-of-beef-size shoulder. The Bitchgun belches flame and drowns out the world. The weapon's concussion shakes the dust on the road into a round, flat cloud floating away from Raj's feet. I hear a huge explosion, and the ground trembles. Raj must have hit the truck's gas tank.

He looks at me and comms, "Scarlet, this is Raj. Consider this area secure."

"Thanks, Raj. Thanks, Lovebird. I'll get you guys

each a case of beer for that one." I finally break the buggy loose from the garden. "Darwin, which way?"

"Take a left, Scarlet," Darwin comms. "Raj, continue down the street to cover Scarlet's flank."

I gun the engine and swerve left into the incredibly small alley. The buggy barely fits. A donkey would barely fit. Sparks fly as we scrape and bounce off the walls. I try to make sure Winter's side hits more often than mine. I take a second to glance at him. His eyes are shut tight, and his mouth moves rapidly. I think he's praying.

"Pray all you want, fucko. Nothing can save you now!"

He looks over at me. His face is slick with sweat and covered in bits of paper, little chunks of tomato, streaks of dirt, and other debris. He breathes in ragged, wheezing gulps, almost audible over the roar of the buggy's engine. Now that I take a good look at him, I notice he looks terrible, like he's about to die from fright. I think I've discovered a new interrogation technique.

"Had enough?" I yell over the cacophony as we smash our way down the alley.

"Yes! Please. Please stop. I will call off my people, only please stop!"

"Darwin, please advise on directions and pursuit."

"Scarlet, right 180. Hostiles are still closing on your location."

I count to 180 feet and bang a beautiful power-drifting right into a fairly large street. It's got space for two vehicles to pass each other safely and even has room on the sides for pedestrians. It feels like the autobahn after that alley. The buggy has overheated, and all the indicator lights are on. I can't tell if they're real problems or if I've simply driven the poor thing insane. Behind me, Raj roars around the corner and follows me for a block before skidding to a halt and getting out of his car, his Bitchgun at the ready.

"Scarlet, straight 3,000. Hostiles seem to be breaking off pursuit."

"Roger that, Darwin. Lovebird, what do you see?"

Lovebird comms, "Negative, Scarlet. I'm already on the ground."

Darwin comms in. "Roger that, Lovebird, we'll get you a ride. Raj, do you have a visual on pursuit?"

Raj comms, "Three vehicles full of competition just stopped in the middle of the street and reversed direction. I think we're good, Shortcake. Keep going. I'll cover your exit."

I slow down and glance over at Winter. He's white as a sheet and drenched in sweat. "Darwin, be advised the target may be having a heart attack."

Darwin laughs. "Scarlet, be advised he's not the only one."

CHAPTER 39

"Still with me?" I sneer at Winter.

He takes a few moments answering. "Yes, I suppose so," he finally replies.

Winter and I are in an abandoned bunker outside of Riyadh. Back in town, Raj is patrolling the road that leads here to make sure Winter's dogs don't come sniffing around. Lovebird has found a quiet place to repair his wounded helicopter. He commed a few minutes ago, saying he should be in the air pretty soon. So far, the DTET is still drawing attention away from the Slaytona 500 we just smeared across the city. Sooner or later, though, the local authorities will know us by the trail of dead.

I try to mentally compel Lovebird to work faster so I can escape this country-size furnace. Poor Raj has to stay here for a few more days. He's going to lurk around Riyadh to confirm that White Stone Research and the Darius Covenant were completely destroyed.

After Winter called off his people, I followed Darwin's directions out of the city and parked my dune buggy behind a smashed-in corner of this blazingly hot bunker. It must be 130 degrees in here. My face is streaked with sweat, my throat is as dry as the Bible, and my legs are wobbling from all the Madrenaline I did today. Every few minutes my hands start to vibrate, and I have to drizzle some Kalmers to make them stop.

Now that this mission is almost done, I just want to go home and see Cleo. I miss the way she smiles when she smooths my hair away from my face. I catch myself

daydreaming about what I'll look like when I'm her age.
I wipe my face on my sleeve and shake my head to clear
my mind. *C'mon, Scarlet, focus!*

I keep watch by a window with a good view of the
road. Except for that strip of dust-covered concrete, all
I see is the bright blue dome of the sky covering a whole
lot of nothing. It's like being in a giant sand-filled frying
pan that stretches to forever in all directions. I haven't
seen any vehicles drive by, but I still have to be wary.
Even though Winter ordered his people to back off,
some of them might take it upon themselves to keep
looking for their boss.

Winter's heart attack was only his reaction to the ex-
cessive quantity of stimulation. Being kidnapped, beaten
up, and then scared shitless by a big dose of Scarlet's
wild driving techniques was too much for him. His face
is still pale, but he's lost that crazed I'm-about-to-die
look. I've got him tied to a bench. He's stared at me
since I put him there. His rumpled, no-longer-white shirt
is dark with sweat stains. His hair, although still gelled
in place, is salted with sand and flaked with bits of debris from all the shit I ran the dune buggy through.

He's about to say something, but then he thinks better
of it. His eyes reveal some bitterness, but it's mixed with
something else. He's checking me out, but his gaze lacks
the urgency of plain old horniness. It's more like how
my martial arts coach used to look at the really talented
kids in his class.

Neither of us speaks for a few minutes while I keep an
eye on the road. Finally I say over my shoulder, "Cat got
your tongue, Imad?"

"I find myself wishing your abilities were not so mis-
guided," he says.

"I could say the same about you, bub."

"My destiny is clear, little one."

"Destiny, my ass." I turn from the window and growl,
"What is your 'destiny,' anyway?"

"To remove se oppressive foreign regimes sat have enslaved my people."

"So you can replace them with your own oppressive regime?" Finally, something to do with all the history I choked down at school.

Winter studies me for a moment and asks, "What makes you so certain sat would happen?"

"Because your people have always been ruled by power-crazed nut jobs."

He grins. "We have sat in common."

"We've only got one thing in common, jackass." I stride across the room. "How did you capture my father?"

"Go to se Devil," he replies.

Big mistake.

My foot crashes into his groin like a wrecking ball. These German Youth boots are terrific for this. Winter cries out, tips over on the bench, and wheezes for breath. I pull out Li'l Bertha and press her barrel down on his right knee. "This crazy demon *bitch* asked you a question, motherfucker!"

He clenches his teeth while he sputters, "All right, all right. By Allah . . ."

I stand back. He stays on his side, groaning in pain. I nailed him good. Guys are total suckers for that move— one of the many reasons women make better spies.

Winter catches his breath. "As you and Extreme Operations have no doubt discovered, I needed technology from Carbon for my Darius Covenant."

"Darwin," I comm, "you can hear this, right?"

"Affirmative, Scarlet," he comms.

I say to Winter, "Yeah, we figured that out. To generate your anaerobic bacteria faster."

Winter raises one eyebrow. He didn't know we'd uncovered that part. "Impressive," he says quietly. He gingerly sits up straight. "My transactions with German intelligence brought me special privileges, but it was not enough to get me se clearance I needed. My contacts refused to even discuss Carbon with me. Then your father created se opportunity I had been looking for."

I cross my arms over my chest. "How'd he do that?"

"His actions during se oil embargo, specifically in Berlin, enraged se Reich. Sey promised anything to se person who could deliver se Beast of Berlin alive." Winter leans back against the wall. He winces as little cartoon stars and planets orbit his groin. "Price was no object. Se bounty was enormous, but it was not money I wanted. I brought a proposition to my contact in se Abwehr. It was accepted, and I began looking for a way to acquire ExOps' star Level.

"Your father was an excellent field agent—intelligent, fast, and capable under pressure. I observed him for years, as did many other people. Philip Nico was se target of many abduction attempts. All of sem failed, with dramatically fatal results. Clearly, to pursue Big Bertha was to sign one's own death warrant. I decided to turn se game around. I would make *him* come after *me*. I felt it would be unexpected, even for him, to be lured in sis way."

Christ. I was eight years old at the end of the embargo. When my dad got captured, I was twelve. All those years, while Dad and I were going to Dairy Queen, this lunatic was planning the end of my father's life.

Winter stares at my face. I'm sporting a ferocious scowl. I unfold my arms and plant my hands on my hips. The muscles in my throat are so tight that it makes my voice hoarse.

"Keep talking, bucko," I grate. It's difficult to listen to this story, but I know how it turns out.

Winter tries to wipe his face on his upper arm, but I've tied him too tightly. Sweat runs through his beard and down his neck. "Soon after I made sis decision, I was contacted by an American intelligence officer. He presented me with exactly se situation I had imagined. He sent Big Bertha after me and provided what I needed to capture him in perfect condition."

My God, it was Fredericks's idea.

I comm, "Cyrus, you there?"

"Yes," Cyrus's comm voice says. "I'm here."

"Did you hear that?"

"I did. See if you can get him to name the American officer."

"But we know it was—"

Cyrus interrupts me. "The Justice Department needs Winter to say it, Scarlet. Ask him who it was."

I rest my hand on the hilt of my knife, making sure Winter can see it, and demand, "Who was the officer?"

Winter licks perspiration off his lip. "He worked through his agents. I never knew his name."

Of course this son of a bitch isn't gonna make it easy.

"Yes, you do, and you know what?" I snarl. "So do I."

Winter narrows his eyes and sits very still.

"Lemme tell ya about that pal of yours, Winty. He's so far up the food chain that he reports directly to the Executive Intelligence Chairman. When we found out about your goddamn petron bombs, the chairman turned to this man to plan our response." I wave my hand over my head the way Jacques does when he tells a story. "You remember that giant-ass cruise missile? That was your pal's idea! In fact, *you* were supposed to be under that sucker when it cratered your lab." I lean in close and hiss, "*That* was his idea, too."

Winter's nostrils flare, and his eyebrows crawl toward his eyes like a pair of angry spiders.

I step back. "What was *not* his idea was pulling you out of there." I poke my chest and shake my head. "He doesn't know I'm here."

Winter's eyebrows press closer to his eyes. His grinding teeth radiate sharp screeching sounds.

"When was the last time you talked to him, Wintergreen?"

Our ongoing surveillance of Fredericks's comm calls tells us it was probably—

"Yesterday?" I yell. "No wonder he knew exactly when to bomb your mad scientist's lair. Man, with friends like that, who needs—"

"All right!" Winter shouts. He's really sweating hard now, and his face has turned pale again.

I comm, "Darwin, where's that damn chopper? Winter looks like he's having another coronary."

"Lovebird's on the way, Scarlet. ETA in three minutes. Keep going. You're doing great."

I tilt my head to one side and hold Winter's glare. "Well?" I say.

"I will tell your superiors."

I slap his face. "He's *my* father. You'll tell *me*, shitbird!"

Winter's responds, "First I want immunity from se U.S. and Greater Germany."

That's it. "How about immunity from getting your fucking balls hacked off?" I unsheathe my fighting knife and step between his knees. I slash the front of his pants open and shove his yucky, uncircumcised penis out of the way. Then I press the edge of my knife against his hairy scrotum.

In the movies, the hero would give the villain one last chance before castrating him. Actually, in the movies the hero probably wouldn't be castrating the villain at all, but either way, this is not the goddamn movies. I immediately begin sawing off Winter's love spuds.

He screams, "*Ahh!* It was Fredericks! *Stop!* Oh, God! It was Jakob Fredericks!"

"Scarlet, stop!" It's Darwin. "We got it!"

Cyrus comms, "Scarlet, if you terminate that asset, I'll kick you straight into hell."

I let go of Winter's man jigglies. My hand is covered in blood. "Darwin," I comm, "you'd better tell Lovebird to step on it."

TO: Administration Supervisor Albright, Extreme
Operations Division
FROM: Office of the Front Desk, Extreme Operations
Division
SUBJECT: Paternity Leave for Special Agent Philip Nico
(L8)

Madeleine,

Please be advised that Agent Nico will start his three-week paternity leave effective today. Philip's wife Cleo gave birth to their daughter, Alixandra Janina Nico, early this morning. The mother and baby are both doing well.

Between the two of us, I think this will be a good break for Philip. He'd never admit it, but his excellent work in Southeast Asia has taken a toll on him. I will assign Senior Analyst Fredericks to cover his Information meetings until Philip returns at the end of the month.

Sincerely,
William Colby

CHAPTER 40

Air travel makes me drink too much. Maybe it's the tedium of it. Jet-setting used to be fun, but now I do it so often that it's a drag. I'm tempted to pass the time by wrestling with the waitresses. I'll bet they're a lot tougher than they look.

Winter sits next to me, by the window. He's taking a chemically induced twelve-hour power nap. I wanted to stick him in pressurized cargo, but the Protectors talked me out of it. Cyrus sent a quartet of bodyguards to accompany me and my big fish back to the States. Two sit in front of me and Winter, and two sit behind.

My hand clings to a glass of schnapps and soda as I watch the clouds drift past the little windows. I'm technically still on duty, so drinking alcohol isn't exactly kosher, but to hell with it. My mission is completed. I could chat up the Protectors, but they're only Level 3s, and I don't feel like regaling them with war stories. Besides, I'm enjoying the fact that I'm actually conscious for this return trip.

I'll finally meet Patrick's replacement when he picks me up at the airport. I'm glad Cyrus had him work from Washington. He did great, but this snatch job was so frantic that there was no way a partner could have kept up. Besides, I wasn't ready to meet him yet.

I once asked my dad how he dealt with his friends getting killed. After a long pause he said, "I make more friends." I can't make another Trick, though. I loved him as much as I've loved anyone except maybe my father. Mom, too, especially lately. Now that she's seen how good I am at my job, I think it's easier for her to accept it. She'll be waiting for me at the ExOps hotel. I'm hoping we can buy another house. We're sort of falling over each other in our little apartment.

I flag down a waitress and ask her how long until we land. She curtly tells me, "About fifty minutes," and then stalks away. What is it with stewardesses? I mean, I *try* to be friendly. When I told this woman to take all my empty soda cans away, I offered to show her my scars, but that made her even grouchier.

My relationship with this particular stewardess went down the tubes when she tried to confiscate my flasks of schnapps. Technically I *am* underage, I guess. But I figure this big-ass handgun strapped to me has got to be worth a few years. Plus, these gals work for American Airlines. They're used to ferrying Levels around. Who are they to tell me I can't have a little drink? Damn aerofascists.

I swig some of my schnapps and review everything that went down yesterday. Lovebird finally got his chopper repaired and flew it to my abandoned bunker. When he got there, he gave me a hard time about my captive's physical state. I laughed in his face and launched into a meticulously detailed description of the gruesome expirations of my previous captured assets. What happened to Winter was nothing. I didn't even cut his hoo-hahs off. He's breathing, and all his body parts are still connected.

Lovebird stopped lecturing me and patched up Winter's paltry fourteen gashes and lacerations. Then we flew to a small airfield. Winter and I boarded a small plane with fake flight manifests and innocently reentered the grid at Riyadh's big airport.

While I waited for the flight, I commed with Cyrus about all the crazy shit Winter told me and my trusty commphone. The stuff about Fredericks was incredible. He really can track a Level's No-Jack module through his commphone. During the Blades job, that bastard forwarded my dad's every move to Kazim Nazari.

Even so, Winter took his time luring my father. Fredericks was impatient, but Winter remained cautious. Winter knew so much about what my father was doing that he thought it might be a setup to snare *him* instead. He also knew Big Bertha would be suspicious if it was too easy to infiltrate the inner ranks of the Blades of Persia.

Winter was eventually convinced that this really was the opportunity Fredericks said it was. Kazim brought my father to Winter's secret residence in Baghdad. There he incapacitated the mighty Level 20 Liberator with a refreshing cocktail of whiskey and neurotoxins. The powerful poison, formulated at White Stone Research Institute, was intended for horses. According to Winter, it barely worked. My father trashed an entire floor of the house before he went down. Then Kazim brought Dad to the Abwehr office in Baghdad.

I asked Cyrus what we were doing to find my father. He said that would be impossible right now since our relationship with Germany has fallen off a cliff. Apparently some crazy American covert agent trashed the Chemistry Institute at Zurich University, used the German Youth program as cover, and then carved a swath of destruction through Riyadh.

She's also indirectly responsible for a dreadful amount of collateral damage. My German Youth group leader insisted on searching White Stone for me instead of stranding me as we expected. When the cruise missile hit, he and his fifty kids were instantly catapulted to the big jamboree in the sky.

The news of this event was uncontainable. The German public is mad as hell, and they've told the chancellor that they're not going to take it anymore. All across Europe the normally factious Josef *Sechs*-Packs have fused into a unified, raging mob. The crap Dad pulled in

'68 landed him on the Reich's ten most wanted list, and this is over fifty times worse.

Our diplomatic relationship with Greater Germany is chronically uneasy, even in the best of times. What we have most in common is that neither of us has *anything* in common with Russia or China. If the alliance between Germany and the United States were breached, both states would be vulnerable to an attack by the combination of the other two superpowers. The reverse is also true. If we could somehow isolate Russia from China, the Germans and us Americans could knock them off one at a time. Then we'd go after each other.

There's plenty of conflict within these alliances, but it's mostly a war of sneaky shits trying to outsmart other sneaky shits. Ironically, Extreme Operations frequently tries to outsmart the covert agencies of our ally, Greater Germany. When this gets too hot, like now, we have to back off for a while.

Cyrus tried to make me feel better and reminded me that we know Dad's alive. The Info people are hatching a rescue plan with our intel from Zurich and the data doozies Winter has coughed up about Carbon.

We already knew about the initial generation of cloning research, or Gen-1. That resulted in the first human clone and knocked the scientific community on its collective ass. The next round, Gen-2, was the pursuit of rapid-growth techniques so a clone could grow to adulthood in a fraction of the time it normally takes. After nearly two decades, the Carbon scientists succeeded in compressing a clone's first twenty years of physical development into only two years. The problem is, the Gen-2 clones have the emotional maturity of a two-year-old. It turns out the experiences that shape our characters still have to be lived through. There's no shortcut. For now.

Earlier this year, Carbon launched Gen-3. They're trying to map the consciousness of a living person into the minds of clones. It's called psychogenesis, and it's the craziest fucking idea since . . . well, since rapid-growth clones. This is why everyone in Washington has wigged out. Each generation of Carbon research results in a scientific advance so significant that it might as well be a miracle. If anybody can invent psychogenesis, it's the lunatics at Carbon.

Gen-3 brings up really confusing questions about the future meanings of maturity, individuality, and mortality. When people get old or very sick, Gen-3 would let them transfer their accumulated abilities and experiences into a much younger clone of themselves. Fifty years later, they do it again, and again, and never die. Their worn-out old bodies will need to be disposed of, but I'm sure the Germans can solve an excess population problem.

Gen-3 also brought up all the nuttiness that's happened to me in the last five months. One of the minds the researchers want to try duplicating is my father's. *What the heck*, they probably thought, *Big Bertha's just rotting away in a Gestapo tomb, anyway. Let's make more of him and see what happens.*

My dad's transfer from the Gestapo to the Carbon Program showed up in one of the reports that Winter accessed. This report surprised the hell out of ol' Wintergreen, since he thought the Beast had been dead for eight years. He decided that his former partner in crime—Fredericks—should know about this, since taking down one Big Bertha was hard enough. If Gen-3 really worked, there would be multiple Big Berthas, all with vivid memories of what they had done to him. Winter had Kazim contact Fredericks through Hector, and the rest has been a nonstop jolt-o-matic thrill ride ever since.

The ride isn't over yet, either. Snatching Winter may only be the beginning, because the Germans are threatening to leave the Pan-Atlantic Alliance. This would expose the United States to the predatory tendencies of Russia and China. Germany, too, unless Berlin decides to join the Asian Pact.

The Capitol Hill bigwigs are pulling all-nighters to deal with this emergency. The man at the head of the table is the president. At the president's right side is his chief strategist, Jakob Fredericks. The slimy fuck is planning our response to this disaster, and until we're out of it, he's considered the most important man in the USA.

Director Chanez has been strongly advised by his friends at the Justice Department that Fredericks is untouchable right now. We can't even let Winter out of the bag, because we're worried that Fredericks will find a way to discredit or even kill his former accomplice. The Justice guys volunteered to stash our star witness until this situation with Germany gets sorted out.

It's likely that ExOps will take an active role in that sorting, but Cyrus wants me to rest before he gives me another Job Number. I had to admit that sounded like a good idea even though I'm dying to find my father.

I finish my drink and stand up to use the bathroom. The tops of the seats try to squirm away from my hands as I stagger up the aisle. I lurch into the bathroom and catch my reflection in the mirror. I grip the sink, lean in close, and take a good look.

Lines. There are lines on my face! I look so much older! Have I been poisoned? Was it some chemical thing in Riyadh? Radiation in Zurich? I pull the skin on my face this way and that, trying to make me young again. It doesn't work. Now I see that my red hair has a white streak on the right side of my head. Where the hell did that come from?

In the mirror, someone with big bug eyes appears behind me. I spin around. No one's there. My hands shake, and I feel faint. I jack a dose of Madrenaline. It's probably not a good idea to mix synthetic adrenaline with all the alcohol I've had today, but I don't care. I cannot let myself pass out in an airplane lavatory. My mouth goes dry and the back of my neck tingles, but the drugs help my dizziness. I close my eyes and grit my teeth because at this point I know what happens next.

Alix

Even though I expect it, the voice almost knocks me out of my skin. My neuroinjector reacts to my stress by giving me a shot of Kalmers. I sit down on the toilet and do what I came for in the first place. I finish and flush. I'm washing my hands when I hear it again.

Alix

This time it sounds like it's right next to me. No, not next to me. I look where it comes from, and I find myself eyeballing Li'l Bertha. Her status indicator reads "ready."

Li'l Bertha is never switched on when I'm on a plane. The first and last part of my preflight routine is to confirm that my sidearm is powered down. I take her out of my holster and check that her mechanical safeties are engaged. Yes, they are, but somehow my gun has managed to activate herself again. While I try to figure out what's wrong with her, it occurs to me that I hear that voice only when she's on.

I feel like a doofus, but I hold her up to my mouth and whisper, "Daddy?" The gun's sensors light up in succession, one after the other. Next I try, in order, "ExOps," "Winter," and "Darius," with no results. Then I say, "Philip Nico." The sensors all light up at once, and I hear a soft, distorted voice, like someone talking through a pillow. I can't make out what the voice says. I try a couple more phrases, then repeat the words that worked before, but now nothing happens no matter what I say. I'll have to take a long look at Li'l Bertha when I'm home. That's another reason for me and Mom to buy a house. I need a shop.

I holster the gun and wobble back to my seat. I lay off the hooch for the rest of the flight. What do I need booze for when I've got terrifying hallucinations built right in? I try to sleep, but for a while I can only think about my dad and about Trick. Eventually the combination of Kalmers and liquor makes me doze off and gives me another one of my weird dreams.

The monk's head is normal again. He sits in his usual spot, but his robe is now black instead of orange. He looks at me for a minute, then recites:

The pestilent horde is consumed,
By you, furious Dragonflower,
Along with the lush, cheering grass.

I sleep through the landing and wake just as we pull up to the gate. I "buh-bye" off the plane and walk through the meat tube to the terminal. Then I mosey around the gate area, waiting for Darwin to spot me. I've only heard his voice, so I expect him to recognize and approach me. Instead, I find him in the airport café next to my gate.

He's reading a newspaper.

He's the last person I ever expected to see again.

He's Patrick.

ACKNOWLEDGMENTS

The fictional world of Shadowstorm is complex, and I needed the help of many intelligent and patient people. They answered my questions and advised me about everything from history and politics to genetics and emergency medicine. To mention them here only scratches the depth of my gratitude. I never would have finished this novel without these generous friends.

To my parents, Carol and George, thank you for enabling my creativity from a young age, for sending me to RISD, and for your support and confidence throughout this long process. Mom: My next series will have fewer curse words.

To my sister, Mary Rose, thank you for guiding me around rookie mistakes, no matter how determined I was to make them, and for all your help getting this going.

To my wife, Natalie, thank you for your years of support and enthusiastic help as I've pulled this together. I love you.

To my teachers and mentors:
• Anne Grolle: my brilliant editor at Random House. Anne has taught me more things in less time than any other person in my professional life. Her creativity, intelligence, and positive attitude made this one of my most creatively fulfilling experiences.
• Tristram C. Coburn: my bulldog literary agent. Tris had the persistence to shovel through a mountain of re-

jection letters and the wisdom not to tell me about them. And I couldn't ask for a better Protector on the business end of things.

• Roberta Grimes: my shield-bearing entertainment lawyer. Roberta's knowledge, experience, and easy-going nature were invaluable in helping me get a grip on the foreign language of intellectual property.

• Keith Smith: entertainment biz veteran and perhaps the coolest guy in the world. Keith generously shared his real-life knowledge and helped me navigate the confusing world of extra-literary rights.

• Jamie Costas: the editor who, even though we didn't wind up working together, convinced me to make Alix the age she is now instead of the age I had her before, which helped the book a lot.

To my advisors and beta readers:

• George S. Almasi: world history, German language and culture, general science, technology, and all the other things fathers teach their sons.

• Paul C. Christesen: history, German language, macro-economics, and general science.

• Andy MacInnis: military history, firearms and ballistics, European culture, and long-time sounding board.

• Steven Sharp: military history, general science, and sci-fi literature.

• Arthur V. Milano: military history, coma recovery, and the inspiration for Raj.

• Kirsten Schwaller-Sigrist: Genetics, cloning and sci-fi literature.

• Diane O'Brien: Medical science and keeping Andy in line.

• Beth Kelley: Medical science, in particular the treatment of gunshot wounds, operating room procedures, and other disgusting hospital stuff.

• Scott D. Packard: Medical science and theoretical future sciences.

• David Hayes: History and literature.

- Len Freiberg III, Maureen Robinson & Krista Snyder: FBI terminology and procedures.
- Lori Freiberg-Rapp, Paul Muller: Military terminology and procedures.
- Jamin Naghmouchi: German slang.
- Paul Owen Powers: Eighty-one inches of Midwestern dynamite. Paul told Tris to read my first manuscript, but left the dire consequences of not reading it to Tris's imagination.
- Megan Kiernan & Seth Coburn: my original models for Scarlet and Patrick.
- Claudia Wilcox-Powers, Laurel Christie, Jim Foley, Gretchen Schwaller-Sharp, Peter Sigrist, Cathy Davis-Hayes, Carol DuBois, Steve Coburn, Mark MacFarlane, Emily Clark, and anyone I can't remember at 3:00 A.M.: Beta-readers, sounding boards, super-supportive cheerleaders.
- Everyone on my Facebook author page. Thanks for following my demented late-night ravings!

I've found great inspiration in the books of Ken Follett, Neal Stephenson, William Gibson, Hunter S. Thompson, Ian Fleming, Robert Ludlum, and Frank Miller, the films of Luc Besson, Quentin Tarantino, and Guy Ritchie, and the video games of Todd Howard, John Romero, and Jason Jones.

Can't get enough of Scarlet?
Then be sure not to miss the next
pulse-pounding novel of the Shadowstorm:

HAMMER OF ANGELS

by

G. T. ALMASI

Coming soon from Del Rey.

Turn the page for a special preview!

"Scarlet, ten left," Brando's comm-voice says, "and stay low."

I dash ten yards up Main Street. My heavy breathing blows little puffs of dust off the floor. Some dirt sticks to my sweat-soaked forehead. I blink hard to get the salt drops out of my eyes.

A turret pops out of a stand of plastic bushes on my left and noisily sprays the air above me with rubber ordnance. I slide on my stomach and aim Li'l Bertha at the bullet-bot. My pistol locks on and comms "Target Acquired" to my Eyes-Up display. I pull the trigger and return fire. My lightweight practice slugs rattle off the turret's metal shell, which signals the Training Control Center that *ya got me, pardner*.

Brando comms, "Next station, twenty right, fly-by."

I jump to my feet and pump my legs for twenty yards. I look to my right. "Fly-by" is IO slang for "don't stop moving," so this next part will be something extra hairy. A bright light flashes from a little house on the right side of Main Street. As I turn to riddle this target, the floor drops out from under me. I've got just enough momentum to grab the far lip of the insta-pit with my free hand. Then my body slams into the pit's wall, and I get the wind knocked out of me.

I hang there for a moment, gasping. My partner

comms, "Scarlet, hurry, we've only got thirty seconds and one more station to get through."

That's easy for you to say, Darwin. I pull myself out of the pit and wheeze on up the road.

"Okay, last one. Fifty-five straight ahead, top speed."

I mentally activate my sidearm's safeties so she won't accidentally fire as I swing my arms as fast as I can. My sneakers slap the floor and my hair blows behind me as I race up to twentysomething miles per hour. I can hit the high thirties with Madrenaline in my blood, but Brando and I are supposed to be able to complete this training sequence without using my Enhances. Each run-through is different, and I've screwed it up three times today. This is the closest we've gotten to finishing.

Brando comms, "Twenty seconds remaining!"

Ahead of me is a clear run to the finish line. All I need to do is jog fifty yards and—

Wrong.

Three bullet-bots drop from the ceiling in front of me. They bounce up and down on long rubber cables, and each bot emits a thin red laser beam. All three beams point at my chest, and the bots fire a volley of rubber bullets.

Brando comms, "It's a bungie screen!"

I hold Li'l Bertha in front of me while I leap and dodge away from the bouncy-bots' bullets and laser beams. Her target indicator is blank.

"Darwin, what's happened? Why can't my pistol get a lock?"

"They've got jammers. You'll have to—"

I charge straight at the left-most bot.

"—find a way around them."

The left-bot locks on to me as it drops to the bottom of its arc. I leap at it and grab the bungie cord above its body. The bot's momentum hauls me off the ground, and I sail up toward the roof.

I swing like Tarzan across the training space and wrap my bot's cord around the other two cables before dropping myself off at the bottom of the next bounce. The bots are still live, but now they can only point in a fixed direction. I dodge the static laser beams and hurl myself across the finish line with less than a second to go.

"*Yes!*" Brando shouts. "Made it!"

I flop onto my back to catch my breath. The view from Camp Gaspy shows that this facility has a very high, curved roof supported by metal trusses. It's like a giant airplane hangar.

"Terrific," Brando comms. "Now for the driving test."

Sure. Whatever. "Gimme a minute," I comm. It takes a minute anyway since Brando has to bring the car around.

A vehicle pulls up next to me. I peel myself off the ground. Oh god, I wish I could use Madrenaline. Brando switches to the passenger seat, and I hop in behind the wheel. Something must have happened to our previous training vehicle, which was a fucked-up black-and-white Dodge sedan, like a former police cruiser. This new car, a white BMW two-seater convertible, is quite a hot little number. The relatively few dents and scrapes tell me this sexy momma hasn't seen much track time here yet. While I coast to the start line, I take in the gorgeous tan interior.

My partner sees how impressed I am with our new wheels and says, "Drug bust."

Ah, of course. Sometimes when ExOps helps local cops, we get to keep the bad guy's ride. If the D.C. SWAT guys can't take care of a situation, or if the FBI is in over their heads, Director Chanez will send one of his Levels out with them. It never takes long after that. Regular crooks can't compete with a million-dollar murder machine designed to help topple whole governments.

I rev the engine and yell, "Think there's any cocaine left in this baby?"

Brando turns up the heater, puts on his seat belt, and smiles. "I doubt it. The mechanics probably got it all."

I pull the Cokemobile up to the start line. In front of us, a pair of giant hangar doors slide open. Brando riffles through his instructions and nods to me when he's ready.

"TCC, Scarlet and Darwin ready for launch."

The Training Control Center comms back. "Roger that, Scarlet. Arming the tree. Go on green."

In front of us is a tall pole that supports two vertical series of lights. Right now the top lights are lit up bright red. I press the clutch down and shift into first. My right foot floors the gas and holds it there.

The light tree flashes down: reds, yellows, *green!*

I slip my left foot off the clutch pedal. A white cloud of tire smoke billows behind us as we screech off the line. The tachometer redlines and I shift into second. We burst out of the hangar at sixty miles per. The sun smacks my face, and my vision Mods adjust their gamma to compensate.

I shout, *"Yeee-hahhhh!!!"*

Brando responds with a wolf howl as we roar down the first long straightaway. The Cokemobile makes it to a buck-ten before I tap the brakes to set up a spectacular powerslide around Turn One's broad expanse. I countersteer and slam full on the gas before I've even passed the corner's apex. Cokey leans into this scandalous driving like a drunk businessman doing the motorboat between a hooker's tits.

Oh, I am totally getting myself one of these honeys.

"Turn Two," Brando navigates, "eighty in, descending circumference, sixty out."

I downshift from fifth to third to transfer the car's weight forward. My hands twist the wheel thirty yards from the turn. All that weight up front makes us plow into the corner. When we're a foot from the pavement's outer edge, I stomp the gas and pull the car's weight back onto its rear wheels. The unloaded front tires suddenly grab the pavement tighter than a Scotsman's wallet and whip us through Turn Two.

"Turn Three, seventy in, ascending circumference, seventy-five out. Sharp vertical rise at apex."

I slither us into Turn Three with my right toes on the gas and my right heel on the brakes. My left foot peppers the clutch as needed to keep our revs up. I do great until the turn's apex. The vertical rise bumps Cokey into the air and screws up my driving line. We fly three feet sideways before we land. I overcorrect and the Bimmer tilts onto her two left wheels. Brando and I both lean as hard to the right as we can. I jiggle the wheel left to get us back on all fours, but now we're headed off the track.

I yank the emergency brake, crank the steering wheel right then left, and drop the e-brake down again. This throws us into a completely sideways skid. I look over my left shoulder to see where we're going.

God almighty, we'll be lucky if there's any rubber at all on the tires after this one. My training has taught me to ignore the natural inclination to slow down when faced with an all-out mental-patient driving disaster like this. If I even breathe on the brakes right now, we'll spin completely out of control. I shove the gas pedal to the floor, dimly aware of Brando as he hangs onto his door handle for dear life. He doesn't say anything though, god bless 'im.

The tires throw out a massive cloud of scorched rubber, and we exit Turn Three at eighty-eight miles per hour.

"Hah!" I wipe the back of my hand across my forehead. "Okay, El Brando, what's next?"

We're so far ahead of the time we need that I only drive like Maniac Junior for the next five turns. Still plenty of excitement, but nothing like the heroics in Turn Three.

We come off Turn Eight and enter the main straightaway, ready for Lap Two. Before we pass by the hangar we receive a comm from the Training Control Center. "Scarlet and Darwin, switch seats before Turn One. Lap Two will be a target lap."

Brando calls out, "Chinese fire drill!" and grabs the steering wheel. I take my feet off the pedals, crouch up on my seat, and haul my partner bodily across the center console. He keeps his eyes forward as his legs unfold onto the pedals. Meanwhile I transfer myself to his seat and pluck my pistol out of her holster.

I snap Li'l Bertha's neural contact into the pad in my left palm, and she connects to my internal systems. Her status cluster appears in my Eyes-Up display to show me how much ammo she has left and her current ordinance settings. I swivel my head around to see what my field of vision will be for this lap. With the convertible top down, I have clear firing lanes in all directions except to my direct left where my partner sits.

Brando brakes into Turn One, smoothly clips the apex, and guns the engine out of the corner. The tires barely chirp.

"You call that driving?" I tease.

"Hey, Miss Hot-Rodder, I clocked the same time as you did without scrubbing a year off the tires."

"Yeah, but you'll never make the highlight reel!"

He smiles and then presses his lips together while he sets up for Turn Two. As he brakes into the corner he comms, "Target! Right side, yellow on red."

I spin my head and aim Li'l Bertha. A red sign with a big yellow dot has popped out of the ground twenty-five yards away from the pavement. I hit it with a short burst, and the target drops back where it came from.

Brando races the Cokemobile through the track's twists and turns and calls out each target. I nail all of them, but I've barely got time to aim and fire before I have to get ready for the next one.

We exit Turn Eight and return to the main straightaway. I sit back, smugly thinking we're done when Brando looks in his side-view mirror and cries out, "Target far left, yellow on black." I swing my head around. The yellow-and-black sign is already behind us, plus it's very low to the ground.

While Brando says, "Crap, we were almost perfect, too," I jump out of my seat and clamber onto the car's trunk. Cold wind hits me like a refrigerated hurricane, but the extra height I get from standing up here gives me a better angle. I hook my foot into the roll bar and sight on our shrinking target. I unload Li'l Bertha at full auto. Just as she clicks empty, the target falls down.

"Got it!"

"Scarlet, sit down! We've gotta get back inside to finish."

We're too close to the hangar. I don't have time to sit down normally because I might roll off the car sideways when my partner turns. If Brando brakes I'll fly off the front. If we overshoot, we'll fail the exercise—*definitely* not an option.

I wrap my arms over my head and dive into the passenger-side foot well. I end up with my legs on the seat and most of my body smooshed under the dash. The engine is much louder down here, and hot air blows into my ear. I feel the car swerve right, accelerate for a few seconds, and then slow to a stop. Past my feet is the hangar's metal roof, and then my partner's face as he leans over from his seat.

"You all right, Hot-Rod?"

"Did you know there are tiny men down here who make the heater work?

"How do they do that?"

"They eat bowls of hot peppers and fart into the duct-work."

Brando laughs and tries to extract me from the foot well, but I'm jammed in here so awkwardly that rescuing me requires him and one of the ExOps training administrators to haul me out by my knees.

"Hey," I say to the admin as I dust myself off. "What's with that last target? It didn't pop up until we were past it!"

The admin raises one eyebrow. "That's because it wasn't actually a firing target."

Brando stands behind me and swacks car-floor crumbs off my jacket. "So we weren't supposed to shoot it?" he asks.

"You were barely supposed to *see* it. We use it to record how you'd react to having missed one."

"Has anybody ever shot it before?"

The admin slowly shakes his head back and forth. I hold my hand out behind me and Brando slaps me a low-five.